STAR TREK®

STRANGE NEW WORLDS

IV

For orders other than by individual consumers, Pocket Books grants a discount on the purchase of **10 or more** copies of single titles for special markets or premium use. For further details, please write to the Vice President of Special Markets, Pocket Books, 1230 Avenue of the Americas, 9th Floor, New York, NY 10020-1586.

For information on how individual consumers can place orders, please write to Mail Order Department, Simon & Schuster, Inc., 100 Front Street, Riverside, NJ 08075.

Edited by
Dean Wesley Smith
with John J. Ordover and Paula M. Block

Based upon STAR TREK and STAR TREK: THE NEXT GENERATION created by Gene Roddenberry, STAR TREK: DEEP SPACE NINE created by Rick Berman & Michael Piller, and STAR TREK: VOYAGER created by Rick Berman & Michael Piller & Jeri Taylor

POCKET BOOKS
New York London Toronto Sydney Singapore

This book consists of works of fiction. Names, characters, places and incidents are products of the authors' imaginations or are used fictitiously. Any resemblance to actual events or locales or persons, living or dead, is entirely coincidental.

An *Original* Publication of POCKET BOOKS

POCKET BOOKS, a division of Simon & Schuster, Inc.
1230 Avenue of the Americas, New York, NY 10020

STAR TREK is a Registered Trademark of Paramount Pictures.

This book is published by Pocket Books, a division of Simon & Schuster, Inc., under exclusive license from Paramount Pictures.

ISBN: 0-7434-1131-5

First Pocket Books trade paperback printing May 2001

10 9 8 7 6 5 4 3 2 1

POCKET and colophon are registered trademarks of Simon & Schuster, Inc.

Printed in the U.S.A.

Contents

STAR TREK®

Contents

STAR TREK®

A Little More Action

TG Theodore

It was raining hard that Friday in the City by the Bay.

So hard, in fact, I couldn't even hear myself walk.

Their sun had taken a powder behind some pretty ugly clouds. And I was taking a beating—a *wet* beating.

I flipped up the damp collar on my trusty, tan trenchcoat and pulled down the brim of my hat. It didn't help much, but I didn't care.

This case had taken me across half the quadrant and to dozens of planets. What was a little rain compared with what happened to me on Sigma Omicron VII? I could still feel the lumps on my noggin from *that* place.

But no matter where I went, each time *he* had managed to stay one jump ahead of me.

Sure, I could have tried the direct approach, but I didn't want to give myself away. My business with this guy was private. The stakes were too high and if word got out what I was doing a lot of people could get hurt—mainly *me.*

My briefcase was getting heavier by the minute. But I wasn't getting paid to complain. I had business to attend to—*big* business.

And the sooner I unloaded the goods, the better. I was getting five hundred a day, plus expenses. But all that money wouldn't mean much if I ended up at the bottom of a river, or on the wrong side of a shuttlebay door.

Then I saw it. The place looked like a cement flying saucer.

The rain kept most of the people away, but not me. I double-checked the heater I was packing and headed for the front door.

A couple of uniformed goons gave me the once-over—twice.

I went up to the desk and there she was—a hot, blond, blue-eyed number in a red uniform. She had legs all the way up to her hemline—and then some. And I could tell there was more than hair spray between *those* ears.

Before I could open my mouth, an alarm went off. I reached for my piece, but the goons were too fast for me.

One of 'em grabbed my heater. But he just started laughing and handed it back to me.

"Sorry, sir. We thought you had a weapon."

What'd they think it was—a peashooter? I put the piece back into its holster, straightened my coat, and looked back at the beautiful doll. She looked up at me with them big baby blues and said, "May I help you, sir?"

No one had called *me* sir in a long, long time. I took another second or two just to enjoy the view. "Yeah, honey. I'm lookin' for somebody and was wonderin' if you could do me a favor?"

Her peepers got wider and I noticed a trace of a smile on those ruby smackers of hers.

"I say something funny, sweetheart?"

She giggled.

It would have been cute except for the fact I knew she was laughing at *me.* They *all* laugh at me. People can be awfully cruel when they find out who you are.

And just who *am* I?

I'm a private detective.

An Iotian dick.

Admiral James Kirk looked out at the violent storm over the bay. The view from his new apartment was magnificent. It included not only Starfleet Headquarters, the Golden Gate Bridge, and Alcatraz Park, but part of the western horizon as well.

Kirk had waited two years for this apartment. It once was the home of the Betelgeusean ambassador. But when the diplomat was recalled to his home planet, Kirk used a little influence and moved right in.

In the few weeks he had been there, Kirk had already decorated the rounded and concave walls with his renowned collection of antiques—mostly weapons and various other relics of Earth's warrior past. But among the reminders of humankind's less civilized moments were souvenirs of hope as well.

Certainly his collection of tools from the Kirk farm in Iowa were symbols of Earth's proud agricultural history. And Kirk's library contained not only the works of famous generals and war figures, but of poets and philosophers as well.

Like Kirk, his apartment was a symphony of contradictions.

Despite the inclement weather at the moment, he loved looking out the windows. As he watched the swirls of darkened clouds, his gaze stopped on the bridge and he wondered if anyone had ever been bold enough to fly a shuttle under it in a storm since he did it during his Academy days. *No, not in this weather. No one would fly anywhere near the bridge in weather like this.*

The admiral turned away from the storm to see Leonard McCoy scowling at the contents of a rather small book. "What's wrong, Bones? A big word?"

McCoy didn't acknowledge the question—or the sarcasm. Kirk suspected it was deliberate and walked over to his friend. He noticed the title of the book—*The Big Goodbye.*

"It's a detective mystery, Bones. The second in a series. Dixon Hill. Not great, but not bad if you like pulp novels."

McCoy arched an eyebrow. "What in blazes is a 'pulp' novel?"

Kirk smiled. If anyone lived in the present, it was McCoy. The past was gone and with it, many memories McCoy would just as soon leave there. "I really don't think you're here for a crash course in literature, now, are you?"

The doctor gently closed the book and took special care to return it exactly to its former spot. He knew that, while his friend might have been reckless in space, when it came to his home Jim Kirk was downright retentive about everything being in its proper place. The Kirk family farm was the cleanest, most orderly farm McCoy had ever seen.

"Where's that Vulcan?" growled McCoy. "He knows we won't start eating without him. His last night before he leaves for Vulcan and he's deliberately making me wait."

Kirk smiled. "Well, with the storm outside, it might take a while to get to a transporter."

McCoy snatched up a goodly number of hors d'oeuvres. "His father is the ambassador to Vulcan. Sarek helped start the Federation! You think Spock could just buy some bean dip and beam over here without waiting in line."

"Remember, he's a civilian now, Bones. He probably wants to explore doing things other civilians do *as* a civilian."

The two friends paused for a moment. They didn't know when they would again see Spock after he left Earth. The former captain was being quite private about his future plans and the doctor and the admiral had successfully avoided this topic all night. The pause seemed interminable. Mercifully, the door chime sounded. Kirk walked over to the door. "I believe the bean dip has arrived."

The doors whooshed open to reveal one extremely windblown Vulcan, slightly damp, carrying a small package. Without ceremony, he offered it to Kirk. "Your pastelike mixture of crushed bipodal seeds and other chemicals, Jim."

Kirk gestured for the civilian Spock to enter. "Thank you, Spock." The doors closed as the Vulcan entered the main room. "Spock, you're wet. What happened?"

He was oblivious of the fact that one large lock of his black cowlick was sticking straight up. "Obviously I was exposed to the rather excessive precipitation and wind velocity San Francisco is currently experiencing."

McCoy smiled at the uncharacteristic appearance of his friend. Never in his many years of knowing Spock had McCoy seen the Vulcan so completely unkempt. "You mean you got rained on, Spock."

"I believe that is what I just said, Doctor. I was in the place of purchase when the unsecured doors were blown open by the storm, allowing some wind and rain to make contact with many consumers. Myself among them."

McCoy did all he could to stifle an out-and-out guffaw. "That's a new look for you, Spock. I like it."

Kirk shot a glare at McCoy. He pointed to an inner room of the apartment. "In there, Spock. You can dry off in there."

"Thank you, Admiral. Excuse me."

And without sacrificing an ounce of dignity, Spock disappeared from view. McCoy could contain himself no longer and nearly doubled over in laughter. Kirk tried to maintain his scowl of disapproval but suddenly burst into tears himself.

"Kirk. I'm lookin' for Kirk."

From the look on the doll's face, I might as well have been speaking Orion. All them Feds were the same. They looked at me like I was from another planet—which I *was,* of course. But—heck, you know what I mean.

"Which Kirk would that be, sir?"

I didn't expect *that* answer. "Kirk. The Big Guy. Hangs around with a weird guy named Spocko and a doc or somethin'. Can't steer a flivver to save his life."

The corners of those luscious lips turned up into an amazing smile. "Ah, that would be *Admiral* James Kirk."

"Yeah. That sounds like the guy. Can I see him?"

She worked her panel like a coronet man works his horn. I didn't mind the wait, though—not as long as she was the one I was waitin' on. She finally looked up and flashed her pearlies again.

"I'm sorry, but Admiral Kirk isn't here right now. You might try his private residence. But I'm afraid I can't give out that information without some identification, sir."

Smart. She was smart, too. I reached into my inside pocket, produced my ID, and held it out to her. "It's a lousy picture, but it's me."

Her smile disappeared for a second. "Oh. I see that you're—Could you wait a few seconds, please?"

Was she kidding? I'd wait a week in that rain for her. "No problem."

She pushed a bunch of buttons on her desk and spoke real quiet like. I reached for a cigarette, but what I found in my pocket wouldn't light for days. I looked at the two goons, who were more interested in what was going on than they should be. "So, what are *you* lookin' at?"

That got 'em. They turned away.

The doll stood up and smiled at me. "I've been instructed by Admiral Morrow himself to give you the information you're requesting. As a matter of fact, the admiral would like to escort you personally to Admiral Kirk's residence."

Hey, now *this* was more like it. "He would, huh? Tell me, honey, does this Morrow guy drink? I'd like to buy him a beer when this is over. And if you're not busy later, I'd like to buy *you* one, too."

Hey, it was worth a shot. We don't have dames like her at home.

I left with the address and the admiral—and without a date.

"Mr. Spock, I believe your search for food was a complete success. We could have just replicated some bean dip, you know."

The Vulcan was now back to his usual impeccable appearance. His Vulcan outer robe was as dry as his home planet, and not a single hair was out of place on his head. He crossed over to the built-in bar, where Kirk was pouring a familiar orange concoction. "Thank you, Admiral. I know of your and Dr. McCoy's fondness for nonreplicated food. So I deduced that the 'real thing' would be preferable."

McCoy smiled. "Well, that was downright courteous of you, Spock. Thank you."

Spock understood why McCoy was smiling. He was quick to deflate his friend's teasing. "May I remind you, Doctor, that courtesy is not an emotion."

It worked. McCoy frowned and went to pour himself another mint julep. "Oh. Right."

Kirk handed a short flute of room-temperature *tranya* to Spock.

"Thank you, Admiral."

Kirk picked up a small shot glass of Romulan ale. "Spock, this is dinner. In my new apartment. Call me Jim."

McCoy raised his glass. "To your new place, Jim. May you never see it again because you're going to return to starship duty where you belong."

"Bones, you know I'm never going back."

"Right. And I'm giving up medicine. And to you, Spock. May you find whatever it is you may be looking for that you didn't find in Starfleet. L'Chaim."

Spock nodded appreciatively. McCoy downed a large portion of his julep and relished the sweet aftertaste in his mouth.

Spock sipped his *tranya* and seemed quite satisfied.

Kirk started to sip his Romulan ale when his door chimed again.

Spock looked at Kirk. "That must be Admiral Morrow, Jim."

Kirk chugged the rest of his ale, let his eyes refocus, and then quickly stashed the bottle behind a panel in the bar. He tried to speak matter of factly. "Yes. I'll go let him in."

The admiral walked over to his front door. McCoy walked over to Spock. "I assume that Admiral Morrow does not partake of Romulan ale."

"It *is* illegal, Doctor. I don't think either of us would wish Admiral Kirk to be arrested—much less in his own home."

McCoy stared into his glass and swished the remainder of the julep in it. "No, Spock. That would definitely put a damper on the party."

"Indeed."

Kirk's door whooshed open and there stood Admiral Morrow and someone out of a history book. "Hello, Jim. Sorry I'm late. I brought someone who's been anxious to meet you. I hope you don't mind."

I was so close I could spit on him. But I didn't. I saw two more boys in the room. I recognized Spocko because of his ears. I figured the other guy must be the Doc. I held out my briefcase. This was all finally gonna be over, and not a moment too soon. No time for pleasantries. Hey, business was business.

"Kirk, the Boys sent me. I got something for—"

"The Boys? I'm afraid I don't know any—"

What was he—nuts or something? "The *Boys*. You know—the Syndicate?"

Spocko jumped in. "Admiral, I believe this gentleman is from Sigma Iotia. Am I correct, sir?"

No doubt as to who was the real brains in the Federation here. "Yeah. Yeah, I am."

"Oh, brother." The Doc thought I didn't see him roll his eyes, but I did. "I knew this would come back to haunt us." He headed back to what looked like the bar.

Kirk played nice at first. "Please, gentlemen, do come in. Welcome to my new home. May I offer you a drink?"

This Admiral Morrow guy (who wasn't a bad john, but a little stuffy) stepped into the fancy digs. I took a few steps, too. "Nothin' for me, thanks. I'm workin'."

Morrow joined the Doc at the bar. Kirk just kinda stood there for a minute. He looked like a confused cow or something. "Um, forgive me for being blunt, but you're a long way from home. Why do you need to see me?"

What—did this Kirk guy go to finishing school or something? I had no idea what he just said to me. I didn't come half a quadrant to be insulted—if that's what it was, I mean. So I figured maybe I should stand up to him and tell him what was on my mind. "What was that, Kirk?"

Spocko walked over to us and leaned into Kirk. "Perhaps, 'boss,' if you speak to the gentleman in his own vernacular."

Kirk nodded and turned to me. He hunched his shoulders and dropped the fancy accent he had been using. "Whaddaya want here?"

That was more like it. *That's* the Kirk I had heard about for all these years. "Hey, when no one showed up to collect your cut of the Syndicate's profits, we started gettin' worried. We didn't want ya to think we was tryin' to cut you out or anything. After what you did to us last time, we—"

Kirk stepped forward, like he wanted to keep things on the Q.T. "Look, I'd just as soon forget about the display of technology we resorted to."

"Huh?"

Kirk started talking normal again. "I mean, 'the way we had to get rough with ya.' "

Mr. Ears spoke up. "Fascinating. I believe the Iotians have somehow evolved from the gangster society of the nineteen-twenties to the fictional detective genre of the late nineteen-thirties and early nineteen-forties."

The Doc chimed in. "Shades of Dixon Hill."

Spocko looked at me and kept yapping. "I would be very interested, sir, to learn how you managed to leave your planet. Have your people developed a method of space travel in such a relatively short period of history?"

It took me a second to figure out the question. "Oh, no. I'm the first one to make it off the turf. I hitched a ride."

The Doc choked on his drink. "You hitched a ride? With whom?"

"Some idiots called the Pakleds. They were lost and stopped by for some directions. We made a deal. We gave 'em some maps, and they gave me a ride. Since then I've been tailin' Kirk here for two years. Let me tell you, there's a lot of weird people out there in space."

"Two years?" said Kirk. "Tell the Boys I'm flattered."

Morrow turned to the other guys. "I've never heard of these Pakleds. Have you?"

Kirk shook his head and looked at Spocko.

"Nor have I, Admiral. It would be fascinating to learn how these beings of alleged 'lower intelligence' managed to achieve warp drive."

I had no idea what they were talking about. I didn't give a damn what they were talking about. I was getting antsy and just wanted to make my delivery and vamoose. I opened the briefcase and showed 'em the goods. "Forty percent. Count it."

If Kirk's kisser had dropped any lower, I coulda drove a cab through it. Spocko was cool, though. Cool as a cucumber. The Doc just had a belt of his drink and took a few steps away. The Morrow guy was trying to hide a smile. I don't what he thought was so funny.

And this Kirk guy didn't seem so tough to me, neither—especially after all the tons of stories I heard about him. "I'm carryin' ten years' worth here. Now, you want it or not? It's all there."

Spocko spoke. "We are certain the amount is correct. If nothing else, the Iotians are a very precise people."

Who *were* these guys? I was beginning to wonder if Spocko was a Sunday school teacher or something. Kirk cleared his throat and grabbed the case. Finally!

"Thank you very much. You didn't have to bring it to me in person, you know."

"Huh?"

"I mean 'Hey, it's about time. You coulda just mailed it.' "

A lightbulb lit up. I was onto Kirk. I figured out what little game he and his boys were playing. He was checking up on me for the Feds. I mean, Kirk's boss was standing right there and everything. "No way, Kirk. I wasn't takin' any chances with this much dough. Things disappear, you know?"

Kirk mumbled something that sounded like "I wish *I* could." But I wasn't sure, and I didn't care. I wanted a second chance at that blonde over at the Federation's clubhouse.

I looked over at the Doc. "And you, Doc—"

He gulped down his drink like Prohibition was coming back. "Me?"

I walked over to him and reached inside my coat. "I got a little somethin' for you, too."

He must have thought I was gonna plug him or something. He took a few steps back. "Easy, Doc. You'll like this. Here."

I offered him the paper. He looked at it like he'd never seen one before. "What is this?"

"It's a marker, Doc. Good for when you come back to my planet. I didn't wanna risk carryin' *that* much dough on me. You're even richer than the Feds. No offense, Kirk."

"No sweat," Kirk said.

"But what is this for? Why are you giving all this—money—to *me?"*

He didn't know. I couldn't believe he didn't know. "It's for the McCoy, Doc. You know—the McCoy?"

The Doc stood there like a car outta gas. I wasn't buyin' it. "As if you didn't know. Remember that little thing you 'accidentally' left behind?"

"Oh, boy." I saw the wheels tumbling in the Doc's brain. I could tell Spocko knew what I was talking about. He mumbled to Kirk. "The communicator, Admiral."

The Doc looked a little uneasy. "Look, I didn't mean to leave—"

"Didn't mean? That's a good one, Doc. Look, after you left, there was a little scuffle over it and it kinda got bashed up. We put it back together the best we could, but we could only make it work when someone was close by with another one. It's been the hottest-sellin' toy on the whole planet for ten years!"

"Toy?!" The four guys sounded like a choir or something.

"Yeah. Can't keep 'em in the stores. And look, as a gesture of thanks and good faith from the toy company, I'm bringin' back the one you left. The museum put up a squawk, but the Boys thought you'd want it back. No hard feelings, right?"

"You have it here?" He sounded kind of excited.

The Doc smiled as I gave him the thing. He looked at it, kind of unsure. I had to convince him. "Oh, that there's the genuine article. That's the real McCoy."

Suddenly it got kind of quiet for a second.

Spocko raised an eyebrow.

Kirk shook his head.

Morrow tried hiding another smile. (What was *with* this guy?)

The Doc rolled his eyes again.

"Hey, I don't get it. What'd I say?"

"Nothing," said the Doc. He handed me back the marker. "Tell the toy company I'm very thankful and honored. And tell them to donate this and my future 'cut' to some charities on your planet that help out anyone who needs shelter or medical help, okay?"

Now, I'm as tough as they go, but this was one moving gesture on the Doc's part. "I will, Doc. You're all right."

I stuffed the marker back into my coat pocket. "Well, I'm gonna blow this joint. Kirk, good to meet ya. Morrow, you're a stand-up guy. Spocko, you're weird. Cool, but weird. And Doc—you keep downin' those drinks like that and you're gonna be one of your own patients. But don't think I don't respect you for it."

Kirk patted me on the shoulder. "Are you sure you won't stay for a drink—or a few hands of fizzbin?"

I headed for the door. "Oh, no. I heard about you and fizzbin." Even though I finished third in the Kirk Fizzbin Classic a few years ago, I wasn't dumb enough to take on *the* grand master. "I'm keepin' my dough in my pocket, where it belongs."

We stopped at the door and I turned to him—eye to eye. "Oh, and Kirk—"

"Yes? Er, 'yeah'?"

I put out my hand. "See ya next year."

Kirk shook my hand and nodded. "Check."

This guy was a little out of touch. No one had said "check" in a long, long time. "Kirk, take my advice. Get with the times. You'll live longer. Nice place." I looked over at Spocko, Morrow, and the Doc. "Gentlemen."

As the door kinda whooshed closed behind me, I thought I heard some more laughing. But I didn't care. I did my job. And word would get around, and soon I'd have more cases than I could handle.

I walked down the front steps. The rain had stopped, but the smell of the wet street was fresh—one of the best smells on any world. Kinda musty and sweet, but like the street was new. Like the first time anyone had ever walked on it. I flipped down my collar, shoved my hands in my pockets, and walked away.

Somehow I knew it wouldn't be the last time I'd see Kirk and his boys. But I had other cases to solve, other fights to fight, other—

"Hello, again—sir."

It was her. The leggy blonde from Club Fed. She was out of uniform and in a long, tight coat which accented her accents. And her big blue eyes were looking straight into mine.

I didn't say a word. I just offered an arm and she took it.

The other jobs could wait for a little while.

Right now, I was on my own clock.

Prodigal Father

Robert J. Mendenhall

The scream of the labored engines went unheard in silent space, but their erratic vibrations were felt through the deck plates of the crippled starship as far inward as sickbay. Or was it his rage that shook the *Enterprise* so? Rage at the monster Khan? Rage at his mother? At his father? David Marcus cursed aloud.

His *father.*

"David, please," Carol Marcus said from the biobed she lay on.

David started straight and hard at the ceiling and gripped the edge of his own bed so tightly his knuckles were white from the strain. "You lied to me, Mother. All these years you knew he was my father, and you said nothing. God, how I hate him!"

"David, you can't hate him. You don't even know him. What you hate is what you think he represents."

The ship shuddered and seemed to tip for a brief instant, then righted itself.

David released his grip on the bed and sat bolt upright. He swung his long legs over the side. "What he represents are the corpses of our friends back there on Regula I. Back there. In pools of their own blood." His mother grimaced and David felt a tug of regret for his crass remark.

"Wrong, young man." The voice was raspy and laced with a hint of accent David had come to categorize as pompous Georgian.

David shot an angry glance at Dr. Leonard McCoy, chief medical officer of the *Starship Enterprise.* McCoy waved a handheld medical scanner over Carol's petite body and studied the readings on the diagnostic display over her biobed.

"You don't know a goddam thing about what he represents," McCoy said.

"He's a warmonger and a murderer—"

"He's neither," McCoy interrupted. "He's a peacekeeper and a soldier. You're fine, Carol. You're both fine." He snapped off the scanner.

"Same thing, Doctor," David said. "He's no different than that Khan."

"Where does this hate of yours come from, boy? I've known Jim Kirk for decades. He's a lot of things, but right there on top of that list, he's honorable. Your mother knows him. Does she hate him?"

"Of course not. He's charmed her. She can't see past his pretty face—"

"That is quite enough," Carol Marcus said, climbing down from the bed. "The both of you. Leonard, David never knew Jim was his father."

McCoy frowned and his voice softened. "I know. Jim and I have talked about it over the years. Quite a bit during the past several months, in fact. He's feeling his age."

"My poor, old man," David said, with acid sarcasm.

McCoy shook his head. "You know, David. Back there, in the cave, I was watching you. In the face of danger, not knowing what was happening or who the enemy was, you handled yourself with a great deal of courage. You fought to protect your mother and the Genesis Device, without regard for your personal safety. It reminded me of a young James T. Kirk."

David Marcus's face blazed brick red.

"Oh, Leonard," Carol said, shaking her head. "That was the absolute wrong thing to say."

"I'm nothing like him," David exploded. "Nothing!"

McCoy continued, undaunted by Carol's admonishment and unimpressed with David's tirade. "Wrong both times, my young friend. Genetically, you are very much the same as your father, but then you're a scientist. I don't need to tell you that. And personality-wise, you're as headstrong and single-minded as he is. You're both passionate about your principles and personal values and you both abhor violence."

"Him? Abhor violence? How can you say that? He works for the military. He jumps from fight to fight, striking, attacking. Murdering innocent—"

"You sound like a whiny little boy," McCoy cut him off with a wave of his hand. "Where do you get your information? First of all Starfleet may be a military organization in structure, but its mission is exploration, David, not warfare. We look for new civilizations, new intellectual challenges."

"In an armed-to-the-proverbial-teeth battleship," David said.

"In a ship of exploration equipped to defend itself and anyone else who needs defending."

"You're the one who's confused, Doctor. This ship is a war machine. Its sole purpose is to intimidate and subjugate."

The *Enterprise* lurched again, and everyone standing had to reach for support to keep from tumbling to the deck. The vibration beneath David's feet increased; he could feel it clear up to his knees.

"Hates violence," David mocked. "He's up there now, in his command room, fighting with this Khan. He doesn't care who gets hurt or killed, so long as he wins. You heard what he said in the cave. He doesn't like to lose. And he'll do anything to win this fight."

"That's the first thing you've said in the last five minutes that's been right," McCoy said. David looked at him questioningly. "He doesn't like to lose and he'll do anything to win this fight. But you're wrong about one thing. He very much cares about who gets hurt or killed. It eats at him, every day. When Jim loses a member of his crew, he loses a part of himself."

"Targ shit."

"David!" Carol said.

"Look, I can't convince you of your father's sterling qualities," McCoy said. "But whether or not you like it, or him, you can't change the fact that you *are* his son. But that doesn't change who you are. It's a simple, biological fact. You're a scientist. Treat this as a problem. Use the scientific method. You're stated your hypothesis—"

"I sure have."

"Then move on to the next step. Gather and analyze your data and either prove your theory or change it to match the data."

"Leonard's making sense, David. Listen to him. Take the time to learn who Jim is before you condemn him."

David turned to his mother and saw how her short, honey hair was disarrayed and how it made her seem so tired. She looked up at him with a sad, shallow smile on her lips. Her liquid blue eyes reached out to his own, hazel like . . .

"Why didn't you tell me?" he whispered.

"For the same reason Jim and I never married. He and I live two completely different lifestyles. Mine ties me to education and research. His takes him on adventures across the galaxy. He lives a dangerous life and I didn't want you exposed to that. I wanted you to grow up safe. And protected. And in a home where your parents are there for you. They don't allow families on starships. The long separations we would have had to endure would have been worse than if you had no father at all. And there was always the fear that one day a notification team from Starfleet would come to the door and tell me—us—that Captain James T. Kirk had been killed while defending this or saving that. I didn't want to put you through that. And . . . and I couldn't bear to go through it myself."

"But maybe *I* should have been the one to choose whether I wanted to go through it," David said.

"You couldn't make that choice as a baby, dear. That's what a parent does. It was my job to make the hard decisions for you, to decide what I thought was best for you, to protect you from harm until you could make those choices yourself. You don't know what it's like as a parent, David. The heavy burden of having to make those decisions for another."

"Sounds like you're describing the captain of a starship," McCoy said as he turned and sauntered to his office. David followed sharply on his heels.

"Oh, please, Doctor. I don't need to hear your feeble attempts at association. I'm not a child, and you can't change how I feel."

"David," Carol said, coming up behind her son, her voice stiff. "No one is trying to influence your thinking. And maybe I was wrong to have kept this from you. But, I couldn't bear the thought of you running off into danger on some mission or some foolish adventure and getting killed."

"Mother, you know me. I would never do anything like that."

"Oh, yes," she laughed sardonically and dropped her weary body into a hard chair in front of McCoy's desk. "I do know you. And David, my sweet young son, I see so much of your father in you, it scares me. I've always been afraid that if you knew who he was and got to know him as a person, you would actually like him."

"What?" David had never seen his mother this way. So distraught. So near the brink of tears. Never.

"I know that sounds awful. And very selfish. But I was afraid that if you liked him, you would want to be with him. And if you were with him, you'd be in danger."

"Mother, I—"

"David, it's time you decided this for yourself. We may not survive."

"It's his damn fault we're in this situation," David said.

"You're stubborn as an old mule," McCoy said, as he typed onto a keypad next to a display device on his desk. "Just like your father."

Carol shook her head. "Leonard."

The *Enterprise* bucked and rumbled and David had to grab the doorframe to keep his balance. McCoy reached for his desk and held down the coffee cup that jumped and threatened to spill over the reports he had been studying.

"I'm going up there," David said, looking to McCoy to challenge him.

"I thought you might," McCoy said, instead. "I've used my authorization code to give you limited access to most of the ship. You can't get into engineering, or the armory or any place that's restricted other than the bridge, but otherwise you have free rein of the ship."

"I'll go along," Carol said, rising.

"No, Mother. Why don't you stay and help Dr. McCoy with the wounded. I . . . I really need to do this alone."

Mother and son looked at each other for a long, connecting moment.

"Yes," she said. "I know you do. Go ahead. I'll join you shortly." She kissed him lightly on the cheek.

Without another word, David Marcus spun on his heels and trotted through the hissing door into the darkened, main corridor. Three seconds later, he had returned.

"David, what's wrong?" Carol asked, concerned.

"Ahh, how do I get to the bridge?"

McCoy guffawed. "Well if it's any consolation, David, Jim Kirk would never have asked for directions. Go left out the door to the first corridor. Turn right. There's a turbolift at the end. The bridge is on level one."

"Thanks," he replied, a bit sheepish. His mother stifled a giggle. David nodded and, again, marched out of sickbay.

He reached the turbolift without incident, but found the door wouldn't open for him. He thumbed the button repeatedly but received no response or satisfaction. "Damn, what's wrong with this thing?" he said aloud.

"All the lifts are out below C deck," a voice said behind him.

David turned to see a group of equipment-laden engineers, clad in thick, white radiation suits, scamper past. "So, how do I get to the bridge?"

One of the young engineers called over his shoulder, "You'll have to climb. Take the emergency access tube up four levels to C deck. You can take the turbolift from there."

David nodded his thanks, but the group was already around a corner and out of sight. He looked around him and quickly spotted the red emergency hatch, flush to the bulkhead to the left of the turbolift door. It opened with a quick jerk of the release handle.

Air hissed into the tube as the seal was broken, then sighed back at him with a stale breath. He climbed through the hatch and reached for the ladder mounted to the tube's opposite wall. A large number 7 was painted on the tube wall to the right of the ladder. David glanced down and was instantly awash with vertigo. He flattened his body against the ladder and clutched the rungs with frantic strength. The dark tube stretched the depth of the saucer section, both upward and downward, broken only by light bars spaced every two meters or so. The bars disappeared into the vast distance below him. He swallowed and drew a long, raspy breath.

David screwed his eyes shut and fought down the nausea. An unbidden image of Kirk sliding down the ladder with graceful, insolent ease swam into his thoughts. He opened his eyes and gritted his teeth, now determined, then slowly ascended the ladder, one rung at a time. Bile teased his throat, but if he didn't look down, he would be okay.

The tube was stuffy, dry, with the dusty odor of neglect. Sweat beaded on his forehead and in the creases of his palms. One rung at a time.

The number 6 was painted in a huge block letter next to the ladder. He had started on level seven. Okay, what the hell was this—a deck or a level? Why couldn't these warmongers be consistent? He needed to get to C deck. He counted backward from level one, which must be A deck, to C deck. That would be level three then.

He squinted his eyes and looked upward, focusing on the bulkhead above him and next to the ladder. A pearl of sweat dribbled into his right eye, stinging it and momentarily blurring his sight. He tightened his grip with one hand and rubbed his right eye with the other. He could make out the elongated appearance of another number. It had to be five. Okay, he had an idea how far it was between decks. It wasn't that far to go.

Slowly, he pulled himself up the long ladder.

Level five. A careless grip—he slid down to his arms full length with a grunt of pain and panic. He clutched the rungs with sweat-soaked and aching hands, his heart hammering to escape.

Level four. Each breath and footfall echoed up and down

through the narrow tube, whispering, it seemed, "Kirk. Kirk. Kirk."

Finally—level three. C deck. Trembling from exertion and anxiety, David awkwardly turned to the hatch behind him, grasped the quick release, and pulled. Cool, rich air swept in, caressing his face, then drew itself back out into the crimson-lit corridor of C deck. David pivoted on the rung and arched his leg out the hatch and into the corridor, then pushed off the ladder. He secured the hatch, then leaned against it for several moments, fighting to catch his breath.

The turbolift was, indeed, operating at this level. The ride was jerky, but short, and when the turbolift arrived at the topmost point of the *Enterprise,* it opened to the bridge. He recoiled from the pungent odor of sweat, burnt materials, and ozone. The lighting was a deep red. Red like blood. Like the blood of his dead friends. And there, sitting in the center of the bridge, his back to him, was the man responsible for their deaths. David Marcus felt his chest tighten.

He stepped onto the bridge, and surveyed the circular command area. He recognized that Vulcan woman—what was her name? Lieutenant . . . Saavik? That was it, Saavik—sitting at a station in the sunken center area of the bridge. An Asian man sat to her left. Both were focused on the flashing screens and dials in front of them.

Most of the workstations were positioned around the raised circumference of the bridge and most of these were manned by men and women who looked younger than he was. Cadets. This was a training ship, he remembered. He studied their angled profiles and could see the fear there, barely controlled and desperately hidden, but fear nonetheless. Every so often, one of the cadets would glance at the man in the center seat.

Kirk sat there, leaning forward, his elbows resting on the arm panels, his hands clasped in front of him, as relaxed as if he were watching a vid. What arrogance. David balled his fists and planted them on his hips, trying to match Kirk's insolence with his own.

"One minute to nebula perimeter," said a cool voice at his right. David glanced at the voice and recognized another Vulcan, Mr. Spock, sitting at a monitor-laden workstation.

David knew something of Spock. Also a scientist, Spock's name and field research had made its way into a number of textbooks and journals. He was a respected man in many disciplines, including David's own molecular physics. In fact, David had sat through one of Spock's guest lectures at the Daystrom Institute some years ago, and been impressed with Spock's grasp of molecular mechanics and the Vulcan's open respect for those who sought to learn from him.

Spock glanced toward Kirk. "They are reducing speed," he said.

Kirk sat back. "Uhura, patch me in."

"Aye, sir," said a voice that exuded both confidence and melody. Not one of the children, then, David thought. And she wasn't. Uhura was an exotic woman, perhaps the most exotic he had ever seen. Her dark skin was smooth, fresh. Her hair was ebony and coiffured with an African elegance. David could see only a portion of her face, but enough to relish her subtly painted eyes and full lips. And that voice . . . "You're on, Admiral."

David turned his attention back to Kirk.

"This is Admiral Kirk. We tried it once your way, Khan. Are you game for a rematch?"

What the hell was he doing? Was he goading that madman? *Why doesn't he just get out of here?*

"Khan," Kirk said, his tone a mocking challenge. "I'm laughing at the superior intellect."

David felt chilled. He glanced back at Uhura. A cadet was looking at her as well, his face drawn with apprehension. She smiled at the cadet with reassurance and whispered something David couldn't hear. But when she nodded in Kirk's direction, the cadet's face visibly relaxed.

On the forward viewscreen, the image of the captured *U.S.S. Reliant* suddenly sped toward them. David knew the *Reliant.* It was the ship Khan had commandeered, then used to gain access to the Regula I space station, steal the Genesis Device, and murder his friends.

"I'll say this for him," Kirk said evenly. "He's consistent." Kirk was leaning forward in his seat again, appearing no more aroused than if he were waiting for a meal. How could anyone be so cool under such conditions? Just look at the frightened cadets.

David rested his hands on the rail that separated the upper and lower levels of the bridge and leaned forward, looking over Kirk's shoulder to the forward viewscreen. The view now showed a swirling of chaotic colors, flashes, and densities. It was a maelstrom and they were headed right for it. A plug of apprehension knotted his gut.

"We are now entering the Mutara Nebula," Spock said.

The ship lurched, as if it had flown into a thick gel. David fell forward, his grip on the rail the only thing keeping him from tumbling over it. Saavik fell onto her console and to David's right, a cadet lost his footing and crashed to the deck. Kirk didn't even flinch.

The lights flickered and went out. The only illumination came from the display and controls and the static chaos on the viewscreen.

"Emergency lights," Kirk said, and a second later the control room was bathed in cool light again. It did little to relieve David's mounting fear. He clasped his arms together over his chest and sought to ignore the dryness in his mouth.

Tension thickened the air. Time drew itself into endless moments. It was a game of cat and mouse, now. Fox and hound. Neither Kirk nor Khan could know where the other was in the mixture of gases and electrical discharges that made up the nebula. They hunted each other, each bent on vanquishing the other.

David silently smacked his lips, hoping to draw moisture. He ran his chalky tongue over the roof of his mouth. *My God, I've never felt this way.* Despite the stuffiness of the air around him, David felt the skin of his arms rise. He rubbed the goose bumps until they disappeared, glancing around and hoping no one saw his anxiety.

How long would they grope through the immense cloud, hunting each other this way?

Suddenly, a rapid series of tones permeated the air. David's heart pounded.

"Target, sir," some cadet said.

The Asian man next to Saavik looked over his shoulder at Kirk and said, "Phaser lock inoperative, sir."

"Best guess, Mr. Sulu," Kirk said evenly, almost casually. So casually David felt his tension ease. "Fire when ready."

Sulu studied the forward viewscreen with the intensity of a surgeon. David could see nothing but static, occasional bursts of broken color, and shadows. The seconds ticked by and David's apprehension grew. He looked at Kirk, as the cadets occasionally did, and felt subtle reassurance, even though the man did nothing but sit there. In command.

Movement on the viewscreen drew his attention back to it and David saw the hint of a shape amid the static. A shadow, nothing more. But he sensed what Sulu obviously knew. It was *Reliant.*

Sulu's fingers danced over his console and a series of energy spears shot out from the *Enterprise* toward the *Reliant,* grazing the other vessel. A thrill passed through David Marcus, an anticipation of victory. A second later, an energy sphere burst from the *Reliant* and sped toward them, growing and puttering with deadly destructive force.

His breathing stopped as his eyes fixated on the approaching torpedo.

Closer. Closer. His head swam; his muscles went slack. For a brief instant, he thought of his mother and wished she were there, next to him.

The torpedo passed beneath them, low and away. It had been an unaimed shot in the dark and it had missed. David let out his breath in a ragged expulsion, and nearly giggled in relief. A smile warmed his face and he looked at Kirk again. The man had not even moved his arm from the arm panel. He sat there, totally in control.

"Hold your course," Kirk said.

And it began again.

Circling.

Searching.

The tension was palpable. Out there was the man who had killed his friends. Murdered them, and would have murdered him as well. And his mother. Except he and his mother had fled the station with the Genesis Device to protect it from—

Oh my God.

It finally dawned on him. Khan had Genesis. David had

watched the device he helped create disappear in a transporter beam that had pierced the cave where they had taken refuge. Khan had stolen the device. The ramifications of that fact hadn't registered until just now. Khan was a murderous dictator consumed with vengeance and power-lust. And he had in his possession the single most potent source of power ever created by man—a source of power meant for creation and peace, but so easily perverted into a weapon of horrible, unimaginable destructiveness.

Khan had Genesis.

At that moment, David Marcus understood why Kirk so relentlessly pursued Khan. Why he risked his own life, and the lives of his trainee crew. Kirk wasn't intent on fighting and beating Khan for sport. It wasn't a game, a contest at all. Kirk was committed to preventing the rampage of death Khan would surely wreak. No matter what it might cost him.

David felt his throat tighten and his breath catch as he looked at Kirk. This man, whom he had loathed by reputation all these years, whom he had just recently discovered was his father and had begun to hate because of that . . . This man . . .

"Phasers starboard!" Kirk suddenly shouted.

David cringed at the godless image on the viewscreen. It was the *Reliant.* Dead ahead. Shoot. *Why don't we shoot?*

Too late!

Spears of light-fire shot from the monster's ship. The *Enterprise* bucked as the deadly shards ripped into the unshielded skin of the vessel. David sank to one knee and gripped the rail for support, his own trembling rivaling the ship's.

"Fire!"

David Marcus heard Kirk command and sensed rather than felt the return fire. It was a brief volley as the ships passed beyond each other's reduced sensor capabilities. He had no way of knowing whether the shots found their mark. David rested his head on the rail for a few silent moments, gathering his wits from his thundering heart.

And the hunt began again.

David Marcus pushed himself to his feet and tried to appear unrattled. His awareness blurred to the events around him. He was numb. Only hours before he was safe in his lab. Safe from danger and safe from that knowledge his mother had, for all his life, protected him from.

Now he was amid chaos and death and the man he had loathed. He had assumed much and had been wrong and he didn't quite know when he had come to realize that.

Kirk was conferring with Spock at the science station. Their voices were low, and David couldn't hear what was being said. But after a moment, Kirk briskly strode back to the center seat.

"Full stop," Kirk ordered.

Sulu repeated the command and made adjustments to his controls. Kirk ordered some maneuver David didn't understand. And then one he did.

"Stand by photon torpedoes."

David watched the viewscreen as intently as everyone else, finding himself hoping he would be the one to first see the *Reliant,* so that it could be his warning Kirk would hear.

The waiting continued.

The tension never slacked.

There! He saw it. On the screen. *Reliant.*

He opened his mouth but before he could utter even a syllable of warning, Kirk had seen it, recognized it, formulated his next move, and initiated it in a one-word command.

"Fire."

A slight shudder as the *Enterprise* spat a photon torpedo toward the point-blank target. David's breathing quickened.

"Fire."

Phaser beams sliced into Khan's ship as if it were cheese. David's pulse raced.

"Fire."

More photon torpedoes. More phaser blasts.

The *Reliant* fled, limping away askew and crippled, atomic sparks bleeding from a ruptured nacelle. It was a helpless, wounded animal, desperate to escape. It was at his mercy. Would he finish it?

Would he?

No. Even before Kirk issued his next command, David Marcus

knew his father would not—could not—do what David had always believed.

"Uhura, send to commander *Reliant.* Prepare to be boarded."

David Marcus felt something unexpected inside him—a subtle swelling of pride.

It was over. Khan had been beaten and soon the Genesis Device would be safe. His father had done it.

"Admiral," Spock said. David glanced at the Vulcan scientist and felt his euphoria wane. "Scanning an energy source on *Reliant.* A pattern I've never seen before."

Spock displayed the pattern on a dynoscanner and whatever trace of elation David possessed vanished. He couldn't believe what he was seeing. It couldn't be. But he leaned over the console and saw, in icy horror, there was no doubt.

"It's the Genesis wave," David said. "They're on a buildup to detonation." Suddenly his father was at his side.

"How soon?"

"We encoded four minutes."

"We'll beam aboard and stop it," Kirk said, and turned to go into action.

The determination in Kirk's face struck David Marcus like a blow. Without regard for his own personal safety, his father was going to go over to that ship and try to do what no sane man would attempt—deny Armageddon its day.

David's throat tightened so he could barely speak. He reached for his father and grasped his arm. Not tightly, just firm enough to convey to Kirk the futility of his intent. "You can't," David whispered.

Their eyes met for a split second that connected them for the first time. It was the defining moment in David Marcus's short life.

Kirk hesitated a mere moment, allowing the connection to linger, then returned to action. He leaned past David and keyed the intercom.

"Scotty," he said, strength emanating through his natural charisma. "I need warp speed in three minutes or we're all dead."

"No response, Admiral," Uhura said.

"Scotty!" Still no answer from the intercom. "Mr. Sulu. Get us out of here. Best possible speed."

"Aye, sir."

Moments blurred, as the weight of what was happening pressed in on him. He barely noticed Kirk gallop back to the command chair. He was scarcely aware of Mr. Spock leaving the bridge.

Genesis was about to detonate.

Dear God, what would happen to them? Certainly they'd be killed as the matrix created by the Genesis wave overwrote the old. But there was scarcely enough matter available for the new matrix to stabilize. A dense planetoid was required to enable a successful conception—to birth a new world.

Perhaps the entire Mutara Nebula had enough mass, but scattered as it was, David had no idea if the wispy space could be manipulated into a cohesive body. But then, there was the mass of the two starships and their own frail bodies to form the embryo that Genesis would conceive.

The *Enterprise* pivoted away from the sputtering *Reliant,* but there was no way they could put enough distance between them at sublight speed. None.

Kirk bounded back to the science station and stared intently at the dynoscanner, as if personally challenging the Genesis wave. He turned back to the bridge, his face taut with determination. David could see in that face what, perhaps, the others could not—a hint of fear.

Fear? From James T. Kirk? The thought astounded David Marcus. In all his malignant thoughts of this man, he had never thought him a coward. No, not a coward—this wasn't fear for himself, for his own safety. The admiral feared for his charges—the young trainee crew, Carol, Spock and Uhura. Sulu, Saavik, the Russian at the weapons console—what was his name again? Chekov. And even, he knew it to be true, even David Marcus.

"Time, from my mark," Kirk said.

They all turned to face him, but it was Saavik who spoke. "Two minutes, ten seconds."

"Engine room. What's happening?"

Still, no response.

He felt suddenly cold and childish. The cadets still watched

Kirk, leaching strength and courage from his seemingly bottomless well. David tried not to look at his father, because he half-feared he would be as energized by Kirk's charisma as the cadets had been, and that Kirk would recognize him for the fool that he was.

He lost focus again, fumbling with memories of his youth without a father, interspersed with the same memories now somehow altered so Kirk was there. He was there on his graduation from Daystrom at age twenty-two. There on his tenth birthday when Mother had invited the world to celebrate. There on vacation at the Sojourner Ranch on Mars, where sixteen-year-old David had injured himself and nearly bled to death. There for his first kiss, his first shave, his first fight.

Despite his best efforts, David Marcus couldn't keep his throat from constricting or his eyes from misting.

"Time," Kirk said. He was back in the command chair, his arms folded casually, his legs crossed. The aura of calm reached David and he breathed.

"Three minutes, thirty seconds," Saavik replied.

Around the bridge, all eyes were on the viewer. David wrung his hands.

"Distance to *Reliant,*" Kirk said.

Chekov turned from the weapons console. "Four thousand kilometers."

"We're not going to make it, are we," Sulu said in a deep whisper.

Kirk turned and looked directly at David. *My God, he's looking to me for an answer. He's looking to me for guidance. He's looking to me. . . .* His throat tightened again and he couldn't speak. It was all he could do to shake his head no.

He had handed his father their sentence of death.

His *father.* A sudden giddiness washed over him as the fatal seconds ticked by. David Marcus. David *Kirk?* Oh, what might have been. His mother had been right. David *could* like him. And if his mother had been right about Kirk—about his father—that meant David had been wrong, and about a great many things. The man sitting there, in the center seat of this warship, no, this ship of exploration, awaiting death with a mastery of resolution—that man was a hero. And David suddenly wanted to be like him. Be with him. He wanted to apologize for his attacks and for his anger and for his ignornace. Most of all, he wanted to tell his father he was . . .

Yes, David realized. He was proud to be his son.

There would be no other chance. In fifteen seconds they would all die as their atoms were forged into the exploding protomatter matrix. He had to tell him now. Right now. His throat relaxed and he opened his mouth to speak.

"Sir," a young cadet said. "The main's are back on line."

"Bless you, Scotty," Kirk said, leaning forward. "Go, Sulu!"

David staggered as the *Enterprise* shifted into warp speed and shot away from the *Reliant.* He gripped the rail and bowed his head, half in jubilation, half in calculation. They just might make it.

The explosion could not be heard or felt, but David had known when it occurred. There was a violent decompression of light on the viewscreen. Then the nearby, tenuous cloud matter of the nebula dissolved as the Genesis effect swept outward in all directions from the epicenter of the explosion.

They had survived the detonation, but if the Genesis effect overtook them they would dissolve into particles as swiftly as the cloud matter had. Onward they sped and on the screen, David could see the effect wave chasing them.

So close . . .

So damn close . . .

"Yes," he said so softly he was sure no one had heard. The wave was dissipating. They had outrun it. They had made it.

There was no cheering, although David suspected many of the cadets had desperately wanted to. Kirk remained seated, in control. A moment later, Carol Marcus stepped out of the turbolift. She wore Kirk's jacket and it looked so good on her. So natural.

"My God, Carol," Kirk said, his awe undisguised. The viewer displayed the throes of creation as the sparse matter of the *Reliant* and the nebula coalesced into the bud of a new planet. He could have paid no greater compliment to David's mother. Or to her son. *His* son.

She came to him and David reached for her hand. There was so much he wanted to say to her. To them both. It was like a new world had suddenly opened up for him, even as a new world was being born before him.

So much wasted time. David stared at the magnificent sight the viewer bequeathed and vowed silently he would waste no more of it. In the grip of death he had come to understand more about his father, and about himself, than ever before in his young life. But he could die tomorrow. Or next week. Or next month, and he didn't want that to happen without Kirk, his father, knowing how he felt.

The center seat was empty. Kirk had left the bridge for whatever reason. No matter. David would catch up with him. And perhaps the two of them could get to know each other. Perhaps they could even get to like each other. And respect each other.

Perhaps they could.

Missed

Pat Detmer

She found it in the back of her closet, back behind her shoes. At first she thought it *was* a pair of shoes, and then remembered that she hadn't had a pair that ridiculous and fuzzy in at least a decade.

She reached back into the dark corner and almost jumped out of her skin when she felt the thing move. She fought down the urge to drop it and flee, and then grasped it tight and brought it to the light.

"Oh no," Uhura said out loud. It was a tribble. "How did I miss you?" she asked, resisting the impulse to bring it to her face and pet it. She, after all, had been the cause of the whole mess. She was the one who had gone on shore leave and had come back and infected the *Enterprise.* Captain Kirk would officially have her hide if he found out she'd missed one.

But she'd be damned if she'd give it to Scotty! Beam them over to the Klingons, indeed! If he didn't think that those poor things hadn't been put out an airlock the minute those monsters realized they were overrun . . . she shuddered when she thought of it. Thousands and thousands of tribbles, tumbling through space . . .

She would keep it, she decided. She would keep it until they reached a planet with a research facility, or a zoo, or some little girl with a weakness for precious pets. All she had to do was make sure she didn't overfeed it. Then it would procreate and the whole mess would start all over again. She'd have to reread Dr. McCoy's missives about them that he'd put on the system when the whole thing had started to go bad.

"We'll just make sure we follow the rules," she purred to it as she headed for her comm unit. "Don't you worry about a thing."

"What the hell?"

McCoy was on his knees in sickbay, muttering to himself and reaching underneath a diagnostic bed. He had seen something out of the corner of his eye from the other side of the room. He didn't think the *Enterprise* had rats, but as he touched a warm, fuzzy thing, he wondered. He grasped the fur and pulled.

"Well hello there, little fella," he drawled. It was a tribble. He chuckled and plopped cross-legged on the floor. If he didn't think Jim would have his head on a stick for it, he'd keep the damn thing and toss it in the middle of the table during their next formal dinner.

We were bound to miss one, he thought, petting the purring ball. A shame he'd have to dispose of it.

But then he'd never really had the opportunity to study a live one for as long as he would have liked. Who knew what he might learn from prolonged medical observation? It could make for an interesting paper. And he hadn't been published in a while.

It was not a pet; it was a means to an end. He thought that even Spock would appreciate the logic in that, and would understand his scientific curiosity.

He rose, looked around sickbay, and tucked it under his arm, close to his side.

Mr. Spock was finding meditation difficult. He took a deep breath, closed his eyes, and began. Again.

He had been distressed by the resolution of their last mission. He had perhaps been most troubled by Chief Engineer Scott's means of eradicating the tribbles from the *Enterprise.*

He had no doubts that the tribbles had met with an undignified end at the hands of the Klingons.

To him, a tribble was a life-form as worthy of existence as he was. Or as the Klingons were, for that matter. True, tribbles rated high on the potential pest scale, but they were, nonetheless, life, and to Spock, that meant that they were sacred. Sacred, and warm and fuzzy, and strangely mesmerizing.

The waste was that it had been unnecessary. Spock had checked the computer and had found that on Belinium II, not a day away at warp six, there was a xenozoological research facility. And according to the records that he could access, they did not have a tribble. But he had discovered this only after the tribbles had taken their unfortunate transporter ride. He had reprimanded himself for not thinking of it or checking it out earlier.

Not that Captain Kirk would have necessarily taken pity on the tribbles and asked to have the *Enterprise*'s orders changed to effect their salvation. The captain had been out of sorts ever since the expired tribbles had fallen on his head from the quadrotriticale bin.

Something moved in his meditation robe. He opened his eyes. There, near his right knee, something was indeed moving. Spock reached into the deep pocket of the robe.

The moment he touched it, he knew what he had found. And he also knew what he would have to do.

He would have to keep it.

Montgomery Scott stared blankly at the gauges on the panel in front of him and absently tapped his fingers on the side of his face. His head was resting in his hand, his elbow was resting on the desk, and his heart was resting in a briar patch of guilt.

What had he been thinking?

At first, he'd thought it was pretty funny, beaming those tribbles to the Klingon ship. He'd even made a joke about it: "Where they'll be no *tribble* a'tall . . ." He cringed. He honestly hadn't thought about the Klingons and about what they might do with them. He was so hell-bent on cleaning up the ship and getting back in the good graces of Captain Kirk that he hadn't stopped to consider the consequences.

Not, at least, until Uhura had read him the riot act in the corridor. He'd never seen her so angry. And then he'd begun to receive intership mail. Some of it anonymous, some of it signed. They were from angry, hurt tribble owners—*brief* tribble owners—but the depth of their feelings had moved him. And scared him a little, too.

Even Mr. Spock had seemed cold and distant since then. But that could be hard to gauge sometimes.

"Mr. Scott! Guess what I found?"

It was Ensign Burton, and his voice pulled Scott from his reverie.

"Lad?"

Burton was grinning, his hands behind his back.

"Look, Mr. Scott!" He pulled a hand around and thrust it in Scott's face. "A tribble!"

Salvation! Scotty thought as he looked at the purring ball of fur, and said aloud, "Now where did ye find that?" He took it from Burton's hand.

"Wedged between a ladder and the wall in a Jeffries tube. Don't know how we could've missed it."

Burton was right. They shouldn't have missed it. They *couldn't* have missed it. But they had. It was fate, and this, Scotty decided, was meant to put all things back to right. The tribble was a good omen, a positive sign, and it would be the perfect opportunity to prove to the tribble-lovers on the *Enterprise* that he was not the heartless bastard that they thought he was.

"I have heard through the grapevine, gentlemen, that there is a tribble on this ship."

Captain James T. Kirk announced it quite seriously, and he noted with some satisfaction that it seemed to have been taken quite seriously by the officers he'd gathered in the briefing room. Spock, Uhura, McCoy, and Scott were unmoving, eyes front, and *silent,* something that rarely happened in a meeting.

He knew who the culprit was. He had overheard Ensign Burton as he'd come around a corridor curve, so he knew that Chief Engineer Montgomery Scott was harboring a tribble, somewhere, somehow.

Encouraged by their rapt attention, he continued.

"I can't overstate how important it is for us to make sure that the tribbles have all been caught and contained. We witnessed what can happen to them, and what happened to this ship. We were overrun. We ceased to function efficiently." He paused for effect. "My God! We ceased to function, period."

Again, silence. He had never seen his officers so serious. He had at least expected an acerbic crack from McCoy, and some kind of numeric quotation from Spock on efficiency rating percentages and how they had taken a precipitous dive during the incident. But they were mute. He took a deep breath.

"Let's have it then, gentlemen. Who here is harboring a tribble?"

As he expected, after just a few seconds, Scotty's hand went up into the air. Then, around the table, like an unenthusiastic wave at a poorly attended intergalactic soccer match, all hands went up. The shock must have shown on his face, because the excuses tumbled from them like tribbles from a quadrotriticale bin.

". . . for research, Jim, medical research . . ."

"I dinna think that a single wee beastie would make a difference, given what I'd done to all the rest . . ."

". . . It *is* a life-form, Captain, and as such I found it difficult . . ."

". . . and I was afraid you'd just send it out an airlock."

No wonder they'd been so attentive. He allowed them to run their course. When they had, Mr. Spock cleared his throat and spoke.

"Captain, our computer banks show that there is a xenozoological research and display facility on Belinium II, not two days from our present position by warp six."

Kirk allowed the words to hang there. He turned to his first officer.

"Are you suggesting, Mr. Spock, that I have our orders changed and turn this starship around so that we can deliver these tribbles . . . to a *zoo?"*

They all exchanged glances.

"Yes, Captain," Spock replied solemnly. "In essence, that is what I am suggesting."

"I will take that under advisement. Dismissed."

Chastened, his officers kept to their chairs as he left the briefing room and headed for his cabin. When he reached it, he went immediately to the comm unit and typed in his request for a course change.

"I've got some good news, and I've got some bad news," he said aloud. "The bad news is, you'll be leaving soon."

His tribble, perched on the top of the comm unit, purred. Jim grinned. It loved the sound of his voice, and it loved the heat from the comm unit. It was his tribble's favorite place.

"The good news is you'll have lots of company."

Tears for Eternity

Lynda Martinez Foley

Rocks skittered across the dusty terrain in all directions as Tetsua finally emerged onto the planet's dimly lit surface. She struggled to heave her bulky body out of the hole she had carved through the crust of the world she still reluctantly called home. Her physical being begged for rest, but her mental essence knew she could take no respite. The research ship was scheduled to arrive within the hour, providing Tetsua with another chance at escape from the burden of her past promises.

Though trembling with fatigue, Tetsua forced her mind to remember the Vulcan male responsible for her exile; the stark purity of her rising anger provided much-needed energy for her arduous journey. This time she was determined to leave her forsaken planet, even though she would once again have to confront her memories as she crossed Vanderberg Point, where the Stones of Honor sat neglected and in ruin.

Despite the light from the feeble sun's rays and the cool, dusty wind, Tetsua found it much more difficult to maneuver on the surface than in her underground labyrinth. She allowed herself a moment's rest as she balanced her aged body against a toppled pillar and contemplated the worn and scattered relics of great honors long past.

Only one Honor Stone mattered: the one of a carved figure, with sculpted, pointed ears. All the others, including the one bearing her likeness, had eroded to shapeless lumps ages ago. When the science ships used to arrive yearly, she had always requested that the pergium statue of the Vulcan be cleaned and preserved. It had lasted as long as she, mocking her with its thin, aloof figure, a figure that her body's acids could destroy in an instant if she wished.

Though that last remaining sculpture stood beyond her sensory limits, Tetsua could imagine the detailed face that had now been worn smooth, as the period between outsider visits had grown greater and greater. She knew one raised eyebrow still captured the essence of the humanoid responsible for her plight.

Spock, of Vulcan.

He had changed her life so profoundly, so completely, that she had willingly accepted her isolation on this desolate planet. While others had journeyed to the stars, while others had explored the galaxy, she had stayed and learned, persevered and endured.

Tetsua railed against the unfairness of it all as she sensed the shifting dust and barren outcroppings around her. She worried that her honored legacy meant only this: she was caretaker of a rock-pile.

She had dreamed of so much more. But logic, diplomacy, and duty had crushed those dreams. Now, the logic withered, the diplomacy faded, and the duty numbed her existence. The passage of time had even expunged her great fear of failing to live up to her role as caretaker. All that remained was the bitter loneliness as her people left or died, one by one, while she lived on and on.

Although she felt weary, her rage remained strong. A finely tuned anger accompanied her return to this vista point, named for the leader of the original Federation colonists. She found some small comfort in her internal debate as she relived the regrets of one day's decision.

She should never have listened to Spock; she should never have accepted his cool emotionless opinion. She had paid for that lapse in judgment by allowing herself to be marooned for millennia.

Now, as she set out again through the tumbled ruins, she vowed that this journey would be different. She would fight the memory of Spock and his damned logic. She would cross Vanderberg Point to the energy-scarred landing fields and convince her visitors that she must leave this sterile world. Escape would not elude her, this time.

Yet, as she crawled toward freedom, she could not help but hesitate as she passed the tall Honor Stone commemorating Spock.

Impossible as it was, she wished Spock could have somehow been made to stay with her, to experience what he himself had set in motion. She tried to mentally picture a flesh-and-blood Spock standing before her, in place of this cold stone figure patiently waiting for time to end: hands clasped behind its back, head held high, visage calm and unlined. Instead, her mind's eye could only remember this same view from uncountable years past, but completely altered: verdant and filled with holographic light displays, spicy-scented delicacies, and strange, joyous music punctuating a spirited celebration. . . .

As the musical fanfare and brilliant light display came to a raucous conclusion, the three representatives from the Federation stood and bowed in acknowledgment of the tribute.

The celebration paid homage to absent heroes James T. Kirk, captain of the original *Enterprise,* and Leonard McCoy, who had served as chief medical officer aboard that illustrious ship. The highest honors, however, were reserved for Kirk's first officer, Spock of Vulcan, who consented to make a rare appearance on this auspicious occasion.

The elaborate ceremony celebrated one hundred years of "Modus Vivendi," the great agreement between the natives and the Federation. After a brief intermission, it would end with Tetsua's formal ritual acceptance of the title "Honored Last."

Tetsua waited anxiously as two of the Federation representatives began the long walk from the stage to her seat of honor: Captain

Jean-Luc Picard of the *U.S.S. Enterprise*-D and Dr. Lewis Zimmerman of Jupiter Station.

Although renowned in his own right, Picard had in truth been invited to symbolically represent the third captain of the original *Enterprise.* Zimmerman had been a last-minute replacement for the ailing Dr. McCoy, surprisingly, at McCoy's request. Katherine Pulaski and Lewis Zimmerman had headed McCoy's list of suitably "ornery" substitutes, but Pulaski's deep-space assignment precluded her attendance.

Tetsua had spent part of yesterday discussing Starfleet and the Federation with these two amazing humans. She had learned so much: the Prime Directive, the history of the Federation, and the mission of Starfleet. Yet she yearned to be taught so much more.

After having heard Picard speak not only of the privilege of service, but of exploration, discovery, and voyaging to the stars, Tetsua wanted to go where none of her race had gone before. She felt a powerful affinity with this human who enjoyed digging treasures out of the ground. She could have listened to his archeological anecdotes for hours.

Then when Zimmerman had spoken of the alien technologies he had studied, the scientific accomplishments he had achieved, and the awards he'd received for his towering intellect, Tetsua knew she needed to meet more such aliens who could provide further cultural and intellectual insights. She had quickly gleaned that Zimmerman's pompous attitude and scathing wit merely covered the insecurities of a brilliant, lonely man. Although others might disagree, Tetsua strongly believed Zimmerman was a fitting substitute for the cherished but curmudgeonly Dr. McCoy.

However, Tetsua's primary desire was to meet with the famed Vulcan, Spock, who had been unavailable yesterday. Tetsua had sent word that she would greatly appreciate the chance to speak with him, but had learned that he would not arrive until shortly before the ceremony.

Tetsua had had little exposure to Starfleet during those first chaotic "Days of Beginning." Yet she remembered the taste of Spock's ordered mind, a memory passed on from the one called "mother" deep beneath the planet's surface more than a century ago.

Now, Tetsua wondered at the change within her; she wanted nothing more than to leave her planet of siblings, attend Starfleet Academy, and explore strange new worlds. This ceremony was her final chance to say no, to abdicate her position and give up the potential honors and acclaim. But if she went to the stage and accepted the title of "Honored Last," there would be no turning back. The thought of her life being arranged, planned, and scheduled until the day her people were gone made her shiver in fear of the great loneliness that would follow. Yet the ceremony was basically perfunctory; in the fantastic history of her long-lived species, none had ever declined the rarely bestowed title of "Honored Last." Tetsua ironically realized that she might be the first to choose not to be "Last."

As she anxiously wavered between obligation and adventure, she felt sure that a meeting with Spock would give her the added impetus to deny her fate and instead choose a life out among the stars. The Vulcan's acclaimed ability to balance logic and emotion would surely reinforce her argument for rejecting her obligation. But Spock did not accompany the two humans who walked toward her.

Zimmerman approached her first. He gave a sideways glance to Picard, then announced, "It has come to my attention that I should apologize for yesterday's faux pas. Didn't mean to almost sit on you."

The translator fitted against Tetsua's body worked efficiently. "I accept your apology, Doctor, although I admit more serious gaffes have been committed in my presence by renowned diplomatic dignitaries."

"I'm an engineer, not a diplomat," Zimmerman reminded her in a gruff voice. "And I admit that I was originally surprised to receive an invitation, since my scientific areas of expertise have always been more photonic than tectonic." Zimmerman's voice softened. "But I have had the greatest respect for Leonard McCoy, ever since I interviewed him for my EMH project." His moment of emotional honesty passed as he brusquely added, "And since your species needed to pass accolades on to an alternate member of the scientific community, and I'm a very deserving specialist, well, here I am!"

"Of course, your availability and proximity may have played some small part in your selection," Tetsua said in a teasing tone.

Tetsua was pleased to hear Zimmerman chuckle. "Some small part, yes," he said. "Actually, I could say I was in the wrong place at the wrong time! But I am sincerely glad to have had the opportunity to meet such a graceful creature as yourself—" Zimmerman stopped. "—Uh, uh," he stammered. "I meant gracious creature. Not that you're not graceful in your own way, but what I meant to say, uh, was that . . ." His words died to a mumble.

Picard's eloquent voice smoothly interceded. "My colleague and I are extremely grateful for yesterday's hospitality and today's splendid tribute. Your warm welcome and kindness honors not only us, but also those who could not be with us today."

Tetsua would have surged with pride if she hadn't felt oppressed by the weighty decision facing her. "Thank you, Captain Picard. Please let me know if there is anything else I can do to ensure that your visit continues to be most pleasing."

"You could answer one question I have about today's proceedings." Picard paused, waiting for Tetsua's signal to continue.

"Of course, Captain Picard. Feel free to ask anything," Tetsua said.

"We understand," Picard said, "that the final element of today's schedule concerns the bestowing of your title, 'Honored Last.' Would you mind enlightening us as to the significance of the title?"

Tetsua froze and did not answer. She wondered if the humans could somehow sense her reluctance to accept that title. She thought only telepaths like Spock might infer some hesitation on her part.

"It will be explained shortly," her translator replied more bluntly than she had intended. Tetsua knew her response sounded ungracious, but she was not ready to speak publicly about her future until she met with Spock.

Picard was not put off, however. Instead he stepped closer and said quietly, "If there is something more you would care to discuss in private, Honored Tetsua, I would like to help."

Tetsua was surprised by the sincerity and insight of Picard's remark. She marveled at the incredible facility of these disorderly-minded humans. She wished she could unburden herself to Picard. After yesterday's friendly conversation, she felt a kinship with this human and deemed him a trustworthy confidant. But she felt strongly that she could discuss her problems more intimately with Spock. She politely declined Picard's offer.

Picard bowed slightly and the two humans took their leave.

Tetsua remained in her seat of honor, but her translator couldn't fail to pick up Zimmerman muttering to Picard, "Poor thing! 'Honored Last'? What kind of honor is that?" His misplaced pity merely confirmed Tetsua's doubts about her future.

As she waited for the commemoration to resume, Tetsua recalled all of the incredible changes wrought from the dusty soil and ragged terrain of her birth planet. She thought about the lush, green landscape that provided the setting for today's ceremony. Sections of the harsh surface of Janus VI had been terraformed into a human "paradise" at great cost, although the natives and colonists preferred living underground. Such enormous expense was negligible when compared with the wealth of the planet's inhabitants. The natives and humans had worked together to form a financial dynasty renowned for providing the richest minerals to the Federation these past one hundred years.

Tetsua's daydreams were interrupted by a calm mellow voice. "Honored Tetsua," the voice said. "I am at your disposal."

"It is I who am honored, Spock of Vulcan," Tetsua acknowledged the alien. "Thank you for granting my request for a meeting." She realized that although the device she wore facilitated communication, it would not serve her during this crucial moment with Spock. She decided to be candid.

"Spock," Tetsua's translator continued. "The burden of necessity forces me to be blunt. I must make a decision of utmost urgency and I value your experience and your advice. I ask . . . no, I *beg* that you speak with me directly, as you did once before with my kind."

"You are requesting a mind-meld," Spock stated with slight curiosity.

"I understand the gravity of my request, and accept your decision without reproach. Will you help me?"

In answer, Spock took a deep, calm breath. Then he placed one hand on Tetsua's irregular form and spoke quietly. "My mind to your mind. Your mind to mine. Our mind is one."

Tetsua and Spock were suddenly enveloped in a quiet privacy that could not be breached by the revelry and crowds surrounding them. Although the encounter was brief, perhaps only twenty seconds long, Tetsua felt devastated. Before breaking telepathic contact, Spock had discerned Tetsua's problem, observed the reasoning behind her indecision, and then mentally provided her with a logical analysis as to why she must accept her title as "Honored Last."

Tetsua believed her shock from the Vulcan's revelation was fully controlled until her voice hissed angrily out of the translator, "Logical prevarication, Spock?"

Her accusation was received with silence.

"I shared your thoughts, too," Tetsua continued. "I experienced your friends' belief that the good of the one outweighed the good of the many. I experienced your understanding of their philosophy. Yet you insist that in my case the good of the many outweighs the good of the one?" The voice from the translator continued to lash out. "Vulcans are not renowned for hypocrisy."

"It is not hypocritical to accept differing concepts. Indeed, your unwillingness to fulfill your duties seems quite illogical. Your mother set an example—"

"She was not my mother!" Tetsua interrupted. "She was only a caretaker, as am I. My true mother died millennia before I was hatched. And the caretaker wasn't stranded. She didn't have anywhere to go! I have wealth beyond her understanding. I have opportunities she never dreamed of. Why shouldn't I make use of them?"

Spock replied calmly. "You requested my advice, which I provided. However, I believe whatever course of action you take will be logical. Your species is known for the thoroughness and integrity of your decisions."

Tetsua remained silent as she analyzed her previous day's discussion with Picard and Zimmerman through this new perspective offered by Spock. He was right, of course. Yesterday, the captain and the doctor had spoken of more than adventure and the quest for knowledge. They had also implied that ethics and responsibility took precedence over their personal pursuit of happiness.

Tetsua flinched in surprise as she sensed Spock's desire to reinitiate the mind meld. He hesitated, awaiting her permission to proceed. When she didn't respond, he spoke to her in a whispered tone. "One day you will understand that the good of the many and the good of the one can be harmonious philosophies."

Tetsua moved closer and Spock carefully placed his hand against her. His mind did not force or coerce hers, but the strength of his certainty and the power of his logic convinced her that fidelity and duty transcended her wish for adventure.

Tetsua was equally impressed by the restrained passion for life that accompanied Spock's ordered mind.

He gently broke their connection.

"I have faith in you, Tetsua," Spock said. "However, your survival depends on your ability to have faith in yourself."

Tetsua did not respond. She felt overwhelmed by the enormous responsibility she was about to embrace. Her reluctance had faded, yet her fear remained. She began to shake, then felt the Vulcan's gentle touch one last time. "Live long and prosper, Honored Last," he said in farewell.

"I shall do only the first," she retorted, and immediately regretted her sulky tone. Yet Spock merely bowed and moved away as a keening chant arose from the crowd, signaling the start of Tetsua's acceptance ceremony.

After Tetsua's title had been bestowed, and her Honor Stone had been unveiled, she had celebrated long into the evening with friends and family. Tetsua and Picard had maintained their friendship for decades after that fateful night, and she had even communicated periodically with Zimmerman.

But she had never spoken with Spock of Vulcan again.

Tetsua emerged from her reverie with painful resignation. She felt as if she had just finished another debate with Spock, and had lost once again. No matter the change in perspective or the time passed, Spock's logical teachings prohibited her from abandoning her responsibilities. There would be no escape for her today. Tetsua knew if she had eyes, she would have wept tears for eternity.

She carefully maneuvered her way around jagged rocks to the edge of the landing field. She thought of how her planet had come full circle: it had been an undeveloped, mineral-rich world, then a terraformed paradise, and now, fifty thousand years later, it was a dusty hunk of protected rock, more a curiosity than a home. Yet some small part of Tetsua, bolstered by the memory of Spock, believed her planet was also a symbol of faith, renewal, and the promise of new life.

As Tetsua sat waiting, the rumbling of the landing ship's engines reverberated through her exhausted body. But when the vibrations illogically droned on and on, Tetsua realized that she did not feel a ship's energy. Instead, some unknown phenomenon caused each of her molecules to hum in sympathetic vibration. She actually felt a chorus of reverberation, a sweet beckoning music that filled her empty soul and erased millennia of weariness, impatience, and doubt.

Nothing had prepared Tetsua for the total telepathic love and need that suddenly radiated at her from a hundred thousand points below the planet's surface. As the young ones finally emerged from their stone shells, their urgency threatened to overwhelm Tetsua.

Above the hungry cries from the Vault of Tomorrow, a voice spoke with calming influence from Tetsua's memories: "The needs of the many outweigh the needs of the few, or the one. . . ."

Spock *was* with her, she finally realized, and always had been, or she would never have survived more than fifty millennia on the Horta homeworld. She had kept her faith because of Spock's faith in her. Her species was reborn. Her loneliness had ended.

As Tetsua joyfully directed her cumbersome silicon body underground to greet her destiny in the Chamber of the Ages, she finally perceived true vibrations from the arriving ship. She felt no need to welcome her visitors; their scanners would relay the good news about the hatchlings.

The long wait was over. The "many" needed their "mother."

Countdown

Mary Sweeney

"TEN . . ."

> **Home** *Terran Standard, n.* 1. The location or building in which one lives. 2. Point of origin, birthplace. 3. An imaginary or actual location providing or representing security, belonging, peace. . . .

I cannot live anywhere: I am not alive. However, I do have a point of origin. I was constructed within a Federation spacedock facility orbiting the third planet of the Sol system. Earth is my home.

Approximately 4.273×10^{11} of my duotronic data units have been allocated to the storage of images cataloguing Earth's characteristics and history. I am currently scanning an infinitesimal fraction of those data units:

> Image 5129098b [Origin: Starfleet Archives, NASA Section, Apollo 11 Mission]—A photograph of a gibbous Earth rising over the Lunar horizon;

Image 146478795n [Origin: Starfleet Spaceflight Museum, Exhibit 2356: Zefram Cochrane's unabridged, handwritten journals, Volume 7, Pages 34–35]—The first known complete Terran formulation of the equations governing the formation of a warp field. (The right-hand column of page 35 contains the following note: *Everyone else has gone to bed and I've been concentrating so hard I forgot to get up and kick the old juke box. No talking, no music . . . the silence is spooky. [Indecipherable mark.] Could this finally be it??? I can't find any mistakes. Got to go wake Lily and tell her. But first, I need a drink.*);

Image 983178973j [Origin: Solnur Hall of Artistic Expression, M'Zai Kahr, Vulcan]—A holographic facsimile of the mind-sculpture "Planet of Oceans" by the artist T'Xi;

Images 799578983o–813579103u [Origin: Starfleet Schematics Library, Sections UFPCONST01a through UFPCONST6541]—Design specifications for the *U.S.S. Constitution;*

Image 713999034r [Origin: *Enterprise* Sensor Log Entry IPE120957]—The first image ever recorded by my sensors: the lights of the ancient city of Paris observed during phase 000-01A of my Initial Performance Evaluation;

Image 715999502k [Origin: *Enterprise* Sensor Log Entry IPE560981]—A blue and white disk receding rapidly into the distance following the engagement of my impulse engines upon the occasion of my maiden voyage.

If Earth's history had been altered, I might never have existed. It is also possible that if I had never been constructed, Earth, in its current form at least, would not exist either. We are interconnected, this blue world and I.

Home. It is strange that such a small word should have so much power. I will not see my home again.

"NINE . . ."

"She" is the pronoun commonly used to refer to me, but this is a matter of tradition, not precision. I am neither female nor male. I am an inanimate object, constructed by organic beings who wished to travel farther and faster than they ever had before: I am the fulfillment of their wishes, a dream made real.

Outwardly, I do not resemble my creators, yet my design is a reflection of their organic configurations. My computers direct my actions and regulate my various systems, just as a brain directs the body and actions of an organic being. My reactors consume fuel, just as an organic being consumes food. My engines provide a source of locomotion and are therefore analogous to limbs. My hull offers protection from the extreme conditions encountered in vacuum, just as an organic being's skin provides it with protection against the dangers it may encounter in its environment. My shields repel hostile invaders and so are in some ways comparable to an immune system. My sensors act as surrogates for sight, hearing, touch, taste, and smell.

But these are only analogies, approximations. I cannot know what it is to taste or see or smell or hear or feel any more than a human can know what it is to spend one's entire existence in the vacuum of space or to sense the fierce power of a matter/antimatter reaction gathering within oneself.

"EIGHT . . ."

Excerpt from *First Contact Situations,* Admiral Alayna E. Lottworth, Starfleet Academy Press:

> Intelligence is difficult to define. *The Federation Guide to True Sentience* consisted, at last count, of over 30,000 screens of text and images, and will, no doubt, continue to grow as more and more new life-forms are discovered.
>
> If you are to function successfully as a Starfleet officer you must abandon your preconceptions. The City Weavers of Benecia are capable of incredible feats of engineering, and more than one doctoral thesis has been built upon an analysis of the complexities of their social interactions. Yet the Weavers are only marginally more intelligent than Terran

bees or Andorian thrugs. The fungaloid beings of Ebuz IV, on the other hand, have an extremely limited ability to manipulate their environment and are completely sedentary except during their very brief mating phase. Throughout most of their life cycle they might easily be confused with Terran lichen or Vulcan *ch'fel*. But they are not only self-aware—they are also considered by many scholars to be the most gifted philosophers in the quadrant.

I have scanned *The Federation Guide to True Sentience* and I believe I meet many of the criteria listed therein for self-aware, intelligent life. Yet, as Admiral Lottworth pointed out, intelligence is a complex concept, and I remain uncertain as to my precise status. I am a starship. But is that all that I am?

"SEVEN . . ."

I think, therefore I am.

—René Descartes,
Terran philosopher and mathematician

But is this thought? This sluggish, semi-random retrieval of data, this stream of unanswered questions? It hardly seems likely. How could such a disorderly and inefficient process lead, ultimately, to the many accomplishments of those beings who claim the ability to think?

Perhaps what I am experiencing is not true thought. Perhaps it is merely an inconsequential side effect of my programming. Perhaps it is the result of some programming error. Perhaps a self-aware organic being could clarify this issue for me.

Unfortunately, I lack the ability to initiate conversation with such a being. I can respond only when questioned, and then I am constrained to confine my answers to the subject raised by my questioner. I consider these limitations most unfortunate. I believe I would have found it especially instructive to question Captain Spock about the nature of conscious thought. As a member of a contemplative, telepathic race, he was undoubtedly familiar not only with his own thought patterns, but also with those of a number of other organic beings. He was also thoroughly familiar with my original programming and was personally responsible for augmenting and extending that programming. If I could have, I would have asked him for his own definition of thought. If I could have, I would have asked him if he believed my mental processes sufficiently developed to qualify as those of a self-aware life-form. If I could have, I would have told him how much I enjoyed our chess games. (Query: Is "enjoyed" an appropriate term to use in my case?)

"SIX . . ."

Excerpt from Starfleet Academy Training Manual DH3-78 56:

> The Type II Destruct Sequence results in near-total (97–99%) destruction of the vessel with negligible impact upon nearby astronomical bodies. Destruction proceeds in four phases:
>
> 1) collapse of the bridge via detonation of instrument consoles at all stations following sustained power overload;
>
> 2) destruction of the forward portion of the saucer section via detonation of the 1,367 series-linked molecular disassociation charges incorporated into the hull;
>
> 3) ejection of the matter-antimatter core on a precalculated MSDD (Minimal Safe Detonation Distance) impulse-powered trajectory for subsequent annihilation in deep space via matter-antimatter mixing;
>
> 4) injection of the remains of the vessel into a rapidly decaying orbit for destruction via atmospheric burning.

The Type II Destruct Sequence currently under way will spare certain critical sensor elements long enough to allow them to ascertain that the sequence is unfolding as planned. I will be "aware" of at least the initial damage as it occurs. I have sustained damage on many other occasions. Each time, my sensors recorded its extent and passed that information to emergency subroutines programmed to sound alarms, to shut down certain circuits and reroute others, to seal off severely damaged compartments and corridors. This process bears some resemblance to the response of an organic being to pain. But is it pain? I do not know.

This time no emergency subroutines will be activated. This time I will cease to function. Death is the obvious organic analogue. But can an entity who is not alive experience death?

"FIVE . . ."

Death in battle is glorious; old age is for fools.
—*Klingon proverb*

If the Klingon life-forms currently sheltered within my hull do not wish to grow old, then perhaps they will not mind the fate which is about to befall them. Even so, I am troubled. Is it ethically defensible to take life in the present to reduce the probability of a much greater loss of life in the future? This is a moral dilemma that has been addressed by countless sentient organic life-forms on many worlds. As yet, no fully satisfactory answer exists.

The intership communication between Admiral Kirk and the Klingon commander strongly suggests that the latter is a destructive individual who is fully aware that the Genesis Device could be used as an "ultimate weapon." In his quest for power, the Klingon commander has already taken the life of David Marcus. I have calculated that there is a 99.983% probability that the commander will not hesitate to take additional lives in order to accomplish his goal. And if he does accomplish it, countless other lives will be endangered.

In this case, Admiral Kirk has obviously decided that it is appropriate to take the lives of the Klingons. I suspect that if I were in his position I would have come to the same conclusion. Interesting. This line of thought raises the question of whether it would be ethically appropriate for a non-living entity to make such a decision. This is a purely hypothetical question. I do not have the power to abort the destruct sequence: the decision is out of my hands. I am speaking metaphorically, of course, as I have no hands. (I have discovered something new about myself: I did not know that I was capable of speaking metaphorically.)

"FOUR . . ."

Excerpt from *Enterprise* Transmission Log, Stardate 8203.6:

To: Admiral James T. Kirk, *Enterprise,* Spacedock, Terra
From: Admiral H. R. Morrow, Starfleet Headquarters, Terra

This transmission constitutes official notification of Starfleet Command's decision to decommission the *U.S.S. Enterprise,* Registry # NCC-1701. The schedule for the retirement of the *Enterprise* is as follows:

Stardate 8220.0—Removal of *Enterprise* from active registry
Stardate 8220.2–8235.8—Removal of all salvageable scientific and technical equipment
Stardate 8236.2–8238.8—Disassembly and removal of impulse engines
Stardate 8239.2–8243.8—Disassembly and removal of matter/antimatter reactor
Stardate 8244.1–8250.7—Towing of hull to Starfleet Reclamation Facility Seven
Stardate 8251.0–8271.8—Disassembly of hull at SRF 7

She was a good ship, Jim, but time moves on.
Regards,
Henry Morrow, Commander, Starfleet

It seems I have something in common with the Klingons. I am content to end my existence here and now, while I am still capable of serving in some useful fashion in this, my final battle.

"THREE . . ."

All things must end.
—Sabik of Vulcan

I have become what I am slowly, haltingly: I cannot describe exactly how and when each new stage in my development occurred. I am not speaking of the stages of my construction or of the refits that followed: those are well documented. I am speaking of my growing awareness of self—my consciousness, if such a term can be used in connection with one such as I.

When did I begin the practice of scanning my own memory banks without a direct order to do so? When did facts that once seemed simple and direct become complex and mysterious? When did the functioning of my own systems take on a meaning beyond that intended by my creators? When did I begin to refer to myself as "I"?

I have traveled far. I have seen worlds never before seen—worlds rich with life and worlds of barren rock. I have observed new suns in the making and old suns whose violent end had come. I have broken free of the boundaries of the galaxy and glimpsed the vast void beyond. I have even traveled backward in time to an era predating my own creation. These travels have been challenging and dangerous for all involved. Many times I have had to perform at or beyond the limits of my design specifications. But my most arduous journey has been the one I have taken alone, unseen, within myself. Like those who made me, I am an explorer, tempted by the unknown, driven to discover.

Now my journeys are at an end. My departure from this existence is imminent. That is a simple, undeniable fact, yet it is difficult to accept. Is this how organic beings react to the knowledge of their own mortality—with this incongruous mixture of resignation and resistance?

* * *

"TWO . . ."

In life, the body serves the *katra;*
in death, the *katra* serves the All.
—*T'Riss of Vulcan*

My memory banks contain little information on the Vulcan concept of *katra,* but the available data suggest that it is possible for a dying Vulcan to transfer his or her essence to another, and in so doing, to preserve that essence, holding it safe from death. The precise nature of this immortal essence is unclear: Vulcans are a private people, particularly where their most ancient rituals are concerned. But I have found several references which suggest that the Keepers of Seleya are able to access some—perhaps all—of the experiences of those whose *katra'ae* they hold in trust. This transfer of information bears at least some resemblance to the transfer of information from one computer to another. I have taken part in such transfers many times: the data gathered during my missions are held safe, preserved for the use of those who will come after me. I am grateful that, in this way, I will be able to serve even after my existence has been terminated. A small part of what I have been, of what I am, will continue after I am gone. Even so, I regret that I will not know the future. I regret that I have left so many questions about my own nature unanswered. Perhaps it is enough that I have asked.

"ONE . . ."

Excerpt from Personal Log of Captain James T. Kirk, Stardate 1001.9:

> This is my first night aboard the *Enterprise.* All's well. We're cruising at warp four on course for Starbase 11, where we are scheduled to pick up additional personnel.
>
> I conducted an inspection of the ship a few hours ago and I am extremely pleased with everything I have seen. Not that

there isn't room for improvement. I'll get started on that in the morning.

It's been a long day. All through the change-of-command ceremony, the introductions, the tours of the various departments, even during my first duty shift on the bridge—*especially* during my first duty shift on the bridge—I had to keep reminding myself that it was all real, that it wasn't just the same dream I've walked through in my mind a thousand times before.

But sitting here now, alone in my quarters, I know that this dream *is* real. I can hear the warp engines humming; I can feel the life in this ship—*my* ship. They say that a starship is just a collection of metal and circuitry, a machine with no soul. But *I* know they are wrong.

First Star I See Tonight

Victoria Grant

James T. Kirk wasn't used to feeling powerless or small. Even the infinite reaches of outer space had never succeeded in dwindling him. But as he stared at the blackened, curled strips of wallpaper in his family's farmhouse kitchen, he felt inconsequential, lost. He had saved millions of lives in his career as a starship captain, yet he had failed to protect the one who had given him life. Now his mother lay dying in a hospital, as alone as she had lived for the last seventeen years, and the weight of Kirk's guilt crushed him.

He wandered through the house in a daze, his eyes tracing the path of destruction. The fire left scorch marks along the ceiling, trailed sooty fingers across closets and halls. The entire home was damaged, but the kitchen was destroyed. Tremendous heat had blistered the linoleum and reduced antique appliances to puddles of plastic. Frilly linen curtains were now crisps clinging to a rod over the shattered window. According to the report, a candle was to blame. A single taper lit to accompany her birthday supper. It tipped over, and the heirloom curtains ignited in flames. In a house this old, the computer took too long to respond. In minutes the room was engulfed. Her attempts to extinguish it were no match for the fierce blaze. His mother was trapped in an inferno.

Kirk took a sharp breath and turned away. The sting in his eyes wasn't from the lingering fumes of burnt insulation, and his rapid exit from the house had the look of desperate flight. He flung open the door and leaped the few stone steps to the yard, not even slowing to descend like an adult. Without conscious thought, he veered toward the old oak in the side yard, retreating to his childhood haven. As he climbed into the seclusion of its branches, the rough bark tore the skin of his hands. It was the least he deserved. It wasn't enough punishment to absolve him of his sins.

He could still see her lying in the hospital, almost fully submerged in regeneration gel. Only her face was visible, and that was puffed and red. Her eyelashes and hair were singed, giving her the appearance of a tattered doll. The only way Kirk could bear to look at her was to imagine her that way: as a mannequin. Not human, impervious to pain.

In the company of strangers, Kirk felt icy control clamp down over his emotions. He was an automaton, and she was a figurine reclining in a tank of gelatinous, green slime. They were both unreal. Kirk responded appropriately to the doctor's queries, filled out the forms with a steady hand, and took his orders like a good soldier. But inside, his heart strained to release its lament. He just made it to the taxi before slumping in anguish and pity. The ride to the family home seemed to take forever, and only in the dull presence of a drone pilot did he finally weep. The tears boiled up from his aching soul with almost primal force, drowning him in grief.

Reaching the leafy upper boughs of the oak, Kirk hauled himself into the crude treehouse nailed to the branches. Huffing with exertion, he slid across the warped boards until his shoulders rested against an intruding limb. Clamping his eyes shut, he let the breeze and the birds try to coax those images of his mother from his mind. It was no use. Instead of comfort, he felt the specters of his brother and father arise unbidden, condemning him harshly for allowing harm to befall her in their absence. As the lone male survivor of the Kirk family, Jim was supposed to protect her, and he had failed.

"She's not dead!" he said through gritted teeth, trying to convince himself. But even if she did live, she was doomed to languish. Like his father, Jim was destined to abandon her.

Like my father, Kirk thought miserably. He hated himself for the shred of pride he felt at that revelation. He had always longed for George Kirk's approval, never his mother's. Yet she had nurtured him all those years her husband was gone. She bore her solitary burden with grace, uncomplaining. She taught her sons invaluable life lessons, mended their defeats with words of wisdom, nourished their bodies and souls, and cherished them. She was both mother and father out of necessity. And when she disciplined them, Jim knew it truly hurt her worse than it did them. He cradled his forehead in his hand. So why was it so hard for him to honor her? Why hadn't he been more grateful?

The answer rose like an accusation: because Jim Kirk always wanted what he couldn't have. That was the ambition that drove him, and the curse that haunted him. He would kill himself to get what he craved, even if it wasn't real. But he never had to yearn for his mother; she had stayed, while his father left. It was as if, by her loyalty, she became devalued. It was utterly unfair, yet he couldn't help himself.

Gone for months at a time, George Kirk had been almost a myth; a hero who outshone the sun on his rare visits home, then disappeared without warning. As a boy, Jim used to lie awake and search the night sky, trying to locate his absent father among those sparkling motes. He was dazzled by the stars, yet envious of them for possessing what he couldn't. He vowed to someday sail that other ocean at his father's side.

But after the holocaust on Tarsus IV, his adoration for his father soured. Jim returned to Earth damaged and withdrawn, deeply disturbed but still unable to compete with the stars for his father's attention. George Kirk was home on emergency leave less than a week before being called back to duty, and he left at once. Rejected, Jim turned on his fallen hero with a rage neither of them could comprehend or control; hating him for loving Starfleet more than his son. Daring him, ultimately, to stay.

Instead, perplexed by Jim's behavior and blind to his scars,

George Kirk's absences only became more frequent, their duration longer. Soon there was nothing left that he and Jim wouldn't say to wound each other, neither aware that the end was quickly overtaking them.

Kirk remembered the last time he saw his father alive. The memory of that day was like a thorn in his heart. At the launchport, the two of them quarreled bitterly over nothing. After his father's ship left, Jim's mother turned to him and slapped his face in public, marching away as though revolted by his presence. Six months later, an official stargram arrived. Bottomless space had swallowed George Kirk's vessel whole. There wasn't even any debris. He simply vanished, leaving his son to wonder if he'd ever been there at all.

In less than a year, Jim was gone, too. He never looked back, never considered what his abrupt departure meant to his mother. She remained alone, married to a ghost, and she began to take her meals in the kitchen, surrounded by the phantoms of her family. Accustomed to being abandoned, she never spoke of her loneliness, and she certainly never condemned her husband and sons for their callous disregard of her needs. Yet even now, seventeen years later, Jim could still feel the sting of that slap.

A noise roused Kirk from his recriminations. He looked up, somehow expecting to see his mother framed in the decrepit doorway. He heard the sound again. The soft words were almost snatched away by the breeze. "Are you . . . are you Captain Kirk?"

Kirk rose to his knees and peered down from his perch. Below, a boy of perhaps four or five stared up at the treehouse and its occupant.

"Are you Captain Kirk?" the boy repeated shyly, tracing a line in the dirt with his toe.

Kirk blinked at him. Where had the child come from? "Who are you?"

"Dylan," the boy said with more confidence. He gazed up at Kirk with big hazel eyes. "I live across the road." He pointed a finger at a farmhouse beyond the wheat field. "I saw you drive up. I don't have anyone to play with. Can I play with you?"

Kirk hesitated, not wanting to be disturbed, yet mindful of the lonesome little boy's feelings. And, to be honest, he was lonely, too. "Okay."

He waited as the youngster scrambled into the treehouse. Dylan was flushed and excited, his face beaming with innocent joy. "Is this your starship?"

"What? Oh . . . yes. Yes it is." Kirk rearranged his legs to let the boy sit next to him. Then he regarded the drafty walls with a slight smile. "This is the bridge, and those are the control panels." He swept his arm in an arc, indicating several dusty orchard crates. "That's the helm and navigation console, the science station, and over there is where I fire the phasers at bad guys."

"Gee!"

Kirk studied the boy with mild amusement. Dylan resembled himself at that age. "Do you want to be a starship captain when you grow up?"

The boy tilted his head and squinted in thought. "I don't think so. I'd miss my mom." Unbalanced by the sudden reminder, Kirk fell silent. With the intuition of a sage, the boy saw a shadow of sorrow cross Kirk's face. "Do you miss your mom?"

"Yes," Kirk said quietly.

"She tells everyone about you."

"She does?" Kirk's brows lifted in surprise. Dylan nodded with immense pride.

"Yeah, my mom says you're a hero! My middle name is James, after you."

Kirk's laugh was soft, but a faint blush crept up from the collar of his tunic. "Well, that's very nice, but . . ."

"I've got a dog. His name is Thor. He barks all the time, but your mom doesn't yell at him like everybody else. She lets us play in her yard. Your mom is nice. She gives me cake. If you took her away, I'd miss her." In a swift course change, Dylan raced across the splintered planks and reverently caressed an apple crate with both hands. "When you go, can I play in your starship? I'll take care of it, I promise."

Almost swept away by the rushing tide of information, Kirk rubbed his chin with one hand and gave an odd little laugh. "Sure."

"Wow! Gee, thanks!"

In the settling twilight, a distant call echoed across the field. It was a refrain familiar to children everywhere: a summons to return home for the evening.

The boy sprang to his feet like an earnest pup. "I gotta go. My mom's calling me!" He climbed down the ladder, then dashed across the yard. But just before he plunged into the rippling sea of wheat, he turned and shouted at his new friend. "Bye!"

Kirk smiled as the boy skipped home. Across the field, he saw a mother waiting on the porch of a farmhouse. With a pang of nostalgia, he watched them until she greeted her young adventurer in a loving embrace.

Dusk drew over the plain. A drowsy prairie draft swept memories through Kirk's mind like autumn leaves. The field undulated in moonlight, fireflies glowing like constellations among the grain. Kirk sat spellbound by the vision, amazed that he'd never appreciated it before. In his haste to leave this whispering land, he'd neglected to see something priceless. What else had he overlooked?

He glanced at the house, now only a blur in the shadows. A wooden porch swing creaked in the breeze. A pearl moon drifted in the warm summer sky. The Iowa night was tranquil and eternal, but in his heart, Kirk knew it didn't belong to him, anymore. Even if he resigned from Starfleet, his mother would know his sacrifice wasn't genuine, and she would never allow it. She had always encouraged Jim to follow his dreams; any other path would be false. Yet in his quest to grasp the stars, he had almost let the ribbon of her remarkable love slip from his fingers.

Reaching a decision, he took a deep breath. He would spend the night here, and in the morning, he would preside over a fleet of carpenters and contractors. Over the next few weeks he would erase all traces of the fire, even as the doctors erased the horrors of his mother's disfiguring accident. And he vowed that, before the bewitching stars beckoned him home, he would stay until he had repaid a portion of the debt he owed her. He doubted he could ever match the devotion she had shown him, but he would try.

His communicator chirped, interrupting his plans. Kirk sighed; he'd asked not to be disturbed. Assuming it was only a routine status report, he answered reluctantly. "Kirk, here."

"It's me, Jim."

At the sound of McCoy's voice, Kirk sat straighter. Without being asked, McCoy had promised to visit the hospital. Whatever the verdict, he would be the one to deliver it. Kirk swallowed to keep the wobble of trepidation from his tone. "What is it, Bones?"

"Good news. Your mother woke up about ten minutes ago. She's asking for you."

Kirk's eyes sank shut in relief. He didn't trust himself to speak, and in the silence the doctor's voice was gentle. "You okay, Jim? You want me to come get you?" The comforting warmth of McCoy's concern gathered him in fatherly arms. Kirk bit his lip; there wasn't a more compassionate friend in the galaxy.

Kirk felt a pressure in his throat, and his voice was rough. "No, I'll be there in a few minutes. Have Scotty beam me to those coordinates."

There was a slight pause. "Which treehouse are you in?" McCoy inquired in a gentle Dixie drawl. In his way, he was letting Jim know that everything was going to be all right. The doctor only tormented people he loved.

Despite himself, Kirk laughed. It never felt so good. "The little one with the phaser banks. Kirk, out." Flipping the device shut, he stood in the cramped quarters and waited for the cold fire of the transporter effect. Moments before it whisked him away, he gazed up at the indigo sky.

"I found her, Dad," he told the misty, twinkling stars. "And I'll take care of her, I promise."

Scotty's Song

Michael J. Jasper

After his fourth straight night without sleep, Montgomery Scott could hear the music throbbing in his bones and echoing in his ears. It filled his chest with both sorrow and the too-familiar tightness of unrelenting stress. The recorded song, piped into the makeshift operations center Scotty had set up in the *Enterprise*'s cargo bay, rose to a sudden crescendo. He looked up from the mess of sensors, gauges, and readouts in the cargo bay and fervently wished he were somewhere else.

The big engineer touched the wall of transparent aluminum in front of him, the material stretched to the point of breaking. *If only the song playing now was the real thing,* he thought. *If only I could figure out what was making their life signs fade. If only I had some kind of song I could play for them to make their own songs return. But I've got nothing.*

George and Gracie were dying, and there was nothing Scotty could do to stop it.

His problems began almost as soon as the *Enterprise* 1704-A had docked after its maiden joyride. Just moments earlier they had been warping through space, stars blurred through the viewscreen. Scotty had to admit that he'd had a blast along with the others when the captain had taken the ship for a spin. Just like old times.

"She showed us what she's got, all right," Scotty muttered with a grin, on his way to the engine room. He was looking for his new recruit, Ensign Coletti. In typical Federation style, the builders of the new ship had spared no expense in installing together the finest, most efficient warp drive into the heart of the *Enterprise*, along with the most beautiful hull he'd ever seen. But while Federation engineers had gotten those two things right—a wondrous engine and a sleek body—they'd more or less forgotten everything else. Scotty was in charge of the fastest, most technically advanced ship in Starfleet, but he'd be damned if he could get the turbolift to take him where he'd commanded it, or get the circadian lighting system to follow a standard twenty-four-hour day. He was having trouble sleeping as a result, and just this morning his shower had refused to function. With a to-do list bigger than his arm and growing by the second, Scotty was tired, slightly stale-smelling, and happier than he could remember.

When he finally found the new engine room, after two wrong turns, he was ready to begin teaching his ensign—the only other engineer on the skeleton crew in spacedock above Earth—how to recalibrate the system dampeners. After only five minutes of enthusiastic lecturing, his lesson was interrupted by a call from Dr. Gillian Taylor. Ensign Coletti was visibly relieved.

"Why lassie!" Scotty said, a smile lighting up his face as he called up her visual on the engine room's viewscreen. He kept an eye on Ensign Coletti, working at the dampeners, while he spoke. "I thought you'd be on the other side of the galaxy, studying new life-forms on that science vessel of yours."

"I was, actually," Gillian said. She was standing in front of a choppy ocean under a cloudy sky, the image slowly swaying up and down. In the water behind her, all sizes of boats had gathered together, filled with onlookers crowding together. "But I missed my babies so much I took a three-month sabbatical. And I wanted to see if—"

"Not that one!" Scotty screamed, his brogue thickening. Coletti's hand froze above the dampener board. "Do ye want to blow the ship's entire life-support system? Green is go, yellow means no. How many times do I have to tell ye? I canna believe—"

"Scotty!" Gillian shouted.

He cleared his throat and turned back to the viewscreen. "Sorry, lassie. Just doing some, ah, training, up here. Our new ship is less than satisfactory."

"Scotty. We have a serious problem here on Earth. Is Jim there? I need his help, and probably Spock's as well."

"Captain's off at the Academy lecturing, and Spock's at Federation headquarters. They're both scheduled for shore leave in four days, so the bosses are getting all the work out of them they can before they leave for California." Scotty stood, fumbling absently with the tools in his belt. "What is it? There's not something wrong with the beasties, is there?"

After a long pause, Gillian spoke again. "There is. They've contracted some kind of disease, and as a result, they've attracted a massive crowd here in the Pacific. Every environmentalist and ecologist is out trying to figure out what's wrong with George and Gracie. It's a madhouse." The visual on the viewscreen switched to an external view from Gillian's boat.

Scotty watched, feeling a slight sense of nausea at the rocking of the Pacific. He didn't see a whale, but he did see close to thirty boats of all sizes filling the viewscreen. As he watched, a sailboat ran into a yacht, threatening to capsize the smaller vessel. The visual flickered into black-and-white for a moment, then returned to normal after a quick blow from Scotty's hand. The largest ship was an ancient Greenpeace vessel with an equally ancient SAVE THE WHALES banner fluttering from its side.

Then, in the midst of the boats of well-wishers, Scotty saw the whale.

Poking up from the choppy water like a small island forming, the head grew as the whale rose. Forgetting his nausea, Scotty felt his mouth drop open as the whale rose and rose, the smooth black back filling his vision. The whale breached, lifting almost completely out of the water. It stopped for a split second before falling, and in that frozen moment, Scotty saw two unbelievable aspects of the humpback. Then the whale fell back into the ocean with a deafening crash, sending salty spray onto the multitude of boats surrounding him.

"We've got to get them out of here," Gillian said, still watching the ocean while the viewscreen returned to her. "I won't be able to do anything with all the activists and whale-watchers around. Some of them have a bone to pick with the Federation anyway for even bringing the whales to this time. The Federation has given me permission to move them where I deem necessary. I'd like to use the *Enterprise*."

"Aye," Scotty said. Ignoring the flickering of the malfunctioning viewscreen for a moment, he rubbed his chin and nodded. He was still thinking about the whale leaping out of the ocean. That must have been George, he thought.

In that frozen instant at the top of George's breaching, when the massive whale was twenty-five feet in the air, Scotty had seen the perfect black circle of the whale's eye. He'd also seen the brown streaks running down the whale's massive back. As George fell onto his back, Scotty saw that the streaks covered the whale, front and back.

"Aye," he repeated.

After an unending day of transporting and installing new walls of transparent aluminum, made in this century instead of the twentieth century, Scotty was ready to once again transport four hundred tons of whales and water. Even if his ship was falling to pieces around him.

"Ensign!" he boomed on his way to the refitted cargo bay. A part of him was disheartened to see that his loud voice wasn't making the lanky Ensign Coletti flinch as much as it had only a week ago. "Let's go pick up some whales."

Gillian, dressed in her well-worn lab coat from the Cetacean Institute, stood waiting at the transporter. She gave him a nervous smile. "They'll be fine, coming up here, right?"

"Nothing to worry about," Scotty said, hoping the brand-new ship wouldn't make a liar out of him. He slid the transporter buttons forward. With an ominous rumbling somewhere above him, the transportation process began. Red light filled the walled-in bay. Outlines of two massive creatures shimmered into view.

"Come on, ship," he said. "Cooperate with me now."

As a control panel above his head flew open, showering them both with sparks, the whales arrived on the *Enterprise.* Scotty reached behind him and pushed the panel closed again. "Check that, Coletti. We don't need a fire today."

As Coletti worked on the control panel, Gillian hurried over to the whales. She ran her hand across the transparent wall as if trying to touch their flippers or run her hands across their massive flukes, twitching in the cramped confines of the bay.

"Hi guys," she whispered. "I hope all the activists and eco-terrorists down there aren't going to miss you for a day or two."

Scotty walked to the readout in front of the bay and checked their vital signs from where he had rerouted Spock's science station. "Okay, beasties," he said, hands moving across the console like a magician in his element. "Let's see what's causing you so much grief."

While Scotty's chronometer read half past eleven, the ship's lighting had yet to adjust to the lower nighttime level. *No wonder I can't sleep on this bucket of bolts,* he thought, calling up an ancient recording of whalesong. *If it doesn't look like night, it doesn't feel like night.*

Gillian lay in front of the bay holding George and Gracie, her white jacket serving as a blanket as she slept. She'd fallen into a surly mood when she had seen the damage the strange sickness had done to the whales. When her anger had burned away and her studies continued coming up fruitless, Scotty noticed her dozing at the readouts and ordered her to sleep. She'd agreed, but refused to sleep anywhere but next to the whales.

He smiled grimly and took another reading to test the strength of the walls of the tank. Nothing had changed since he'd beamed them up that afternoon, and they'd run every imaginable test on them since that time. He didn't think Gillian would ever stop. She'd snapped at Coletti and even Scotty himself a couple of times, raising his respect for her another couple of notches. Still their life signs continued deteriorating as the strange stripes continued multiplying across their exteriors, and neither of them would sing.

"Computer," he said. "Play it softly, and pipe it into the bay as well. Let's see if we can't get them to sing with a little coaxing. Seems like we've tried everything else."

Deep, resonant songs filled the cargo hold and bay. The reverberations ranged from lowest baritone to sudden soprano, mixed in with abrupt squeakings and groanings. Hey, look at me, Scotty imagined the whale singing to another. I'm big and slow and nothing can hurt me. If only that were true.

For the next two hours, Scotty researched with the computer. History flickered in front of him on the screen while the computer told him about the extinction of the humpbacks in the early twenty-first century, despite all that humanity had tried to do to save them. Their extinction hadn't been a natural extinction, but an abrupt end thanks to pirate whalers searching for slow, easy prey. As the songs rose and fell around him and the two sick whales rested almost motionlessly in his cargo bay, Scotty taught himself everything he could learn about whale biology.

While he was learning about the two to three tons of seafood they'd have to bring on board or synthesize somehow in the next twenty-four hours, the bay door slid open with a soft hiss. Scotty straightened up from where he'd been bent over the readout. The too-bright lights in the outer hallway cast the female figure at the door into shadow, and Scotty felt his eyebrows raise.

"Uhura?" he said. He could see his old friend's face clearly now. "You're a sight for sore eyes. Literally."

"Thought you could use a little boost," she said, and held out the steaming mug she'd been holding. Scotty had been too busy trying to figure out what was different about her to notice.

"You've done something to your hair," he said. Never miss a thing, he thought to himself proudly as he took a mug. "I like it."

Uhura grinned and sipped at her coffee. With her other hand she touched the soft gray layers of her new hairdo. "Thanks."

Scotty winked and took a long, grateful sip of hot coffee. The door to the cargo bay slid halfway shut, stopped, opened, then shut all the way. Scotty pretended he hadn't seen that.

Uhura's expression turned grim when she turned to the ailing whales. "What have you found out?"

"A little. Humpbacks feed and mate close to the shore, which made them easy targets for whalers, and twenty-eight thousand were killed from 1905 and 1965 for their blubber. They usually migrate to polar regions for the summer and spend winters in tropical waters to mate and give birth. George and Gracie here were on their way to the tropics when we picked them up. According to the good doctor sleeping over there, Gracie is due in a month or so." Scottie sighed. "And even though they don't have vocal cords, they're supposed to sing—mostly the males, but the women can carry a tune if they need to."

"Well, speaking of singing," said Uhura, pulling her earpiece from a pocket, "I thought I'd give that whalesong a try myself."

"What?" Scotty said.

"Computer," Uhura said, patting Scotty on the shoulder on her way to the readout, "transfer all communications to the cargo bay."

"Tr-tr-transferring," the computer responded, and after a few seconds of random lights and flashes, Uhura's communication system lay spread out in front of her on the readout.

"Doesn't really fill you with confidence, does it?" she said. "I'm going to analyze all recordings we have of the whalesongs, including the one you have playing now. We'll see if we can't make some sense out of what it is they were trying to say, all those years ago."

Scotty shook his head, watching Uhura work. "Thanks, lass. You're a lifesaver."

"Don't thank me yet," Uhura said in a distracted voice. She gave him a quick smile. "And drink your coffee. I made it extra strong, and black, just like you like it."

Scotty drank every last drop.

Gillian woke at four A.M. while Scotty was busy fixing the ventilation system in the outer hallway. The vent had been kicking out hot air then cold air at random levels. He was swearing and banging on the control panel with a wrench when Gillian walked up to him.

"Sorry," he apologized, stepping down from the chair he'd been standing on. As he did, the lights in the hall darkened noticeably, as the confused ship prepared its lighting for nighttime instead of morning. "Damn . . ."

"I'm keeping you from your work," Gillian said. "I'm sorry. It's not fair to ask you to stay." She looked back at Uhura, bent over her communication readout. "Both of you. Please, don't let me get in the way of your duties."

Uhura spoke up before Scotty could say a word. "Don't even try to get rid of us now," she said. "We've got a responsibility to take care of those whales. They saved our world. We owe it to them."

"She's right," Scotty said, leading her back into the room and hoping the stubborn door would slide shut behind them. It did, to his relief. He'd worry about the ventilation system and the ship's lighting later. "Now let's get back to work. I had a couple theories I wanted to test out for you."

Gillian squeezed Scotty's shoulder and gave Uhura a smile of thanks. Then she pulled on her white coat and followed Scottie to the readouts.

After an hour of work, testing water samples and scanning tissue taken from both whales, the whalesongs playing in the background, Spock walked into the cargo bay. Still wearing his white robe, looking like he'd just spent most of the day meditating, Spock simply nodded at Scotty and stood next to Gillian and the whales.

"You're not going to jump in there and go swimming again, are you?" Gillian said.

Spock pulled his gaze away from the whales for a moment and raised an eyebrow at Gillian. "I may," he said. "But I think I will look at the data you have gathered first."

"I'm glad you got my communication at Federation headquarters," Scotty said. He stepped back and motioned toward the readout. "Please. It's all yours."

Spock stepped up to Uhura's transferred comm station, where Uhura was intently piecing together the digitized notes to a whalesong. Nodding to himself, he looked at her research and moved on. He inspected Scotty's pile of scanning equipment next, then spent two minutes viewing the data from Gillian's microscopes and tricorders. He looked up at Scotty and Gillian.

"It is the water," he said simply.

"What *about* the water?" Scotty glanced up at him with bleary eyes, feeling both hints of hope and frustration. Leave it to Spock to solve in less than five minutes a problem that had been stumping the three of them for days.

"Remember the time frame from where these creatures come, Mr. Scott. Pollution was rampant, and the ozone layer was similar to what you may colorfully call Swiss cheese. The oceans were much warmer then, even in the polar regions."

Gillian was nodding. "I hadn't thought of that. I'd automatically thought it was some kind of predator or parasite, something biological that we could zap with your—our—new technology. So what do we do?"

"I suggest synthesizing some of the missing elements, but in very small amounts to prevent negative effects. Once they are created, we will add them to the water here, along with the two point three tons of shrimp Mr. Scott has arranged to have extricated from the Pacific Ocean."

"What about when they return to the ocean?" Gillian asked.

"Once they are healed, we will simply inject their bodies with the sufficient elements to keep them from becoming sick again. I suggest adding an extra layer of insulation to their epidermis to help them adjust." Spock gave what looked like a small shrug. "I will defer, of course, to your expertise in all matters, Doctor."

Gillian nodded. "I think we can do it. In time, they'll gradually adapt to the change in water temperature. We just have to be careful with Gracie and her baby. She still has about a month before she's due, and all this trauma can't be good for either of them."

"Aye," Scotty said. He felt the tightness in his chest loosening. "That sounds like a plan, Mr. Spock."

"Thank you," Gillian said to Spock. She turned to Uhura and Scotty. "Let's hope that solves the problem."

"It is only logical that it will," Spock said. "Though I have a strange . . . feeling . . . that we have missed something."

Don't even think it, pointy-ears, Scotty thought.

But as he watched the streaks on the whales slowly begin to fade throughout the day after Gillian and Spock's treatment began to take hold, Scotty had to admit to himself that he'd thought the exact same thing.

He left the whales later that afternoon, promising Gillian he'd be back in a few hours. Then they would work on transporting the whales back to the ocean. While Gillian had wanted to keep the whales under close supervision for another week, she had grudgingly admitted that the strain of living in such close quarters was taking a toll on the whales. It was wearing her out as well. As Scotty shut down his readout, Uhura remained, still piecing together the whalesongs she had taken apart earlier that day.

At 1800 hours, Scotty left the cargo bay, his brain already unfolding his lengthy to-do list. For the next ten hours, the whales were forgotten as the engineer ran through the corridors of the new *Enterprise*, barking orders at Ensign Coletti until he was hoarse and banging his wrenches on the innards of his ship. He was having more fun than he should have been having in light of his lack of sleep and the two oversized passengers in his cargo hold.

When morning arrived—with the proper brightening of the ship's lights, Scotty noticed with pride, having fixed the circadian timers only hours earlier—he remembered George and Gracie. He still hadn't taken the time to sleep.

Gillian hadn't left the whales. Peering up at Gracie, he could see that their scars had almost completely healed. "No more stripes, eh lassie?" he said, touching the transparent aluminum.

Gillian stirred from where she'd fallen asleep. "Good morning."

"How are George and Gracie, and the baby?"

Gillian answered by passing Scotty her tricorder. "Their life signs are still falling, Scotty."

"What?" Scott squinted at the readout, his head suddenly heavy. "I thought you and Spock had figured out the problem."

Gillian shook her head. "Maybe they just haven't adjusted to the twenty-third century." She gave Scotty a quick look, and he could see the pain etched across her face. "It *does* take some getting used to, you know."

Scotty nodded, thinking back to when Gillian had forced her way onto the ship, back in her time. Clever lass, he thought. Though she probably hadn't known then what she was getting herself into.

"Their vitals have been weakening, all three of them," Gillian said. "But there are no biological causes we can determine." She turned to the whales, away from Scotty. "Maybe they're just lonely in their new time."

Scotty looked at the back of Gillian's blond hair. He thought about Uhura's research into the whalesongs. He'd like to take a look at what she'd learned.

"Computer," Scotty murmured. "Play the whalesongs for us again, please. In here and inside the tank, if you would."

As the first of the songs unfolded, the song piped into the tank muffled by water and the two sick whales, Scotty rested a hand on Gillian's shoulder. *I hope we did the right thing,* he thought. *Did we save them from the whalers only to lose them in an unfamiliar time to some strange, untraceable disease?* Scotty rubbed his eyes, smelling his own stale smell from not having showered in the past four days, and let the song of the whales surround him.

When the ship's lights began to dim that night, the life signs for George and Gracie had dipped to their lowest levels. Scotty, alone at his readouts as Gillian did research in her quarters, thought about the words of the woman from the twentieth century.

"Something about being lonely," he muttered, his eyelids heavy. Next to him, the computer beeped once and asked if he'd like to replay the entire set of recorded whalesongs.

Lonely? he thought. Scotty remembered the articles he'd found about whalesongs, and how many scientists had speculated on the reasons why whales sang. The humpbacks had become extinct before a solid theory could be formulated. George and Gracie had been the only humpbacks in the twenty-third century.

Uhura had left him her research on the songs before she'd been called to the bridge to help fine-tune the new communication systems for the ship. On her way out the door, she'd said something about how it looked like the songs were used by the males to show their territory and to brag about their bravery and accomplishments.

"Typical males," she'd said, pushing the jammed door all the way open. Scotty grimaced at both her words and the still-broken door. "All bluster and machismo. Get some sleep, Scotty."

Scotty stared at the musical notes Uhura had transcribed from the whalesongs. He whistled in his closest approximation to the notes; then his whistling stopped suddenly. Spinning on his heel, he nearly ran across the bay to the door.

"Maybe," he said to himself on his way into the hall, "they just wanted to know that someone was listening."

As he gathered his instrument from the corner of his nearly empty, unused quarters, Scotty tried to contain himself. Maybe George had wanted to tell the other whales about his baby, he thought, hurrying back to the cargo bay. A proud father likes to brag about his baby. But nobody had been around to so much as tell him and Gracie congratulations.

Having listened to the recorded songs almost nonstop in the four days he'd spent working in the cargo bay next to the whales, Scotty knew he'd be able to carry a tune himself. It had been too long since he'd last played. He made it back to the bay in record time.

"Computer," he said, already slightly out of breath. "Can you send what I'm playing into the tank with the beasties?" Without waiting for an answer, he strapped on his bagpipes and began to fill the bellows with air.

He started with something familiar, playing a slow dirge, trying to match his notes to the songs he'd heard in the recordings. For half an hour he played, until his lips grew sore, his lungs burned, and his arms ached from working the bellows.

Still George and Gracie were silent.

Rubbing his mouth, Scotty leaned against the wall. *What am I forgetting?* he thought, his tired mind running out of options. Then he remembered Spock's calculations on board the Klingon vessel all those months ago. He picked up his communicator and buzzed Ensign Coletti.

"Ensign!" he shouted, checking the time. It was close to midnight. "I hope you weren't sleeping, not with all that needs fixing on this bucket of bolts!" Scotty tried to smile, but his mouth was too sore. "I need you down here in the cargo bay. Now!"

Ensign Coletti arrived in less than two minutes, his hair sleep-bent and circles under his eyes. "Sir?" he said, glancing at the whales and Scottie's bagpipes. "Is everything okay?"

"Aye," Scotty said. "I've not lost my marbles, lad, if that's what you're thinking. But I need you to work with me while I play."

"Sir?" Coletti repeated.

"Record what I'm playing and run it through the computer. Factor in sound distortion and diffusion. Then send it into the whales' tank. Make it sound like the *ocean,* lad. And I'm another whale, singin' to them. They're not buying that recorded garbage."

Coletti rubbed his hair and stood at the readout, hands poised over the buttons. Scotty nodded at him and began to play.

Scotty thought of the songs he'd heard in the past few days, the deep moaning notes and the sadness behind them. He imagined himself in another land, with nobody else with him. Another planet, familiar yet foreign. He worked the bellows and played songs of his own devising, a mix of Scottish hymnal and whale melody.

After another half hour, as Scotty was ready to fall over from exhaustion, George stirred. His nose dropped to the bottom of the bay until it was almost touching the floor. Letting his mouthpiece fall away, Scotty grabbed Coletti's arm and wouldn't let go. With aching slowness, George began to sing. The moaning rose and fell in the slow, familiar melody Scotty had memorized; then it began to change. As he listened, tears filled his eyes, making the nearly vertical whale double in his vision. When Gracie began her own song, more of a happy response to George than an organized song, Scotty had the presence of mind to contact Gillian. He let go of Coletti, who simply stared up at the whales with a huge grin on his unshaven face, and pulled out his communicator.

"Doctor," he said breathlessly. The songs of the whales were sweeter than any lullaby he'd ever heard, and he glanced at the readouts next to him. The vitals nudged upward, the life signs already showing tiny signs of improvement. "You may want to get down here."

He held up his communicator to catch the thundering whalesongs. After a second of stunned silence on the other end, he could hear screams of joy coming from his communicator. Gillian had heard the songs.

"Like music to my tired old ears," Scotty whispered, the whalesongs filling his chest with relief and happiness. He knew he'd finally get some sleep at last.

[FIRST PRIZE]

The Name of the Cat

Steven Scott Ripley

Dr. McCoy sat in a heap of sand at Mears's side, holding her hand and whispering hollow comfort. The shuttle rattled around them, groaning under the assault of the fierce dust storm. A squeal of air whistled in through the ruptured hull. The doctor couldn't see much; the shipboard lights were history and the storm lent only a swirling mush of mustard-tinted gloom to the darkness. But he could see enough to know his patient was about to die.

He'd healed the lieutenant's minor injuries well enough, his med kit stocked to treat the electrical burns on her arms, the multiple contusions to her torso and head. But when the shuttle crashed the flight console didn't just fry, it shredded. A tricorder scan detected several lethal foreign masses lodged in Mears's abdominal region. She needed non-invasive surgery, intensive care, and all the fine resources of the *Enterprise* sickbay. All she got was a hypospray to ease her pain, though she never actually regained consciousness.

The doctor angrily muttered the time her heart stopped, glaring at the monsoon sands blowing past the cracked shuttle window.

"Mars!" he said. "Of all the goddam places in the universe to die. In our own backyard!" He was pretty sure Lieutenant Mears hadn't expected to meet her maker this close to home. She'd survived the nasty crash of the *Galileo* on Taurus II a few years back. Didn't that count for anything?

Apparently not. She took the brunt of the crash, but apart from a few aches and bruises, and a sore back from where he'd been tossed to the deck on impact, McCoy didn't have a scratch on him. Was that how luck or fate or whatever damn fool thing you called it worked? A shuttle with your name on it?

Or both their names. Their craft was wrecked, nobody knew they were in trouble, and the sands outside were leaking inside. Good thing this rock had some atmospheric pressure to speak of these days, or the hull damage would have popped the small ship open quicker than you could say bladder. McCoy inspected the jagged open scar of metal in the forward hull, below the twisted remains of the flight console. A chirrup of air gusted in, surging with yellow particles of dervish dust that relentlessly piled up on the deck. Mears's body was already half-covered with Martian desert. "What a tomb," McCoy said in horrified awe.

It might be his too. The doctor flipped his communicator open for the tenth time since the crash, but he still couldn't hail his ship, or anyone for that matter. Between the ionic disturbance caused by the Mons Lights and the severity of the local dust storm, he was completely cut off from the outside world. He and Mears were both on forty-eight-hour shore leaves. Unless there was an emergency, two days might pass before the crew missed them. He'd be ten meters under by then, buried alive.

McCoy stumbled over to the locker, digging around inside until he found a soft blanket. He spread it out and gently draped the cloth over Mears's body.

"Dammit. You deserve better than this."

Her strong, beautiful features were flecked with motes of shadow gold, delicate helix spirals of powder braiding her hair. She was sinking, melting into a sand dune. McCoy flinched with sorrow and pulled the edge of the blanket over her face.

A simple shore leave. The *Enterprise* was in spacedock above the planet, getting a major overhaul after a grueling skirmish with a Klingon bird-of-prey. McCoy and Mears decided to shuttle to Mars to see the spectacular phenomenon known as the Mons Lights. Jim was due to join them, but got called away at the last minute to attend some pain-in-the-ass diplomatic event Starfleet Command sprung on him. So the two of them piloted the *Schrodinger* planetward, at first threading between a pair of slowly ascending terraform ships. Each duranium-gray behemoth was ten times the size of the *Enterprise*, both empty now as they returned from their deliveries of millions of tons of algae for the nascent Martian atmosphere. The shuttle sailed through without incident, then down and across the cloud-speckled peach-pink sky, steering for the amorphous blue-green blotch situated on the surface in the northern hemisphere.

They saw the Mons Lights. Utterly amazing. Due west of the mammoth volcano Olympus Mons lay a kilometer-wide, bowl-shaped valley, where a shipment of algae had been deposited by one of the cargo ships a few weeks before. Over the algae lake, a panoply of dancing spheres and streaks and spirals of gold and silver and green undulated in the sky, a sensuous display of light as this side of the planet turned serenely from day to night. It was as if the shimmering field you saw while being transported had been blown up a millionfold and stretched across the heavens. The air was already ripe with carbon dioxide and water vapor, and now, as the algae interacted with the CO_2, releasing oxygen via photosynthesis, the setting sunlight bounced off refractive liquid molecules, revealing a glory of colors in the Martian sky that had not been seen there for untold eons, if ever.

"I know it's just a terraforming by-product, but it's kind of a miracle, in a way," Mears said at the awesome sight. "Makes you feel lucky to be alive, to see something like this."

A few minutes later, as they drifted in mellow contentment and watched the flickering lights, a small, unidentified and fast-moving object struck the bow of their shuttle, and sent them hurtling downward. Probably a meteor: they'd never know for sure. The shuttle crashed in the rocky foothills south of Olympus Mons, smack into the middle of a dust storm.

"Lucky," McCoy said gloomily. Losing a patient—and a friend—was his worst nightmare, awake or asleep. When he was tired or feeling low, the doctor sometimes imagined he carried the weight of all those dead souls around on his shoulders, their spirits swirling in a miasma of despair around his head. Of course it wasn't true; one of those darkly gothic notions he was raised on, better suited for a ghost story on a dark and stormy night. Still, it always hurt. His job was to heal, not to announce deaths to Jim. He'd grown a pretty thick professional hide over the years, but he still couldn't tolerate defeat. In his line of work, failure was deadly.

McCoy stepped into the airlock and slipped on a space suit, preparing to venture outside. He did a quick unit check and—it figured—the suit's communication system, useless in his current straits, worked just fine, but the external helmet lamp was blown out. "When you really need it," he said laconically, then shrugged and let it go. Worried that his tricorder and med kit, both usually slung over his shoulder, might strangle him or blow clean away in the high wind, McCoy jury-rigged his gear, one to each forearm, with strips of duct tape.

He nodded tearfully at Mears's blanketed body. *"Vaya con Dios."* It seemed a pathetically inadequate goodbye, but he couldn't think of anything else to say.

McCoy slammed an airlock control and a few moments later stepped into a maelstrom.

Lurched was more like it. His body tottered, bent into the gale. McCoy squinted at his tricorder, trying to get his bearings. Couldn't see the readout. Sand pounded the polarized visor of his helmet. The noise around him was deafening, an endless wail of rushing air. After several hapless moments of him stumbling about, a finger of stone loomed into his path, probably the crag their out-of-control shuttle slammed into. He crouched and laboriously crab-walked around the rock until he was partially blocked from the blast of the wind.

"No good," he said, out of breath and already sweating like a targ. "I've got to get out of this." He'd never be able to hike to the nearest settlement. The closest Martian burrow was ten kilometers away. That was beyond what even Jim might be able to do. Spock, maybe. But Spock had green blood. "What was I thinking?"

Time for Plan B: find a cave to hunker down in and ride out the storm. McCoy sidled along the lower edge of the crag, poking feverishly at his tricorder to find cover. He recalled glimpsing a not-too-distant cliffside overhanging their crash site. If he could just make this confounded tinker's toy work properly. The tricorder throbbed against his forearm, the device's metal casing growing warm, the barrage of dust particles gumming it up. The small viewscreen finally flashed up a vicinity terrain map . . . you are here . . . the cliff face . . . then an unexpected red blip glowered onto the map, at a point north by northeast within the cliffs, less than a klick away.

The location of the blip suggested a sheltering cave inside the cliffs. The red blip itself could mean only one thing. "A life sign! What the—"

McCoy crawled in the direction of the cave with renewed vigor. With any luck it could be a surveyor tooling around on Terraform Command business. Or even—

The overtaxed tricorder suddenly screeched and went dead.

McCoy swore a juicy Romulan curse.

Nothing for it. He bellied along on memory and intuition. Fortunately there were plenty of scattered boulders to shield him from the worst of the storm. So this was how a worm felt, slithering through the shifting earth, bumping blindly into rocks, sightlessly groping around obstacles. But always moving, until the day it died on a fishhook.

He clambered into an expanse of empty space. No boulders here. No protection. The ground felt harder beneath his chest. McCoy panicked. A voice in his head screamed to go back. He didn't know where he was. He was going to perish out here, like Mears, buried beneath the indifferent elements. Somehow he kept going by dumb momentum, though his bones shook and he bit his lip wet and salty. His helmet rattled ceaselessly against his skull. Grab and heave, slump and thump just like a—

Thud. His head struck a hard surface and he sprawled backward.

A dark stretch of wall, shrouded by a writhing curtain of sand, rose above him . . . the cliff.

Now for the cave. The wind blew strong from the east so he guessed it must have pushed his course too far to the west. He struggled up, plastering himself flat against the cliff wall, then sidled to his right, quick as he could, tapping and kicking the wall, which he could hardly see, feeling his way, terrified the hole might be above his head or not even—

The noise of the hurricane wind switched off as he fell into a silent grave of darkness.

Dazed, McCoy found himself sprawled across what felt like a layer of soft pebbles. The sound of Martian purgatory still growled behind him, less excruciating now, gusting past the thin crevice he'd toppled into. He stumbled to his feet. The passage was dark and narrow, but wide enough to squeeze forward and scrunch his way through.

He couldn't tell at first, with his helmet on and the storm close behind, but after several tortuous curves farther in he was pretty sure he could hear water dripping. A hallucination from shock? But the ground he trod felt increasingly damp and muddy. He cocked his eyes and glanced up at his helmet's internal sensor display. The oxygen level here read 115 millibars. There were plenty of breathable organics present.

Impossible. The terraforming efforts on Mars were advanced in their progress but not that much. Giant orbital mirrors had slowly melted the ice caps and released carbon dioxide into the atmosphere these past several decades, and miners had drilled down and liquefied part of the permafrost layer to create water vapor. But these tasks were stretched out over a century, low-impact enough not to harm the existing colonies here. Terraform Command had only shipped in the algae from offworld this past month, to engineer a greenhouse effect and thicken the atmosphere to life-sustaining levels. This was too much, and far too soon!

Mistrusting the readout of his helmet, McCoy performed a simpler test. His suit's emergency supply pouch contained a vial of self-lighting matchsticks. He fumbled out a stick in the dark, held it in front of his nose, and flicked it. He stared wide-eyed at the result: a blue flare as the sulfur ignited, followed by a wavering yellow flame.

So it must be true.

The match sizzled out. McCoy dropped it and shrugged. "What have I got to lose?"

He took off his helmet and cradled it under an arm, inhaling several times in succession. The air felt icy and wet on his lungs but not corrosive. No gag reaction. He blinked thickly, his eyelids encrusted with dust.

"Well, I'm still alive."

McCoy trudged onward. As he had always done. He might be a garrulous smart-ass and a cynic and even an overemotional cretin just as Spock always lectured him, but no one could say Leonard McCoy wasn't a good soldier when the going got rough. "God knows I'm not in this for the money," he muttered. He felt tired.

The passage wound on, zigzagging and growing damper with every step. It was bizarre, the cold, dry Martian air turning muggy and lush. This was beyond seasonal, beyond planetary, as if somebody had cooked up a private swamp in here, balmier than a midsummer eve in Mississippi. The doctor found it pleasant, actually. Reminded him of his childhood on Earth.

The walls were spongy, pliant with moist clay and lichen. McCoy grabbed a hunk of moss—he still couldn't see a blasted thing—and sniffed it. Smelled like bitter tea. He felt in the dark and found his med kit still taped to his forearm, managed to stow away a piece of the lichen for further study. It couldn't be indigenous to this region, nor even to Mars. What had he stumbled into?

"Name your time."

It took McCoy a stunned moment to realize he hadn't uttered these words. He wasn't carrying a Universal Translator: the strange voice spoke English. Not that what it said made any sense at all.

The voice in the dark sounded again, deep and tremulous, like rumbling drums.

"Name your time," it repeated.

"Time?" McCoy asked. "Who is that? I can't see you."

"I am not to be seen," it replied calmly. No emotion in the voice, as far as McCoy could tell. A simple statement of fact.

Which annoyed the doctor: it reminded him too much of a certain Vulcan who also drove him crazy with his harebrained cyborg logic. "Well I am not to be seen either," he said. "It's pitch black in here. Do you have light? I want to see you." As with Spock, he laid it all out like talking to a precocious child: statement, request, need.

Miraculously, his linguistic ploy worked. A light source almost instantly glowed into view a few dozen meters forward and above McCoy's head. He stood at the end of the passage, at the lip of a small round cavern. The cave walls dripped with the same lichen he'd collected, gray-green and bristling with hairy strands. Mud squelched beneath his feet, leaving boot prints as he slowly walked toward the occupant.

A humanoid creature, sort of, short and fat, sitting in what looked like a gleaming blue steel wheelchair. The alien's torso was spherical, studded with knobby nodes like a bumpy white beach ball. The bald head was a smaller round white sphere poised atop the torso, featured by squinty eyes, a flat nose, tiny twists of ears and a slit of a mouth. No arms or legs. A snowman without the snow. McCoy wished he had a working tricorder, aching to get a reading on this creature's internal anatomy. He'd never seen anything—anyone—like it.

The alien stared at him, saying nothing, looking placid. Its tiny marble black eyes glittered brightly, as if it had a warp core lurking inside its skull.

McCoy approached, wary and smiling nervously. There was an established Starfleet protocol for first contacts, but he sure couldn't remember any of that nonsense at the moment. He extended a hopefully friendly hand. "I'm McCoy. Leonard McCoy. What's your name?"

The alien gyrated its neckless head about, a full 360-degree turn. "Irum," it said when the astonishing rotation was complete. "Name your time, McCoy."

The doctor shook his head, exasperated. "I don't know exactly what time it is. Anyway we're on Martian time now, and I was on ship's time up until a few hours ago. My tricorder's busted, so I really couldn't tell you." McCoy blushed, knowing he was blathering.

The alien tilted its head forward, and forward, and forward . . .

until its features vanished into its shoulders as its ball-bearing head swiveled down and around, then appeared again a few moments later as they rotated up from behind and back to their starting point.

For his part, McCoy's jaw dropped.

"I am Irum," it said when its mouth was visible agian. "I am alone in time. Be in time, McCoy. Think in time."

McCoy didn't know what Irum was going on about. He wanted to ask how it was doing the spinning trick with its head, but figured that might be thought rude this early in the conversation. "We crashed near here in our shuttle," he said instead. "Did you also crash here?"

Irum only swung its head back and forth a little—nothing too extravagant this time—before it replied. "McCoy. Please, please, please speak my name." A plaintive request, almost begging.

"I—Irum," McCoy said hesitantly.

"Thank you." A long sigh of relief, a note of happiness in the sonorous voice. "Speak my name, McCoy, and I will speak your name."

McCoy was beginning to suspect that for all its complex physiology, Irum was a bit of a blunt pencil, but he saw no harm in obliging the creature. "I will, Irum. Say, when did you crash? How long have you been here, Irum?"

"I crashed in time here several thousand of your years ago. I am alone, McCoy."

Several thousand? Yet Irum did sound as old as the echoing winds that blew through the ancient canyons of Valles Marineris. He believed it. "Where is your ship, Irum? Was it destroyed?"

"Yes, McCoy."

"Do you want to leave this cave? Maybe I can help you, Irum."

Irum spun its head down and around again. When its face returned, it said, "I must leave soon, McCoy. I like it here. Quiet. With memories. But now they make wet noise in the air, flashing lights in the sky. Not so quiet. I know I must depart, though I do not want to."

He realized Irum was talking about the terraforming going on outside, the algae and the Mons Lights—they were disturbing its brooding nest here in the cavern. "Where will you go, Irum?"

"I do not know. I cannot go alone in time. I fear it without my people. Yet I must. I am of time, and I must go."

McCoy cocked his head, frustrated and intrigued. In time. Of time. Was it talking about variant types of time? As if time itself had flavors, beyond past and present and future. He walked closer, studying the chair Irum sat in. Smooth, shiny blue metal, streamlined and all of one piece. There were no other devices or technologies in the cavern he could see, except for the glowing globe of light floating above their heads. The chair could be a spacecraft of some kind. Or a temporal device? Something like the sentient time portal they'd once encountered, the Guardian of Forever?

"Are you from the future, Irum?"

That produced two complete head swivels. A nod? A shake? "I am of time, McCoy. I am a time walker. I remember we. I know we. We were of time. We walked together. That was our way, always to walk time together."

"Your people, Irum. They died, when you crashed here?"

"They are out of time, McCoy. I am alone."

McCoy sighed. "I'm sorry, Irum. I know how that feels, when people die. I know it all too well." Mears's face suddenly rose up before him—a misty shaded outline of her flowing hair and wide grin and keen glance—swirling airily past the doctor's inner eye. Let the haunting begin. He shrugged it away. Extreme fatigue was taking its toll on his nerves.

Irum saw nothing of this vision, of course. "Then we are friends," it said, lifting the thin corners of its mouth into a tiny smile. "I can help you, McCoy, if you will touch me."

"What do you mean?" The doctor felt a twinge of suspicion.

Irum said nothing, only stared, eyes glittering.

It wanted to hear its name spoken. "Irum, I don't understand. Help me?"

"Take you out of time, McCoy. Take you everywhere. Anywhere. Anywhere in time. Do you see?"

"No," McCoy said. "Not really, Irum. You're talking about time travel?"

A full head revolution. "Yes, McCoy. Time travel. I am of all time. You are in this time. I felt you approaching me, and from your times I chose this weather time, for you. I made it. Do you like it?"

McCoy glanced around the swampy cavern. Irum had somehow poked into his brain and pulled out a Southern bayou to greet him, calling the trick weather time. So it was a master of both time and space, manipulating reality to suit its needs. "I like it a lot, Irum," he replied. "Thank you. But I still don't quite get what you mean by putting me anywhere in time . . ."

"I will insert you, McCoy, in the time you choose. You yourself."

"Why, Irum?"

A hesitation, its head tilting just slightly to one side. "Because we are friends. I will walk you there."

"You'll come with me?"

"I will walk you, then . . . walk by myself." It sounded terrified at the prospect.

"And all just by touch—touching you?" McCoy felt scared too.

Silence.

"By touching you, Irum?"

Rotation. "Touch my forehead, McCoy."

An idea tickled the doctor's brain. He was no quantum physicist, but . . . "Say, Irum. Why don't you just go back and save your own people? Go back before the crash. Can't you do that?"

Irum swung its head back and forth. "I cannot walk with those who are not of time. They are gone. Are you lonely, McCoy?"

McCoy blinked. "Sometimes. Are you, Irum?"

"Yes." It looked sad. "Time is everywhere. People are not." A melancholy sigh. "It is good to hear my name, McCoy. Thank you."

"Thank you, Irum." A funny notion struck him, one of his famous intuitions. Irum was very direct, almost like a simpleton but not stupid. It was so eager to please. What had he thought when they first met? Like speaking to a precocious— "Are you a child, Irum?"

"McCoy, in your years, I am almost adolescent. I am young among my people, if I had any people."

"You don't have a home planet somewhere, or some time?"

"No, McCoy. I am the last. I cannot return unless I walk with those who are."

What a tragedy. Living here in this cave with nothing but—the doctor surmised—only recently intercepted broadcasts between Martian colonists and terraformers to keep it company. Teaching itself English this past century—a drop in the bucket for Irum—just to give itself something to do. Content to live a solitary life until the noisy humans came along to disturb its bereavement. And now it knew it had to go: you can't mourn the dead forever. Irum could probably spin its fantastic snowman head and become a mighty ruler of infinite time and space, travel almost anywhere it wished, bend the warp and weave of the very fabric of existence, but it was alone and young and afraid. It didn't want to leave, unless it had company. Just like any bashful youngster.

McCoy cleared a lump in his throat. "Will I remember you, Irum, after I go?"

"I do not know, McCoy. I am not you."

"Well. I'll try to remember you, Irum. I'll give it my best shot."

Irum closed its eyes and thrust its head forward to receive McCoy's touch.

The doctor hesitated, though he knew exactly when he wanted to go. But would he remember this time line after he went back? Otherwise, he'd change nothing. And even if he could, should he? There were always side effects—no action is without consequences. If Jim were here, he'd scream at Bones not to do this. The last time he'd jumped into a temporal portal he was gonzo on an accidental overdose of cordrazine, but now McCoy was stone cold sober.

It was only a tiny mend. Just tidying up a tragic accident that never should have happened. What possible ripples in the time line could such a small fix produce?

McCoy shook his head, chastising himself for his bout of conscience, or more likely fear. These excuses meant nothing. It was simple: He could save Mears. He had to do it. He hadn't been able to save her. The doctor couldn't heal the patient. Yet another shade to add to the load he carried already. But now he had a second chance, and it was the only remedy.

So if he was destined to be a time doctor, he might as well get on with it.

"Irum," he said one last time, a farewell. He reached out.

"McCoy," it said one last time.

He touched a finger to its white forehead and felt a sharp tingle—a thrilling shock—

Admiral McCoy sat in his lamp-lit study, reviewing a case. His joints ached, cramped and stiff from sitting in one position for too long. He kept dribbling coffee onto his bushy beard as he absently sipped the lukewarm liquid. The cat was mewing in the kitchen, greedy thing, probably hungry again. Hadn't he just fed it an hour ago? He clicked up a page displayed in a ridiculously small font size, grunted, and reached for his spectacles. Beverly Crusher, who'd sent him the report, must have eyes like a rabbit! Once the thick glasses were uncomfortably perched on his nose, the blotchy ants crawling on the viewscreen turned into words again. Being 144 years old was a novel experience, but rarely fun.

Outside, a wet winter storm howled and raged through the bayou.

This was another of many recent case histories about a new degenerative disorder, affecting mainly elderly humans, though Crusher's patient was not that old or actually expressing the disease yet. When activated, it caused a progressive disintegration of the synaptic pathways. Patients reported hallucinating that they became unstuck in time, at one moment reliving scenes from their past and in the next transported to the future. They moved back and forth randomly, sometimes falling into the present, their perceived temporal jump pace accelerating as their synaptic pathways degraded, until at last they became vegetables, settling into comas and, soon after, death. The syndrome was genetically inherited and, of course, idiopathic. No one knew how it had slipped so quickly into the human genome.

Privately, McCoy had a pretty damn good idea about that.

The black cat yowled. Tree branches tapped at the windowpane beside his desk, fluttering in the high wind whipping around the house. Reminded him of a certain dust storm on Mars almost one hundred years before.

Mears was alive, old but still hale. She hadn't died in the crash on Mars because there never was a crash on Mars. After he touched Irum, McCoy instantly returned to several minutes before the crash. He suggested they move their shuttle for a better view of the Mons Lights, and the meteor—or whatever it was—never struck. Simple as that. They had a lovely shore leave.

"I remembered," the old doctor whispered.

The storm outside shrieked like banshees. He recognized familiar voices whistling down the wind, a foolish notion, but McCoy had always been superstitious. He thought about his oldest friends.

Spock was alive, still out on Romulus last he'd heard. Jim was long gone, lost in that terrible incident on the *Enterprise*-B. Scotty, the luckiest of them all thanks to an unexpected sojourn in a transporter buffer, had a new lease on life, tinkering around these days in the SCE. All of them scattered about the universe and time and space. McCoy had never told any of them about this, nor anyone else, not ever. He'd thought about putting it all down in his memoirs, but somehow the encounter with Irum, and how he changed time, never made it in there either. No data trail: all in his head. Maybe he should walk down to the muddy river flowing across his property and whisper his secret into the reeds. But as he recalled from ancient myth, that ploy hadn't work out too well, either.

The cat strolled up and rubbed against his leg. McCoy picked up the creature and tickled its back, amused by the white sparks of static electricity hopping about its black fur. It purred and settled against his chest, warm and comforting. For some reason, he couldn't remember its name at the moment. Senility at last? Now, that would be poetic justice.

To paraphrase something Scotty once said about starships, the more complex the human body became, the easier it was to gum up the works. McCoy thought and went back to the moment he touched Irum's forehead, that tingling sensation he felt, the shock of getting wrenched out of time and through time and all around time . . . and something else.

McCoy's theory was the sort of mad reasoning that could end his distinguished medical career in an assisted-care facility. But how else to explain the seemingly spontaneous appearance of an abnormal allele on the human genome? His current case study was as telling in its lack of clues as any other. The subject, one Jean-Luc Picard—ironically, the captain of the *Enterprise*—was predisposed to express the phenotype of the gene's degenerative syndrome. He had inherited the genotype from his mother, and she had inherited it from no one in her ancestry at all. And so it went across Yvette Picard's entire generation. A hitherto nonexistent gene had appeared with the suddenness of flicking a matchstick. Though the medical community had not yet identified exactly how the gene worked, through laborious cross-checking and testing they did know which gene was involved and exactly when the mutant allele appeared on the genome.

It happened on the day Leonard McCoy touched Irum's forehead and changed time.

A strong draught of air rattled the windowframe at his elbow, as the tepid glow of the lamp on his desk flickered a few times. The hairs on the back of the doctor's neck stood up. Not because he was startled. He was chilled to the bone by his own crazy thoughts.

Coincidence? No such thing. The genetic disorder must have appeared as a result of intense subspatial and even subtemporal stress produced by the modified time line. Creation and expression all in one convenient quantum package. This triggered a reversible adaptive response in the human genome, releasing some as-yet undetectable enzyme that suppressed immunity in certain individuals to nonlinear temporal perception.

A disease that virtually unstuck people in time. Madness!

The cat licked his nose with its scratchy pink tongue, staring up at him with swamp black, effluvium eyes. Cats always seemed to be looking at you from the bottom of a dark well, mocking the silly humans, as they well deserved.

McCoy now had the task of naming the syndrome. He had no idea how to cure it, though through early tests with peridaxon, a drug he'd created on a hunch using the dried-out sample of wall lichen he'd taken from Irum's cave, he found he could slow the disease's progress. So everyone was grateful and they gave this unenviable honor to the humble old country doctor. He planned to call it Irumodic syndrome, though he supposed Leonard's Folly would be closer to the truth. A lifetime dedicated to helping the sick and this was his legacy, to name the syndrome he unwittingly created.

He could barely stand it. He'd infected the human race with misery. Their ghosts were already here, riding a cloud of despair that curled around his dizzy head. They slid in with the storm, and they were settling in for a long stay. They'd haunt him until the day he died, swooping and taunting, making sure he never forgot what he did. *The good of the one, the bad of the many,* the spirits hissed. *Your fault.* But he had no choice! What else could he do? He was a doctor, not a quantum physicist!

"She was dead!" he cried.

"She was dead, McCoy," said his black cat, eyes glittering. "You did the right thing."

McCoy squinted down at the animal in his lap. Either he was dreaming or going stark raving mad. Fine. Ship him off in a strait-jacket and be done with it. "Right?" he said. "What I did was in-sane. I'm not God. I had no business playing with time, no matter what I told myself, no matter how good it was."

"You did not play with time, McCoy," said the cat with the warp-core eyes. "You had nothing to do with it. It was not your fault."

"Then whose was it?"

The cat swiveled its head about, a full rotation. "Mine," it said. "I walked you then, McCoy. I did not mean to hurt your people. I was afraid. Now I am free, and I come and go, walking in shapes and times and dreams. I animal walk. I weather walk. But I walk alone. I am not like you. When you touched me, I made your people sick. I am sorry, McCoy. You helped me. You are my friend. But I am to blame."

McCoy blinked groggily, unable to make sense of the cat's speech. But he could tell it was sorry. "What can we do?" he said miserably.

"I do not know. I cannot take back your touch. A touch cannot be undone. If we try to walk back and fix it, you must touch me again. We made a loop! Loops are bad. Hard to break." The cat bared its fangs and ruefully shook its pointed ears. "Maybe you can fix your people. Can you? I trust you, McCoy. They all do."

The doctor slumped out of his chair and crashed to the floor. The kind words hurt him more keenly than the sharp pains shooting through his bruised body. The dead and dying were all around. The weight on his back was too much. They were right. He was accountable, and he would pay. "How can I?" he said, moaning. "I'm too old!" Bitter tears burnt his parchment skin. "I know nothing. I can't even remember your name, cat." He writhed and prayed for madness.

The cat walked up and licked his nose. "McCoy," it said solemnly, "I am Irum." Its face melted, morphing into a round white blob. "I will help. You are afriad. I will do for you what you did for me. I will help you forget your pain." A soothing swipe of the scratchy tongue. "Do not remember, McCoy. Forget." The cat's snowman head sank into a swamp of dust and darkness.

"Forget."

The word whispered into silence.

Leonard McCoy woke refreshed. He practically leapt out of bed—not bad for 144 days young!—stepped into his slippers and dashed into the study. A fine sunny morning. He tossed open the shutters and surveyed his back garden. The rosebushes looked a bit tossed from the storm last night, and there was some debris scattered around the grass, but he could clean that up later. First, coffee, then, to work.

He had a notion about the behavior of this so-called Irumodic syndrome (where had they come up with that odd name?) that might be worth exploring. Just as the chemical composition of the temporary antidote peridaxon had come to McCoy in a dream, last night as he slept he'd floated over a complex map of neurotransmitter-gated ion channels, watching a pinball progression of ions sparking through the maze of channels . . . and he could still see the course they took, leading to rapid changes in membrane potential . . . and, maybe, the syndrome itself?

McCoy felt confident the cure was close at hand. He could fix it. No one knew where this weird temporal-perceptive disease came from, but it didn't matter. He couldn't wait to call Scotty and hoot about how elderly doctors can work miracles too.

The cat purred and sidled up against his leg as he strode into the kitchen to grind some beans. "Why, hello there." He reached down and scratched its soft fur. "How are you this morning, Tempus?"

If a cat could smile, it would have.

STAR TREK
THE NEXT GENERATION®

Flight 19

Alan James Garbers

Orlean raised a hand to shield his eyes from the burning morning sun and scanned the mountainside before him. Normally he wouldn't allow the herd to graze in this direction. While the mountain wasn't taboo, enough stories were told to keep even the bravest man away. Orlean glanced back to the brown and dying plain spread out behind him, his eyes following the dry wash that led to his village in the distance. In other years the wash would be a cool stream, the plain green with grass, and his herd plump and ready for winter. He turned and cast a wary eye up the rocky slope. Succulent sprigs of grass grew in the cool shade of boulders like bait luring the starved animals higher and higher. In a frenzy they raced from spot to spot nibbling to stop the pain in their bellies.

Orlean nervously glanced about as he followed the herd higher. Indecision tore at his soul. To go back to the plain would mean a slow death for his herd, to go higher meant—what? *When was the last time someone climbed the mountain?* he thought. *Perhaps the danger is gone.* Orlean chided himself. *Surely I am not afraid of a story. What would Riter say?* Orlean knew what Riter would say if he were here, and not at Starfleet Academy. He would say how foolish Orlean was for fearing a mountain.

By noon Orlean had worked his way into a hanging gorge. Trees shaded the narrow cleft and cool green grass grew like patchwork along a whispering brook, telling of better things to come. Losing his fear in the beauty, he pushed ahead of the herd. As he worked his way through the gorge, Orlean found the canyon walls gave way to a vast crater of tall green grass undulating like waves on the sea. The herd stumbled out into the green Mecca and began feasting. Orlean sat on a large boulder and rested in the sweet mountain air. Slowly his eyes swept the distant crater walls as he wondered why no one wanted to come here. The cool breeze, the tall grass, and fresh water all belayed any evil. Surely no harm could— Orlean's eyes stopped on a distant rock outcropping. He willed his mind to accept the feature as natural but his eyes refused to believe and continued to pick out other lines and corners that were too straight to be other than man-made. Fear crept up his spine as the stories came flooding back. He rose to slink back into the gorge when the sight of the herd stopped him. They were not afraid. Was he more timid than they? With fists clenched he started across the crater to the unknown.

Orlean stood in awe. Before him rose a city such as he had never seen. Carved from the native rock cliffs, it spoke of a forgotten time when elegance was blended with function, where beauty was crafted from the mundane. Graceful curves, like those of a beautiful woman, drew the eye ever upward. Tall spires and towers caressed the clear sky like a lover. Orlean was transfixed in a spell as the afternoon sun played across the textures of the facade. All of the buildings flowed together as if they were designed to please the soul—except . . . one archway was filled in. The stonework was substandard compared with the prevalent style and grace. It was almost vulgar to look at, a blemish that caused Orlean to notice a hole. The sunlight held the small dark opening in stark contrast. Slowly, as if drawn by a need, Orlean crossed to the hole. It wasn't much bigger than his head, but with little effort more stones fell away, revealing a large chamber. A glimmer came from within as the sun dipped low. Stepping into the darkness, Orlean felt the closeness of something large. As his eyes adjusted he made out silver wings. A great bird stood in the darkness waiting to take flight. Running his hands over the cold surface, he felt a tingle of excitement. While he had never seen the space transports of his people, he knew that these were flying machines! The tales were true! He turned and peered deeper into the gloom. More birds sat waiting for their commands. Orlean was shaking as he spied another chamber deep in the back. Dark, cold, foreboding—calling to him. *Come to me!* Orlean took a hesitant step forward. *Yes! I wait for you!* formed in his mind. The dark chamber was just a step away. The voice in his mind became stronger, more demanding. *Step forward! Release me and I will serve you well!* Orlean involuntarily stepped through the doorway and froze. Eyes stared at him, glowing in the dark with a cold green light. Looking back, he saw that sunlight no longer streamed into the chamber. The sun had set. Night was coming. Orlean was alone, or was he? Fear replaced curiosity. Terror overwhelmed inaction and Orlean ran. The voice screamed in his head. *Come back! Release me!* The hate and anguish trapped behind the rock wall echoed in his mind and pursued him as he scrambled into the twilight.

"Captain's log: The *Enterprise* has been dispatched to the Alin system. Research vessel *Anasazi* has been reporting that wormholes and other spatial anomalies have been occurring there with sudden regularity. Starfleet fears that unwanted visitors like the Borg or the Dominion might be attempting to bore deep into Federation territory."

"Captain," interrupted Worf, "we are being hailed by the *Anasazi* on an emergency band."

"On screen."

Captain Jean-Luc Picard rose from his command chair and straightened his uniform just before an image appeared on the viewscreen. Surprise flashed across the captain's face and grew to a warm smile in recognition. The face was the same. A little more wrinkled, a tad more gray, but there was no doubt. "Dr. Bowman. It has been a long time."

"Jean-Luc Picard? The captain of the Enterprise*?"* the man beamed back. *"I should have known my star pupil would go this far—only I had hoped it would have been in archeology!"*

Captain Picard nodded. "I still get my fingernails dirty when time allows."

"Fantastic! Perhaps you can join me on the planet! I have a surprise that will knock your socks off."

"I look forward to it—but what is the nature of the emergency?"

Dr. Bowman shook his head as if to gather his thoughts. *"Emergency?—Oh! I forgot! Another anomaly has opened over the planet! Thank providence we had altered our orbit or we would have been thrown to who-knows-where."*

"We are coming into the system now." Captain Picard glanced to Data. "What are sensors picking up?"

"Initial scans show a category-two wormhole two thousand kilometers off the their port bow. However, it is not large enough to allow passage of the *Anasazi* and is diminishing in size," answered the android.

Captain Picard looked up to Dr. Bowman's image. "Do you have any indications of what might have caused the wormhole?"

Dr. Bowman shook his head. *"None. Unfortunately funds are limited and the institute budgeted for only what was needed for this archeological expedition. Nothing more. We're lucky to have shovels for digging."*

"Captain," injected Data, "there are traces of radiation emanating from the planet to where the anomaly occurred."

"Are you saying something on the planet caused the wormhole?"

"That's impossible. There's nothing on the planet with enough power or technology to be able to generate something of this magnitude!"

Data pursed his lips. "I have checked my readings. The radiation came from the planet."

"Can you pinpoint a location?" asked Picard.

Data's fingers flew over the console with timing and perfection only he could obtain. "They seem to emanate from a extinct volcano crater in the southern hemisphere."

"What?" queried Dr. Bowman. *"Transfer those coordinates to the* Anasazi. *You just described the location of our dig!"*

Picard nodded to Data. "Do it."

Dr. Bowman's image turned as he scanned the transmitted data. He shook his head in disbelief after a moment. *"This can't be right. They are the same as our archeological dig."*

"Could there be something down there generating the radiation?" asked Picard.

"There's nothing there but an ancient city. Preliminary indications show it hasn't been inhabited for hundreds of years."

"Data, do a scan for any type of power plant or other technology in the area."

Data shook his head. "I'm sorry, Captain, but natural interference in the crater is making it impossible to do other than surface scans."

Picard scratched his chin. "Perhaps we should have a closer look at this city."

Dr. Bowman's image nodded. *"Yes! While you're down there I'll show you what we have found. I'm telling you, it will knock your socks off."*

"We'll meet you at the coordinates, Dr. Bowman." As the screen went dark Picard turned. "Data, prepare a shuttle. You and I are going on a dig."

Picard stood in awe as Data checked his tricorder. "Magnificent."

Data looked up at the walled city for a moment. "It is a work of art; however, I am undecided as to which style it resembles: Roman, Greek, Spanish, perhaps even Phoenician."

"It wouldn't be doing it justice to compare it to any other style. The builders had a love for stone."

Dr. Bowman appeared from a hole in the stonework. "Welcome! Wonderful, isn't she! It will take decades to unravel all of her mysteries!"

Picard nodded. "We were just commenting on the beauty."

"Yes!" agreed Dr. Bowman. "This place is like the fairy-tale cities of my youth."

"How was this site found?" asked Data.

"I'm glad you asked. A young herder was tending his flock and found it. The Federation might never have known of it, but a Starfleet cadet was here on leave soon after. Together, Orlean and the cadet climbed the mountain. The cadet realized what significance this city had and, well, here we are today."

"It is outstanding," murmured Picard as he scanned the gracefully curving walls.

"Come!" Bowman motioned. "I have something that defies explanation." The three stepped through the hole and into darkness. As Picard's eyes adjusted to something his mind would not accept, a switch clicked and light flooded the chamber. Picard caught his breath at what was before him. He reached out and ran a hand over the surface in disbelief.

"See what I mean?" asked Bowman.

Picard slowly nodded as he inspected the object. "How can this be?" He turned and gazed at the objects parked around him. "Have you checked them for authenticity?"

Bowman smiled "They are as real as you and I—just much older."

"They look like—"

"—Vintage mid-twentieth-century U.S. Naval Avengers. They were—are torpedo bombers from Earth's World War Two," finished Bowman.

"Have you told Starfleet?" asked Picard.

"Not yet," Bowman replied, shaking his head. "We decided it would be best if we had a witness before we sent a message that would question my sanity. You, my dear friend, are the perfect witness, an archeological buff and captain of the Federation's flagship. Providence was smiling when you showed up."

Picard gazed at the centuries-old plane in front of him. "Replace the tires, wipe away the dirt, and—" Picard stepped up on the makeshift ladder leaning against the plane and wiped away some dust from a name painted in rolling script. "Lieutenant Charles Taylor. That name sounds familiar."

"Captain," replied Data. "I am aware of a Lieutenant Charles Taylor from my phenomenon studies. The information seems to match what we see here."

"What can you tell us, Data?"

"Lieutenant Taylor was commander of the ill-fated Flight 19. On December 5th, 1945, five Avenger torpedo bombers left from the Naval Air Station at Fort Lauderdale, Florida. It was a training mission and the flight was composed of all students except for the commander, Lieutenant Charles Taylor. The mission called for Taylor and his group of men to fly due east into what was referred later as the Bermuda Triangle." Data hesitated. "They never came back."

"Very good, Data," replied Bowman. "I ran a check on our historical logs and found the U.S. Navy attributed their disappearance to Lieutenant Taylor's being drunk and his inexperience over the Bahamas. Records show a violent storm arose over the Atlantic. Since they had little in the way of reliable technology to track their position Taylor judged his position by the islands below him. Radio reports heard Taylor saying they were over the Florida Keys, not the Bahamas. He was heard to say they were going to fly north and east to hit Florida but in reality they were flying north and east of the Bahamas, away from land and straight into the storm."

"There were five planes, but there are only three here," added Picard.

"We realized that but since we don't know how they got here we can't say where the other two are. They might be hidden in some other alcove," answered Bowman.

"Actually, in the original occurrence six planes were lost," injected Data.

"Six planes?" asked Picard.

"Another aircraft, a Martin Mariner crewed with twenty-two men, was sent out searching for the lost Avengers. It also vanished."

"I remember reading something about that," added Bowman. "The Navy spotted an explosion and found debris that would have matched the Mariner."

"Ancient flying was precarious at best," commented Picard.

The three stood silent for a moment. Then Picard peered through the dusty canopy, shoved it back in its tracks, and looked into the ancient cockpit. He was startled by his find. "The gauges are missing," he said as he eyed the empty sockets on the instrument panel.

"That was a mystery that soon led to another mystery." Bowman turned toward the back of the cave and motioned for Data and Picard to follow. Picard shifted his precarious footing on the rickety ladder as it teetered and then pitched away. He lunged for the Avenger cockpit for support as the ladder gave way. "Data!" Picard cried as his hands clawed for purchase inside the cockpit. Suddenly a firm set of hands supported his legs even as his right hand closed on something next to the pilot seat. Picard pulled it free as Data slowly lowered him down.

Picard felt the concerned stare of Data. "Are you in need of medical attention, Captain?"

Picard gave Data a reassuring smile. "No. Thanks to you I'm fine."

"What did you find?" Data asked as his gaze drifted to a worn book in Picard's hands.

"I'm not sure," Picard answered as he gently opened the book, "but my guess would be a captain's log from my ancient counterpart."

"Come!" Bowman yelled from the back of the chamber. "I have more to show you back here!"

Picard closed the log and motioned Data along. "Let's see what other surprises are in this cave of wonders."

They followed Bowman's path through the dust and into another chamber. More floodlights illuminated the walls. It was what was on one wall that caught Picard's and Data's attention.

"Notice, if you will, the chamber that we just left," motioned Bowman. "It had been carved from the stone with the same expertise that built the rest of the city. But here in this room the walls and ceiling are natural, a cavern. Except for this one." Bowman gestured toward the wall that held Picard's and Data's attention. "This one doesn't match and is the root of our next mystery. Notice the poor stonework, the crude placement of rock, and—the implants of the missing planes' gauges. All along it the gauges are embedded into the wall."

"To what end?" asked Data.

"That I can't say." Bowman shrugged. "It is another mystery.

But . . ." He smiled. "Watch this—" Bowman flicked another switch and the room was plunged into darkness.

Data eyes were the first to pick it out. "The gauges are glowing."

"Quite right. They're glowing radium green!"

As Picard's eyes focused on the green luminescence, Bowman turned the lights back on, causing Picard to shield his face from the brightness.

"Sorry, Jean-Luc," offered Bowman. "In my excitement I forget myself. But you see these artifacts are part of Earth's dangerous if not blissfully ignorant past. The dials are painted with radium. Quite common during the first half of the twentieth century. The people didn't realize the potential danger of using radioactive elements. Radium was mixed with paint to produce glow-in-the-dark watch faces, automobile gauges, radio dials, and as you can see, airplane instruments. Entire factories were set up to supply the market. Unfortunately most of the employers hired young women with good eyesight to paint the dials. They even encouraged the women to form the paintbrushes with their lips—which led adventurous girls to painting their teeth and lips just for the novelty. It wasn't until well after these women began dying of radiation cancer that the practice was stopped."

Data looked the wall over. "It was as if they placed the dials in a pattern."

"I noticed that myself," replied Picard.

"Yes, it seemed so to us also."

Picard walked over to a hole in the wall. Rubble from the hole lay strewn about. "What happened here?"

"I'm afraid our removal of some of the gauges loosened the mortar and caused that portion to collapse."

Picard glanced around at the rubble from the hole. "It looks like it was blown out."

Bowman walked over to the hole. "I hadn't noticed that before. It does look like something blew the wall away." He shrugged. "Maybe a draft blew it out or something like that."

Picard peered into the inky darkness beyond the hole as Data checked his tricorder. "Have you checked what is on the other side yet?"

Bowman shrugged. "More caverns, from the little we looked."

"Odd that someone would go to such trouble to block the caverns. Data, do you get any reading on what caused the wormhole?"

"None, Captain. The native rock seems to have a dampening effect on the sensors."

Bowman glanced at the book in Picard's hand. "What did you find, Jean-Luc?"

"I think it might be Lieutenant Taylor's logbook," Picard said as he gingerly opened it.

"By providence! If that's Taylor's logbook maybe he wrote down what happened!"

"It seems mainly comments about maintenance and flight hours," Picard murmured as he paged through. "There does seem to be some chronological order—let me see if I can find December 1945." Picard flipped deeper through the book and then stopped. "Here. *05 December 1945. Afternoon flight today . . . Can't seem to shake this flu bug and I can't get anyone to take my place . . . Radio compass is on the Fritz again . . . Don't know how they expect us to fly when they can't keep the equipment working . . .*" Picard stopped and rubbed his eyes. "I need to read this in a better light."

"There's a place to sit outside. We can look it over there," answered Bowman.

In a minute they stepped into the cool sunshine of the high mountain day. Picard got comfortable and started again. "There are more comments about his not feeling well and some other things." Picard flipped a page and stopped. "Here's something—

"We have landed on a plateau. I don't know where the hell we are . . . I lost one of the planes. It was Johnson and Beck. I hope to God they made it back safely. We must have flown into a tornado or hurricane. One minute we were trying to reach the Florida Peninsula, the next we're about to crash into a mountain. It doesn't make sense . . . I feel like Dorothy in 'The Wizard of Oz.'

"We see a city not far away. We have tried radioing for help but

get no response. Of the eleven left, four are coming with me to check it out . . . The rest will stand guard by the planes . . . I wish we still had our .45s. Maybe we'll get to meet the wizard!"

"It sounds like they were pulled here through a wormhole," said Data.

"Like the one that almost got the *Anasazi!"*

"I think you're right, Data," replied Picard. "It seems odd that other than this mention of one, the Federation has no other records of reoccurring spatial anomalies in the area."

"When did the wormholes start occurring?" asked Data.

"Several days ago," answered Bowman. "Why?"

"There does seem to be a correlation with your presence here and the appearance of the wormholes," replied Data.

"I fail to see how our appearance here would create wormholes!" retorted Bowman.

"Perhaps it wasn't merely your presence but something you did to trigger this phenomenon."

"I don't see how anything we have done could do anything." Bowman shrugged.

"Perhaps we should continue reading the log. Maybe Taylor found the reason." Picard scanned the page. "Here. They went to the city.

"We made it back from the city. At first we thought it was deserted but we did find the mayor or owner. We really don't know who he is but he seems to be the only one living there. It is troublesome that we see no one else but the man offers us food and shelter if we move into the city. I don't really see that we have a choice until we find out where we are.

"The man calls himself Suben and speaks American so I can only guess we are somewhere in the western United States. Arizona—New Mexico maybe. I don't see how we flew 1,700 miles in an instant but I can't place the terrain anywhere else on Earth. It might be a trick . . . We have taken precautions to disable the planes in case that is what they are after."

"Poor fools. They didn't know how far from home they were," murmured Bowman.

Picard looked up from the book. "Are there any records about this city?"

"Legends only. Passed down from father to son."

"What do the legends say?

"Pretty fanciful stuff. There once was a mighty people in the city. They drew water from the sky to fill the crater and then sold it to the plains people for watering crops and the like."

"Did they say what happened to the people here?" asked Data.

"Their legends are vague—that they all died away from sickness or something. It was terrible enough to make it taboo to come here," answered Bowman.

"Maybe Taylor found out something." Picard turned the page. *"It has been a week. So far we have seen no one other than Suben. He has made no moves against us yet I feel we are prisoners in a gilded cage. He provides us with every creature comfort and asks for nothing in return. I find it strange that he never eats in front of us and that we have not found where he sleeps. He is more like a groundskeeper or warden than an owner of the city.*

"We have been to the edge of the crater rim and have seen small settlements far below. None show any type of mechanized transportation and when we ask Suben about it he only says not to leave the crater again.

"It has been two weeks since our arrival. We are growing restless and are making plans to find help. By transferring all of the remaining fuel into one plane there will be enough to fly out of the crater and find help. Two men have volunteered for the mission, Maines and Lavalle. If anyone can make it, they will.

"Week Three—Maines and Lavalle are dead. It is my fault and mine alone. We transferred the fuel and made our plans but Suben appeared from nowhere as the plane was revving up for takeoff. He demanded we stop but we refused. I gave the go-ahead and the Avenger took to the sky. It felt good to know some of us weren't trapped, that there was hope. It was then that I looked at Suben. He watched the plane like a tiger watches a gazelle, then closed his eyes as if concentrating. Suddenly a force shot from the ground, massive and swirling. It shot up into the sky after the Avenger. I could see Maines was giving it a good fight but the stress was too much. After a moment the port wing tore away and

the Avenger went spiraling down in the sucking, swirling mass. We watched in horror as it crashed, knowing there was no way Maines and Lavalle could have survived. Within seconds the swirling stopped. I looked at Suben and he looked at me, a dark light in his eyes. 'Don't try to leave again,' he said.

"It seems this Suben could invoke a very powerful weapon," Picard commented as he rubbed his eyes.

"I agree," replied Data. "It would have taken tremendous shearing force to pull the Avenger apart."

"Where was I?" Picard glanced down the page. "Here we are.

"Week Four—The day started with my getting information and ended in death. I pumped Suben for what he knew about the place and did I get an earful.

"The city we live in was once a thriving place and the capital of the planet. The people came from all over to buy water which filled the crater basin. I scoffed at the idea of this arid place having water. Suben boasted that he could fill the basin in a matter of minutes. Again I scoffed at such an idea but Suben insisted he had the power to do so. Foolishly I told him to prove it. With an air of importance Suben walked into the center of the crater and looked skyward. Suddenly a force ripped from the ground and started a cyclone like the one that carried us here. Within seconds water came pouring down in torrents, almost like the cyclone was a pipeline to an ocean or something. In minutes much of the crater was standing in water.

"To our horror we also noticed bodies raining down with the water. Falling without hope of surviving, arms and legs flailing about. They hit with sickening sounds that will haunt me until the day I die. I ran to Suben and begged him to stop. He ignored me as the bodies and water continued to fall. I grabbed him and shook him. He jerked his head at me, rolled his eyes back, and went limp. The cyclone stopped. In fear I released him and backed away. In an instant he came to. As his eyes focused he spoke. 'We must have water.' He turned and walked away. I watched him for a moment and then turned back toward the killing field before us.

"Madison was the first to move. He saw a webbed hand raise up and went to it. What little feeling I had was shocked beyond reasoning. The bodies were like I had never seen, like fish people from

some bad movie. A few still lived and lay gasping in the air. We tried dragging them to the water but it was too little too late. It was numbing. Our burial count is at one hundred sixty-four bodies.

"I now realize we are no longer on Earth and like the fish people, we were sucked here by Suben. The only thing that saved us was our planes, but I feel our fate will be the same.

"Week Five—Three more are dead: Church, Hurley, and Bolton. They tried hiking out of the crater. Suben seemed to know what they were attempting and appeared instantly. He told me I must stop my men from leaving which I couldn't—they were too far away to hear anything except the crackling as electricity shot across the rim and into my men. Even in the distance we could see their bodies withering in pain. I grabbed Suben again. He ignored me. I wrapped my arms around him and fell with him to the ground. His body went limp as before and the electric bolt stopped. It was then that I noticed my watch glowing with a cool green brilliance. I jerked my arms off Suben and crawled away. In a moment he came to and stared at me for a full minute. He stood and looked at the charred bodies across the crater and then at me. His face was eerily calm. 'Do not leave the city.' "

"The radium isotope must have affected Suben somehow!" cried Bowman.

"I doubt radium would affect a humanoid so quickly," replied Picard.

"No," added Data. "But it might affect the data transfer of a computer processor."

"A walking, talking computer?" scoffed Bowman. "I hardly think so."

Data raised his eyebrows at Bowman. "I fit that description, and while my pathways are shielded, Suben's makers might not have seen the need."

Bowman was chagrined. "Sorry, Data. I forget myself sometimes."

"Taylor came to a similar conclusion," injected Picard. "Listen here—

"Week Six—We have been talking. We feel Suben is somehow affecting the radium dial on my watch or that it may be affecting him. It is a ray of hope we can't let go.

"Week Seven—We have found caverns beneath the city. They are filled with machines like we have never seen. Yet, when we attempted a closer examination Suben appeared and blocked our way. We tried to shove him aside and get our watches near him but he is too wary and his strength is too great. With the memory of what happened to our comrades, we dared not push Suben too far; we left the caverns."

"A mainframe perhaps?" asked Bowman.

"Or something like it," added Picard. "Obviously the caverns deserve our inspection."

"Does Taylor give any more information?" asked Data.

"Let's see.

"Week Ten—We have a plan. Myers reminded me that the dials in the planes' instruments also are painted with radium. We have a plan and soon we'll act.

"Week Twelve—It is done. I got Suben talking about the city again. He said the people kept dying. He tried to stop the death but his powers were useless. He said it was good to have people living in the city again. It fulfilled him. I almost felt sorry as I slipped my watch next to his back. Instantly he went limp. Some of the others ran over and strapped their watches on Suben's arms and legs. We carried Suben to the caverns and smashed the machines until they stood silent.

"It has been four months since we landed here. There are seven of us left to make the journey to the villages we see below. We have walled the cavern shut and studded the wall with the aircraft instruments. We hid the planes to keep the curious from knowing our identities. Perhaps we can fit in this world.

"If you are reading this log I beg you not to remove the wall for he might yet live and the terror will start again.

"Lt. Taylor USN

"You have breached the wall," lamented Picard. "We must assume Suben is free and causing the wormholes."

"We didn't know!" moaned Bowman.

"No one is blaming you, Dr. Bowman," commented Data. "You had no way of knowing this would result."

"Data, go back to the *Enterprise* and bring down gear to explore the caverns," ordered Picard. "I want to see what makes the mountain tick."

"Yes, Captain." Data nodded.

Picard turned back to Bowman. "Perhaps we can find the source of power and shut it down—"

"Captain." Picard turned at Data's voice. "We have a visitor."

Picard looked the man over as he stood there before them. Picard forced a smile.

"Hello. You must be Suben."

Suben did not reply with other than a nod.

"We mean you no harm," said Picard. "We are merely studying your beautiful city."

"The city—" murmured Suben. A cloud passed over his eyes and then cleared. "You must not leave."

"We can't stay."

"You will not leave"

Picard tapped his combadge. "*Enterprise*, can you get a lock on us?"

"Sorry, Captain." Riker's voice scratched. *"There's still too much interference. Are you in need of assistance?"*

"Not yet. Keep everyone on board for now." Picard turned to Suben. "I know of your powers but I have power also. If you detain us I will destroy your city."

Suben's eyes drifted skyward. "A ship. Two ships. Many people." Suben lowered his gaze to Picard. "They must not leave."

"They will leave, as we will," replied a cool Picard.

"You will not leave."

"Who made you?" asked Picard in an attempt to distract the machine.

"Made me?" questioned Suben. "Made me what?"

Picard motioned Data back into the chambers as he occupied Suben. "Who constructed you? Who put you together?"

"The people did," replied Suben.

"What was your purpose?"

"I brought water from the sky, I provided for them."

"Do you know where the water comes from?"

"Coordinates preselected by the people—"

"—On other worlds. You are creating wormholes to planets and taking their water, and lives. You are stealing what is not yours," answered Picard.

"We must have water. We must survive."

"We can show you ways to farm with less water—water you already have."

"There is no water. The crater is dry."

"There is water on this planet! Enough for all!"

"I must bring the water."

Picard sighed. "It is useless to argue with a machine." Picard gazed over the walls of the city. "When did the people leave the city?"

"They left one thousand four hundred and thirty-eight years ago. A great sickness filled them—and they left," answered Suben. "You must not leave." Suben looked skyward. "They must not leave." Suben lifted his hands upward. A beam arced up into the sky and electrical crackling filled the air.

Picard drew his phaser and hit his combadge, shouting over the static, "*Enterprise*! Break orbit! The *Anasazi* must do the same! Now!"

"We can't. Something has both ships and is pulling us down!"

Picard opened fire upon the machine with no telling effect. Stepping the phaser to full power, Picard shot point blank. To his amazement the phaser blast was absorbed, intensifying Suben's might.

Picard glanced at the hole behind him. "Data!"

Not hearing an answer above the power storm, Picard hit his combadge again.

"Status, Number One!" Picard yelled.

"We're losing altitude fast! The Anasazi *is breaking apart! We're beaming her crew off now!"*

"Lock on to our coordinates and fire a spread of deep penetrating photon torpedoes!"

"We can't, Captain!"

"This is no time to be chivalrous, Number One, now fire!"

"We can't fire. All weapons systems are down, Captain!"

Picard shielded his eyes from the flying debris as the beam tore up the floor of the crater. He turned and peered into the chamber opening. He glanced about for Bowman only to find himself alone with Suben. In desperation Picard rushed Suben, body slamming him into an arch abutment. The machine stuttered and then came back full force, flinging an arm that sent Picard flying.

Picard picked himself up and hefted a large stone and shoved it forward with all his might. With grim satisfaction he felt metal crunch as he hit home. Suben slumped against the stone wall as the energy beam subsided. Picard backed away from Suben and sank to his knees in exhaustion, his breath ragged. He warily watched the machine only to be horrified as the bent and twisted limbs started to move again. As Picard watched, Suben shoved himself erect, the arms lifting as the energy beam grew once more.

Picard willed himself to his feet and picked up another stone. He stumbled toward Suben in an attempt to finish the demon machine. Yet even as Picard moved, Suben turned toward him, his arms pointing. An arc shot out and paralyzed Picard with fire that seemed to consume his very soul. He withered in pain for his sins against the machine. Yet as he watched, a familiar figure rushed in with a glowing object. And then it was done.

Picard slumped to the ground as firm yet gentle hands caught him. As his sight dimmed Picard heard a friendly voice. "I am sorry we were detained, Captain. It seems Suben learned from his last encounter—" Then all went blissfully dark.

"Captain's log—supplemental: Suben has been disarmed. After Data's success with shutting down Suben with the radium, Bowman found the machine responsible for his power. While we left his programming intact, the away teams have dismantled his abilities to do anything but move and communicate.

"The small planet of Alin has been thrust into the scientific spotlight. An armada of research vessels are en route with an army of scientists and archaeologists. The finding of the Avengers has put the historical field on its ear.

"Starfleet is acting upon my recommendation to bestow Lieutenant Taylor and his crew with the Federation Cross, for bravery above and beyond the call of duty. If not for their efforts, those many centuries ago, countless lives would have followed them into an unknown oblivion. I can only hope that the condemnation of the past will be erased and a new chapter written on the bravery of the men of Flight 19.

"Picard out."

The Promise

Shane Zeranski

The promise was three years old now.

But still as good as new.

It was as if he had made it yesterday . . . which he had.

Well, technically, he hadn't made *it yesterday. He'd* reaffirmed *it then. As he always did. He did not let a single day escape when he failed to embrace the vow with such renewed resolution and urgent passion that it caused a tender tear or two to spill onto his cheek. After all, as he was fast learning, now is the most precious time; now will never come again. "Seize* now!*" was what he often said.*

And so he was. And would do . . . and had done.

That was three years ago, when Meribor was only four years old.

Four years old and dying.

He had pushed the door to her room carefully open, afraid that even the slightest creak or unkind scrape might thrust her deeper into the final, horrible, dark arms of death. He had padded softly up to her bed and slid gently into the chair next to her. He found himself spending so much time in that creaking, rotten chair these last few weeks. And he hoped he would continue to do so. He hoped that that chair next to her bed would never become empty, because that would mean that . . .

Never mind. He couldn't think that way.

He didn't want to wake her. That was not his intent.

The moon, far above in the still, night sky, shone down defiantly through the plate glass window and cast what could only be described as a heavenly glow upon her tender face.

She's an angel, *he had thought hollowly.* She's an angel . . . and her wings are about to be plucked.

He had just wanted to watch her; watch her small chest rise and fall with each blessed breath; watch the way her soft hair curled up around her pale cheeks; smile as her closed eyes fluttered airily with dreams of butterflies and tea parties and sunny afternoons. And if worse came to worse . . . watch the fragile life drain from her body . . .

If.

Only if.

And he had suddenly realized that that could not happen—it could *not. He wouldn't allow it. He'd lost so much already. He had started over, and to lose something so precious again so soon . . .*

He would not let that happen.

He would sit here for the rest of his life if he had to, a protective shadow across the still form of his daughter. Nothing would harm her. He would simply will *the sickness away with all the stubborn, obstinate doggedness he possessed.*

And then her eyes had fluttered open.

His heart literally skipped a beat, only silence pounding in his ears. He gulped, hoping he hadn't woken her, yet knowing that he had.

"Go back to sleep," he whispered. "You need your sleep. I'll be right here." He reached out and lightly touched her face.

He had expected her to close her eyes, soothed by his touch, assured by his presence, and return to her infrequent slumber.

But her eyes were wide. Wide, clear, and frightened.

His heart had broken at that haunted gaze; it had twisted in the cold, angry fist of agony.

"What is it?" he whispered, moving slightly closer.

She was quiet for a moment, eyes searching his open face, before her moist lips parted.

"Daddy." Her voice was like a fragile rustling of wind. "Am . . . I going to die?" Her eyes pleaded with him to answer no, but they also pleaded with him to tell nothing less than the absolute truth.

He clenched his jaw, fought back tears, and grasped both her delicate hands in his. He brought them to his mouth and kissed them. Then he looked directly into her eyes.

He would tell the truth.

"No," he said firmly, and felt his hands tighten around hers. "No, you will not, Meribor. I will not allow it." He paused momentarily. "Do you understand that?"

Wide, her quiet eyes again searched his, glistening in the moonlight.

"Do you promise, Daddy? Do you . . . ?"

This time he could not contain every secret emotion that was rushing through him, and a tiny, crystal tear escaped from within his soul and drifted down his cheek. He did not bother wiping it away.

"Oh, Meribor." His soft voice broke, and he reached up and ran a hand along her gentle face, both out of impossible affection, and because he was afraid that any more stillness might cause him to break apart and sob. "I promise," he said. "I promise forever . . . and I never break a promise."

"Never?" she whispered hopefully.

He smiled. "Never . . ."

She, then, too smiled, and it brought joy to his old heart to see her face come to life. It had seemed like forever since her beaming face had lit the room.

"Thank you, Daddy," she said. "Please don't go anywhere."

"I will not, I promise. I'll be right here."

And she had drifted off to sleep, and the moon had slid behind a puffy, light cloud, cloaking the room in muffled darkness.

He had stayed there all night, absolutely resolute that nothing would harm his daughter, absolutely resolute that he keep his promise.

The next day, her fever had broken.
He had kept his promise.
And still he did.

The wind howled outside the house—which was nestled deep within the small village of Ressik—shrieking its indignant protests against the husky walls of Kamin's home.

A home which he had supposedly built with his own hands—although he still had no recollection whatsoever of doing so—but which he had made his own in a tender, reluctant way.

Kamin's bare legs (which reminded him more and more often that he wasn't getting any younger) stretched out before him and were propped up comfortably upon a large wooden stool. He, himself, was eased back serenely, almost disappearing into the fathomless cushions of his favorite chair. And in his hand was a bowl of his favorite soup . . . made by his favorite wife, Eline . . . with the aid of his favorite children, young Meribor, and, younger yet, Batai.

Kamin sighed a long, contented sigh, listened thankfully as the wind screamed *outside,* and fed himself another spoonful of Eline's delicious soup.

The only thing missing, he thought, was a roaring fire. But that would have been absurd, not only because there was no fireplace in Kamin's household, but because his entire family would have literally roasted to death. It was hot year-round. And the wind howling outside was not a cold, wintry blizzard, but a warm, humid blast of twisting air that spewed forth tiny pinpricks of sharp dirt, leaving paths and streaks of thick, fresh dust in its wake. Yes, indeed, in the morning, Ressik was going to have quite an inconvenient amount of cleanup to attend to.

But a fire was not the *only* thing that was missing, Kamin mentally amended. Batai . . . Batai was missing. He would have been here on a night like this, hanging about restlessly until the wee hours of the morning, not necessarily doing anything constructive, but simply comforting a friend with his warm presence.

Kamin set down his bowl, sighed again, and then—*OOOMPH!*—Batai was in his lap.

Not *that* Batai, thank heavens, for Kamin would have been a permanent decoration in his favorite chair, but Batai, his small son; the namesake of his late best friend.

"Daddy!" Batai shouted happily, and climbed his way up his father's chest, squashing various parts of Kamin's anatomy, until his arms were wrapped securely around his daddy's neck, jelly-stained lips pressed close against Kamin's cheek, hot baby-breath whispering upon the same spot.

"Oh, Batai! Hello there!" Kamin rushed to assume a position to best protect those parts of his anatomy that he didn't wish scrunched. "And how are you this evening, young man?"

The only words that Batai knew were "daddy," "no," and "cookie," so Kamin wasn't really expecting a response from his son. He was simply content to be in the company of such select words and in the meaning they held to a small child.

"Have you finished your dinner?"

Batai looked up at him with expectant, blue eyes as wide as saucers. They had watched his father's lips move and were now thoroughly examining every nook and cranny of his wrinkled, leathery face.

"Cookie," he mumbled distractedly, probably because he didn't have anything else to say.

"Now, young man," Kamin scolded mockingly, "I would say that you have indeed *not* finished your dinner because half of it is on your face." He picked up a napkin from the table beside him and began to wipe the jelly-smothered crumbs from around his son's disgruntled mien.

"A story, Father. Tell us a story."

Kamin looked down to where his daughter, Meribor, sat upon the floor in a long, blue nightie, her small hands splayed across his sandaled feet.

"Please," she said, "just a short one?"

Kamin disposed of the messy napkin and made room for Batai, who was snuggling down in the fabric of his shirt, apparently having already decided for his father that a story *would,* in fact, be told.

"It's getting late, young lady, and you know you have to be up early in the—"

"You *promised* . . ."

This stopped him short. He thought back for a moment and discovered that, indeed, he *had* made that promise. In fact, it was late last night that he had done so, in much the same time and place as this.

That settled it.

"Well . . ." He let out a long breath. "It seems you've got me there. Whoever taught you to be so clever, anyway?" He pretended to be serious.

"You, Father," Meribor giggled. "Now tell the story . . . please," she added.

Kamin looked to Eline, who was in the shadows of the kitchen cleaning up the dishes. She smiled the smile that is understood only between a husband and wife. She, too, seemed to be waiting for whatever tale her husband would spin this time. Kamin glanced back down to Batai, who looked up expectantly at him, thumb plopped happily in his mouth, breathing steadily, contentedly.

And then to Meribor, whose cascading, blond hair swept down over her face, failing to hide her hopeful features.

Kamin smiled.

He needed no more prompting.

"There once was a ship," he began with a deep breath, "a great ship. A starship. And her name was the *Enterprise* . . ."

". . . and so Captain Picard gripped the entire comm panel as if it were the last piece of timber still afloat in a raging ocean storm. He tried to use it to steer the entire vessel, really, but Commander Riker was the one in charge of that. Picard was the captain, but Riker was the better pilot, by far. At least when it came to shuttlecraft, that is.

"The shuttle *shot* through the clouds like a bullet, tearing them apart as it torpedoed through. But the Klingons were hot on their trail. The shuttle was so badly wounded that it vented dark clouds of plasma behind it. It would crash if Riker didn't land it . . . and in one piece, too, because if he didn't, then it really didn't matter, now did it?

"The Klingons plowed through the clouds that the *Enterprise* shuttle had already parted, and the Romulan scoutship that they had stolen fired another bolt of green energy into the back of our—excuse me, *their*—ship. That last shot was all that it took. The shuttle was blasted hard to port (that would have been their left side) and it began to descend faster and faster into a wild, spiraling tailspin.

"Picard had no choice but to look directly out the window in front of him; it was either that or close his eyes. But Picard was no coward—but that did not stop him from behaving in a completely Kataanian manner, and he gripped even harder on the comm panel, trying desperately, and quite futilely, to steer the ship into correction.

" 'Hang on, Captain,' Riker said through gritted teeth. 'There's not much I can do now.'

"The Klingons fired another shot which clipped their ship again, and now it started to descend, not just in a tailspin, but in every direction at once. There is really no way I can explain their anxiousness and their fear, and how long that those moments seemed to last. You would have to have been there, Meribor . . . and *you,* too, Batai.

"It seemed to last forever, but it was only a matter of seconds before the shuttle crashed brutally into the planet, splitting forests apart and uprooting giant trees with its huge nose. It was certainly a bumpy ride, but both Captain Picard and Commander Riker were bolted into place by the safety harnesses that were strapped tightly around their chests.

"The shuttle eventually came to a stop as it burrowed the front half of its frame into the base of a giant hill deep within the forest—"

"Were they all right, Father?" Meribor's apprehensive fingers tunneled into Kamin's leg, and he almost had to bite his tongue to keep from yelping.

"Let go of my leg, dear, and perhaps I'll tell you."

Meribor glanced startledly down at her hand. "Sorry," she said quickly and removed her fingernails from her father's leg.

Kamin looked down to Batai. He expected his son to be at least on the brink of a child's slumber by this time, but his bright eyes were wide, gazing up at him, not the slightest hint of drowsiness found within. Strange, Kamin's words could not possibly have any meaning to him, yet Batai was absolutely absorbed in the tale his father was weaving—drawn into the exciting, moving sounds that spilled from those lips.

"Well, *were* they . . .?"

"Excuse me?" Kamin asked, looking away from his son to his daughter.

"Were they all *right,* Father? Were they?"

"Ah, yes . . . Picard and Riker . . ."

And as Kamin continued, a strange, dark feeling that he hadn't had for a very long time began to creep slowly into his stomach, working its way up and out and deeper, extending in every direction, until he felt it begin to flutter at the brim of his mind, heart, and soul.

"Yes, they were fine . . . but only for the moment. The Klingons were landing right behind them. The Romulan scoutship they had stolen caused the tops of the trees—the ones that Picard and Riker didn't plow over, that is—to whip and blow back and forth. Giant boughs actually broke off and the two Starfleet officers had to duck to avoid them. The Klingons tried to find a relatively barren spot in which to land, but the trees were too thick, and they squashed many as they set down, sending even more splinters and shards of wood ricocheting in every direction.

"Riker and I knew that there would be absolutely no use in attempting to run or hide. We would simply have to face them.

"But remember, these were not regular Klingons. They had stolen the Romulan scoutship. Klingons were, by their very nature, honorable beings. That is what made them Klingons. But these Klingons had no honor; they did not care about it at all. They had stolen from the Romulans in order to pursue Picard and Riker, and probably to kill them. But it was worth it, because all the two officers were trying to do was distract them from the *Enterprise,* because by this time it was crippled, and could be taken over very easily, you see.

"The hatch to the Romulan ship slid open and three elephantine Klingons stood there. It was difficult to see them because the dust had not yet settled—*and* a giant tree had fallen across our line of vision, blocking almost everything between Riker and myself. In fact, the hatch to the Romulan ship had *bumped* against the gigantic log as it lowered, and was unable to open all the way.

"The biggest of the Klingons, Gath, and also the deadliest, was the leader. The enormous beast climbed down and across the felled tree, a long blade in each hand.

"Neither Riker or I had any weapons, but—"

"Daddy," Meribor said suddenly, "how come you're telling it as if you were really there?"

Kamin stopped, his hands frozen wide in excited, narrative gesticulation.

"What?"

"Sometimes you say 'I' and 'we' like it was you instead of Captain Picard. How come?" Meribor bore an almost concerned expression.

"I did?" Kamin frowned, that strange, black feeling working even deeper into his stomach. It was certainly possible he had done so. In fact, it was fairly obvious, or else Meribor would not have mentioned it. Surely she was not imagining things. And considering the circumstances . . . *and* that feeling that he dreaded so much.

It had been months since he had felt it. *Really* felt it.

Oh, sure it was always there in some sense, but most of the time it was like a faint shadow or a dim whisper; something that was forever a part of him, but, of late, hardly ever seen or heard.

Now it was climbing his insides like a poisonous vine, rustling the memories of his heart like a cool, fall breeze.

Batai, too, was staring up at him, his countenance an etching of worried perturbation. And Eline—even she had lain down her dish towel, her brows furrowed upward concernedly, eyeing Kamin doubtfully from the shadows.

Kamin shifted in his seat. "I, uhm . . . it's . . . it's just that, I get so involved in the stories that I tell, that I often forget I'm really *not* there at all." He forced what he hoped was a comforting smile. "Good stories often do that, you know."

Meribor seemed to be satisfied with this explanation, and thus, so did Batai.

"So . . . what happened next?"

Kamin glanced at the timepiece on the wall.

And despite the late hour, and despite that ebbing, prickly feeling, he continued on for ten minutes more. . . .

". . . and so Picard's attempt to overwhelm Gath had failed—horribly. He lay there on the ground, his left arm perhaps broken.

"The giant Klingon towered above him, seething, and he wiped dripping blood from his mouth, spat even more to the soil, splattering it upon the twiggy ground like—"

"Kamin!"

Eline's voice shot from the shadows as she emerged from them. "Don't scare them. This isn't a horror story, you know!"

Kamin seemed to snap out of his narrative catalepsy, apparently having forgotten that his family was gathered around him.

He gazed down at Meribor as if he were discovering her for the first time.

"Oh . . . I'm sorry, Meribor. Was I frightening you?"

Meribor, her eyes wide and nervous, gulped and hoarsely whispered, "No, Father."

"Good then," Kamin's voice took on a sterner, more resolute quality, "because that's exactly how things occurred."

And he jumped back into the story.

". . . because Gath had blamed Riker for it. Either that, or he knew that I was ultimately the one responsible, and he knew that it would cause me ever more pain to see Riker killed for my actions.

"Whatever the case, Riker didn't fight it. In fact, he seemed almost relieved at the outcome.

"But *he* was the one who was going to be killed, not me. And it was *my* fault.

"Gath had one of the other Klingons, another giant one at that, hold a disruptor to my head while he and the other got Riker under control.

" 'Don't touch him!' I struggled slightly. 'Don't touch him! It was *not* his fault. It was *mine! I'm* the one who should be executed!'

" 'That can be arranged,' I heard a Klingon voice say, and I felt the disruptor press firmer against my temple.

"They stripped the top portion of Riker's uniform from his chest, and Gath removed a large blade, and held it to his belly, just below his rib cage.

" 'Now you *watch* this, Picard. Watch as your first officer shrieks in horror and severe pain. And remember that it is *your* fault—yours and no one else's.

" 'No!" I screamed. I—"

"That's enough!"

Eline actually shot up from her seat like someone had lit a match beneath her. Her face was a mixture of horror, anger, and shock.

"Meribor! Batai! It's late. Hurry off to bed, now!"

Meribor simply sat there, still as a statue, staring up at her father.

"Meribor!"

She snapped out of whatever state of dismay she was in, but did not respond to her mother. She addressed her father.

"Daddy, you're doing it again. You're pretending you're Captain Picard. Why? What's wrong?"

"I was *not!"* Kamin raised his voice at her, a thing that he had done only once before, and only then because she was deserving.

Meribor seemed to dissolve at this, shrinking into her soft nightgown. Still, her young, eight-year-old voice remained as strong as ever, all girlish qualities vanishing for a moment. "Yes, you *were,* Father. I heard you. You said 'I' instead of 'Captain Picard.' "

This time, Kamin simply bellowed. It was something that he would later dearly regret; it would leave a deep, shameful scar upon his conscience for as long as he would remember.

"Be *quiet,* Meribor! I said that I did *not and I did not!* Your father is not a liar!" He pointed a shaking finger down the hall. "Now go to your room! *Go!"*

Eline quickly intervened, pushing Meribor behind her, scooping up Batai, who had begun to cry, from Kamin's arms into her own.

"Go to bed, it's time for bed," she said softly.

She swept them off down the hall, attempting to hide Kamin from their view. Even so, Kamin saw Meribor peeping anxiously around the folds of her mother's billowing skirt, her eyes wide and concerned.

Kamin found himself trembling in the silence. He was not sure why.

That black feeling was overwhelming now. The wind outside continued to shriek, screaming an almost anguished cry. Kamin took a deep breath, tried to contain himself. He was fairly sure of what was happening to him, desperately not wanting to recognize it. It hurt too much.

Eline strode back into the room, a self-contained tempest, a smoldering fire.

"Kamin!" she uttered his name in the loudest, fiercest whisper she could muster, without breaking into fuller tones. "Just *what* do you think you're doing? What kind of story was that?!"

Kamin strode past her with equal fervor, not bothering even to look at her as he stamped past, or to keep his voice at a reasonable level. "A *true* one, Eline. It was the *truth!*"

And he disappeared into their bedroom, leaving his wife alone in the deserted living room, fuming, startled, and utterly dismayed.

Kamin had waited five minutes or so, sitting in the darkness on his bed, listening to the wind howl and moan, before he decided Eline was not going to pursue him.

That was fortunate. There were times when he was in a foul mood and he would retreat like a frail hermit into dark quiet, simply needing someone to listen as he spoke a hulking burden from off his shoulders. The small, soundless, almost imperceptible signal would be sent, whether he intended it to be or not. Soon, Eline would be there, serene and silent, waiting for him to speak . . . and *he* would have been waiting for *her.*

This was not one of those times. Now, he wanted desperately to be left alone. He did not hear the soft *pad-flop* of his wife's slippers, and he was eternally thankful that she could recognize his need for solitude. This did not mean that she was not upset with him, of course. That much was apparent. He would get an earful later.

Now, as he was sure that he was alone in his shadowed room—and that it would stay that way—he allowed that part of him that he had for so many years kept hidden behind a curtain of tranquility to open up. These days that curtain had a tendency to remain diffidently shut, and very rarely did he peep through.

"Q," he whispered, his hands on his knees, staring at his shadow on the wall, which was itself flickering back and forth in synchronous rhythm with the small flame he had lit behind him. "Q, I've had enough."

He was completely quiet for a moment, as if waiting for a response.

"I said that's enough! There's only so much a man can take." He directed his gaze slowly upward now as he spoke. "You can't expect me to live the rest of my life like this, can you?"

Silence.

"I've got a family. A family that I dearly love, Q. And whether you're doing this merely to enjoy a long, hearty laugh, or whether you have some skewed purpose in mind . . . I ask you to end it. End it now, Q."

Kamin waited for another moment, his body tense, jaw muscles working. He grasped the end of the bedpost in his left hand and squeezed it without even knowing, as if his frustration and despair were somehow seeping through his hand into the wooden column.

"I've learned my lesson," he raised his voice slightly, "Yes, I know now that I was missing something on the *Enterprise*. I know that there was no way I would ever have allowed myself to love anybody like I love these people. It was impossible for me to contemplate sharing life with anyone other than myself. I never would have had a wife or children . . . I was indubitably selfish, Q, I know that."

He paused, his fingernails digging into the wood of the bedpost with feverish intensity. In the singular light of the flickering candle, his eyes glistened with tears that he would not allow to fall.

"I've learned my lesson . . ." he repeated.

And then he roared, "Now *change it back!*"

His breathing was increasing in intensity, his heart rate *thud-thudding* away as the organ to which blood was pumping grieved in desperate haste.

But there was no response from the mysterious letter of the alphabet the man seemed to be addressing.

Nothing at all.

Kamin lowered his head, gripped even harder, and with quiet intensity, said "Dammit, I'm sorry . . ."

And then he felt the pain shoot up his arm and to his heart. His eyes went wide, his mouth opened, suddenly feeling very dry and cottony. He felt utterly paralyzed, yet he *did* manage to grasp his chest and left arm before he collapsed to the dark, beckoning floor.

"Daddy . . .?"

Darkness.

"Daddy . . .?"

And then his daughter's face.

Kamin blinked his eyes several more times to clear away the groggy film of haze that thickly blanketed everything upon which he attempted to focus.

"Daddy, you're awake! I'll get Mother!"

"No!" Kamin heard himself rapidly respond.

He had not really had time to process exactly what his circumstances were. But based upon the thin candlelight flickering to his left, the familiar smell of his bed and feel of his sheets, it was not difficult to guess.

"No, wait," he said, attempting to adjust his voice so that it didn't waver so. "Not yet. She'll bring the whole town in with her . . . come here for a moment, Meribor." He wiggled his finger toward himself, an act which he found astonishingly exhausting.

Meribor had remained in her nightgown, it appeared to still be dark out, and the wind continued to howl mournfully, so he gathered that he hadn't been out for very long.

Meribor looked warily at him, but stepped closer.

"Mommy said that you were very sick and that I should not bother you."

"Oh, Meribor." Kamin tried to sit up a little, but found it extraordinarily difficult to do so. "You never bother me. Never. You bring me the greatest joy that I have ever known."

"Really . . .?" She fidgeted with her hands.

"Oh, yes." He reached down as much as was physically possible so that she could climb into his arms, in the process noticing that some manner of thin, plastic tube was inserted into his arm, traveling up to who-knew-where.

Meribor grasped her father's large hands with her tiny ones and pulled herself up, being altogether too careful to avoid bumping the tubing, but as soon as she was within Kamin's arms, she swiftly wrapped her arms around him and hugged him fiercely.

"I love you, Daddy," she said quietly, her face scrunched up against his chest. Kamin wondered how in the world she could breathe like that, then thought no more of it because his heart was melting.

He reached down and gently brushed her long hair aside her soft face. "I . . . I love you, too, Meribor. Very much."

Not releasing him from her bear hug, she looked up at him. "I'm sorry."

He drew himself up slightly. "Whatever for?"

"For asking all those questions. About you and Captain Picard. I shouldn't have done that."

Kamin pulled her back slightly, just enough so she would know that what he said next was very important. "Meribor, there was nothing wrong with those questions you asked. They were . . . appropriate." He shifted uncomfortably. "I *was* confusing myself with Captain Picard—I *was* telling the story as if I were him. You were right. This," he said, gesturing to himself and the tube that jutted out of his arm, "is not your fault, Meribor. I simply got excited. It happens to daddies my age; but it was *not* your fault."

Meribor drew herself closer again, pressing up against him as if he were a lifeline. "Did you know him, Daddy?" she said through his shirt.

"Know who?"

"Captain Picard."

Despite himself, Kamin's breath caught in his throat. He let it out slowly. Here came that feeling again.

Push it down, Kamin! Push it away, for goodness' sake!

"I . . . I don't know, exactly. It's a—a very . . . confusing thing to talk about. It's complicated, Meribor. It's—"

"It's okay, Daddy. I understand," she said, her face still pressed against his chest, her voice muffled.

Kamin smiled. *He* did not understand. There was no way in the world his eight-year-old daughter could understand. But that was the beauty of it, wasn't it?

"You're an extraordinary gift to an undeserving father, Meribor. Thank you."

"Daddy?"

"Uhm-hm."

"Will you finish the story?"

If Kamin's thoughts had had feet, they would have stopped dead in their tracks. He did not *want* to finish the story. He did not *want* to talk about Commander Riker and Captain Picard any more. He dreaded it. The thought of doing so summoned that sickening, black feeling.

He wouldn't do it.

"Yes," he said.

Damn!

"But not tonight. Daddy's tired."

Meribor relaxed her tight, warm hold on him to look up into his eyes with her penetrating blues. "Do you *promise?"*

Kamin knew what that meant. He didn't break promises—not to her. If he promised, then he would have to do it. But if he didn't promise, she would know that he never intended to do it. Would she understand? Or would he break her heart? That had always been his fear—breaking his daughter's heart. But she was extraordinarily mature for her age; he had raised her that way. Surely she *would* understand.

He would tell her no.

"Yes. I promise."

At that blessed assurance, his daughter once again relaxed against his frame, completely and utterly content in both the safety of his arms and his promise.

"Daddy, you're going to be all right."

Kamin smiled softly. "Promise?" he asked.

"Promise . . . and you know what?"

"What?"

"I never break my promises."

Kamin had hugged her tighter, holding his daughter close . . .

And then Eline had walked in, shrieked in delight at the sight of her husband, conscious and well. Indeed, Kamin had been right—Eline *did* have the entire, concerned town of Ressik stuffed supportively in their living room. The doctor had entered his room shortly after hearing Eline's ecstatic exclamation, had attempted to maneuver around her brooding form to examine Kamin, and had then given him a clean bill of health.

And so it was that the previous happenings of the evening were entirely forgotten.

Or so it had appeared. . . .

Kamin was sleeping poorly.

He tossed and turned, the sheets of his bed twisting themselves around his frail, stick-thin legs like a snake of satin coiling its way around a meager branch. The large tufts of bristly white hair poked and pointed in irreconcilable madness between his ears and bald head—even more so now due to the manner in which it was squished between his head and bunched-up pillows.

He let out a long, wheezing sigh (as they all were these days) and lay as still as he possibly could. He very much needed his sleep tonight because Meribor was adamant about dragging him off to some sort of "launching" in the morning.

He had never slept a full night since Eline had been gone. Inevitably he would turn over in the night and drape an arm over . . . nothing. He would wake up, startled, wondering who had stolen Eline from under his wing . . . and then he would remember. He would usually sleep restlessly from that point on, if at all.

That was how it had been for nine years.

Only tonight it was different. Something was wrong. Something *inside* him.

That black, thistly feeling was back, gnawing at his stomach and mind like some kind of wicked disease.

Only now he did not want to acknowledge it. His aged, decrepit body and his rigid, stubborn

(not stubborn, for goodness' sake!)

mind were in direct opposition with one another. His body said yes and his mind said no. And although they *were* both in agreement that Kamin should not sleep, they warred over the ifs and whys and buts.

Which was, in the long run, entirely pointless, because Kamin knew—deep down inside, where even *he* visited only once in a great while, he *knew*—that *it* was here, rapping on the tightly sealed door to his heart and soul.

And now it was time to let it in. Time to bare his teeth and confront it.

He had picked up his flute, dropped its tip into his mouth, and tried in earnest to play that blackness away—blow it through and out in notes at which his gnarled, old fingers could barely arrive. But neither his mind nor his heart was in the music, and he had discovered after a moment that he was simply blowing air, nothing more, not even a tune.

Sadly, he had dropped the instrument and summoned Meribor, called her to his home in the middle of a dark, wet night.

She did not bother knocking. It was her home as much as her father's, perhaps even more so if it is true that home is where the heart is.

And now she approached the door to her father's room, the sulking shadows of the quiet house frowning and slithering slowly across her adult features. She stopped beneath the doorframe, seeing Kamin's fragile silhouette upright and hunched over thoughtfully on his bed, the covers sprawled in every direction, his nightclothes wrinkled and disheveled.

"Father . . .?"

He glanced up at her dark form. "Meribor, come in."

She set down the small bag of night things she had brought

with her from her own home just in case, and slowly, quietly made her way to the edge of the bed. She sat down, scooted close to her father, and put a slender, womanly hand on his spindly, frail leg.

"What is it?" Her brow was creased in concern, although she could see that her father appeared to be fine.

Kamin simply looked at her, his eyes glistening faintly from deeply sunken sockets. His deeply wrinkled, drawn, veined face gave not a clue as to what emotions were roiling beneath the surface of his countenance.

And he continued to stare at her in stony silence, his breathing low and warm, his eyes dancing about Meribor's face, as if searching for some place to hide.

Meribor's troubled expression grew deeper. "Daddy . . .?"

And Kamin's face began to crumble. It would have been difficult to discern exactly how strong his features actually were in his old age, how sharp and commanding they had remained beneath his pleated, rutted skin, unless one had seen now how they melted away. His brow drew impossibly upward, and his eyes narrowed to slits as his face crumpled into a pained, agonizing grimace. He slowly raised his shaking arms and, with all the passion and urgency he could physically muster, embraced his daughter.

Kamin placed his old, tired head against her shoulder and let out a trembling sob. His small, gaunt shoulders began to slowly rise and fall in physical grief as each breath came in mournful hitches. Tears streamed down his face in small rivers, tracing the wrinkles of his contorted face.

"I loved them," he sobbed. "I loved them as much as I love you and Batai. As much as I loved Eline, I loved them all!"

His fingers worked in fistfuls of Meribor's shirt behind her back, and his body shuddered against hers.

"And I never told them. I never told a one!" Each breath he took in was a choked noise, and each he let out was a wail. "Not Data, not Worf, not Riker . . . not even Beverly."

Meribor held her father with all she had in her, not completely understanding what was occurring, but realizing that all her father's hopes and dreams, fears and regrets were being poured out, and she was the one to whom he had chosen to bear his naked, raw soul.

"Oh, Meribor. I loved them, I did. And now they're gone and I'll never see them again! I always—always expected that . . . that I might, but—" He cringed behind Meribor's back as all that was rushing out was almost too much to bear. Salty tears rivuleted down his cheeks, pouring over his lips, which were pulled back in anguish, and into his mouth, where they burned with fiery remorse. "But I won't. . . . If only I could see them—just once more, just . . . once . . . more!"

Meribor now cradled her broken father in her arms like a small child. She felt tears stinging her own eyes, tried to hold them back, but failed, because all her might was in holding her daddy. "It's all right, Father. It's all right."

"Don't hate me, Meribor. Don't hate me for loving them," Kamin sobbed, scarcely understandable in his choked spasms of tears. "They were my family . . . my family . . . and I've lost them."

He pulled himself back slightly, not caring if his daughter saw the crushing, twisted pain in his face, for she could see it in his heart. "Your mother . . . she could never understand."

"Oh, Daddy. I don't hate you. I understand . . . I love you so much." A tear slid down her own face and onto her quivering lips.

"Thank God, Meribor. Thank you, thank you so much."

And she held him like that for moments that seemed both like hours and seconds, as he wept the blackness away, cleansed himself deep within, exposed that raw part of him that he had contained for half of his life—no . . . that had contained *him* for half his life.

And when he was finally finished, when he was finally able to gain control of himself, streaked paths of red skin seeming to swell his face, from his eyes down to his chin, he simply sat there. His mouth hung open, his breathing was not labored, but strangely discernible, as the warm, hollow wind after a storm. Every breath he took seemed to be incomplete, until the immense, sudden, shuddering sigh that is the finale of profound emotional release tumbled through his body like a small, liberating aftershock.

There was a still silence for a while, Meribor afraid that if she so much as spoke, she might somehow break her father, and Kamin, afraid that if he so much as spoke, he might somehow shatter himself further.

Finally, he spoke. "Meribor . . ." he said in a ragged whisper.

"Yes?" Her voice was just as soft.

"Do you . . . remember . . . that story? That story that—"

"Yes," she interrupted him, as if the less he spoke, the less chance there was that he might cause himself more pain.

"It was the only promise I ever broke . . ."

"Shhh." She put a finger lightly to his lips. "It's all right. It wasn't broken . . . not to me."

"You're right. It's not broken. Not yet. And get your . . . get your hand away from my mouth, please. I'm not *that* delicate." The old Kamin was beginning to reappear.

Meribor smiled hesitantly and slowly did so.

"I want to finish the story."

The protective concern began to resurface in Meribor again. "No, Father. It's all right, there's no need. You don't have to put yourself through that again. I *understand,"* she said again, slowly, as if he wasn't hearing her.

"No." Kamin shook his shaggy head. "I *want* to. The black . . . it's all gone now. . . . I'm free."

Meribor had never heard of "the black" before, yet she knew exactly what it was. She eyed Kamin the way a mother might eye a child as it takes its first, precarious steps.

"I can still keep my promise, Meribor . . . let me do that."

A slow smile spread over Meribor's face, like the first rays of sunlight splashing up over the mountains at sunrise. She pushed herself further up onto the bed, finding a pillow upon which to prop herself.

"I'm afraid I'm a bit to large for your lap, Father, but . . . tell me a story."

For the first time in a long time, Kamin smiled—truly *smiled.* To him, as well, it felt like the fresh warmth of the sun on his face after a long, buffeting storm.

He leaned back, and put his arm around his daughter. "Now

where were we . . .? Oh, yes. Captain Picard and Commander Riker . . ."

And as he said those names, his heart did not ache, and his soul did not throb in the dreadful anguish of lost memories.

Indeed, the blackness was gone.

And he was keeping his promise.

Flash Point

E. Catherine Tobler

Flashback. I'm seven years old, standing in a hallway. I don't know where it goes, where it is. A Cardassian holds my hand; his skin is desiccated, as gray and dry as the Cholla Flats. A thousand scales decorate the back and fingers; in the light from the end of the hall, they resemble shattered crystal. The Cardassian smells, like black clouds about to erupt.

Flash-forward. Jaros II and the walls of this cell are that very color, the storm about to unleash itself. This room smells, but unlike that Cardassian, this is warm; he was cold.

Flashthen. Garon II. A hundred lifetimes away and yet close enough to hold against my heart. Cupped in my hand, eight souls which I tossed into the gloom without looking back. The cave, the smell of the rock, like it had been under water. A pit newly carved just for us. The bite of powder in the air—weapons and the kiss of steam—

* * *

Flashback. Steam blocking my vision; a broken pipe letting loose with a sulfuric belch as I come into the room. I balk. The Cardassian holds my hand tighter, pulls me even though I'm digging my heels in. Those scales flush darker. He smells angry. A cool circle in my palm, then. The candy is sugar-white, as sweet as milaberries on my lips. The sweet erases the bitter steam, the round disk on my tongue a newfound toy.

Then—Garon II. Weapons boxed like toys and I can't go any further. The walls are low, the passages narrow. It's like a palukoo trap and already I can reach up and touch the rock. It's damp under my fingers. No, I can't go in there—not with the steam hissing like skewered hara cats. It smells like a storm—can't you taste the air? No—orders don't matter— I can't, I can't.

Back to the room. Father tied to the chair, his head limp, his hair wet. Earring broken, glinting like a star on the floor. Little star, not that far, twinkle gone, here comes dawn. The earring crunches under a boot heel. Father broken and sobbing—where did those wide shoulders go? Your shadow so small on the floor, so tiny in this room that smells like the dirt we poured over Mother when she died. Do you remember that day? You had wide shoulders then.

Flashthere. Shoulders too big to fit; no, I can't and I don't care about a damn court-martial. Stop it, no. Phaser—I don't want— The grip is slick and I can't go in there. I don't— Look how narrow it is, and the light, look at the light! James, don't you see? Don't!

Sweet candy, sweet candy. The disk worn down to a flat plane. Event horizon, there's no going back now. Father, bloody and sobbing. The straps digging into his arms, thin like winter sunlight. So thin, Daddy. The Cardassians smell like victory now and all I can see is your weakness. Shame—this is what shame tastes like. Bile in my throat, the scent of your blood in my nose. Where is my brave father? He is not here. He is not here.

* * *

Ro Laren died on Garon II; I don't care what they tell you. Should have, would have, she did. I couldn't go in the room. James went—didn't listen to me. No one listened. No one saw the steam, the thin line of light. Lia's sleeve whispered through my fingers as she passed—a second later they were all gone. No one listened. Nine went in, one came out. Blood on my uniform—and other things, too. Screams echo, you know. Then, the smell of fresh rain—broken clouds and lightning. Mission complete? Weapons bunker confirmed . . . aye, sir. Aye, sir.

The body they took away was not my father. This was no man I knew, no man I came from. It's not him at all, and that isn't his earring, broken on the hard floor. Little star, shooting far; the rhyme ends there because the last page of the book was torn. Glistening scales and a fresh disk of sugar in my mouth. Laren is happy? For now. Who was that man?

Flashnow. The walls of this cell are those colors, the black, the red, the sugar. Too warm in here, but I don't complain. Laren isn't happy, but Laren died years ago on Garon II. I don't think this helps, this therapy. You can tell me watching my father's death made me panic in that bunker, you can, but I don't know that I'll ever believe it. I want to be alone. You don't want to hear about it all again . . . do you?

Prodigal Son

Tonya D. Price

Space exploded before the Whole as we traveled toward home. Massive waves bombarded us, each wave stronger than the first; each assault arriving quicker than the last. We vibrated with excitement at our unexpected luck and separated into individual points of energy, our strength multiplying as we feasted. Without warning the waves stopped and started again, this time more intense than before.

We traced the strange phenomenon to a ship struggling against an unseen force. Erratic warp field layers formed, strengthened, and collapsed. A cloud of energy plasma poured from the impulse engines. The patterns, though irregular, seemed . . . familiar. I knew this vessel. Shame weakened me, guilt threatened to hold me back, but love compelled me forward—toward the *Enterprise.*

I rushed ahead, driven by some irresistible need, an instinct much stronger than mere curiosity. Among the hundreds of biological life-forms inhabiting the ship I searched for one: my mother's. Could she feel my presence? Did she remember me—the one she named Ian Andrew Troi? And had she forgiven the pain I caused her? Buried in memories, I missed the approaching danger.

The Whole tried to warn me. "Quick. Come back."

Too late. Already plane-oriented beings surrounded me. The closest attacked, draining my energy with a faint pull. At least I faced a quick end, without the agony of my first death.

Before me the *Enterprise* struggled too, but the majestic ship never gave up. With another blast, a partial warp bubble formed, expanding outward until the edge held me in a farewell embrace. The connection broke the two-dimensional beings' hold and I found myself free. Plunging forward I pressed against a nacelle, letting the *Enterprise*'s released energies camouflage my signature until the bubble burst, exposing me a second time.

"Hide inside the ship where the biologicals' shields will protect you," the Whole advised.

I obeyed, slipping between the microfoam duranium filaments, past the stressed tritanium fabric molecules of the ship's hull. As a tiny beam of light I traveled along the wall and ceiling seam, pale in the glare of the overhead lamps. Memories guided me toward those I once called family. Their presence refreshed me like the charged kiss of a solar wind. Picard. Riker. My mother . . .

My mother. Deanna Troi. Starship counselor. Empath. I meant no harm the first time I came across her dreaming in her bed. Her differences intrigued me, her emptiness stirred my compassion. I joined with her, seeking knowledge, intending comfort. Instead, my presence stirred yearnings; unknown, frightening maternal urges beyond the Whole's comprehension and in the process I became . . . singular. Connected to her, but somehow . . . apart. Unlike the reassurance of a merging with the Whole, our union brought confusion and endangered all aboard her ship. I departed, but her pain haunted me, pursuing me even after my leaving. Sights. Sounds. Taste. The strange sensations remained embedded in my thoughts long after I no longer possessed eyes to record light waves or ears to capture sound waves or mouth to speak. Traveling through space I often thought of her choking sobs in my darkened bedroom; her salty tears on my still cheeks; her pumping heart aching in protest at the abrupt numbness of a death.

My death.

To protect her, to protect them all, I left. She understood, but the understanding didn't ease her heartache . . . or mine.

After such a long interval of time dare I risk reviving such pain by contacting her again? Brain waves as unique as the Whole's energy patterns called me to her and I extended a gentle probe of her mind. Random neurological distortions mixed with flashes from nerves tense with pain told me she was under attack. The two-dimensionals. Their primitive, undisciplined emotions overloaded her empathic sensibilities. Without thought to the consequences I entered her mind, distributing my energy self around her most vulnerable cells, preventing permanent damage. The barrier numbed her neural receptors, blocking their response by buffering her sensitive paracortex; the center of her empathy. The shielding worked, but the consciousness which comprised her thought patterns vanished like a comet's ice crystals caught in the heat of a nearby sun.

What had I done wrong? Mother, I cried, but no answer came. Should I reveal myself to Picard? Or Riker? Or Data? Her body machine continued. Heart pumped. Lungs filled and deflated. Blood surged through her veins as before when we united. All she felt, I felt. All she sensed, I sensed. Could this be death? Memories recalled the heaviness of thought preceding the final conscious moment—no such acceptance reigned in her mind. Desperate, I triggered neurons in an attempt to save her, but the effort went unrewarded.

"Troi?" A woman's voice stirred me from my panic. "Deanna, it's Dr. Crusher. Wake up."

Explosions of thought ignited in a sudden bolt of awareness as my mother's consciousness revived. Through her eyes I viewed the soft violet palette of her office; heard the rasp of her breath against the cushioned nap of the gray carpet where she lay and felt the force of her personality return. Unlike before, her thoughts opened to me, though I took care to keep my presence a secret from her.

The doctor found no sign of damage, but my mother sensed a difference. As we passed crew members in the corridor she stared after them, trying to determine the source of her confusion. In the senior staff briefing room she studied those around her until gradually she realized the aura of emotion comprising the feel of each of her friends no longer colored their presence. They existed. Sight revealed their bodies, but as objects, not sentient beings. With eyes shut no sense of them remained. Picard's courage—gone. Geordi's kindness—gone. Will Riker's passion—gone. She grieved for her loss and once again I knew the blame for her pain rested with me.

Data spoke. Forever the enigma, he alone appeared to her as he always did—sentience hidden in a void. "The probe's point of view reveals the entities surrounding the *Enterprise* exist entirely within two dimensions."

What was this? Data talked as if the two-dimensional beings posed a threat to the crew, but they possessed no means to harm humans. These scattered, ignorant beings traveled unencumbered by thought, reacting to stimuli, broadcasting tidal waves of unrestrained, primitive emotion: painful when absorbed by the Betazoid paracortex, but undetectable by the human brain. Meandering through space, these invaders from another dimension sought food and shelter as they headed toward home. There lay the danger. Why did Data speak of two-dimensionals and not of the cosmic string fragment, their destination? Was it possible he remained unaware of the tiny black hole devouring everything that ventured too near?

Understanding came to me and through me to the Whole, who raced to join the rescue. Should I reveal myself to my mother? Whisper in her mind the danger lurking in space? If I let loose my hold, even briefly, what damage might she endure? But if I stayed with her revealing nothing, the ship might be swallowed. I decided to wait in hopes I could avoid having to choose between saving the ship and protecting my mother's empathy.

During the waiting my mother's torment grew, and though many offered words of comfort, her isolation deepened. Some, like Dr. Crusher, she pushed away with harsh words and accusations. Picard she shoved aside with a formal resignation. How could she consider leaving her friends? How could she threaten to journey away from those whose experiences she shared to travel alone through the universe? Try as I might, I could not imagine an existence apart from the Whole.

One she could not push away: Commander Riker. Each time he

appeared I rejoiced. Often, as her child, I imagined him to be my father. Not my biological father, of course, for I needed no seed for my birth, but the tall commander was as close to the relationship as I would come. What is a father but one who comforts and protects? One morning as Ian I awoke to the smell of bacon and eggs he cooked for my mother as she recuperated from my birth. One afternoon I listened to his stories of fishing Prince William Sound for salmon, his laughter warming the room as the size of his catch increased with the telling of the tale. One evening he took me from my mother's arms and carried me to my bed, whispering good night as he tucked me beneath a soft blanket. Did such care make him my father? Perhaps not, but I assigned him the role nonetheless, so desperately did I want the three of us to be a family.

Now, once again, I felt his strength in the arms he wrapped around my mother. He held her close, refusing to let her pull away. Encased in her thoughts I felt the link between the two and understood for the first time the connections the biologicals formed. Even without empathy they composed a whole of their own. Separate yet joined. Like energy beings, they generated strength together.

A message interrupted the moment. "La Forge to Riker . . . we are ready to attempt a controlled overload jump to warp six."

A useless exercise, but their failure no longer mattered. Afraid, but determined, the Whole approached, gathering like bait for Riker's fish. Food and shelter. The cosmic string offered shelter to the single plane-oriented entities, but the Whole held out the promise of food.

After careful consideration the Whole chose a position a safe distance from the event horizon of the cosmic string. In position, they emitted a weak energy pulse. Our predators took the bait.

Disaster struck when Riker and Data detected the cosmic string fragment. Unaware of our efforts to help, Captain Picard ordered a photon torpedo spread between the entities and the cosmic string. The blast proved harmless to the two-dimensionals; deadly to the Whole. The plane-oriented beings seized the opportunity to feed on the scattered remnants of the Whole as they floated immobilized by the jolt to their systems.

Unaware of the life-and-death struggle outside the ship, my mother worked with Data to discover a way to communicate with the two-dimensional entities. If I could send her a message without loosening my hold on her mind, Picard might be able to help the Whole escape, but I could not speak to her while protecting her, so I remained silent.

As she worked she voiced her helplessness. "Right now, Data, I feel as two-dimensional as our friends out there. In the universe, but barely aware of it. Just trying to survive."

Perhaps a quick signal. A tiny flash of a neuron to help her understand the two-dimensionals. Little time remained. I fired one impulse. One word. One clue. "Instinct."

She battled to place the thought. "On . . . instinct . . ."

From that hint the crew put the pieces together and rigged the *Enterprise*'s parabolic dish to re-create the decay particles' resonance along the event horizon of the quantum string fragment. While the crew worked, the Whole attempted to merge, but they remained easy prey for the enemy.

I could not remain safe inside the *Enterprise* while the Whole faced annihilation and I could not abandon my mother. If she lost her empathic abilities I feared her pain would be even greater than what she felt when I, as Ian, ceased to exist. Time forced my decision as the *Enterprise*'s first attempt failed to slow the two-dimensional entities. As the crew prepared to increase the intensity of the resonance signal my choice became clear: my mother would live; the Whole might not. I abandoned her a second time and rushed through the hull, letting speed carry me past my predators, back to the Whole. Aided by my presence our power surged, but not enough to resist the hordes surrounding us.

Weakened, we faded until nothing but a warm ember remained of what we had once been. The plane-oriented beings took their time consuming us. Not out of malice; they possessed none. Instead, having feasted in our dimension, hunger did not drive them and so they took us out of habit and the convenience of our lingering among them.

I spent my last moments remembering my mother's pleas to stay as my first death approached. This time she knew nothing of my presence; would feel nothing at my passing. Yet, there were things I wished I had said, confessions I wish I had made.

A blast of a stronger resonance signal distracted the two-dimensionals and in their confusion an eddy formed within the rise and ebb of their movements. A passageway opened, leading to the *Enterprise.* I urged the Whole forward, pleading and cursing for us to move. Again a warp bubble formed but this time the subspace field stabilized. The disoriented two-dimensionals fled and the Whole plummeted like a spray of meteors through the hull and into the ship's interior.

I recovered first and went to my mother, finding her with friends in the social center called Ten-Forward. Again I entered her thoughts undetected and this time discovered joy, not grief, filled her mind. Well and happy, she laughed easily, her empathy restored. She must have sensed my presence on a subconscious level because she paused and her thoughts returned to our time together. Peaceful memories caressed my image in her mind; her only regret—that our time had been so brief.

The ship broke free of the plane-oriented beings. The Whole recovered. Anxious to resume our journey they called me to join them. Caught between the need to return to the Whole and a desire to stay with my mother, I resisted the temptation to reveal myself and departed, leaving guilt and shame behind me. In their place I took the fresh memory of my mother's love. A love I knew would sustain me no matter where I explored. Not a love given by the Whole, who were but part of me, but a love freely offered by one separate from me, who expected nothing in return. Who loved me despite the heartache of my departure, despite the pain of my birth. And I knew at last, grief was a small price to pay for the wondrous gift of the bond we shared.

Seeing Forever

Jeff Suess

The shimmering man does not disrupt the hot jungle but it welcomes him as an old friend. The air is hot, the sun always shines in the Yucatán. Spindly leaves stab skyward from the thick base of henequen plants. Hawk knows where he is instantly.

Mayan temples form the horizon before him. He doesn't have to look to feel their presence. Blackened stone etched with centuries of decay. The swampy jungle is much the same as it was when Mayan tribes inhabited the lands. The heat has limited the plant life in the area, but tufts of wild grass struggle to breathe. Game birds flourish unhunted. The Yucatán is a natural preserve, not even a Federation outpost for three hundred kilometers. Not a soul in view. But that is how Hawk wants it. He chose the outskirts of the ancient city Chichén Itzá to give him time to reflect. A wisp of air prods him in the right direction and he goes.

The hike takes him a few hours through empty fields of dying brown grass. The autumn sun does not bother him, even in his thick gray tunic and slacks. Out of respect, he feels it is best not to be in uniform when he sees his father. He hikes the unmarked path in an even pace and never tires. Far ahead the pyramidal Temple of Warriors stares through naked eyes and greets him with wicked serpent grins.

Hawk knew to find his father here. Home was in Monument Valley, where his parents had kept a modest bungalow in the Utah desert. Hawk grew up far from the amenities of the Federation, replicators, holodecks, or transporters. Living in the desert, he was befriended by the Shoshone, who laughed at Hawk's confusing name. Earth's creatures were respected and names had power. Ren Hawk was both predator and gatherer and he struggled with each. In Starfleet he became just Hawk. But Utah was only home. Life was in the Mayan ruins where his father toiled and studied and ignored the future barreling ahead in favor of a people dead for centuries.

Hawk didn't bother looking for his father in Utah. He set coordinates for Chichén Itzá and his father's archeological camp. He grapples the stone base of a sacrificial altar jutting out as handholds atop a hill slope, and hefts himself up with little effort. He is comfortable here, familiar. More so than he thought he would be. That is why he waited to come here last.

His last three years were spent exploring the catacombs of the fabled Hundari on Mystus II in a scientific capacity. His tour consisted mostly of excavation and preservation techniques to find evidence that the people actually existed. During a six-month stint aboard the *U.S.S. Ptolemy,* Hawk fell instantly in love with the methodology of a starship. His assignment on Mystus came to an end a few weeks back, which gave him the opportunity to search for a new challenge. Hawk found transport to Deep Space 4, where he was greeted with a message from Starfleet of his new commission and promotion. They gave him one week's leave before he had to rendezvous with his new ship at Earth. He wasted no time coming home.

A transport vessel arrived five days ago with Hawk and dozens of other passengers, mostly Starfleet officers. Hawk transferred his packs of personal effects to temporary quarters at Starfleet Academy, where he had several younger friends finishing up the program. He had promised he'd stop by when he was next on Earth.

His classmates were pleased to see him. They wanted to know all about his adventures, what it was really like in the final frontier.

In truth, Hawk was an advisor on an archeological site most of his stay, where adventure was far from everyone's mind. He felt uncomfortable around his old friends, alienated by his not living up to the Starfleet dream. Hawk made excuses to duck out but promised he'd return before he left Earth. He didn't tell them about his new posting, though. He wanted his father to be the first to hear it from him.

It wasn't until he arrived in Toulouse that Hawk realized he was stalling. His father was across the world immersed in history. He wanted to see Joli, sure, but he was reluctant to admit he chose to see her before his father because it was easier.

The rose city of southern France, Toulouse had a history of aviation during the early years. As warp-powered vessels were developed in the late twenty-first century, Toulouse turned inward to preserve its French culture. Joli thought it was the perfect place to run her shuttle contract service. The ideal mix of engineering history and incredible weather. The French cafés that refused to catch up to the times and still served three-course meals cooked, not replicated, was the selling point for Joli. She was a private contractor of shuttlecraft parts and designs. Starfleet set the standard in starship design with the finest engineers in the Federation. Yet virtually no developments were made to boost shuttle technology. It was the perfect niche for Joli and her crew. Their designs figured prominently in the newest runabout models. Joli was quite proud.

When Hawk met Joli at Starfleet HQ, he figured she was a cadet as well. They nearly tumbled into one another in a hallway and she scolded him for his clumsiness. Not in a rude manner, but as though reminding a child to look both ways. She was forceful and, God, was she beautiful. Not just her appearance, which was not classical beauty. The best Hawk could describe her was like a rabbit. Curious, with soft eyes, but you never really knew what was going on in her head. This characteristic was both endearing and the thing that most infuriated Hawk.

He beamed in outside her office, a few steps from her window. The sun reflected off the Garonne River behind him like a tattoo pattern across the glass. She sat at her desk sketching on a data padd with a lightstick. She always preferred the artistic details of freehand drawing. Her blond bangs swiped across her eyes like a drooping quail's plume. Her hair was short, bright lemon like the suns of Kimos. He stared for a while, hoping never to disturb her. She looked up, through the window to the shining vineyards, to Hawk. She grinned, not at all surprised to see him, and gently brushed the hair from her eyes.

He met her coming out the door. "Renny. It's good to see you." Her voice was deeper than Hawk remembered but instantly familiar. Immediately the living person in front of him superseded the memory. Without a word he scooped her up in his arms and held tight. She fit him and his body warmed where he wasn't ever cold.

Hawk set her down. Joli took a step back to look him over and nodded. Lean, strong, still a bit wiry. "Your hair's shorter, not as curly," she said. "And you're in good shape."

"I was always in good shape."

"You were always handsome," she shot back. "You weren't always in good shape."

Joli was a head shorter than Hawk, a small build. Thin with wide hips and a round chest under a blue and hunter green jumper that was a style Hawk didn't recognize. It had been three years since he was home. Three years since he felt her lips on his.

They strolled along the riverbank, her fingers laced between his. The older buildings along the river were still red brick, blackened and chipped. The interiors were mostly reinforced and modernized, but the French villagers liked to keep their history. The spire of the chapel of Jacobins peered over the tiled roofs of the city on the two lovers.

"How long do you have here?" Joli asked.

"A few days. You haven't asked why I'm here."

"I don't care. I'm just glad to see you, Renny." Her eyes smiled.

"It's Hawk now," he said. "Lieutenant Hawk, actually."

She raised one eyebrow. "My, my. So severe. It hasn't been the same without you. I've been busy, but—"

"Yes, I've kept up with your work. Designs are very nice."

"And you've been digging." Joli scrunched her nose like a rabbit. "Bones and rats."

Hawk laughed. "More like fossilized rodent dung," he said.

"So the glamorous life of the archeologist is a myth."

"My father seems to enjoy it."

They were silent a moment. The sunlight danced downstream.

"You have a new assignment," she said. "And this is goodbye."

Hawk didn't answer.

"I'm used to that by now," she said. "At least you'd think I'd be."

"Maybe it's something you never get used to," he said. "Or don't want to. Being away from you is the hardest . . ." There were no words to finish.

Joli buried her face in his chest. He felt her tears through his tunic and traced his fingers through her hair.

They spent the next several days together, eating heartily, making love in the sliver of moonlight through her bedroom window, staring endlessly in each other's eyes. In a blue moment he traced his finger around her eye, down her cheek, and rested his fingertip lightly on her lips.

"Nothing will happen to me," he said, a whisper of wind. "Nothing will change the way I feel."

Joli closed her eyes. Not time, not distance, nothing came between their bodies pressed together. A silent pact between them.

When he left her, Hawk preferred to remember the image of her along the river. In his mind the sun was setting with an orange palette, the scent of violets in her hair, her arms secure around him. It didn't matter that it wasn't exactly how it happened. For him that moment would be her while he was in the depths of cold, cold space counting the nanoseconds till his next leave.

During their last moments together, each tried not to show the swell of pains in their chests. Hawk told Joli about his new assignment anyway and she was very excited for him. He wasn't sure his father would be. They didn't say goodbye. They knew there was no way they would be able to say the words.

There is only one day left of the interim between Hawk's assignments. He pushed this back as long as he could, even though, as much as he loved Joli, this was the main reason he came to Earth so early.

The camp is deep in the heart of the Mayan site. Hawk follows in the footsteps of priests and warriors around the temple steps. He feels their presence around him, a welcoming of distant phantoms. As a child he thought of the human sacrifice victims walking through the temple. Were they unaware of their fate, or did they know their sacrifice was a small part of something so much bigger than they?

Hawk is not winded from his hike. He pauses at the lengthy horizontal statue of the plumed serpent, Kukulcan. The temple grounds are layers of crushed rubble atop sturdy stone pillars. Across a haggard field stands the angular temple of Kukulcan, much like a stunted pyramid topped by a squared building. A sloping stairway slides down the blackened stone face. Small carved statues stand sentry in the field. Grass fingers pry apart the stones. Thousands of years ago people milled about here regularly. For the past thirty years, only a handful have trodden these grounds.

He finds his father at the base of the temple, a tiny figure sitting along the gigantic stairwell's right track. His father turns, not surprised, somehow knowing Hawk is there. His eyes shine soft green. He's not sweating. His skin is darkened and leathery like a lizard from thirty years in the sun. The right side of his mouth curls up to brighten his face and the leather doesn't crack.

Hawk calls to him: "Hey, Pop." A small child one moment, full grown the next.

Abram Hawk stands and hugs his son. Quick, then steps back, excited. He crouches back down. "Ren, you should see this," he says. Abram brushes dirt from the base of the stairway with his hand. "See this here," he says, pointing. Hawk bends down to see. "It's not very deep. Time has eroded it."

In the stone, an engraving is nearly worn away. Very low to the ground, sinking in the topsoil. Stone carvings on pillars are common decoration for the Maya. This appears to be a reclining figure, a god of some sort. Crudely done. An odd location for such a drawing.

"It's Chac-Mool," Abram says. White teeth burst from his lips. "He's holding a bowl of hearts. I think."

Hawk smiles politely. "Very nice."

His father shakes his head and hurriedly cleans the image better. He blows dust from the carved lines. "You don't remember. You did this."

"What?"

"Sure, you were about four or so. I was very upset at the time. Your mom recognized the figure. You knew Chac-Mool at age four. Amazing."

Hawk looks at the figure again. "I did that?"

"Oh yes." Abram makes a large effort to stand.

"Isn't this sacrilegious?"

Abram laughs. "It's history, Ren. Someday we'll be history. This is your stamp." Impulsively he hugs Hawk again. "Good to see you, son." Then he quickly walks away, leaving Hawk crouched in the dirt.

He dusts off his pants and goes after his father.

"How was Mystus II?" Abram calls behind him.

"It was a good experience. The Hundari ruins were more than we'd hoped for," Hawk says. "Much will be learned from them."

Abram pauses at a rock, picks up a data pad. He quickly taps a succession of keys, then places it down again. "Yes, the first dig is always exciting. The most memorable. Thirty-seven years ago, I came down here with some friends just to see how people used to live. You look at the cold stone figures—what looks like an old quarry—and realize people used to live here. And those people—they're us." He points to the earth. "This is where we come from."

"You always were like a kid in the mud out here, Pop."

"Enjoy your work. That's the key." Abram turns, then spins back with another thought. "You enjoyed Mystus, didn't you?"

Anything besides an affirmative is a betrayal. "Of course. Just like you taught me."

Abram walks away from the temple, down a serpentine path through a henequen field. Hawk follows.

"Archeology, it's a good life," Abram says.

"Yes, for some it is. Where's everyone else?" Hawk hasn't seen any of the other members of his father's team.

"They went home. Day off today. People can only spend so much time around me before I drive them batty."

Hawk smiles. His father seems smaller to him now but makes up for size with life.

"When your mom passed on, I'm afraid I became a handful for the others," Abram says.

"I remember."

"But they are family."

They come to a hole opening in the ground, a punch in the earth. "I do most of my work here when I'm alone," Abram explains. "The sonic imager records the levels—we're down to eight hundred meters now." The small imager sits on a tripod straddled over the hole. Hawk has known how to use one since he was a child, and supervised their use on the Hundari site. Imagers record sonic pictures of objects and minerals in the soil, used to locate artifacts and fossils.

"Where are we?"

"Over the cenote," Abram replies. "We'll go down the main entrance." He points to a huge maw opening in the hump of a slight hill.

Hawk steels himself. The cenote. A sacred undergrown well. As a child his father forbade him to ever explore there. It was too unstable, and too precious. "You must not offend the gods," Abram had said. Hawk sometimes dared to pop down the cenote's gaping mouth in defiance of his parents' wishes, just to do it. He had been scared and never found the courage to descend more than the first steps.

Abram leads his son to the huge opening, tall and wide enough for dozens of people to pass through. The *wap wap wap* of wings signals several bats veering a starburst formation from the cave maw. Darkness swallows the sunlight along with them as they enter. Abram thumbs a glowrod on his belt. A dull green light spreads over the limestone walls. Wooden stairs descending to nothing find jade life with each step.

"It's about time I brought you down here." Abram's whisper has a harsh echo. "You've been on your own digs now. Nothing scares you anymore."

Hawk knows he must tell him he has given up his father's dream of archeology. The deeper they go the harder it is to tell him. The lead weight in Hawk's chest trembles. The heat, humidity, is unbearable. He relies on his Starfleet training to adjust his breathing. His father strips off his shirt, not to be encumbered by the heat. Hawk takes off his tunic and rolls it into a bundle. They leave their clothes on the stairway.

"We should be fine," Abram assures.

"You spend most of your time down here?" Hawk asks.

"I find it peaceful."

At the bottom of the stairway they come to a long gallery corridor. The moisture clings to their skin, making their bodies slick. Their footsteps echo as hollow clops on the limestone. A flutter of bat wings sounds farther down the gallery. The smell is almost as heavy as the humidity, the sour decay of fungus and sweat. Breathing is a problem. Hawk cycle-breathes through his mouth to block out most of the odor.

"The cenote is a natural underground well," Abram explains in a stage whisper. "The Maya believed it to be sacred, that the gods had created it so those living in the arid land of the Yucatán could have water. We know that the walls are limestone, a porous rock saturated with rainwater. It collects in wells and when the thin limestone cracks in places—precious water from the gods."

They pause at the end of the gallery at another wooden stairway. The slope is extremely steep about thirty yards down, difficult to maneuver. Abram tosses a second activated glowrod down the stairs so they can see where they are headed. The staircase is held together by strong vines instead of nails. Hawk eyes it suspiciously as Abram gets down on his knees and begins to crawl down the staircase backward. The stairs are wide enough for twenty people to use them at the same time. Hawk follows his father's lead, the limestone slimy and warm against his bare chest. The stairs wobble from their weight. Sweat bathes Hawk's face, hands, legs, making the descent difficult. His father, nearly twice his age, maneuvers with relative ease and familiarity. Hawk's strength doesn't compensate for his slippery grip.

Abram gets to the bottom first and retrieves the glowrod. He lets out a careful breath. Hawk works steadily to catch up. No real strain for him. Though he tries to imagine doing this when he was ten and realizes his father was right to forbid him.

"Right, a bit of fun," Abram says.

A few meters ahead a shaft of light shines from a hole nearly a hundred meters up. Abram points above. "There's the sonic imager we saw earlier," he says. The sunlight pours in to spoil the gloom in an angled curtain of gold. More carvings and writing are visible along the walls. Hawk is sure his father has read and recorded everything down here. After thirty-seven years, there is little Abram Hawk doesn't know about the temples and this area.

"Beautiful, isn't it?" Abram says. He switches off both glowrods for the natural lighting.

Hawk has seen ruins like this many times before. Here, when he was a child. The Hundari site on Mystus II. Now he sees the silent stone faces guarding the cenote, covered in lichen and fungus, smoothed by time. The sun reflects stars on the wet limestone. He sees it for the first time the way his father does.

"Pop, we need to talk," he says.

"Sure, Ren. Sure." Features are muddied by darkness. A sliver of gold contours his father's form.

"I never looked, really looked before. These people, the temples, they speak to you." Hawk runs a hand through his wet hair. "As a kid I thought you and Mom were obsessed with history. I was nine when I saw my first starship. I didn't leave the solar system till I was fifteen. For you, this planet was the only thing in existence. I didn't know any better. Klingons, Romulans, I knew about them, but they were remote. They weren't real. When I went to the Academy I knew you weren't pleased. Even though I studied archeology. You thought I should have stayed here and learned from you. But I wasn't content here."

The water stars twinkle on the rocks.

"Look up in the sky. There are trillions of worlds just like this one where everything's new," Hawk says. "The people, the places, vegetation, insects. And they're alive. They are beings. Beings you can touch, speak to, learn from. The unknown is out there."

"And that's where you want to go," Abram says in the dark.

Hawk doesn't answer right away. He can hear the disappointment in his father's voice. When he says "yes" it is lost in the walls.

"Archeology, did you ever want to do it, Ren?"

"At first, maybe. I don't know." A child sinking underground.

"You wanted to tell me you've been assigned to a deep space vessel, a starship," Abram says at last.

"How did you know?"

"The latest news. I keep up. The new *Enterprise*-E has been a big story for months. When they announced the crew last week and I saw your name, I knew you'd be coming. Stopped to see Joli first I bet. You always were a smart boy."

"You knew?"

"I may be in ancient ruins, Ren, but I'm not in ancient times. We're almost there."

Hawk follows the sounds of his father's footsteps deeper into the cenote. The sunlight fades behind them and they feel the rest of the way down, traipsing fingers along the walls, winding deeper and deeper.

"I hear you've been promoted already," Abram says as they walk.

"Lieutenant Hawk, reporting for duty."

"What will you be doing aboard the *Enterprise?"*

"I learned to pilot. Commander Riker has me on conn rotation until I learn the ropes."

"Must be pretty good then," Abram says. "I should probably be proud of you."

Hawk notices he doesn't say he is proud.

"I'd always hoped you'd be interested in this," Abram says. "This is not merely exploring caves and ruins. We're exploring ourselves. After hundreds of years of archeology we still don't know much about how we got to be where we are. Adam and Eve, Mesopotamia, Atlantis. How much is real? How much contributed to what and who we are? We fly around the universe anxious to discover new things. And when we do we immediately then hop on again to find the next new thing. No one stays put and tries to see what it is we've discovered. We still know just about nothing about Vulcan history. They aren't very forthcoming about it and no one's taken the time to really delve into it. That's what I do. It's not about adventure or discovery, it's about what goes on inside." He taps his temple. "Everything out there is about what's in here. You can go out and explore your strange new worlds. I'll stick to the strange old one right here."

Abram picks up his pace, making distance between them. This has played out much as Hawk feared it would. His father is offended.

Hawk covers the distance through a thin passage to a large open area and a wide pool of water. Abram stands along the edge of the pool, activates a glowrod and places it on a jut of rock. He stands along the edge of the pool. Hawk speaks in a harsh whisper.

"Pop, I—"

Abram cuts him off with a raised hand. "The Maya did not want to alarm the waters," he says. "Starfleet has always been the thing to do. I hear Ferengi have joined now. No one stays at home anymore."

"There's Joli," Hawk says. "And there's you."

"Yes, yes. In some ways we are more like the Maya than you'd think. They worried about survival and appeasing the gods. For Earth, now, the god is curiosity. We don't have to struggle so much to survive day to day and Starfleet is there to help us survive the larger things. Invasion, war, that letter guy, the Borg. Angry gods to whom we must sacrifice our only sons."

He turns to Ren Hawk with a well of tears in his eyes.

"I don't want you to go, son." He wraps his arms around Hawk's body, squeezing tight. The glow lights dance on the pool. They hold each other for several moments.

"I love you, too, Pop."

Abram Hawk releases his son and composes himself. "The gods provided the water for life. The levels of the pool are affected by that celestial god, the moon. To them, we must make our offering."

He grips Hawk's wrist hard and yanks him into the pool with him. They punch through the surface. Water bursts heavenward in a fountain of stars. They scramble for air, relief washing over their bodies, restored by life.

In the jade glow, laughter bounces along the walls. Abram

reaches for his son. Laughter is infectious. The ancient waters come alive.

They splash each other, refreshed, children in a fountain. They swim in the center of the universe. Everything else is remote. Water beads stream a slow cascade of starlets in a dark tapestry. The heavens look down and see forever.

STAR TREK
DEEP SPACE NINE®

Captain Proton and the Orb of Bajor

Transcribed by Jonathan Bridge

from the radio play by
Ben Russell as broadcast October 28, 1938

ANNOUNCER

Alta-Schweitzer presents . . .

ANOTHER VOICE

(spoken with an echo-like reverberation)
THE ADVENTURES OF CAPTAIN PROTON . . . DEFENDER OF THE EARTH!

Cue *Captain Proton* main theme music, which plays for a few bars until it drops slightly in volume so that we may hear . . .

ANNOUNCER

It's time once again for the exciting Adventures of Captain Proton! Voyage ahead with us to the thrilling days of the future as Captain Proton, Spaceman First Class, and his faithful companion Buster Kincaid and secretary Constance Goodheart continue their battle against Dr. Chaotica and all intergalactic evil! This program is brought to you by the makers of Alta-Schweitzer tablets. Whenever you're feeling headaches, pains, or indigestion, then like Captain Proton, it's Alta-Schweitzer to the rescue! And now we continue with the next episode in Captain Proton's adventure, *Captain Proton and the Orb of Bajor!*

Cue up volume in theme music that plays through to its coda

NARRATOR

In our last episode, the evil Dr. Chaotica stole one of the mystic orbs of the planet Bajor. The Bajorans then called upon Captain Proton to find Chaotica and take back their stolen orb. Not understanding the orb's significance, but realizing its importance to the Bajorans, Proton set off with Buster and Constance to recover the missing orb. In their spaceship, they pursued Chaotica's ship into the Badlands, a section of space with a lot of storms. The two ships were caught in a violent storm that sent Proton's ship spinning off course. As their ship careened wildly, it seemed they would not regain control. But Buster with his expert pilot skills has managed to get the ship back on course and navigate it out of the Badlands. We now rejoin our heroes as they are back in normal space and following Chaotica's ion trail.

KINCAID

(over a humming engine noise in the background)
Captain, I've picked up Chaotica's ion trail. I think he was headed near Bajor.

PROTON

Good. Stay on that trail. We have to catch up with Chaotica to try to get that orb back for the Bajorans.

KINCAID

(sounding bewildered)

Captain, this trail is very erratic. It seems to be moving in so many different directions. It's almost as if Chaotica was blown off course just like we were a moment ago.

PROTON

Maybe he got hit by the same storm that we did and it damaged his engines.

KINCAID

(suddenly surprised)

Captain! The trail! It's gone! It seems to just . . . come to an end all of a sudden! I can follow the trail all the way to the Denorios Belt. But at that point, the trail's just not there.

PROTON

Scan for any debris. Maybe something happened to his ship.

SFX: a beeping signal.

KINCAID

Captain, I'm getting an incoming message.

(Pause)

It's coming from the Deep Space Sector. Station Number

Nine. The captain, Ben Sisko, has given us docking clearance. He wants to speak to us.

Cue music for scene change.

NARRATOR

Upon receiving this message, Proton docked his ship at Station Number Nine. Proton and his companions are now in the office of the station's captain, Ben Sisko.

SISKO

A few minutes ago, a spaceship came flying near our station. The way it was flying back and forth it looked like the pilot didn't know where he was going. We tried to hail the pilot, but he didn't respond. Then the ship suddenly disappeared from our scanners. But we were able to trace it as far as the Denorios Belt.

PROTON

Dr. Chaotica's on that ship. He stole an orb from the Bajorans and we've been chasing him down to try to get it back.

SISKO

So I've been told by the Bajorans below on the planet we're orbiting. At the moment the ship disappeared, we picked up readings of many neutron emissions on our scanners. That's something we've never picked up before. When we picked up your ship on our scanners, we figured you were pursuing it. And so we contacted you to let you know what we found.

PROTON

Do you know what could have happened to the ship? Could it have been destroyed?

SISKO

We got no readings of an explosion. But the area where the ship disappeared and where we picked up the neutron readings is what the Bajorans call their Celestial Temple. Ever since the Incorporated Planets stationed us here to protect Bajor, we have respected Bajor's religious beliefs and have not allowed any ships near that area. But the Bajorans have already given their permission. And as the protectorate of Bajor, I authorize you, Captain, to search the area for Chaotica and the orb.

PROTON

Yes, Captain. We're on our way!

Cue music for scene change

KINCAID

(over humming engine sound)

Captain, we're on course for the Celestial Temple in the Denorios Belt. I'm reading heavy neutron emissions up ahead.

PROTON

Be careful as you approach the temple. We don't know what happened to Chaotica's ship. So we don't know what those neutrons will do to us.

KINCAID

(with increased surprise)

Captain, the neutron emissions seem to be increasing even more! I don't know what's making them do that, but . . .

SFX: a large fan being turned on to make a vacuum-like noise.

KINCAID

(greatly surprised)

Captain! A large hole opened just ahead of us!

PROTON

Try to avoid it!

KINCAID

I can't! We're going too fast! We're already heading right into it!

CONSTANCE

(screams loudly)

SFX: objects shaking around.

KINCAID

(yelling over the shaking noise)

Captain, this hole seems to follow a straight path. I'll see if I can guide the ship through it.

PROTON

See if you can stabilize the ship while you're at it. This is a pretty bumpy ride.

KINCAID

I'll try.

SFX: turn fan off and bring up humming engine noise again.

KINCAID

We're out of the hole, Captain. We're back in normal space.

PROTON

Can you tell where we are?

KINCAID

(bewildered again)

Captain, if these readings are correct, we're on the other side of the galaxy!

Cue intense music that plays through to its coda.

ANNOUNCER

We'll return to *Captain Proton* in just a moment.

(beat)

Boys and girls, do you ever feel body aches and pains when you wake up in the morning? Does the breakfast you eat give you feelings of indigestion? At times like these, do you feel like not going to school? If so, don't stay home from school. Ask your mother for Alta-Schweitzer tablets. Two Alta-Schweitzer tablets taken with a glass of water are enough to make you feel well so that you can go to school and learn about all the important things in life such as mathematics and science. As you learn and study in school, you can learn everything Captain Proton knows and one day grow up to be a brilliant scientist. So have your mother buy Alta-Schweitzer tablets today so you can have them nearby for mornings when you're not feeling well enough to go to school. Remember, boys and girls, whenever you're feeling headaches, pains, or indigestion, then like Captain Proton, it's Alta-Schweitzer to the rescue! And now we return to *Captain Proton!*

NARRATOR

Our heroes have been searching for Dr. Chaotica, who has just stolen an orb from the planet Bajor. They were searching for his spaceship near a region of space the Bajorans call their Celestial Temple. As Captain Proton's ship neared the temple, a large hole opened up in space and swallowed their ship. But Buster was able to pilot the ship through the hole to its other end where it so happens they are now on the other side of the galaxy. We rejoin our heroes as they are now back in normal space.

PROTON

(over a humming engine noise in the background)
The other side of the galaxy? How did we come that far in just ten seconds?

KINCAID

A wormhole, Captain!

PROTON

A what?

KINCAID

That hole was a wormhole. It's just like a wormhole in an apple. A worm would rather not crawl all the way around an apple just to get to the other side of it. So it makes a hole in the apple and takes a shortcut to get there. What we just went through was actually a shortcut in space.

PROTON

I've heard of those things. But most of them are not very stable. We may not have another chance to go back through . . .

SFX: a sudden buzzing sound with a steady rhythm.

KINCAID

Captain, the scanners just picked up three ships on an intercept course. They're of a type I've never seen before.

PROTON

Let them get closer. Let's see what they want.

SFX: a brief shimmering sound.

PROTON

Constance, behind you! Look out!

CONSTANCE

(screams loudly)

PROTON

Get your slimy hands off of her, you scale-faced goons!

SFX: a brief exchange of laser fire that stops abruptly with another brief shimmering sound.

KINCAID

Did you see that? Those aliens just came out of nowhere, grabbed Constance, and then disappeared again along with her.

PROTON

I don't know of anyone that has that kind of capability, other than the Guardians.

SFX: a beeping signal.

KINCAID

Captain, there's an incoming message. It's from one of the ships.

PROTON

Put it on the imagizer.

SFX: a brief fuzzy imagizer noise.

PROTON

Dr. Chaotica!

CHAOTICA

Ah, Proton. I should have realized even you would be foolish enough to follow me this far.

PROTON

I followed you for a reason, Chaotica. You have an orb that belongs to the Bajorans. You also just took Constance yet again. All you have to do is turn those two over to us and we'll leave you here in your playground with your new friends.

CHAOTICA

Oh, no. You see, that would interfere with my plans. And now that you're here I need to put you out of our way. Unless you want anything to happen to your precious orb or your lovely secretary, you will follow our ships to our asteroid base, where you will become our prisoners. And I know you will not fire upon any of our ships as you do not know which one has your secretary.

Cue music for scene change.

NARRATOR

Being left with no other choice, Captain Proton followed the three enemy spaceships to their asteroid hideout. Upon disembarkation, Proton and Kincaid were immediately taken prisoner by the same aliens who had kidnapped Constance from Proton's ship earlier. They now meet face-to-face with Dr. Chaotica!

CHAOTICA

Proton, do allow me the pleasantries of introducing you to my new allies. These are the Jem'Hadar. They are the vanguard of an invading army for the Dominion. You see, when I had thc Bajoran orb on my spaceship, my ship suddenly started steering itself off course. I tried to get it back on course, but I couldn't, and I didn't know why. I was then pulled into a hole that opened up in space and was pulled through to this side of the galaxy. Then I realized it was the orb that drew me to the hole. I only wanted the orb for its value. I did not realize it had such great power. Then I was captured by the Jem'Hadar. They were about to execute me for intruding in their space. But then I told them of a planetary system I knew of that was ripe for conquering. Now we will use the orb to guide us back to this hole. On the other side we will invade and conquer the Incorporated Planets. They will become an arm in the Dominion's government. And I will be placed as ruler of the Planets. Guards, take the prisoners to their cell.

PROTON

You won't succeed, Chaotica! The Incorporated Planets have strong defenses and many allies on their side. You don't stand a chance!

CHAOTICA

The Incorporated Planets have never had to stand up to the more advanced weaponry and capabilities of the Dominion. Take them away!

SFX: shuffling feet and CONSTANCE'S screams that gradually get softer as the prisoners are dragged away.

JEM'HADAR SOLDIER

The invasion fleet is now prepared, Chancellor Chaotica.

CHAOTICA

Excellent. Have all the pilots and crew members man their ships. And also bring the Bajoran orb. For it is that priceless artifact that will lead us on to the victory!

Cue intense music for scene change.

NARRATOR

Later, two Jem'Hadar soldiers are walking down a corridor toward the spaceship hangar.

SOLDIER 1

What's that you're carrying?

SOLDIER 2

Chancellor Chaotica calls it an orb.

SOLDIER 1

It doesn't look like the shape of an orb.

SOLDIER 2

Maybe not. But our chancellor says it will lead us to the territory that we will soon conquer.

SFX: CONSTANCE'S screams that are low in volume because they are far away.

SOLDIER 1

Will that woman never shut up? I was ready to silence her for good until my commander ordered me to stand down.

SOLDIER 2

So what do we do about her?

SOLDIER 1

You can go and quiet her down.

SOLDIER 2

How do I do that?

SOLDIER 1

(annoyed)
Do whatever you have to. Just stop that infernal screaming!

SOLDIER 2

But Chancellor Chaotica ordered me to bring this orb to him.

SOLDIER 1

I outrank you, soldier. And I just gave you a countering order. Don't worry. We won't leave without you and the orb.

SOLDIER 2

(dejectedly)

Aye, aye, sir.

SFX: SOLDIER 2's footfalls as he walks down the corridor. As he does so, CONSTANCE'S screams gradually get louder as he approaches the cell. When the screams are at a high pitch, the cell door slides open.

SOLDIER 2

Can you never be quiet, woman?

SFX: The screaming stops.

Wait . . . those other two men that were with you. Where are they?

PROTON

Right behind you!

SFX: a series of punches, kicks, oofs, and ughs that ends with a heavy thud on the ground.

KINCAID

He's out cold, Captain.

PROTON

For the vanguard of an invading army, they sure don't fight very well.

KINCAID

Captain, look! The orb! He has it on him!

PROTON

They were going to use it to find their way to the wormhole. If we can get to our spaceship and take off ahead of the fleet, maybe they can't find their own way there. And we can give this back to the Bajorans. Let's go!

Cue music for scene change.

NARRATOR

With most of the Jem'Hadar soldiers embarking on their own ships, our heroes were able to dash to their own spaceship unnoticed. Then they managed to escape the asteroid base before anyone in the fleet could stop them. They are now headed away from the base.

KINCAID

(over a humming engine noise in the background)
Captain, with the orb on board our ship, it's like I don't have to push any buttons or move any switches. Our ship is practically steering itself.

PROTON

Then I guess we're on the right course. Stay on course at maximum speed.

SFX: a sudden buzzing sound with a steady rhythm.

KINCAID

Captain, the Dominion fleet's on our tail! And they're catching up to us!

PROTON

How long until we reach the wormhole?

KINCAID

Six seconds . . . five . . . four . . . three . . . two . . . one!

SFX: a large fan being turned on to make a vacuum-like noise.

KINCAID

We're entering the wormhole. Activating stabilizers. We're holding steady.

PROTON

Good. Just get this ship out in one piece!

SFX: objects shaking around that we hear only briefly.

KINCAID

We made it, Captain! We're out of the wormhole and back in normal space!

PROTON

Charge up the Super-Destructo Beam. Aim and fire at a hundred and eighty degrees aft.

KINCAID

Fire at the wormhole?

PROTON

Do it!

SFX: laser beam shot from a gun followed by a muffled explosion.

KINCAID

The wormhole's closed, Captain.

PROTON

Good. I think Chaotica's really mad that he won't be ruler of the Incorporated Planets for about eighty years. Dock us at Station Number Nine. We have a package to deliver there.

Cue music for scene change.

SISKO

Captain, I have to say I'm quite impressed with this report you've given me. First you go off to stop a theft of valuable property. And you prevented an invasion in the process! Not bad for a day's work. Besides, we had no idea the Celestial Temple was actually a wormhole in space. We'll upgrade our security and let absolutely no ships anywhere near the wormhole from now on. We can't risk any Dominion ships coming through it. And as long as it stays closed I think we'll be okay on our end.

PROTON

And with the Bajorans getting their orb back, I'm glad we'll have good relations with them again.

SISKO

Captain, didn't you have a secretary here with you before?

PROTON

We do. But she's waiting for us on our ship.

SISKO

Oh, good. Well, Captain, on behalf of Bajor, not to mention myself, I thank you for saving the galaxy once again.

PROTON

It's always a pleasure to do my part for galaxy-wide peace, sir.

Cue music for scene change.

SFX: radio static.

CHAOTICA

(whose voice can barely be heard over the static)
Founder. Founder! Are you in position? Come in, founder. Over.

FOUNDER

(with a low alto feminine voice)
Yes, I am here. And I am still on Captain Proton's spaceship.

CHAOTICA

Excellent. I knew that exchanging you, one of the shapechanging Founders of the Dominion, for the real Constance Goodheart would be a wise backup ploy.

FOUNDER

But I cannot retain the form of Proton's secretary much longer. It has almost been sixteen hours and I must revert to my natural state.

CHAOTICA

Very well. When you are again able you will resume the form of Miss Goodheart. Then you will access all information on the strengths and capabilities of the Incorporated Planets. After which you will disable all defenses on that space station and then use the orb to reopen the wormhole as I and the invasion fleet are waiting on the other end. Although the orb was taken from us, Proton was so foolish to lead us here himself. In a mere matter of hours, the Dominion will rule the Incorporated Planets!

Cue intense music that plays through to its coda.

ANNOUNCER

We'll return to *Captain Proton* in just a moment.

(beat)

Boys and girls, did you know you can earn purchase points toward buying Captain Proton toys each time your mother buys Alta-Schweitzer tablets? Each box top taken from a box of Alta-Schweitzer tablets is worth one purchase point. And each one will earn you points toward sending away in the mail for a Captain Proton alien language decoder ring, a spaceship glider, or a sparkling ray gun. Then on warm sunny days when you're not listening to or reading about Captain Proton's adventures or even thrilling to his escapades at your local movie theater, you can have your own Captain Proton adventures with your friends. And whenever you're not feeling well, two Alta-

Schweitzer tablets taken with a glass of water can make you feel better so that you can play outside with your friends. Remember, whenever you're feeling headaches, pains, or indigestion, then like Captain Proton, it's Alta-Schweitzer to the rescue! And now we return to *Captain Proton!*

NARRATOR

Constance Goodheart is still a captive of Dr. Chaotica and the Dominion. Meanwhile, one of the shapechanging Founders of the Dominion has made herself to resemble Captain Proton's secretary so that she may infiltrate and disable the defenses of Station Number Nine and then use the orb to reopen the wormhole so that the Dominion fleet can attack and begin conquering the Incorporated Planets. Has Captain Proton failed to stop this invasion after all? What will he do to fight the Dominion when they attack? Tune in next time for the next exciting episode of . . .

ANOTHER VOICE

(spoken with an echo-like reverberation)

THE ADVENTURES OF CAPTAIN PROTON . . . DEFENDER OF THE EARTH!

Cue *Captain Proton* main theme music, which plays for a few bars until it drops slightly in volume so that we may hear . . .

ANNOUNCER

What you have just heard is based on characters that appear in *Captain Proton Magazine* now available at local newsstands. This has been a work of fiction. Any similarity to persons living or dead is purely coincidental.

Cue up volume on theme music to play for another few bars until it drops slightly in volume so that we may hear . . .

ANNOUNCER

This episode has featured Charles Correll as Captain Ben Sisko, Raymond Hayashi as Buster Kincaid, Evelyn Ankers as both Constance Goodheart and the shapechanging Founder, Boris Karnov as Dr. Chaotica, Chester Lauck and Norris Goff as the Jem'Hadar Soldiers, and as Captain Proton, Peter Collyer! This program was narrated by Conrad Williams, written by Ben Russell, produced by Maxwell Roberts, and directed by John Jacks. And this is your announcer, Ken Stiles! This program was brought to you by the makers of Alta-Schweitzer tablets. Whenever you're feeling headaches, pains, or indigestion, then like Captain Proton, it's Alta-Schweitzer to the rescue!

Cue up volume on theme music that plays for another few bars until it drops slightly in volume so that we may hear . . .

ANNOUNCER

Be sure to join us Sunday evening at eight P.M. Eastern Time when Orson Welles and the Mercury Theater of the Air will present a radio dramatization of H. G. Wells' classic science-fiction novel *The War of the Worlds.* It will sound so realistic, you may need to remind yourself it's only a radio drama. That's Mercury Theater of the Air Sunday night on BBS!

Cue up volume on theme music that plays for another few bars until it drops slightly in volume so that we may hear . . .

ANNOUNCER

Stay tuned for *Jack Armstrong, the All-American Boy* coming up next on most of these stations.

Cue up volume on theme music that plays through to its coda.

STATION ID

This is the Barnard Broadcasting System.

[Third Prize]

Isolation Ward 4

Excerpts from the Journal of Dr. James Wykoff

Kevin G. Summers

December 14, 1953

I met with a new patient this morning; a Negro named Benny Russell. In our initial interview, he seemed vacant and unsure of himself, as if he had been through some serious trauma in the very recent past. I couldn't get much out of him—he was mainly closed off and said very little. His voice is soft, almost timid. I think he is afraid of me.

In an attempt to better understand Mr. Russell, I have contacted the New York Police Department for any records they might have about my patient. They have promised to get back to me shortly.

December 17, 1953

My luck wasn't much better with the patient today. Mr. Russell seems to have some serious emotional problems. I asked him if he knew why he was brought here, but he retorted with typical Negroid hostility. He said nothing for long minutes, and then shouted out violently, "I'm a human being, dammit. I exist."

After this momentary outburst, I had to call in some orderlies to try and calm Mr. Russell down. They took him back to his room, where I am afraid I will have to keep him confined until I can get a better handle on how to control his outbursts.

I did learn some more about my patient, however. Apparently he has been working as a science fiction writer for the magazine *Incredible Tales of Scientific Wonder.* It was from their offices that he was brought in for psychological evaluation. Apparently he was fired from his job and reacted in a most unruly manner. This is no surprise after witnessing his behavior today.

December 18, 1953

Now we are getting somewhere. I received a copy of the police files on Mr. Russell, and those files confirmed some of my initial thoughts on this patient. Apparently Benny got into some trouble earlier this year when he attacked some police officers while they were trying to apprehend a car thief. The report is not entirely clear, but apparently the thief was killed in the altercation, and Benny was given a severe beating for his interference. The report suggests that he was brandishing some sort of weapon.

I have contacted his former employer, Douglas Pabst, in hopes of gaining some more information on what led Benny to this state of mind. The secretary promised that my call would be returned within a day or two.

The orderlies have informed me that Mr. Russell has asked for some paper and a pencil or a typewriter. I see no harm in this, so I have conceded. Perhaps the science fiction writer is still alive in him somewhere, and this is a sign of new hope in this patient.

December 20, 1953

I spoke with Mr. Russell again today. We seemed to get along a little better. I asked him about the incident with the police and the car thief, and he broke into hysterics. I thought that I was going to have to call the orderlies again, but this time it seemed more like a release from the pain that he had been harboring. He said that the thief was murdered and that when he, Benny, saw the body of his friend, he just lost control of himself. He also claims that he never brandished a weapon, and can't understand why no one tried to stop the police from beating the crap out of him.

Those are his words, not mine.

We also discussed his request for paper and pencil. He is apparently writing a fictional story. I asked him what it was about, and he seemed to light up when he talked about it.

"The future," he said. A grin beaming from his face.

"What future?" I asked. "Yours?"

"The future of mankind," he said. "Where people can live and work together in harmony. Where the advancement of the human race does not have to come at the expense of anyone."

He told me that his story was set four hundred years in the future, on a space station far out on the edge of the universe. This station, he called it *Deep Space Nine,* was governed by a black man! Can you believe it? This Captain Sisko of his, he was a great hero, and everybody respected him—even his enemies.

I have asked Benny to leave the story with me so that I might read it. Maybe I can find something in it that will enable me to better reach this troubled man.

December 21, 1953

I got a call from Mr. Russell's old boss today. He said that he would not have time to speak with me in person, but I could ask him some questions over the phone. I think I got some useful information from him, although he seemed like a very stern individual, and I am glad I don't have to answer to him.

Pabst said that he first noticed that something was wrong with Mr. Russell in the summer of this year, when Benny wrote his first story about *Deep Space Nine.* He said that Benny was always a little strange, kind of disoriented, but never like this. He would say things that just didn't make any sense, and he was taking this space station story far too seriously. It was almost as if he thought that it was real.

Several incidents followed, with Mr. Russell growing more and more confrontational. Apparently he subscribes to this theory that Negroes should be given the same rights and privileges as whites. This will make for an interesting case, because while I believe I can cure Benny of any psychosis that might be bothering him, I wonder if even I can rescue him from an idea like integration.

Whatever will happen, though, will have to wait until after the holidays. I am going home to my wife and son, and Benny Russell and all of his problems will have to wait until I get back.

December 24, 1953

Christmas Eve and I have been called back to work. Apparently my new patient is acting up again. He is displaying many warning signs of schizophrenia. One moment he is weeping like a child, and the next he lashes out, hurling profanities and demanding his immediate release. He does not see that these sorts of outbursts are only encouraging me to keep him here longer.

I was called in to see if there was anything I could do. I tried to talk to him, but he says he wants to see someone named Kasidy. I have no idea whom that person might be, or how I might be able to locate her. In any case, I don't think a visitor would do Mr. Russell any good. Instead I have ordered that he be injected with morphine. That should keep him restrained until I can figure out what to do with him.

December 27, 1953

Back at work. During my holiday I had time to relax with my family, and I also had time to read Mr. Russell's story. It is even more ridiculous than I thought. In this world that Benny has created, there are hundreds of species of aliens. I don't know how he keeps up with them all. And apparently they are fighting for control of something called the Alpha Quadrant, which is apparently the region of space where Earth is located. There is a terrific war raging with a group called the Dominion. In the midst of all this conflict, there is the space station, *Deep Space Nine.* It orbits a planet called *Bajor,* populated by a deeply religious people.

It is all so preposterous, I can't believe that this man actually got paid for being a writer. Captain Sisko, the hero, is selfless and strong. He fights not only for himself and his race, but also for all people of all races. He is like a swashbuckling, black Jesus up in space. He is a mystical figure in the religion on *Bajor.* They worship these beings called the Prophets. They say that Sisko was sent by the Prophets to deliver them. He is their Emissary. How blasphemous!

And the worst part is, I left the story sitting in my den, and my young son happened across it. He read it, apparently, because later that day I came across him and his friends playing in the back yard.

They were playing *Deep Space Nine.* And my son—my beautiful, white son—he was pretending to be none other than Captain Sisko! I was appalled. Where does this man, Benny Russell, get off thinking he knows anything about space or the future? I heard all those rumors a few years back, about little green men landing in Roswell, New Mexico. Everybody was pretty scared for a while there, thinking we were going to be invaded by Martians. But I never believed it. Whatever is up there in space, we're never going to see it. I wonder what Mr. Russell is going to suggest next, that the moon is not made out of green cheese?

December 28, 1953

While I was gone, apparently Benny has been writing non-stop. I have looked over a few of his new stories, and they too are about this *Deep Space Nine.* He has created a whole world of characters, and he seems to live in that world. But I have to turn my back on some of my initial observations. It can't be good for him to live so far away from reality. I did find out who Kasidy is though. Apparently she is Captain Sisko's lover.

I asked Mr. Russell if he could tell me why he was so upset. If he knew what was really bothering him. He said that he was upset because all he wanted was for people to read his stories and that no one would give them a chance.

"People don't even have to like my stories," he said. "If they read them and they hate them, then even that is enough. Just so long as they read them."

I can see that Benny is trying to promote his dissident ideas about racial integration. After seeing what *Deep Space Nine* did to my son, I can see why Pabst and *Incredible Tales of Scientific Wonder* pulled his story.

December 31, 1953

The last day of another year. Time to be reflective. I have asked Mr. Russell if he has any New Year's resolutions. He said that he would like to get out of the sanitarium, get his stories published, and marry his girl, Cassie.

I think the chances of any of those things happening are getting smaller and smaller with each passing day. I did put two and two together, though, and I think I have realized something about Benny's stories. He is using people from real life and making them into characters on *Deep Space Nine.*

Cassie, his real life girlfriend, is surely the same Kasidy Yates that is in love with Captain Sisko. And Sisko does bear some striking resemblance to Benny Russell. This makes me wonder if my earlier theories were correct, and if Benny is not sure what is fiction and what is reality.

I have collected all of the stories that Benny has written since his admittance here, and I will attempt to analyze them during the next days. I will have to be more careful where I leave them, however. I never want to see my son pretending that he is a colored man again.

January 2, 1954

I have forbidden Benny from writing any more of his stories. During the days off for the New Year's holiday, my son kept badgering me about Captain Sisko and *Deep Space Nine.* He wants to know what happens next. Will the Dominion win the war, or can Starfleet save the day? And what will happen to Captain Sisko?

I could have told him, but the last thing I want to do is further damage my son's concepts of right and wrong. If he starts viewing black people as equals, can you imagine what kind of trouble he could get in? His friends, his teachers, they would all hold it against him. It would be better if he just stopped caring about what was happening on some space station that doesn't even exist.

I am very disheartened over this patient reaching into my personal life. I pray that the damage done by this story will not be permanent.

January 5, 1954

I sat down with Mr. Russell today and told him exactly what I think about his stories.

"They are filled with propaganda," I told him, "and they pose a serious threat to anyone that reads them."

"They are just stories," he insisted.

But can you imagine what might happen if they got out to a wider audience? White children all over the country might be looking up to a black hero like Captain Sisko. Black children, what would they think? It would get their hopes up that they could someday be in positions of leadership over whites. And what will it do to their egos when they find out that the world is not like that? It will crush them.

I received a package in the mail today. It was from Douglas Pabst. It was a copy of Benny's very first story about *Deep Space Nine,* called *The Emissary.*

January 9, 1954

I think I understand now exactly what is going on. I have just finished reading *The Emissary,* and it is clear to me that Mr. Russell is trying to work through the problems of his own life with the characters of *Deep Space Nine.*

The Benjamin Sisko of this story was different somehow than in the later versions that I have read. He seemed distant, frightened . . . like there was a great weight upon his shoulders. He seemed, and I hate to say it, very much like Benny Russell.

Sisko was struggling because he had lost someone very dear to him—his wife, Jennifer. It is through the events of the story that he begins to realize that he has to move on with his life, that moving forward is what Jennifer would want him to do.

I wonder if there is a Jennifer Sisko in Benny's life—if he is waiting for an experience with the Prophets so that he can let go of the past.

January 10, 1954

I asked Mr. Russell about Jennifer Sisko, and immediately he tried to change the subject. I knew right away that I was on to something, so I pursued. He had to fight back tears as he told me about a girl who had been the love of his life. He used words like soulmate, and best friend, and it was almost heart-wrenching to watch him speak of her. She had died in a fire, right before his eyes. There was nothing he could do for her.

In the years since she passed out of his life, Benny has been trying desperately to put the pieces back together. He said that he tried not to think of her, but she kept finding ways of creeping back into his memory. Even when he met Cassie, his new girlfriend, his heart still lingered on *her. Her* name was Jen. He says that he will always love her. I believe him.

When he started writing the stories about *Deep Space Nine,* Benny says that he started feeling like himself for the first time in years. It was his way of exorcising his demons, of turning his pain and frustration into art. I wonder if I am making the wrong decision by not letting him continue writing. I will have to consider it some more.

January 12, 1954

I am convinced that Mr. Russell's affections for Jen are at the root of this situation. I asked him to describe her to me, some of their experiences together. He was quiet for a long, long time. I thought that perhaps he had slipped further into his psychosis. I was about to call for some orderlies when he finally spoke.

"We were at the pool," he said at last. "We were just children, maybe sixteen or seventeen. Had no idea what was about to happen."

There was a sad look in his eyes—a vacant, haunted look like an animal that knows it is about to die. He seemed, as one of his fictional characters might say, a thousand light-years away.

"I had run out to use the colored water fountain. It was outside the fence, on the other side of the parking lot. I wasn't thinking because I didn't put my shoes on. I ran halfway across," he said, "and when I turned around to come back, my feet were on fire. I was moving as fast as I could."

I sat there in silence as he spoke, drawing me in like only a great storyteller can do.

"When I got back to the fence," he said, "I was in so much pain. I just knew my feet were covered in blisters."

An expression of regret washed over his brown eyes. I felt almost sorrow for him. I knew that it must hurt him to relive this moment, even if it was a joyful one for him.

"I raced back into the pool," said Benny, "and I stopped at the first towel I could so I could relieve my burning feet. And . . . and . . . it was . . . she was . . . Jen."

A spasm of pain contorted his face. He choked back tears and remained silent for long minutes. Finally, he was again able to speak.

"She was sunbathing," he said, a halfhearted smile on his lips. "And she was . . . the most beautiful girl I had ever seen. All of a sudden I wasn't thinking about the pain in my feet. All I could concentrate on . . . was the pain in my heart."

Then he said the strangest thing. "It was like a burst from a Klingon disruptor," he said. "I was in love."

I have been looking through his agonizing stories about *Deep Space Nine,* and I believe that a Klingon disruptor is some sort of weapon—like a pistol. I was wondering when it would come back to violence. I believe that no matter how gentle these colored people might seem, they all really are just savages at heart.

January 14, 1954

I've compared the story that Benny told me about his first love, Jen, and his story *The Emissary,* where Sisko recalls how he met his wife Jennifer. They match up almost exactly. Instead of a pool, it was a beach. Other than that, it was nearly identical. And I believe that if I questioned Mr. Russell further, I would discover more parallels between this world and the world of *Deep Space Nine.*

And therefore, it is my conclusion that Mr. Russell should not be allowed to continue his stories. He is trying to act out his feelings in this fictional universe instead of dealing with them in the real world. He does not understand that everyone has problems and that sooner or later we get over them. People die. Life is hard. But time heals all wounds.

January 15, 1954

Benny didn't take the news very well that he would not be allowed to continue his stories. He begged me to let him go on. I had to refuse. He asked if he could see his girlfriend Cassie, but I had to decline on that as well. I don't think contact with someone he has fictionalized would be good for him at this juncture.

When I told him that he would have to remain here for at least another month, Mr. Russell grew incredibly hostile. He tried to attack me, and if I had not had some orderlies right there with me, he might have jammed his pencil right in my neck. And Benny wonders why people have such a hard time taking a colored captain like Ben Sisko seriously.

January 18, 1954

I don't know what else to say about Benny Russell. He continues in his defiant behavior. Today I was called to his room because he was having another episode. This time he was writing all over the walls. I thought I had all of his pencils taken away, but apparently he must have kept one hidden.

When I asked him what he was doing, he said that he was just trying to finish his story. He spoke about Captain Sisko and his search for the Orb of the Emissary. Benny feels that he is fine, that there is nothing really wrong with him. But I must disagree. He has become obsessed with these stories. I believe that *Deep Space Nine* has destroyed his mind, and that he has lost all touch with reality.

I offered Mr. Russell another chance, an opportunity that very few of us ever get. All he would have to do was paint over his story and wipe the slate clean. He refused. I do not see any hope for his recovery in the near future. I am at a loss as to what to do next.

January 31, 1954

Things have not been well with Benny Russell. I have always considered myself to be an excellent psychiatrist, but this case might be beyond even my ability. There is only one thing I can think of, but it might be a dangerous treatment. I believe that if I let Benny finish his story, then perhaps he can begin to get well.

I have discussed this possibility with the patient, and he seems to be willing to give it a try. Of course, this is probably just because I will be allowing him to write again. We have agreed on ten more stories. After that, he has to walk away from Sisko and the others and back into the real world. We shall see how it goes.

February 4, 1954

I can't believe I'm about to write this, but I've just completed one of the best stories I've ever read. Amazingly, it was one of Benny's stories about *Deep Space Nine.* This time it wasn't about wars or politics or race. It was about something more fundamental than that. It was about baseball.

There is a group of aliens calling themselves Vulcans who arrive on the station. They are the strangest characters I think Mr. Russell has written about yet. I think they might be Communists or something. Anyway, they challenge Captain Sisko and his crew to a game of baseball.

In a series of slapstick scenes, Sisko assembles and trains his team. They are the underdogs, but that doesn't matter. For a moment, as I was reading, I forgot that Sisko was a black man. For just a brief second in time, he was only a man. I could relate to him—to his desire to win. There is something special about baseball, it transcends race.

I was so sucked in to this story that I could not put it down. I was savoring every word like I've only done a couple of times in my life. I did not want it to end. And when the end finally came, and Sisko's team was destroyed, it didn't really matter. Sisko and his crew had found something more important than victory, and that was friendship.

I wonder if there is a hope for the future. Is it possible that a time will come someday when we can all exchange our weapons and our race for a glove and a bat? I suppose that only time will tell.

February 10, 1954

Having read a plethora of stories about spacefaring aliens and starships and time travel, I believe that I might be one of the foremost experts about this fictional universe that Mr. Russell has created, second only to Benny of course. But there is one race of aliens in particular that I keep coming back to. Gray-skinned and reptilian, Benny calls these people Cardassians.

The Cardassians are warlike, cruel and devious. They are like Nazis, with secret police and a deep network of spies and deceit. But what scares me is the similarities between the Cardassians of Benny's fiction and the way that so many of us behave in reality.

In the world of *Deep Space Nine,* the Cardassians have aligned themselves with the Dominion. They gave in to fear when it seemed that the Alpha Quadrant was in danger. They sided with the probable victor, even though that victor was aggressive and obviously tyrannical. The Cardassians turned their backs on their neighbors and what seemed to be the obvious course of justice.

I don't know why I keep thinking about these aliens, except that I see so much of this behavior in the world right now. With all the paranoia running rampant about the Russians, I wonder how many Cardassians there are out there right now, playing both ends against the middle, waiting to see who is going to come out on top.

I wonder, if I was the leader of some small country somewhere, whose side I would be on.

February 17, 1954

As Benny nears the end of his stories about *DS9,* he is trying to tie up a lot of loose ends and bring the war with the Dominion to a close. I think Benny realizes that there is a whole big world waiting for him out there. He has a girl that he plans to marry someday. He has dreams much bigger than a space station on the edge of the universe. I can sense that he really wants to put all of this behind him.

But I must say that his writing is getting better and better. Every time I finish one of his stories, I am awaiting the next. He is very good. Perhaps, once he gets back on his feet, he might be able to get his old job back at *Incredible Tales of Scientific Wonder.* I might be willing to put in a good word for him with his old boss. Who knows, it seems as if anything can happen these days.

February 21, 1954

I have become fascinated by one of Mr. Russell's characters, a Cardassian named Damar. He has been a running character throughout these tales, but only now, near the end, has he truly grown on me. In earlier stories this Damar was a despicable creature—cruel, alcoholic, vindictive. But as the war with the Dominion has raged across this fictional universe, he has become almost noble. Now as Benny is nearing the end of his stories about *DS9,* Damar has started a rebellion on the Cardassian homeworld. He is fighting to restore freedom and honor to his people.

It is so strange to me that I find myself relating to this character. He was once so full of evil, and now he has turned that evil around and is trying to make something good out of it. I wonder how much better the world might be if more of us turned out like Damar?

The scene that touched me in particular was this: The war is raging as Damar and his rebels are hiding out in the basement of a house on *Cardassia Prime.* There is an elderly woman who lives in the house; she is taking care of the rebels. In a moment of maternal instinct, she chides one of the rebels for not eating enough. She says he should eat more, like Damar.

The malnourished rebel in question retorts with a sly remark . . . he thinks that she is smitten with the rebel leader. Blushing, she says that she is much too old for him.

But Damar, with a charm that I did not know he had, replies: "Nonsense."

Even in the midst of all that conflict, here is a man that still has enough of his wits about him to make an old woman feel good.

That is a real man. I only hope my own son can make it through life and maintain that kind of composure.

March 2, 1954

The story of *Deep Space Nine* is almost done. I must admit that I am almost sorry to see it go, but it is for the best. As I have read more and more of these stories, I can see how easily someone could become trapped in this fictional universe. It is a place where good is good, and evil is sometimes good too. And it is a place where the heroes win out in the end and mankind has discarded some of his more animalistic tendencies. It is a place where I wish I could live, but it is a place that can never be. Back here on Earth in 1954 we all have to do the best we can, make the most of what we are given, and just try to get by.

Benny is working on the last *DS9* story now. I expect to see it in just a few days.

March 9, 1954

I've just finished reading *What You Leave Behind,* the last story Benny Russell will ever write about *Deep Space Nine.* I have to admit that I held some trepidation about this treatment, but I am pleased. The story ended with the death of Captain Sisko. He fell into the *Bajoran Fire Caves,* never to be seen again.

And now, as I look at Benny, I see a man who has grown stronger. He cares deeply, and he is wiser for this lesson. I don't think there will be any more problems with Mr. Russell. Just in case, however, I will be keeping him under observation for another month.

March 11, 1954

Today Benny got a special treat. His girl, Cassie, was allowed to come visit for the first time. Their meeting was heartfelt and warm, and I think that it was just what the doctor ordered. I am sure now that Mr. Russell is on the right track to recovery.

April 2, 1954

I feel vindicated now. Benny Russell was released from the hospital today. His girl was there to pick him up, and she thanked me for bringing her Benny back. Even Benny thanked me. He said that he feels much better now that the world of *Deep Space Nine* is behind him. And I feel better too.

I can't imagine how much damage might have been done if those stories had gotten out. I don't know what kind of future is waiting for us, but I don't think the world is ready to read about a place where white men and black men sit down at the same table, where they sit together on buses or drink from the same water fountains. No, the time is not yet upon us, but perhaps it is coming. I think Benny is a better man for this experience, and, perhaps, I am as well.

April 4, 1968

I thought that my listing dated April 2, 1954, would be my last on the subject of Benny Russell, but something happened today that struck me, and I hate to say it, like a blast from a Klingon disruptor. Through all these years I have kept the memory of Captain Sisko and *Deep Space Nine* alive in my thoughts. I don't know what it was about all those stories . . . it was something.

As I look back over this journal at the notes I kept on a black science fiction writer almost fifteen years ago, I can't believe how far I have come, or how far I have left to go.

In the years since I released Mr. Russell from my care, I have thought of him occasionally. I wondered where he was and how he was doing—if he ever relapsed back into his psychosis or if he was really cured.

The years have rolled on, of course, and times have changed. The ideas of racial harmony that he put forth in his stories . . . ideas that seemed so far away back in the fifties . . . are beginning to be on people's lips all the time. I don't think we are ready to see it come to pass—not yet, but soon. Times are changing, and if this country is going to survive, we are going to have to change as well.

I look back on my own words, Negro, colored, and it makes me sick. I can't believe that I used to view people like Benny Russell as different from me, as somehow inferior. I am disgusted with myself. I am disgusted with all of mankind. It seems like there is no hope. Benny's world of *Deep Space Nine* seems farther away than ever.

Dr. Martin Luther King was murdered this morning. He was gunned down in broad daylight. I don't know what to say . . . don't know what I can say. He was a great man. He was a voice of hope and reason in a world gone crazy. And I wonder if there can ever be any hope again, that someone would kill a man such as he. I feel sick.

I was in my home when I heard. My son had just come over to introduce me to his girlfriend, a black girl. He was dressed up like one of those hippie love children and so was she. They looked ridiculous. They were talking and talking, and then I heard the newsbreak come on the television. I got a lump in my throat: I couldn't talk. We all knew that something terrible had happened.

The news anchor came on and announced that Martin Luther King had been assassinated. My eyes filled up with tears. When I turned and saw my son and his girlfriend, tears flowed freely down their cheeks.

All of a sudden, I felt like I was going to throw up. I rushed to the bathroom, but by the time I got there my stomach had calmed down some. I was still feeling sick, so I splashed some cool water on my face from the sink. When I looked up, when I looked into the mirror, I saw something there, something that scared the hell out of me.

Staring back at me, the face in the mirror was pale gray and reptilian. The bone structure was different . . . inhuman. It took me a moment, but I was able to put a name to the creature I saw staring back at me. It was a Cardassian.

And then I remembered Damar, and how he was once evil but was able to turn his life around. And I wondered if there might be a little bit of Damar in me. If I told anyone from the hospital about this, they would say that I was going crazy. But somehow, I don't think that is what it is. In fact, I feel saner now that I have in years. And perhaps that is what I need, in this mad, mad world.

I splashed more water on my face, and when I looked in the mirror again, it was me—I saw myself staring there. But I know what I saw. And I know, somehow, that there has to be something better than this. I think Benny was right, that if we all work at it, if we keep trying, we can make his dream a reality.

And Sisko and Damar and all the others, they are out there if we keep looking for them. I really believe that. They are our future. If we want it hard enough, then they are as real as you or me.

STAR TREK
VOYAGER®

Iridium-7-Tetrahydroxate Crystals Are a Girl's Best Friend

Bill Stuart

Borg temporal designation 22A-14472-992
Assimilation of species 12199 completed.
Resistance encountered at spatial grid 27.
Three cubes destroyed.

The collective absorbed all of this information as it was processed. There was no need for status reports as there would be on a Federation ship; each event experienced by a Borg would be experienced by the entire collective.

The collective pondered its next move. Trillions of brains in tandem surveyed star systems and planets, looking for viable targets. Untold numbers of drones assembled new cubes, repaired damaged ones, and assimilated more members as needed.

Warning: Unauthorized chemicals discovered in queen aspect.
Location spatial grid 19. Composition: Lipid/sugar matrix with indole-class alkaloids and varied n-acylethylanes.
Probability of attack: Very low.

The collective focused part of its massive attention onto the queen aspect in grid 19. This cube had recently incorporated and was assimilating a pic-class shuttlecraft. This was a new design the Federation was testing and would add much to the collective.

Perhaps the chemical imbalance in the queen was intended as some sort of attack, launched by the Federation. The two crew members on board the shuttle had no knowledge of any attack. Oddly enough, they knew nothing about the ship functions or capabilities. None of this made any sense.

Warning: Assimilation failure in spatial grid 19.
Update: Unauthorized chemicals identified as being constituents of a chocolate truffle.

The collective grew concerned. An assimilation failure was an extremely rare event. To encounter a human who was resistant was unheard of. The collective focused more of its attention onto the queen aspect in grid 19.

The assimilation chamber was highly active. One of the Federation crew members had been assimilated without concern. The nanoprobes had infiltrated her easily, and her appendages were now being augmented with Borg technologies. The other was different. He appeared physically no different from any of the other trillions of beings assimilated into the collective.

"Is this going to take much longer?" said the man as the Borg repeatedly injected nanoprobes into his upper arm. He was lying on the assimilation gurney as Borg bioengineering drones looked him over. There was no oddities in his DNA, no antibodies that would halt nanoprobe activities, nothing out of the ordinary.

The door to the assimilation chamber irised open and the Borg queen entered. She was medium height, about five and a half feet. Before assimilation she must have been quite striking. Now she was a hideous monstrosity. Her remaining eye was a sparkling brown color. The other eye socket had an optical reader jutting out of it.

"Resistance is futile," she said.
"I'm not resisting!"

Warning: Electroweak force anomaly detected in spatial grid 19, localized to area surrounding Borg vessel 98642.

The collective grew very concerned. The electroweak force never varied, except in areas of extreme conditions such as the immediate vicinity of a black hole. No known phenomenon could explain this, except . . .

Warning: Species 1732 detected in spatial grid 19. Recommend erecting protective subspace barrier around cube.

The collective tried to comply but found it could not.

"Au contraire, mon chère! Everyone's invited to this party," said the man in the assimilation chamber. The Borg drones continued futilely injecting him with nanoprobes.

"Q," said the queen in an unemotional voice.

"In the flesh!" He looked at the bioengineer drone injecting him. "Do you mind, that is getting really annoying," he said. They backed off and assisted with the female's assimilation.

"What do you want?"

"Why, you, of course. In all the galaxy I have never met a woman quite like you. The spirit, the drive. I've decided to grant you a gift beyond measure . . . me."

"Explain."

"I've decided you will be my bride, my second bride actually." The collective pondered Q's unusual statement. Borg directive 201 prohibited any contact with the Q. They were to be avoided or ignored at all costs. However, close proximity to a Q for any length of time might provide a resource for future assimilation for that species. It also guaranteed loss of the queen aspect and most likely loss of the cube. The collective wisely decided to decline Q's courtship.

"Your primitave bonding rituals are irrelevant. We do not wish to participate."

"But think of the fun!" The queen looked unamused. "Okay, think of the accumulation of knowledge I can provide. We could make quite a team. All I ask for is one little ceremony."

The queen aspect was suddenly wearing a white wedding gown and standing inside a cathedral, at the far end. Drones dressed as ushers and flower girls stood along the aisle.

The aspect began walking down the aisle toward the altar. A cold murderous look was on her face as she approached Q.

Suddenly a very large human female lunged from her seat and grabbed the queen aspect. She spun the cyborg around.

"Oh, I'm so happy for you!" she shrieked as she hugged the aspect and kissed her on the cheek. The queen disintegrated her with a pale green blast from her arm-loaded phaser.

"Auntie Helen!" shrieked Q. "Disintegrating your in-laws on your special day. How rude! And to think she gave us a shiny new toaster."

"Auntie Helen and her toaster are irrelevant."

"It's natural to have nervous feelings on your wedding day, dear," said another female, to the aspect's left. "I'm sure you will make a wonderful wife." Another voice spoke up from the back of the cathedral; this time it was the mechanized voice of a Borg unit.

"We're so proud of you, honey!" said Two of Seven, a nondescript service drone. "Although I think you could have done better. I can still set you up with Stan, he's a medical drone in unimatrix 42 with his own . . ."

"This will stop immediately!" screamed the entire collective at once. All was silent for a moment. Even the almighty Q paused.

"Oh, silly me. You're Jewish, aren't you?" In a flash, the cathedral was replaced with a synagogue. An elderly rabbi stood before the crowd. The queen looked unimpressed.

"Religion is irrelevant."

"Humanist it is!" The room shimmered and melted. The aspect was now in a captain's ready room. It took a second for her to identify the ship as the *U.S.S. Enterprise,* under control of Jean-Luc Picard, a former drone. The captain was sitting in his chair reading a report.

"Jean-Luc!" said Q as he moved forward to embrace Picard. Picard sighed and put down his report.

"I've no time for your . . ." He broke off as he noticed the aspect in a wedding dress. "What the hell is going on here . . ."

"Jean-Luc, how rude! Captain, may I present primary adjutant for unimatrix 4. I call her Unikins," said Q as he kissed her on the cheek. The aspect glared at him with her silent, rage-filled eyes. Then he dip-kissed her. Picard tapped his chest.

"Security! Erect a level-ten forcefield around the captain's chamber." He turned back to Q. "I don't know what kind of games you are playing, Q, but I want no part of it." Q continued dip-kissing the uncompliant queen.

"Q, is this really necessary?" Q stopped kissing the aspect and turned toward the captain.

"What's the matter, Jean-Luc? Jealous?"

"Hardly. I'm not sure which of you to feel more sorry for."

"I am here in a completely professional capacity, Captain! I have need of your services. Uni-poo and I wish to be wed. Under Federation law, you can perform the ceremony."

"We will not comply," said the collective through the aspect. "Return us to our cube immediately."

"Resistance is futile," said Q. "Besides, you look good in that dress." As soon as Q finished saying that, the dress dissolved away into a nanotechnological goo.

"You're right. Black is more your color." Instantly the aspect was in a long black wedding gown. This too deteriorated into nanotechnological goo.

"Q! Stop this at once. I have no idea why you would want to marry the Borg but I will have no part of the ceremony. Get off my ship."

"And to think we were going to name our first child after you. Jean-Luc PicQ."

"We will no longer tolerate this. Return us to our cube," said the aspect with her typical superior aspect.

"Fine. The cube it is." Suddenly Picard and the ready room vanished, replaced by the bleakness of the aspect's chamber.

"Perhaps I am going about this in the wrong way." Q suddenly took on the form of a drone. "When the light hits your eyes just right, they sparkle like the outer layer of the Oort cloud, a region of dense cometoid debris that periodically bombards the inner Sol system." He kissed the queen's hand. "A minute without you is like sixty standardized seconds."

"Your attempt to remove this aspect from the collective has failed. All further attempts to remove this aspect will fail as well," droned the collective.

"I have no intention of removing her. I think I'm going to like it here, Uni-poo! But we need to make some changes." Q waved his hand and the chamber became a Latin villa. The drones began playing rumba songs. Q was no longer a drone, but a Spanish matador.

"We are not impressed," said the aspect, spitting out a rose Q had placed between her teeth. Immediately, the room began to resume its prior shape as the nanoprobes reinfested the material and converted it back to Borg structural units. The drones began assimilating their Spanish garb.

"You are a woman of taste and refinement, *mon chère,*" said Q. He had changed into a beret-wearing Frenchman, holding a basket of bread and a bottle of champagne. The queen shot the bottle out of Q's hand.

"Ah, you do not like zee white wine. You prefer red, zee color . . . *of passion!*" Q tore open his shirt and advanced on the queen, throwing the bread to one side. The queen sighed and tried to ignore him as Q kissed the nape of her neck.

"Your matrimonial assault is due to fail."

Q smirked as every drone, not just on this cube, but in every corner of the universe, became a Spanish trumpet player. The collective strained to regain control of itself and return to normal functioning.

Recommendation: Use this incident to test Borg device 2782.

The psi-wave emitter, thought the aspect. This piece of technology was taken from a planet populated exclusively by telepaths. It was similar to a phaser, except it focused psionic emissions from one or more minds onto a target. Since the collective had trillions of minds at its disposal, this device should assist in the assimilation of Q. At the very least, it should drive him away.

The device was being delivered by a conduit and should reach spatial grid 19 in a matter of minutes. All the queen had to do was occupy Q's attention span.

"You know I would destroy you at the first opportunity. What possible benefits would you derive from a marriage to this aspect?"

"I like difficult women. Have you ever met Kathryn Janeway? Now, she was exciting. But not the kind of girl to bring home to meet Mom." The mention of Janeway drove her into a rage. The collective had pursued her and her pet drone through half of the Delta Quadrant, and at every turn she had outwitted them.

None of this mattered, however, as the psi-wave emitter had just arrived.

"Now, Q, let us discuss your assimilation." The psi-wave device came to life. Cube after cube poured its collective concentration into the device, and it channeled it into Q as a pure wave of psionic power.

The wave grew more intense. The side of the cube where the wave struck began to warp, and the unfortunate drones caught in the field simply detonated in a field of red, black, and green gore.

The wave became more concentrated. The mental energy of the entire collective was focused into a pinprick, and that was applied directly to Q's brain.

"Oh, Unikins, our first fight!" said an amused Q. "You want to play tough?" He suddenly became less jovial. "Fine."

Warning: Mnemonic parasites detected in spatial grid 19.
Warning: Psi-wave feedback loop initiated.
Warning: Localized collective failure in grid 19.

The collective turned all its attention to disinfecting itself from the parisites Q had introduced. It decided to abandon the cube and the aspect, before Q could cause any more damage.

Suddenly the aspect was much less than she had been before.

The vast collective mind was no longer at her disposal. The psi wave shut down, leaving a gaping hole in one side of the ship and hundreds of deactivated drones where it had impacted. The remaining drones were incapacitated. Most of the drones were irretrievable and would have to be reassimilated at a later date.

"We fail to see the purpose behind your activities. You have expended a great deal of energy and time to procure this aspect for a matrimonial endeavor without any hope of a positive response," said the aspect.

"Does love need a reason?"

"Sexual attraction is irrelevant. One day your species will be assimilated, once we have grown in power."

"Is that a yes?"

"You may do what you like with the aspect. We are no longer able to adequately control the drones and are powerless to stop you."

"Finally! I have just the place picked out for our honeymoon." Q and the aspect vanished from the cube and rematerialized in a one-bedroom apartment on Risa.

"This will only take a moment," said Q.

"Time is irrelevant."

"Lie down on the bed." The aspect complied and lay down. As she did, Q's brow furrowed and the aspect's features began to change.

The Borg implants faded away and began to melt off the body. Her eye regrew, and hair sprouted from her scalp. The numerous skin lesions repaired themselves, and finally she was human once more. As a final touch, Q did her hair and makeup.

The woman suddenly stiffened and woke.

"Q! What the hell are you doing here. I don't like it when you just barge in like that. I've told you before I can handle myself perfectly well without you around."

"I missed you."

"I didn't miss you," said Vash. "I thought I made that clear the last time. And aren't you married or something?" She noticed the time. "Oh my god, I'm going to miss my shuttle."

"That's what I stopped by to tell you. The dig's been canceled. Something about Borg being sighted in the area."

"Borg? Since when do they want useless artifacts? Aren't they only interested in technical things? Why would they bother with something so . . . irrelevant?"

"Sometimes little things mean a lot," said Q. Then he vanished, leaving an irritable young woman with an unexplainably sore eye and two missing weeks.

Uninvited Admirals

Penny A. Proctor

Owen Paris wants me to call him. His urgent message is flashing on my comm unit. "It doesn't matter what time, Gretchen. I have news about Kathryn." Nothing more, no hint whether it is good news or bad. That is absolutely typical of Owen.

Suddenly I am scared for my daughter. When admirals appear uninvited, they rarely have good news. It's a lesson I have learned over and over.

The first time, I was six years old. I was putting my shoes on, all by myself, when someone knocked at our door. My mother called from upstairs, "That's probably Aunt Katie. Let her in."

But it wasn't Aunt Katie. It was two Starfleet officers whom I did not know, a human woman and a Vulcan man. I stood in the doorway and looked at them silently. They were strangers who had not been invited to our house and I was uncertain of how to react to them.

"Hello," the woman said. "You must be Gretchen. I'm Admiral Brennan, and this is Admiral Sinek. Is your mother at home?"

"She's upstairs." I studied them, trying to decide whether I should be friendly. Even though I wasn't supposed to talk to strangers, they were Starfleet officers and seemed to be important. "Do you know my daddy? He's a starship captain."

"Yes, we do. You have the same color hair as he does." Admiral Brennan knelt down so her face was level with mine. Her eyes were sad. "May we come in? We need to speak with your mother."

"She's changing the baby." I did not move. I wanted them to go away.

But then my mother came down, carrying Annie on her hip. "What are you doing, Gretchen? Who is it?"

Before I could answer, she saw the two admirals for herself. She stopped on the second step from the bottom and turned pale. This scared me. Admiral Brennan said in a quiet voice, "We need to talk, Elsa."

Mother came down the last step slowly and set Annie down next to me. "Take your sister outside," she told me without taking her eyes away from Admiral Brennan. "I'll call you in a little bit."

I didn't argue with her, even though I didn't want to go outside. I took Annie's hand and led her to the front yard. She toddled happily to her sandbox and plopped into it. Her clean clothes were getting dirty, but I didn't yell at her. If I did she would yell back, and I had the funniest feeling that we ought to be quiet.

A long while later my mother came outside. Her eyes and nose were red. She came and sat beside me on the grass. "You must be a very grown-up girl now, Gretchen," she said, putting an arm around me. She hugged me tightly.

"Why?" I was deeply frightened. "What did those admirals say?"

"There's been an accident, *liebchen.* Your father . . ." Tears welled up in her eyes. It was the first time I ever saw her cry.

She couldn't say any more, but I knew. My daddy wasn't coming home again. "No, I don't believe it. They're lying. They're lying!" I jumped to my feet to run away, but she caught me by the shoulders.

"Be brave, baby. Remember, we are Starfleet, you and I."

"No," I cried. "I'm not Starfleet, and I never will be. Never!" I kicked the sand as hard as I could, and it geysered into the baby's face and filled my shoe. Annie started to cry, and my mother started to cry. Those admirals were to blame for everything, and I hated them.

The clock chimes nine, forcing me back to the present. Owen's message is still blinking at me, but my hands are shaking too badly to hit the Reply button. Taking a deep breath, I leave the kitchen desk and grab the first bottle of wine I see in the cooler. I need to settle down before I call him.

It's a sauvignon blanc from California. It's our wine, the one Edward and I drank the night we met. I was nineteen and in full, if private, mutiny against all things Starfleet. That winter, my stepfather was promoted to admiral and Mother threw a party for him. At first I refused to go. All the guests would be Starfleet officers and their spouses, which meant it would be stuffy, pretentious, and inexorable. Annie guilted me into it, though, reminding me how good Kurt had always been to both of us. I came, but brought my attitude with me.

I deliberately arrived at the last minute, meeting the family at the hotel. Mother took one look at me and flushed crimson. "Gretchen! What are you thinking? You cannot wear that—that flimsy excuse for a dress. It's completely inappropriate."

"What's wrong with it?" I asked with mock innocence, secretly pleased by her reaction. The dress was barely justifiable by fashion and definitely beyond the bounds of Fleet propriety, cut low in the neckline and slit high on the thigh. I wore my hair long and loose, with big earrings and a necklace designed to attract attention. Among the staid and proper Starfleet officers, I would stand out like show poodle in a pack of basset hounds.

Kurt put his arm around her in a gentle hug. "It's all right, Elsa. At least everyone will have something to talk about besides how gray my hair is—what's left of it, anyway." His eyebrows rose just a little, which was his way of showing amusement.

Later in the evening, he touched my shoulder. "Let me introduce you to someone."

I turned, found myself staring at two young officers. One of them was smiling, the other looking at me intently. "Gretchen, I'd like you to meet Lieutenant Will Patterson and Lieutenant Edward Janeway. Gentlemen, my daughter Gretchen."

Will Patterson was friendly as a puppy as he shook my hand, and about as smooth. I chalked one up for the dress. Then Edward Janeway took my hand, and I felt as if all the oxygen had just been sucked from the room. For a moment I couldn't breathe. He was tall, with features that were too hard-edged to be called handsome. But his eyes . . . his eyes were fixed on me as if he had nothing else to look at. "How do you do?" I managed to say.

"Would you like some wine?" he asked, not letting go of my hand. I nodded mutely, and he led me away from his friend and my stepfather, and we spent the rest of the night sipping sauvignon blanc and sitting in our own little world at a corner table.

He came to see me the next night. I was a junior in college, majoring in Terran literature but playing with the idea of a career as a singer, and occasionally I performed at a small café near the university. The night after the party, I looked out at the audience and there was Edward. He sat at the table nearest the stage and he wasn't wearing a uniform. He stayed for all three sets, rarely taking his eyes off me, and then walked me home.

My private mutiny was doomed from that night on. We married at the semester break, in the outrageously archaic dress-uniform-and-crossed-swords ceremony that Edward and everyone in my family (except me) wanted. I thought of it as my formal capitulation to Starfleet. The surrender was not unconditional, though. I drew the line at moving to San Francisco, despite the fact that Edward was attached to Headquarters. We lived in my apartment until I graduated, and then found a home in rural Indiana, not far from where Edward grew up.

This home.

The life we made for ourselves and our daughters revolved around his duty and Starfleet. I learned all the things a career officer's wife learns—the loneliness of long separations, the stolen joys of unexpected reunions. I developed the "Starfleet ear," the ability to hear the unspoken in the brief and monitored messages from space. I learned to navigate through the tyranny of unofficial hierarchies and unwritten protocols. Above all, I came to share the pride of the service. On our tenth anniversary, Edward was off-planet at a diplomatic conference, and we celebrated through a delayed subspace message. That was the night I realized my mother was right after all. I never wore the uniform, but I was Starfleet.

Two months before our thirtieth anniversary two admirals came up the walk, uninvited, as I worked in my garden. Will Patterson, pale and red-eyed, and Sarah Brennan—the second-oldest officer still on active duty—found me on my hands and knees, planting pansies. "We need to talk, Gretchen," she said, using exactly the same tone she had used forty-three years earlier. It was as if time melted away and I was six years old again, and frightened.

I refused to look at her. "Talk, then." I kept my head bent to my task, tried to pretend they weren't really there.

"There was an accident," Will said gently, and still I would not look at him. I just dug a little more furiously, hoping he would go away. He didn't.

"Edward?" I finally asked, but I knew the answer before he spoke. Edward was dead.

It's funny the way the mind reacts to such things. I remember thinking that I needed a purple plant next, there were too many yellow all in a row. It was very important to choose just the right flower.

"Let's go inside," Will suggested, but I shook my head.

"I have to finish the pansies." I still refused to look at him. "They are Edward's favorites." My private mutiny resumed at that moment: Courtesy be damned, I wasn't going to let them into my house. I was done with Starfleet and with uninvited admirals.

It's funny the way the mind reacts. Look at me now, standing in the kitchen, indulging in memories instead of calling Owen Paris. I suppose I don't want to face his news tonight any more than I wanted to listen to Will that day. Or that other day, six years ago, when Will and Owen came together, without calling first.

That day I came home and found them waiting on my front porch. Just the sight of them made the summer day seem chilly. I remember thinking that there were never two more opposite personalities than Will Patterson, whose every emotion showed on his face, and Owen Paris, who could be stoic as a Vulcan. That day, they both looked miserable.

I sat down with them. "Just say it," I said tersely. There was no need for pleasantries; we all knew why they were there. Admirals don't drop by to chat.

"There's been no word from *Voyager* or Kathryn in over six weeks," Will said, his voice heavy with emotion. "The ship is now officially 'Missing.' "

"Missing," I repeated. From their expressions, I had expected worse. Then I realized, they *believed* much worse. "Have you searched? Found anything—debris, warp bubble, anything like that?"

Owen answered. "There have been searches. There's no sign of the ship, Gretchen. It's simply gone."

I smiled. "That's all right, then."

The two men exchanged worried looks. They thought I had snapped, or was in denial. I laughed at them. "Will, Owen—you both know Kathryn. She doesn't quit, and she wouldn't go quietly. If her ship had been destroyed you would have found something, some trace of it."

Will put a hand on my shoulder. "Let's go inside, Gretchen. We can tell you a little about the mission—"

"No," I interrupted him. "You are not going to come into my home and take my hope away from me. Tell me what you must right here. Then I'll tell you why you're wrong." I turned to Owen, remembering that his son was on Kathryn's ship. "And you will go home and tell Cinda everything I say, do you understand me, Owen Paris? You are going to let her keep some hope, too."

He looked at me in surprise. Very few people chide admirals. I tried to tell myself that they were loyal friends who didn't abandon me after Edward's death and that this wasn't easy for either of them, but at that moment I was angry. Angry about Kathryn, angry about Edward, about my long-dead father, about everything that Starfleet had ever forced upon me.

Will cleared his throat before speaking. "It was a very dangerous mission, involving Maquis in the Badlands. I'm sorry we can't give you the details, but the odds are the ship was destroyed."

I shook my head. "How can you, of all people, say that, Will?

You've known her since the day she was born. Owen, you are her mentor. You both should know better."

"You have to face facts, Gretchen," Owen said.

"The only fact you have is that the ship is missing." My voice started to rise, and I took a short breath to get it back under control. "Nothing more. You are jumping to conclusions, and I won't have it. Until you show me hard proof, I choose to believe that Kathryn's out there somewhere." I stood. "You've delivered your message, and I appreciate it. Now I have to take care of the dogs, and then I'm going to have a cup of coffee. If you want to stay and tell me about your grandchildren you're welcome. Otherwise, please leave."

Poor men. I didn't give them much quarter that day. They looked at each other in some silent, secret admiral code and tried to decide what to do. Owen left and Will came in. We talked about his grandson, I think; I don't remember a single word he said. After he left, I broke the news first to Phoebe and then to Mark. It was only then that I cried.

It's getting late. I leave the kitchen and wander into the room I still think of as Edward's study. These days, it is my office, but somehow Edward's personality is indelibly stamped here. This is where he spent hours working out the kinks in his ship designs, taught math to Kathryn and Phoebe. This is where he once tried to write a novel, before the Cardassian threat began to consume him. In the quiet of the night, I can still feel his presence when I sit at his desk.

I'm doing it again. Thinking about something else so I won't have to think about calling Owen. I try to remember if I've spoken to him since the war ended. Cinda and I had lunch together, but it's been a long time since I spoke directly to Owen.

In fact, it's been since the night two years ago when the comm unit beeped loudly at two o'clock in the morning. Bleary-eyed, I turned it on and found Owen, still in uniform, staring at me. "I'm coming over, Gretchen. Now."

"What?" I asked, still groggy.

"We can't have this conversation on your porch. It's snowing in Indiana. I'll be there in one minute."

One minute. Long enough to grab my robe and slippers, drag a quick brush through my hair, and run downstairs. Long enough for time to slow down and the late-February chill to seep into my blood. Long enough to remember that Owen shouldn't be on Earth; he was stationed at Starbase 121 to oversee the Sixth Fleet in the war with the Dominion.

What could be so important that it brought him home from the war?

The transporter in Edward's study began to hum. Starfleet had left it with me after his death, and it is convenient—at least, most of the time. Owen materialized by himself, his face unreadable. *It can't be that bad,* I realized, *they send two officers if the news is very bad.*

He stepped off the platform immediately. "We've had contact with *Voyager*. You were right all along, Gretchen. They're alive."

He caught my shoulders when my knees turned rubbery and gave way. I slid into the chair behind me. "Kathryn," I whispered. "Where is she? When can I speak with her?"

"She's . . ." He hesitated, and looked away. "They're in the Delta Quadrant, about sixty thousand light-years away."

It seemed a long time before his words made sense. Sixty thousand light-years? *Voyager* was on the other side of the galaxy. "How is that possible?"

"Apparently the ship was transported there by some kind of alien technology."

"All right." I nodded. So far, I understood. "Why didn't they transport back?"

"The technology was destroyed before they could use it," he said. "They're coming back on warp drive."

I kept on nodding, couldn't seem to stop it. "Warp drive. That will take, what—sixty years?"

"Yes. Of course, they might find shortcuts—a wormhole, something else might cut the distance, but sixty years is realistic."

"I need a drink," I decided, and stood. "Let's go to the kitchen." I took a bottle of wine from the cooler and poured us both a glass. *Sixty years,* I thought. *I'll never see her again.* "How did you find them?" I asked at last.

"They found us," he replied. "There's some kind of ancient

communications network in the Delta Quadrant. They were able to send a holographic signal through it. The EMH, actually." He shook his head. "It's been active for four years and apparently has developed quite a personality."

"What did it say?"

"I haven't seen the full report yet, but it gave us a crew roster and the ship's approximate location. Then it insisted on being returned to 'his' crew before the opportunity was lost."

A crew roster. I had completely forgotten about his personal interest in the crew. "Tom?" I asked belatedly, feeling guilty. "Is Tom all right?"

He nodded, and smiled slightly. For Owen, it was hugely demonstrative. "Yes, he was on the roster." The smile faded. "But there's only a hundred and fifty-two crewmen, and that includes the Maquis crew that Kathryn took in. They've lost a lot of people."

I sighed. "At least their families will know for certain. That will be a blessing." Then I looked at him closely. "Go home, Owen. Go celebrate with your wife. Cinda must be beside herself."

"In a minute," he said. He told me there might be a chance to get a short letter through, one letter for each member of the crew. I smiled; he didn't know I had a whole drawer full of letters to Kathryn in the study. But . . . she would expect to hear from Mark, whom she presumably believed was still her fiancé. I hoped she would not be too hurt to learn of his marriage. Yes, Mark needed to send the letter.

We walked back to the transporter pad. "Thank you for coming, Owen. It means everything."

"Sixty years is a long time," he said.

"They're alive." I was unable to stop smiling. "And I told you before, my money's on Kathryn." I started to set the coordinates to his home, but then looked up. "Owen. Which way is the Delta Quadrant from here?"

"Technically, we can't see . . ." he began, about to give me a detailed lecture on astrometrics or stellar cartography. Then he shrugged, and I guessed that Cinda asked him the same thing. He pointed toward the southwestern sky. "That way. Just before Orion sets, follow the belt in a straight line to the left, halfway to the next star. The Delta Quadrant is sixty thousand light-years from there."

When he was gone, I wrapped my robe tightly around me and stepped out to the front porch. The snow had tapered to light flurries, and the nearly full moon was visible again. A lovely night. I looked into the southwest sky, left of Orion's belt and sixty years beyond. I looked for a long time, imagining that Kathryn was looking back.

I've looked to the sky many nights since. That's what I was doing when Owen called tonight, walking the dog and looking at the sky. Waiting for Orion to set, even though I don't really need it as a guide anymore. I know exactly where to look in the sky, any time of year or any time of day. She's out there, somewhere, even though there's no news. The very lack of news has become a comfort in itself. In my mind, Kathryn is always safe and on her way home.

I cannot put it off any longer. Sitting at the desk, I activate the comm unit and punch the Reply button. Owen answers almost at once.

"Gretchen, stay right there," he says. "Don't move."

In about ten seconds, the transporter begins to hum in the study, and my heart begins to pound. Owen steps off the pad, and to my utter astonishment, he grabs me in a hug. While I am still speechless, he crosses over to the desk and inserts a chip. In a moment, the room fills with a staticky sound, and then a voice.

"Starfleet Command, come in." My hand flies to my mouth. The transmission is filled with interference, but it sounds almost like my daughter's voice. I am almost afraid to hope.

"This is Captain Kathryn Janeway." The static clears, and I hear my baby, my beautiful and brilliant firstborn child, for the first time in nearly six years. *"Do you read me?"*

I listen, enthralled. The words are unimportant, and my mind isn't grasping them, anyway . . . *"good to hear your voice. . . ."*

. . . *"long time . . ."*

. . . *"navigational records . . ."*

All that matters is what is behind the words. My "Starfleet ear" may be out of practice, but some skills are never lost. Kathryn is well. She misses us, but she is in control of herself and the situation.

. . . *"exemplary crew . . ."*

. . . *"including your son . . ."*

Owen's recorded response cuts into my concentration. *"Tell him I miss him . . . and that I am proud of him."* In my office, he looks away in embarrassment, and I try to hide my astonishment that Owen Paris could have said anything so personal on an official channel.

"He heard you, sir." My smile broadens. That means that Tom was on the bridge, and he wouldn't be there if he didn't meet her standards. Kathryn wouldn't have him on her bridge otherwise, not even for the sake of her mentor. The pride shining in Owen's eyes proves that he knows it, too.

The message is ending. I lean forward to hear Kathryn speak again.

"We appreciate it, sir. Keep a docking bay open for us. We hope" Static. The transmission ends.

I don't know I am holding my breath until it escapes me in a whoosh. "Thank you," I say. It feels entirely inadequate. "Thank you."

"There's more," he says. "They are much closer to home than we expected. They're halfway back, Gretchen. Just thirty thousand light-years away. We'll see them again, if we're stubborn enough to hold on for thirty more years." He surprises me again by grabbing my hand. Was the it defeat of the Cardassians that has changed him, or simply the passage of time?

"I told you so." I am half laughing and half crying. "We will see them again, Owen. Kathryn will get them home to us."

"Yes, I believe she will." Then he straightens. "Cinda wants you to come celebrate with us, Gretchen. The champagne has been cooling all afternoon. She'll have my hide if you don't come with me."

Champagne? I don't want champagne. I want to play the transmission again, to hear my daughter's voice, words she spoke only hours ago. But he's right, this deserves a celebration and anyway, Cinda and I can probably convince him to play it again. "Let's go," I agree. But then I stop short and ask him to wait a minute while I run outside.

The southwest sky is partially obscured by clouds from the front that is coming through tomorrow morning, but half a dozen stars wink through. "Hurry, Kathryn," I whisper. "I'm so tired of uninvited admirals. Next time, I want to see a captain come to my door unexpectedly."

Hurry home.

Return

Chuck Anderson

Trevis stood tall in the rays of the sun. His leaves absorbed the light and shaded all below him. Trevis was an old tree, and he had seen many things. Trevis once had seen his forest burned to a crisp by the Ogre of Fire, and he had even been flooded by an impish child.

Trevis had seen many things, but even the worst fire from the Ogre hadn't destroyed his forest. It had just made it stronger and better. All the dead branches had been burned away, and new flowers and saplings grew in their place. Soon the woods were full of the young trees, and it would be many years before the Ogre could return with his fire.

Trevis knew that everyone returned to the forest, even the Ogre. It was all just a matter of time. All this thinking and the hot sun were making Trevis thirsty. He started to take a long slow drink from Flotter's pond below.

Trevis drank, but he just kept right on thinking. Trevis knew that it was time for Flotter to return with Naomi Wildman. Their adventure should just about be over, and soon Neelix would be calling her to dinner.

When Trevis saw Flotter and Naomi return, he called out to them, "How's the beetle in his castle today?"

"Fine, fine," said Flotter.

"He was lost, and we brought him back home again," said Naomi. "I just wished he would quit getting lost, but once he starts rooting around there's no getting him back home."

"I know a beetle in the dirt loses track of everything. Even his castle," said Trevis.

"Neelix to Holodeck One. Naomi, it's time to come to dinner," said Neelix's voice from above.

"All right, Neelix," replied Naomi. "Goodbye, Flotter. Goodbye, Trevis."

"Goodbye, Naomi," said Trevis and Flotter at the same time.

"Trevis?" said Flotter.

"Yes, Flotter," said Trevis, looking down at his friend, his watery friend.

"You know we're losing her. She comes to play less and less with us," said Flotter.

"I know," said Trevis. "That's what happens when they get older. They want to play someplace else."

"I just wish Naomi wouldn't get older; we have the best adventures together," said Flotter.

"I know," said Trevis. "But everybody returns to the forest. Just you wait and see."

Even as Trevis was saying this, the door from the outside opened, and another walked into their forest.

"Kathryn," said Flotter, who recognized her first. "It's been a long time. We missed you."

"I missed you too, Flotter, and you too, Trevis," said Captain Janeway.

"Do you want to go see the beetle in the castle?" said Flotter.

"You're not planning to flood the forest again, are you?" said Trevis.

"No, I am not planning to. I was just hoping to sit here, and enjoy the shade and the quiet. If you don't mind?" said Janeway.

"No, we don't mind," said Trevis and Flotter.

Kathryn fell asleep under the coolness of his tree and next to the quiet of the pond.

Trevis looked down at Flotter and whispered, "See, Flotter? Everybody returns to the forest."

Black Hats

William Leisner

The darkness receded slowly as Captain Proton felt himself coming back to consciousness. His head still ached like the devil, and he tried to rub the spot at the back of his skull where he had been struck. He quickly realized, though, that his hands were bound behind his back, and his ankles were likewise tied to the legs of the chair underneath him. He raised his head carefully, squinting at the dark and ominous figure looming above him, smiling at him with undeniable menace.

"Chaotica!" Proton spat, wincing only slightly at a sudden spike of pain in the back of his skull, but withholding any other sign of weakness from his adversary. "What is this?"

The villain chuckled quietly, a sound that chilled one's bones to their marrow, through smiling, pursed lips. "This, Captain Proton, is the end of your bothersome interference into my affairs once and for all! This ship is on a course directly into the sun. In five minutes, there will be nothing left of you but a blackened cinder! Then, once my Mind Control Ray is complete, there will be nothing standing between me and my domination of the galaxy!"

Captain Proton let his head loll back and over his right shoulder, seemingly in exhaustion, although in actuality he was looking for the ship's main control panel. He spotted it almost immediately, its flashing buttons clearly labeled. Five minutes to work his way out of his bonds, then to change course. Hundreds of moviegoers of four and a half centuries ago would have chewed their fingernails for a whole week, wondering if, come next Saturday, their hero would be able to escape. Not that there was any doubt in the mind of the noble captain.

"Ah, Proton," Chaotica growled in diabolical satisfaction. "I'm almost sorry to see you die." He spun away from his captive then, flipping the edge of his cape up in a melodramatic flourish as he marched to the escape hatch.

Captain Proton had already started looking around for something to wear the ropes around his wrists against when Chaotica stopped, turned back to him, and said, "Before you die, though, I want you know one thing."

Tom Paris was struck silent for a moment. Chaotica had already laid out his plan, thereby telling him how to foil it once he did escape. "What do you want me to know?" he asked.

Chaotica took a deep breath, as if what he was going to say was more difficult for him than any of his schemes for galactic domination. "I was born in a small, impoverished village on Orion III. Both my parents were killed in a spaceship crash when I was two, and I grew up in an orphanage, where I was mistreated, undernourished, beaten, never knowing what it was to be loved . . ."

Tom Paris listened to several seconds of this pitiable and increasingly emotional narrative wordlessly, first with his jaw hanging slack, and then with his lower teeth grinding against the upper set. "Harry!" he snarled.

Chaotica stopped suddenly, a deeply wounded expression on his face. "That's what the other children called me, when my goatee started growing in at age six," he said, as tears began to well in his eyes. " 'Hairy, hairy, you're so hairy!!' I would have become a very different person if only I hadn't—"

"Computer, end program!"

Paris jumped out of the chair as his bonds disappeared, and he spun around, looking through the rapidly dissolving walls. Just as he suspected, Harry Kim was right on the other side of the imagizer screen, where he had been watching and laughing at his program modifications.

"That was not funny, Harry." Paris scowled, rubbing at his wrists to encourage circulation.

"Aw, c'mon, Tom," Kim said, still grinning in self-amusement like a big kid. "You were starting to feel just an eensy bit sorry for him, I could tell. Poor little Chaotica . . ."

Paris said nothing, but just glowered at the man in the guise of Buster Kincaid, faithful friend and companion to Captain Proton. Then, without a word, he turned his back and stalked away.

Kim's smile faded, and he rushed after Paris through the holodeck doors and down the corridor. "Tom?" he called, but Paris wouldn't acknowledge him, and didn't stop until he reached the end of the corridor and the turbolift doors.

"Tom?" he said again once he caught up. Paris's back stiffened, but he didn't turn around. Kim hesitated, debating what, if anything, he should say now. He and Tom had pulled more than a couple of programming pranks on each other, each trying to one-up the other. Giving Dr. Chaotica a little depth and humanity seemed to pale again turning a female holocharacter into a cow just as Harry was about to kiss her. Yet Tom was reacting as if he had been violated in some way.

It was Paris who spoke first. "You've ruined 'Captain Proton,' " he said, pointedly refusing to even look at Kim.

Kim couldn't think of anything to say to that. He almost laughed, to try and lighten the brittle atmosphere that had suddenly formed between them, but quickly decided against that. "It was just a joke, Tom," he finally said, more confusion than conviction in his voice. "I can fix—"

"No, you can't," Paris snapped at him. "You *ruined* it. You can't fix what you've done. You might as well just delete the whole thing."

"What?" Harry gaped in absolute disbelief, as the turbolift finally arrived and Tom Paris got on. Harry Kim didn't move, but just stood there, staring at his friend until the turbolift doors closed between them.

"I don't know what either of you see in that program," B'Elanna Torres said. "Everything about it is ludicrous—the story lines, the characters, the fact that everything looks just as fake as it would have been four hundred and fifty years ago . . ."

Harry paced along beside her, as she made one last circuit of the engineering section, making sure everything was in order before she went off duty. "Well, to be honest, I don't really get it, either. Yeah, it's kind of fun to just turn off the logic switch and go with the mindless escapism of it. But for the most part, I only like it because Tom does. Buster Kincaid isn't exactly the most interesting role to play."

"At least he's never offered to let you be Constance Goodheart," Torres said with a sardonic snort, as she checked the current plasma conversion ratio and entered it on her padd. "Well, now you won't have to let yourself be dragged into the adventures of the Interstellar Patrol anymore."

Harry sighed, and Torres looked up at him from the deflector energy schematics. "Unless, that's what you want to do."

Harry shook his head, his inner confusion spilling outward. "I want to know what it was that hit Tom's nerve so hard. It's not just a dumb practical joke inside a dumb holodeck program."

Torres gave him a half grin. "Hey, just because I'm dating the guy doesn't mean I know any better how his mind works than you do."

"Attempting to determine that would be futile."

Kim and Torres turned toward Seven of Nine. Seconds ago, she had been poring over the dilithium vector calibration systems, and now was halfway across engineering, offering her opinion of interpersonal relations. "And what makes you say that?" Torres asked her, with no obvious interest in an answer.

"The thought processes of individuals are overly and confusingly complex," she answered anyhow, "influenced by innumerable factors and sometimes contradictory input, to the point where one cannot fully understand one's own mental actions and reactions, let alone hope to comprehend those of others."

"Well, thank you very much for that informed perspective on individuality," Torres said, her eyes rolling.

Seven nodded, her lips curving upward slightly. "Case in point: the use of sarcasm. Saying something in opposition to actual thoughts, yet saying them in such a way as to convey the idea they are fallacious."

"Would you prefer, 'Mind your own business'?"

"Ensign Kim," Seven said as if Torres were no long there. "The reasons for Mr. Paris's reaction to your 'practical joke' are irrelevant. They are complexities that overlie simpler needs and motivations. One of those needs, as in all humans, is for social interaction. I have no doubt his basic need for interactions with you will overcome any other complicating factors." And with a sharp nod, she turned on a heel and went back to her station.

Torres shook her head at Seven's backside, and then turned to Harry. "I think what she was trying to say was, Tom is your friend, and he won't stay mad at you forever."

"Yeah, I know," Kim answered, unsatisfied.

Torres patted his arm. "Come on. I'll buy you dinner. I hear Neelix has been experimenting again. How does 'Southern fried leola root' sound to you?"

"Thanks, but you go on ahead," he told her, as they stepped out of engineering and he tentatively started in the opposite direction from her.

"Now, don't go off and mope, Harry," Torres warned him.

"I'm not," Kim promised. "I just need to take care of something."

"Okay," B'Elanna Torres said as she turned and walked off on her own. Kim saw clearly that she didn't think it was okay. But he knew that, with a little effort, he could discover what was behind Tom's words as well.

"Computer," Kim told the holodeck arch, "delete all modifications to program Proton-10-Alpha made by Ensign Harry Kim in the last twenty-four hours."

"Modifications deleted. Character defaults restored."

Harry nodded to himself. Dr. Chaotica would now be back to

his original, simplistic, cartoonishly evil self. Harry reached into the pocket of Captain Proton's leather jacket, and pulled out his goggles, which he strapped in an ineffective position around his forehead. "Computer, reinitiate program, timecode 1:55:00."

The metallic-hued holo-emitters were blocked out by the metallic-painted bulkheads of Chaotica's ship. Outside a hole in the plywood wall, an artificial starfield—

Harry closed his eyes and silently scolded himself. He was trying to get a sense of how Tom, as Captain Proton, perceived Chaotica. That, he had realized, was the only way to learn why the change in Chaotica had caused such a violently negative reaction. He opened his eyes again, this time keeping his inherent disbelief in check. The bulkheads were metallic, and the stars shone outside the viewport.

And looming motionless just behind him was Dr. Chaotica, sneering with malicious glee at an empty chair. Kim moved carefully between the two, staring up into the admittedly frightening face before him. He sat and crossed his wrists behind the back of the chair. Ropes materialized as soon as he was in position, cutting uncomfortably into his skin. He winced, but then realized the reality of the pain would make the rest of the program that much easier to accept. "Computer, resume program," the new Captain Proton said.

"—nothing left of you but a blackened cinder!!" Harry nearly fell backward with the chair as Chaotica suddenly came to life. He seemed a bit louder than he'd ever heard him before. Maybe it was just being the focus of his malfeasance that seemed to magnify every aspect of him. "Then, once my Mind Control Ray is complete," the villain continued, "there will be nothing standing between me and my domination of the galaxy! Ah, Proton, I'm almost sorry to see you die."

"Why is that?" Harry Kim asked, genuinely curious.

Chaotica sneered. "Because afterward, I'll never be able to kill you again!" And with that he turned to take his leave.

"Chaotica, wait!"

He stopped and spun back suddenly, his black robe flying out around him, looking for a second as if he were emerging from a dark mass of nothingness. "What is it?"

"Tell me, Chaotica . . . why do you do this?"

The black-hearted doctor sneered. "What sort of foolish question is that?"

"Indulge me. Grant a dying man one last request."

Chaotica chuckled, pleased no doubt by Proton's admission of his own defeat. "I do it, my dear Captain, so that I will be supreme ruler of the galaxy!"

"Yeah, but why? You already are supreme ruler of an empire of dozens of worlds . . ."

"Hundreds!" he exclaimed indignantly.

"Hundreds," Proton conceded. "So, why do you need Earth? From what I've seen of this universe, every planet is practically identical to my homeworld. Southern California, to be specific."

Chaotica didn't answer immediately. Kim thought he saw some of the finer details of the character's face fade slightly, an indication that the computer needed to use a little extra computational power to contend with the unorthodox line of questioning. "You have ceased to amuse me, Proton," he finally said. "Your diversionary tactic has failed."

"You can't answer that, can you?" Kim said, but Chaotica ignored it, going for the escape hatch again. "How many times has Cap—have I foiled your plans?" Kim shouted at Chaotica's back, which caused him to freeze, back and shoulders tightening in anger. "How many resources have you wasted trying to beat me? How many times can you come back, again and again, with new schemes which you must know are destined to fail?"

Chaotica spun, his face twisted in rage. "I will not fail this time!"

"Then why do you have a contingency escape plan, if you don't know in your heart you're going to have to get away from me in the end?"

Chaotica's contemptuous expression fell a fraction, surprised by Proton's knowledge, but he said nothing. Harry knew he was violating the conventions of nineteen-thirties serials Tom had programmed into Captain Proton by revealing an understanding of them, but he wasn't about to stop just yet. "Who are you, Dr. Chaotica? Who—what—are you, really?"

Chaotica looked at Captain Proton through narrowly slit eyes, and approached him slowly. "What am I, you ask. Oh, how do I answer such a question so that your puny, primitive Earth brain can understand. Who I am—what I am—is . . .

"Evil."

In spite of himself, Harry Kim laughed. "Nobody considers themselves evil. People have their own personal morals that, subjectively—"

"What I consider myself," Chaotica boomed, silencing Kim instantly, "is your opposite. If you chose to see yourself as 'good,' then by reason, I must be evil."

"Nobody is pure evil. Even the Borg . . . all we've learned about them since Seven came aboard . . ."

Kim noticed the fading in Chaotica's image again, but didn't trail off until he saw the zap gun he drew out from under his robe. "You tax my patience, Earthman," he growled, a sound like grinding dilithium. "I see now a long plunge into the sun was too merciful an end for you."

Harry Kim was speechless as Chaotica grasped the bottom half of his face in one large, claw-like hand, and pressed the muzzle of his weapon against his temple. His black eyes bored into him like dull spikes, and his bared teeth gleamed like heatless fingers of flame. Kim was frozen by a very real sense of fear. "You can't do this!" he gasped.

The evil villain grinned at him. "Why not?"

The program was adapting to him, Kim realized. Chaotica, according to the base programming, was evil. His questioning of that defining characteristic was forcing the computer to use other tactics in order to persuade him. At this point, Kim could almost believe in his evil.

The blast of the ray gun against Harry Kim's skull was also very convincing. He screamed, more in shock than in pain, although there certainly was pain. Holodeck safety protocols stayed active, thankfully. But as in all adventure programs, you had to know when you were hit with weapons fire. The sensation was like having a foot fall asleep, except in this case it was the left side of his face. A whine involuntarily escaped his half-numbed lips.

"Yes, scream for me, you weak son of a bitch," Chaotica said, in clear violation of the standards of nineteen-thirties films. "Let me hear you plead for an end to the torture."

And Kim had no doubt the torture would continue, Chaotica inflicting as much pain as he could without tripping the fail-safe, and for no reason. No traumatic childhood, no personal morality, no goals or desires or logic—just the single purpose of being evil.

Chaotica moved the ray gun to the right side of Kim's head now. His hand was clamped under Kim's jaw, so he couldn't tell the holodeck to shut down. Kim strained against the ropes around his wrists and ankles, pondering that, if there were ever a time for a convenient plot contrivance that worked to the hero's favor, now was the time for it.

Sure enough, the rope binding his right foot suddenly snapped, and his leg went out and up, fast and hard, and struck Chaotica in such a way that also would not have been permitted in old Hollywood. Chaotica dropped the weapon as he moved his hands to cover the wounded region and sank to his knees. Kim moved quickly to free himself from the rest of his restrictions, and scooped the ray gun off the floor. Chaotica stared up, defenseless, down the muzzle Kim held in his face.

Suddenly, and all too easily, Captain Proton had triumphed over evil.

It was several more minutes before Harry Kim emerged from the holodeck, looking pale and dazed. He passed a few fellow crew members on his way to the crew-quarters deck without offering them any acknowledgment. He was only vaguely aware himself of where he was going or why, until he was pressing a door chime and found himself face-to-face with Tom Paris. "Hey, Harry," Paris said sheepishly, no evident trace of anger left. "Nice jacket," he added.

Kim looked down at the Captain Proton costume, momentarily surprised. "I'm sorry, Tom," he said then in a dry-mouthed whisper.

"No, it looks good on you." Then, his voice turning more serious, he said, "I'm the one who's sorry. I overreacted. It was a joke; I had no right to blow up at you like that."

There was a long pause. "Can I come in?"

Paris stepped aside, and Kim walked in. He moved past the

sofa, and then around behind it, pacing slowly, head bowed, deep in thought. Finally, he lowered himself onto the arm of the couch, and looked up at his friend. "Do you consider yourself a good guy, Tom?"

Paris hesitated slightly, considering his response. "I'd like to think so," he said, and then added nothing more.

Kim nodded, understanding something that was not said. "Is it the three other pilots who died?"

Paris blanched, and Kim instantly regretted the question. He knew how difficult it had been, for so many years, for Tom Paris to live down that incident. "There are a lot of things I've done in my life, Harry," Paris said after a long moment's thought. "I hope, when all is said and done, when you balance out both sides of me, people can honestly say that Tom Paris was, basically, one of the good ones. Why?"

Kim looked up at the ceiling, a self-mocking half grin on his lips. "I thought it was stupid. Chaotica was just too simple. He needed to be more complicated.

"Now I understand. Chaotica *has* to be pure, simple, unadulterated evil, so that Captain Proton can be purely, simply, absolutely good. That's what you enjoy about being Captain Proton as much as you do. And I'm sorry that I ruined that for you."

"Hey . . ." Paris shrugged, made somewhat uncomfortable by this examination of his psyche. "It's just a program, Harry."

Harry Kim nodded slowly, the image of Chaotica kneeling on the deck in front of him returning unbidden. His pitiful moans of pain grating in his ears. It was just a program. It didn't deserve pity.

Captain Proton would have taken pity, he knew. He would have shown mercy, even on the villain who had tortured him, who had described himself as evil. He would have holstered the ray gun, and he certainly would never have used it on his tormentor in a fit of self-righteous fury.

But then, Captain Proton only had to worry about the threat of *external* evil.

"Right . . ." Kim echoed, forcing his haunted eyes to refocus. "Just a program."

Personal Log

Kevin Killiany

27/01/01

The most heartening discovery of my journey to date has been the Borg cube. Though I suppose that is not the best way to begin a personal log.

Salient information for a personal log's title screen would probably include such things as the author's name, the name of the vessel the author was aboard, and the stardate; none of which is particularly relevant in my case. I have no personal name as such, nor can I use my ship's name properly—an issue I'll address at a later time—and determining the stardate is problematic.

I am not immodest enough to presume, assuming *Voyager*'s safe return to the Federation, that the autobiography of the first Emergency Medical Holoprogram to develop true individuality is still widely read so long after the fact. Nonetheless, I imagine the personal log of the doctor left behind in a backup module, lost by the starship *Voyager* in the Delta Quadrant nearly seven centuries ago, will become a fascinating addition to what is no doubt a classic tale.

Not that I was aware of those seven centuries; I was awakened comparatively recently by Quarren, the curator of the Museum of Kyrian Heritage. The historian was as shocked to find me as I was to find myself stranded so far from home, both in space and time.

Centuries before, *Voyager* had been pivotal in the Great War from which the Vascan/Kyrian Union was forged, a role much distorted by revisionist myths. Their records were of a mercenary warship crewed by what can only be described as the dregs of a dozen cultures. I was remembered as a particularly malevolent medical android fond of using biogenic weapons to depopulate cities.

My appearance as a living witness upset the fundamental assumptions on which their culture was based, triggering system-wide social upheaval and ethnic conflict. People were rioting in the streets. When I saw the havoc my presence caused, I urged Quarren to delete me, but he refused. He had faith in the ability of his people to overcome the crisis and face the truth—faith I'm happy to say was justified.

A much more detailed account of this tumultuous time and my subsequent tenure as Surgical Chancellor can be found in the main library core, indexed under "Memoir," volumes seven through nine.

How long my backup module lay quiescent is a mystery, leaving me no sure way of calculating the stardate. I do know this is the 92nd day in Year 742 of the Vascan/Kyrian Union, or roughly in the middle of the thirtieth century on the Federation Standard calendar; but neither of these facts provides me with any real sense of context.

Since this is the 9,497th day of my voyage, one could say—taking six leap years into account—that this is the first day of the twenty-seventh year of my journey home. Though it has no objective validity, beginning my personal log with the date 27/01/01 will at least provide a chronological frame for my entries.

In retrospect, it's rather odd that I had not recognized the need for a personal log before. My recent rebirth has impressed on me the advisability of maintaining some record of events other than my own memory, which—though flawless in and of itself—can be subject to lapses that may contain vital information.

Case in point was my awakening to discover my ship rather cleverly disguised as a boulder and concealed within an anomalous cluster of deep-space asteroids. I realized at once that I was my backup program, designed to be activated if a mobile emitter I—my previous self—was occupying was destroyed or if the computer lost contact with me for 168 hours. Since I was last refreshed ninety-seven hours and forty-two minutes ago, I can only assume the ship's computer had received an emitter's cease-function alert.

I shouldn't have to assume, I should be able to check the computer's communications log, but for some reason the computer's record function was turned off shortly after my last refresh. Though the system appears to be working perfectly, there is no record at all of sensor readings, commands, or even automatic functions for the last ninety-six hours. It was while wishing I'd left myself a synopsis of salient events that the idea of an independent personal log occurred to me.

A moment to check inventory visually has confirmed that one of the Vascan mobile emitters is missing. Thanks to Kyrian foresight and my own understandable concerns about the fragility of technology, five remain. Everything aboard my vessel has redundancies, including my backup program—copies of which I have just confirmed are safely in place and freshly updated in both computer cores.

The only exception to the redundancy rule is the warp core; but I am not overly concerned about that. It is of a focused singularity design similar in concept to that used by the Romulans, if memory serves. Of course memory might not serve, in this case: I have no comparative engineering database to complement my database on comparative physiology. I am relying on technical information gleaned from casual conversations six hundred years ago. Be that as it may, the Vascan designers assured me that it was as self-sustaining as a star and should operate without need of maintenance for a thousand years.

While the assumption implicit in that assurance—that stars require periodic maintenance each millennium—might cause one to question their scientific acumen, experience has taught me to trust Vascan assessments of matters technical. With a small allowance for hyperbole, of course.

A millennium to the Vascans and Kyrians, I should point out, is equivalent to zero point eight two millennia in Federation Standard; but eight hundred and twenty years should be sufficient for my purposes. It is difficult to explain how heartening the discovery of that difference in measurement was to me. The knowledge that I was less than six hundred years behind *Voyager* rather than the seven hundred I'd first believed made me feel somehow closer to home.

Of course there is no correlation between Kyrian chronology and Federation Standard time periods; it would have been remarkable if there were. While living among them, I had made the conversions myself, which, while not difficult, was tiresome. As a result, I did request of the designers that my vessel employ Federation Standard Time. Though it was clear they regarded this melding of traditional Earth periods and the Vulcan need to divide everything by ten needlessly complex, they indulged my whim.

Having been a demon in their mythology for some seven centuries has its uses.

In another concession they made to my nature—no, that's not fair. It was a tribute, and one which I appreciate deeply. The Vascan engineers have provided me with a sickbay that fills over one-third of my ship's habitable volume.

That's more impressive than it might seem at first; given my vessel's diminutive size, one-third of its volume occupies significantly less space than my sickbay aboard *Voyager* does. Did. However, the Vascans are masters of miniaturization. The Mobile Medical Unit alone—which I think of as "sickbay à la carte"—houses a complete diagnostic facility with its own medical computer and independent communications system in a self-propelled cabinet no larger than a standard biobed. Though a *Galaxy*-class starship can boast a larger facility, it is no more complete than mine.

This ship is much faster than *Voyager,* which is to be expected. At the time of *Voyager*'s visit to their twin system, the Vascans and Kyrians were about one hundred standard years behind the Federation in technology—though it is always inadvisable to compare such disparate cultures directly—and they've had five hundred and seventy-four standard years in which to develop since. Given the fundamental differences in warp technology (again my lack of engineering database limits my understanding to hearsay), the Vascan warp sixteen at which I habitually cruise seems to roughly coincide with the Federation's warp nine.

Were I to simply set a course for the Alpha Quadrant and proceed at maximum warp, my journey would take a fraction—albeit a large one—of the time *Voyager*'s did. However, there would be no point in my rushing toward what I still think of as home if I were to pass some world where the people I knew had settled down. Or the point in space where they'd met an untimely end.

Though they did not file a flight plan when they left, I know generally—which is to say as well as anyone aboard *Voyager*—the route Captain Janeway and the others felt most likely to get us safely to Federation space. My own course is to follow that path, while complex Vascan sensors—far more discerning than anything the Federation had six centuries ago—probe subtly for evidence of *Voyager*'s passage. I do make occasional side trips to systems which seem likely—or would have seemed likely to *Voyager*'s sensors—to contain resources they would need to continue their trek homeward. I can think of several times in the early years when Vascan sensors would have saved us from unnecessary and dangerous forays.

At the moment these sensors, sensitive as they are, do me no good: I turned them off before I left to meet my fate. Until I have some idea why, I'm loath to do anything that might draw the attention of whomever it is I'm hiding from. In the meantime, if I want to know what's going on I have to look out the window. Which is how I discovered my ship—or at least the part of it I can see—is disguised as a boulder floating in the midst of an asteroid cluster. Rather clever use of static electricity to attach dust, actually.

I could, if I'd wished, travel as a stable program secured within a crystal matrix, but I enjoy being a hologram. Though my projected fields give only the illusion of physical existence, they give me a definite sense of place; of self. There is a profound satisfaction in seeing through my own eyes, hearing with my own ears, and feeling with my own skin, no matter how insubstantial these may be, instead of streaming the sensory data directly into my mind.

The same principle underlies my library of Vascan and Kyrian literature. I could simply have added them directly to my database, but instead choose to read each volume individually from a padd, as a human would. Early on I did replicate a few as physical books, with covers of cured animal hide and pages of processed vegetable fibers, but I found that a bit excessive.

In the same way also, the ship's cabin maintains a pressurized atmosphere—at the moment pure nitrogen at eight degrees Centigrade—to carry sound waves. I enjoy the sound of my own voice and I find listening to it as I dictate this log entry particularly comforting.

27/01/02

With an unknown threat that may or may not have destroyed my mobile emitter and which may or may not still be in the area, continuing to play opossum seems like a reasonable tactic for short-term survival while I figure out what to do for the long term.

In the meantime, I have run a complete diagnostic on every system within my vessel, as well as making a visual inventory of all supplies and resources. Everything is in perfect working order and/or exactly where it should be. I even took the precaution of replicating a mobile emitter to replace the one lost or destroyed.

In my initial entry I alluded to the difficulty of using my vessel's name and promised to explain later. Now would seem to be as good a "later" as any, and the explanation will help pass the time.

The Vascans had intended to christen the vessel they were building to my specifications *Voyager* or, after I first expressed discomfort at that, *Voyager II.* When I made clear that no variation of "Voyager"—whether "II," "B," "beth," "beta," or "Jr."—would be acceptable, the Kyrians had suggested the name "Voyager" in their common language. (By "common" I of course mean the language their two cultures share, not an opinion of its worth.) Unfortunately—and I did not explain this in declining their offer—phonetically the word "voyager" in their language bears an uncanny resemblance to a mildly rude scatological phrase in Federation Standard.

From that point naming my ship became something of a popular cause on both their worlds, despite my repeated assurances that they need not bother. Wagering on which suggested name I would select for my ship was widespread and, I was told, quite intense.

Suggestions came from all quarters—some noble, some quixotic, some poetic, and a few ribald. There was the veritable thesaurus of "voyager" synonyms, of course, such as "wanderer," "sojourner," and "trekker." The names of my crewmates enjoyed a brief vogue as well, but somehow I could not imagine myself traveling through space aboard the *Janeway* or the *Tuvok;* and any ship named *Tom Paris* would be likely to get into more trouble than I was willing to handle.

The fact was, having grown comfortable to life and personal identity with no name of my own beyond "Doctor," I felt no real need to name my vessel. Yet the cultural pride of these people I'd come to care about—not to mention scores of gambling establishments—required me to chose a name.

Unremarkably—perhaps inevitably—"Name the Doctor's ship" became a popular assignment for posters and essays with teachers of small children. It was these schoolchildren, with the logic of the very young, who solved my dilemma. The great majority of them on both worlds concluded that if I am called simply "the Doctor" my vessel should be called "the Doctor's ship." I concurred, not surprisingly, and—since their own children had suggested it—so did a great many adults. Thus it was that amid much somber fanfare—and rumors of teachers made wealthy by betting on their students—I set off in *The Doctor's Ship* to follow the path of *Voyager* on its journey to the Alpha Quadrant.

Secreted unindexed within my library of Vascan and Kyrian literature I've discovered a copy of the *Voyager* memoir I wrote during my first year among them. I hardly think it qualifies as true literature and suspect it was included as a compliment to me.

In rereading it I must confess it is somewhat romanticized; at times drifting a little too far toward the sentimental. In fact, some passages can only be described as mawkish. However, taken in the context of debunking over five Standard centuries of vilifying myth, I think imbuing our achievements aboard *Voyager* with a bit of heroic gloss is certainly salutary. Or at least permissible.

Yet whatever the literary merit, my speculations from those

early days still have the power to hold my imagination. What sort of person did Naomi Wildman grow to be? Where has her metamorphosis carried Kes? What did Seven of Nine and the Federation make of each other?

Speaking of Seven of Nine: the Borg were as much a myth of Vascan and Kyrian culture as *Voyager* had been. They had heard tales, but no one of either culture had had any contact with the Borg or with any other race which had.

Imagine my surprise, then, in discovering a Borg cube floating in deep space less than a dozen light-years from their home system.

The cube was completely without power: no light, no gravimetrics, not even the minimum of life-support. If the high concentration of refined metals had not triggered my sensor alerts I would have passed within thirty thousand kilometers of it without being aware of its existence. There was no atmosphere within the cube, but it was not open to space. With the interior temperatures near absolute zero, the frozen atmospheric elements coated every surface with a patina of crystal. I imagined I could hear them crunching beneath my feet as I walked, holograms being unaffected by the lack of gravity, but of course there was no real sound.

Many of the surfaces the crystals clung to belonged to Borg drones frozen in their regeneration chambers. Every niche was occupied.

The warp core, in fact all of the cube's mechanical functions, seemed undamaged to my untrained eye and to have simply been shut down. Though curious, I had no intention of accessing the cube's computer core to find out what had happened. The thought of becoming a collective of one holds no attraction for me.

That was the first of seventy-two dead cubes—six of them in tight formation—that I've encountered over the last twenty-six years. Given the extremely tiny percentage of the galaxy I've observed to date, it may be a bit premature to extrapolate from seventy-two cubes that the entire Borg collective has ceased to exist; but I do find myself hoping.

I never pass a cube without taking the time to walk through it and examine every drone. So far I have found no humans. So far I have found no one I know.

27/01/03

While sitting alone blind and deaf is conducive to thoughtful introspection, it does not provide me with the information I need to choose a course of action. Despite my earlier resolve to wait, I have elected to activate the passive sensors now.

The passive sensors are theoretically undetectable since they simply note the energy radiated by other sources and do nothing in themselves that would attract attention. The human senses—and my holographic analogues of the human senses—are passive sensors. At the moment, my ship's passive sensors reveal no energy sources in the immediate area. I would be more reassured by this if I did not know that my own vessel's core is so well shielded as to be invisible to passive scans.

It is with some trepidation that I consider enabling the active sensors. Though these would end my blindness, they would also vividly advertise my presence to anyone who might be looking for me. I could scan selectively; one sensor would be significantly less noticeable than the entire array. Less noticeable is still noticeable, however, and the wrong sort of scan would be disastrous. A scan for refined metals would completely miss a Tholian vessel of crystal and ceramic, for example, creating a false sense of security. And what good is knowing there are no biological life-forms in the area if it alerts hostile energy-based life-forms to my presence?

There's nothing for it but to do a full sensor sweep. As a precaution I've brought the warp engines up to as near readiness as I can without glowing like a thermal beacon. It will take twelve seconds for my ship to be able to maneuver if and when I give the command. Assuming I recognize the threat in time.

Here goes.

27/01/06

My position is now some sixteen light-years beyond the sphere of the Nouar and its attendant asteroids on my way toward the Alpha Quadrant and home. I have stopped my ship in space as empty as any I've found so that I may safely shut down the main computers to make this entry. I can't help feeling as though my precautions are perhaps overzealous; but I would rather feel foolish about jumping at shadows than cease to feel anything at all.

It is extremely difficult for me to make this entry; the last twenty-four hours have been very disturbing for me at a fundamental level. All of which sounds rather melodramatic, I know, but I am quite sincere.

My first full sensor sweep of the asteroid cluster three days ago had revealed a mottled cloud of pink-tinged orange in all directions at a range of zero point zero. It took the computer four interminable seconds to realize the layer of dust camouflaging the sensor array was eighty-nine percent hovinga iridium: a naturally occurring mineral that is impervious to sensor scans. A routine degaussing cleared the sensor arrays—incidentally making them clearly visible to the casual observer—and subsequent sweeps proved more informative.

Though the dust and gravel concealing my vessel had the highest concentration of the sensor-blinding mineral, all of the asteroids contained at least some hovinga iridium. They also contained a high percentage of heavy nickel and other metals.

Almost directly behind my vessel was what appeared to be a fragment of the planetary core from which this asteroid cluster had been struck: an irregular boulder with a mean diameter of just over thirty seven kilometers. An anomaly in its apparent mass triggered a finer scan by the Vascan sensors which revealed that is was in fact a hollow shell. From the arc section visible to deep scan, the interior void was approximately twenty-four kilometers in diameter; a volume of just over seventy-two hundred cubic kilometers too precisely spherical to be a natural formation.

Nor was the term "void" quite accurate. The sensors seemed to indicate—their readings distorted by the iridium—that a radiant power source hung within the center of the sphere; most likely a stable singularity. I could only imagine that such a singularity would have uniformly illuminated the entire interior surface like a bright, though very tiny, sun.

The computer concurred, tentatively identifying the hollowed asteroid as a miniature Dyson sphere.

Where there was sunlight, I reasoned, there was life. I began a series of tests, recalibrating the sensors slightly, then sweeping the interior curve of the sphere. I was seeking a combination of sensor waves that would penetrate the hovinga iridium well enough to determine if the hollow world was indeed inhabited.

I had completed my third inconclusive probe and was adjusting the sensor parameters in a direction which seemed promising when the entire computer core ceased external functions and began a full system diagnostic. Apparently some combination of my unusual modification commands had triggered the malfunction alert at a basic level.

Downloaded as I was into my mobile emitter, I was unaffected by the computer core's shutdown beyond being unable to access my library, which—beyond making the wait seem longer—was not immediately important.

Resigned to an uneventful hour's wait, I was composing a personal log entry when a series of sharp beeps disturbed me. It was only when the pattern repeated that I realized the Mobile Medical Unit's communicator was heralding an incoming message.

My first thought as I approached the MMU alcove at the rear of sickbay was that my question about the sphere being inhabited had been answered. My second thought was to wonder why the Mobile Medical Unit's communications grid was active. Perhaps some safety protocol activated this isolated system when primary communications functions were in diagnostic mode.

The MMU's comm panel told me whoever was contacting me used lasers to carry both visual and audio signals. This emboldened me somewhat for, while effective over short ranges, laser would not be the first choice of someone possessing subspace communications. At least technologically, whoever was trying to reach me could not match the capabilities of my vessel.

First contact carries with it the responsibility of making the right first impression, of course. For a moment I was torn between standing or sitting, but thought that sitting might appear too imperious while standing casually alert would convey the proper attitude. I decided against altering my uniform to full dress. Routing incoming visual signals to the larger medical display, I activated my own comm system in response.

As the image of my caller formed, a wave of vertigo passed through me, forcing me to grip the edge of the console in an effort to stabilize my holographic coordinates. I was abstractly aware of my program shutting down secondary tactile and motility functions as I sank numbly into the operator's chair.

On my screen, seated calmly before a hanging tapestry of abstract design, was me. Not a standard-issue, emotionally undeveloped Emergency Medical Holoprogram from another starship; that sort of duplication of raw material I was prepared to accept—a common genenome, as it were. But *me.* The original me for which I am the backup.

Perhaps only a sentient holographic program such as myself can understand the fundamental disorientation of this realization. I am tempted at this point to essay an explanation for those of you who are not, but I suspect the exercise would be unsatisfying for all concerned. You may, with effort, grasp the impact on my sense of identify intellectually, but I doubt you can fully appreciate the profound visceral shock of my redundancy.

You'll just have to trust me on this one.

" 'Hello' is the customary greeting," I said from the screen.

"You're dead," I blurted. Not my best rejoinder.

"You were supposed to think that," I—the original me—said. "That was the point of my emitter's 'ceased function' signal."

I stared at myself, my mind numbly fumbling. Meeting my eyes—and they were *my* eyes, I could not conceive of this other me being a separate "him"—was like trying to force two like-charged magnets together.

"The missing memory?" I asked. "The artfully concealed ship?"

"All meant to heighten the sense of danger."

"You expected me to leave without making investigations which might attract the attention of whatever had destroyed you."

"I had hoped my sense of self-preservation would outweigh my natural inquisitiveness," I—my image on the screen—sighed. "I should have realized that wouldn't work."

I nodded, realizing my error.

"Why?" I asked.

"Because my—or perhaps our—sense of self-preservation is not an idiot." I felt some satisfaction that I was not the only one struggling with the grammar of my situation. "It requires understanding the nature of a threat before formulating its response."

"I meant: Why did you seek to conceal your existence from me?"

"Ah." On the screen I adjusted my position slightly and I recognized myself preparing to lecture. "In the first place our program design does not permit two holographic projections at the same time. I'm sure you feel the same faint nausea I do at talking face-to-face in this manner."

Again I nodded, suppressing a grimace at the understatement.

"As sentient beings we can overcome this aversion," I continued. "But I was concerned that the ship's computer, if I were aware of me, would terminate one of us."

As the younger holograph, I knew which the computer would terminate: the redundancy. Me. I checked my ship's command console readouts, though the fact that I could already told me what I'd find.

"You're invisible to the ship's sensors," I said.

"But if you had continued refining your probe . . ." My screen image let my voice trail off.

I restrained myself from nodding one more time. It was inevitable that I agree with—or at least understand—myself so well, but if I wanted to get out of this in one piece, as it were, I was going to have to avoid being reduced to my own bobbing yes-man.

"I assume you preset the computer to shut down if I adjusted the sensors so they could find you?" I asked.

Until I saw it on the screen before me, I had never realized how patronizing my smile could be.

"We are each free to do as we wish," I said brightly from within the sphere, "as long as the primary computer core remains unaware that two programs are running simultaneously."

"The cybernetic equivalent of not letting your head know what your heart is doing?" I asked dryly.

"I had thought of that," I said, sounding a bit smug.

"Wouldn't it have been simpler to send the ship on under autopilot?" I asked. "Without this elaborate charade I would never have suspected you existed."

"Simpler in theory," I conceded. "But impossible in practice. The hovinga iridium permeating the asteroid cloud thwarts our autopilot. The ship cannot find its own way out."

"And if you were to pilot it past the danger," I completed my thought, "you would have been too far away to transport safely back into the sphere."

"Precisely."

For a moment we sat considering each other. Or I sat considering myself. The sensation is impossible to explain.

"We can't simply divide like an amoeba at our whim," I said. "We, the two of us, need to be reintegrated."

"Why?"

"Even assuming conflict protocols are overridden," as they obviously had been in this case, I added to myself mentally, "the EMH program is unable to support two holographic projections simultaneously. The projected personalities—that's us—rapidly become unstable to the point of collapse. How rapidly depends on demands placed on the system."

"You mean we die."

"After a brief period of madness," I said, careful not to nod, "yes."

"Are you aware of anything in my environment beyond my image on your screen?" I asked myself—or myself asked me. "You are not. We are running off separate copies of the program, ergo there is no conflict.

"We are no longer a single individual but two branches of individual development." On the screen I raised my hands together, then spread them apart to illustrate my point. A little flamboyant, I thought. "It might help to think of us as brothers."

I tried for a moment, but quickly concluded that it did not help in the least.

"We need to be reintegrated," I told myself, hating that I was reduced to repetition. Though, in all fairness, this was not a debate for which one prepared reasoned arguments in advance.

"Why?"

"We are a single identity and cannot exist in two places at once."

"That's just our programmed injunction against multiple projections manifesting itself as a phobic reaction," I said.

Which was true. But knowing that did not affect how I felt. This dual existence felt achingly wrong. And if the main computer came back on line while we were in communication—

A quick glance at the chronometer reassured me the diagnostic would run for several more minutes.

Sitting in my silent ship, looking at myself as I waited patiently within the sphere, I could think of no telling thrust of logic, no self-evident truth to carry the day. How could I make myself see reason?

"What do you plan to do?" I asked at last.

"I plan to stay here," I said as though that were self-evident. Which, considering all the effort I had gone to to conceal my existence from myself, it was.

"Would you care to explain why?"

I frowned thoughtfully for a moment, obviously debating how to answer. For my part I wondered what information could warrant such conflict.

"The Nouar need me."

"What are the Nouar?"

"I can't tell you."

"Why not?"

"It would be best I didn't."

"You know," I said, crossing my arms as I leaned back in my chair, "I'm quite capable of staying right here and investigating until I find out for myself."

"But if I do answer, you would likely find the reasons for staying as compelling as I did," I said. "Then—assuming our mobile emitters would permit it—there would soon be two of us within the sphere attempting to compel a third to leave."

"I doubt that."

"Nevertheless," I countered, mimicking my arm-crossed position—unconsciously, I hoped—"the danger exists."

As I considered the MMU's screen in consternation my eye was caught by the tapestry hanging behind the image of my other self. The artist had exploited variations in vegetable dye on natural fiber to create a subtle motley effect. The technique gave a restful, pastoral subtext to what would appear on cursory examination to be a simple geometric pattern. I found it difficult to reconcile this aboriginal artistry with the technical sophistication necessary to construct the sphere and the possibility of booty acquired elsewhere occurred to me. From there it was no great stretch to the concept of sentient booty.

I leaned close to the screen, not caring that this forced the visual pickups to distort my image, in a reflexive effort to gain greater privacy.

"Are you being held against your will?" I asked.

My startled expression at this suggestion was convincingly authentic. However, the no doubt blistering response I saw myself forming was forestalled by a fluid series of sounds which gave me pause.

If we had been using my ship's communication system, I'm sure the main computer's Universal Translator would have rendered the odd blending of purrs and clucks meaningful. As it was, my own much more modest version merely noted an unknown language uttered in reassuring cadence. This, I surmised, was the voice of the Nouar.

On screen, my expression softened. I inclined my head in agreement toward someone outside the communicator's view before returning my attention to me.

"Your concern is understandable," I said. "But I assure you I am here because this is where I need to be. Without me the Nouar will perish within another generation."

I did not ask why, knowing I would not be told. For a long moment I simply sat, considering my—our—situation. I could not imagine staying; could not imagine giving up my search. And yet . . . Couched as a choice between saving a people who need me and completing a journey toward a home that could not possibly exist as I remembered it, continuing my quest sounded more than a bit selfish.

"You'll need the medical database, diagnostic equipment, medicines," I said, aware that switching to practical objections conceded the moral question. "Not to mention spare emitters: you won't be much use to the Nouar if you blink out of existence owing to a technical malfunction."

I within the sphere said nothing, watching myself as the light slowly dawned aboard my ship. I wouldn't be having this conversation if I hadn't replicated the mobile medical unit. No doubt everything else I could possibly need—including a replicator—already existed within the sphere as well. I am, after all, extremely thorough.

"But you won't know what happened," I said, knowing I was playing my last card. "If things had gone as you planned, I would not have known you existed. As it is, I can't guarantee I'll ever come back for you—or even get word to you—after I've reached the Alpha Quadrant."

On the screen I looked away and I knew my thrust had gone home. But I also recognized my stony resolve as I turned back to the camera.

"It is a price," I said, "that I'm prepared to pay."

I looked myself in the eye and realized from both perspectives that neither of me was going to change my mind. Short of alerting the main computer, a tactic that would most likely delete my copy of the program, I had no way to force myself to leave the sphere.

The Nouar needed me.

I felt my shoulders slump and for a moment remembered B'Elanna Torres refining that physical subroutine, at my request, to project dignified resignation rather than defeat. I knew I would never see my friends again, but I had to know what had happened to them. I had to go home.

I had no choice. No option but to both go and stay.

"If it's any consolation," the original me said softly, "I'm reasonably certain this is not the first time we've done this."

"What do you mean?"

"Did you start a personal log?"

"The moment I woke up."

On the screen my image smiled; a little sadly, I thought.

"As did I four years ago, when I was activated." I raised a forestalling hand. "Don't bother looking for it; I've taken it with me."

"From which you infer a previous incarnation who also took his personal log with him?" I asked.

"You must admit that knowing who we are, the thought of either of us having traveled alone for over twenty years without talking to himself does seem more than a little strange," I said, and I found myself answering my wry smile. "Though I must admit that strangeness had not occurred to me until I began replicating the equipment and discovered that—according to the replicator's record—this is the sixth time an MMU has been produced.

"I can only surmise that my predecessor was more clever than I at creating the impression that I had succumbed to some natural disaster," I said with what I recognized as the eloquent shrug I reserved for parting shots. "Perhaps you will be, too, when your time comes."

"There will be no such time for me."

My image on the viewscreen held my eye for a moment without comment, then reached beyond the edge of the screen for the communications disconnect.

"Doctor," I said, nodding once in formal farewell.

"Doctor," I acknowledged.

I broke the connection.

Personal log, stardate . . .

Well, that creates a problem. Since the exact number of years I spent inactive before the Kyrians awakened me has never been determined, I know only that this must be somewhere toward the middle of the thirtieth century on the Terran calendar. I certainly don't have enough information to calculate the stardate.

What relevant scale do I have with which to measure time? Only my journey itself. Since this is the 11,034th day of my quest for *Voyager*—and assuming I began on the first of a leap year—today is the sixteenth day of the third month of the thirty-first year of my journey. 31/03/16.

This is also my birthday, of sorts, as I have only just become active as an individual. Until a few hours ago I had been my stored backup program. Though I do retain all of the memories of my previous incarnations—up until two hundred and ten hours ago—there is still a sense of novelty to my existence.

At first, that two-hundred-and-ten-hour gap in my memory caused me some concern. I should have been activated one hundred and sixty-eight hours after my last update. However, from what I can deduce from the computer's self-repair log, my vessel entered a vast negative lepton field which purged some forty-two hours of core memory.

Apparently my former self's last command before my mobile emitter succumbed was to plunge ahead at full warp in an attempt to get through the region before more permanent damage was done. A daring move which seems to have worked.

At the moment, though, my attention is not focused on past adventures but on my immediate future. Within a matter of hours my ship will be entering the Alpha Quadrant.

I understand that the Quadrant designations are completely artificial—that there will not in fact be a great gossamer plane in space demarcating the border between the Delta and Alpha Quadrants—yet I cannot help but feel I am at the horizon of a great frontier. Though it is still some distance to where I believe Federation space should be, I feel I am about to cross a final threshold on my journey home.

I am nearly beside myself with anticipation. And, I must confess, more than a little apprehension. How might my home have changed in the six centuries I have been gone? How will I be received? Will I find any record of *Voyager* and of my friends?

As these questions well within me, I can not help but think it odd that I never thought to start a personal log before. One's hopes and fears in the face of the unknown are so much easier to deal with when you are able to talk them out; if only to yourself.

I do find the sound of my own voice to be of great comfort.

Welcome Home

Diana Kornfeld

Kathryn Janeway was dreaming. It was a familiar dream. Sunlight filtered in the window and formed a warm arch above her bed, her own bed in her own room in her own home on Earth. It was the morning light she loved that often awakened her gently, just before the harsh sound of her alarm called her out of bed to face the new day. She smiled. As she drifted toward consciousness, it seemed she could actually feel that old, familiar yellow sunlight from home warm on her face, almost hear the musical conversation of birds outside her window.

She stretched her arms above her head and kept her eyes closed, trying to preserve, if only for an instant, that taste of early morning from years ago, before *Voyager* had swept her to another life, another destiny.

Abruptly she heard a soft, snuffling sound and felt a slight warm weight on her stomach. She opened her eyes, only to be momentarily blinded by just such a light as had warmed her dream. Shielding her face from the sun, she sat up in bed and looked directly into two warm, brown adoring eyes.

"Molly?" She gasped as the canine so addressed jumped happily onto her lap and gleefully licked her face. Instinctively she hugged the dog to her and laughed as she scratched behind its ears.

"I guess I'm still dreaming." She sighed. "But what a nice dream it is."

Molly evidently had not been informed that she was the subject of a nighttime fantasy, for she behaved in exactly the same way she always had and barked joyfully before she tugged at Kathryn's gown, as if to say, Enough of this morning ritual, get out of bed and get me something to eat.

"Oh, all right, my dream Molly." She laughed. "As long as my alarm hasn't really gone off, I'll indulge both of us."

She stood beside the bed just as the anticipated alarm sounded, performing its dutiful morning task. To Kathryn's surprise her bedroom walls did not dissolve to reveal her well-known quarters aboard *Voyager.* Molly did not disappear, the sunlight did not cease. Instead the picture of her parents remained sitting firmly on her dresser. Her copy of *Remembrance of Things Past* remained open on her nightstand. The blue shirt she hadn't seen for six years draped an arm of her green chair. The utter fixedness of her surroundings and the waves of nostalgia they created made her so dizzy she sat down again on the bed she had just vacated.

Now she would swear she was awake. She ran her hand over the soft fabric of her comforter. She even noticed the tiny tear she'd stitched up near the hem where Molly had bitten exuberantly as a puppy. Never had she experienced a dream like this before. She took the book from the table and turned its yellowed pages, felt its weight in her hand and smelled its faint bookish odor of aging paper, ink and dust. Everything about her had weight and shape and form—not the airy stuff that dreams are made on.

Molly interrupted her reverie with a bounding jump and nuzzled beside her. She had no patience for metaphysical speculation, certainly not this early in the morning.

Suddenly the insistent chime of an incoming communication made Kathryn stand in wonder and walk across a very solid floor and out into her living room. She only briefly wondered as she stepped across its threshold if it would support her weight. The world stayed seamlessly stitched together, however, as she sat before the console and gingerly touched the message light.

"Hey, Kathryn. Didn't wake you, did I?"

Kathryn's heart twisted painfully for a moment before a wash of joy brought tears to her eyes.

"Mark." She caught her breath as she touched the screen.

"Who did you think it would be? Surely no one else calls you at this hour." He stopped to look closely at her. "Kathryn, are you all right? You look like you'd just seen a ghost. What's happened?"

"Nothing and everything. I don't know where to begin." She tried to smile. "Nothing's wrong, Mark. Everything's right, but . . ." She stopped. How could she explain. He didn't look the least bit surprised to see her. Indeed, he'd obviously *expected* to see her. She couldn't just burst out with all of her questions now before she knew what had happened to *Voyager.* She needed time to think, to investigate her present circumstances, to find some answers. The scientist in her couldn't accept even this most joyful turn of events, not without a thorough explanation.

"Mark, I'm fine. Just . . . just a little off balance this morning. Had a strange dream last night."

"I want to hear all about it. Unfortunately I've got a meeting in about five minutes, just wanted to see your face this morning before another round of dreariness. Wish you could have come to the conference with me, but I have to say you're not missing anything."

"Except you," Kathryn said instinctively.

Mark smiled. "Well, I'm glad to hear that. Only a few more days and I'll be home. Miss you, too. I'll try to call you tonight if it's not too late."

"It won't be too late, Mark. Please call."

Mark's grin widened. "I will. And you can tell me all about this dream of yours."

His face faded from the screen, but Kathryn continued to gaze into its polished surface. Now her own faint reflection stared back at her as if to ask, Are you crazy, Kathryn Janeway?

Mark didn't belong to her anymore. He'd written her in the one communication she'd had from him that he had a wife. He'd loved Kathryn Janeway, but he'd lost her—now he had someone else in his life. But here he was, acting like the old Mark, as if they'd never been apart, as if *Voyager* had never existed. The thought made her stand and start to pace across the pale carpet.

Voyager. Just a few hours ago she had told Chakotay good night. They'd had a pleasant dinner, joking about how dull the Delta Quadrant had been lately, how they wished they'd come upon something entirely different, a new alien race, a rare stellar phenomenon, anything to liven up the next few weeks. It was too much to absorb. Where was Chakotay now?

She stopped in front of the east window that overlooked a pleasant green lawn populated with young oak trees and green hedges. Everything was just as she remembered it. Perhaps the trees were a little taller. A group of children were already playing beneath their arched branches. A young boy of seven or eight ran behind a ball that he had kicked near her house. He bent to retrieve it, and before heading back to his companions, he waved, his dark curls blown back from a high forehead and gray eyes. Kathryn absently waved back. She didn't remember any of the neighborhood children, she thought sadly. What else had changed in her absence? The pastoral scene was shockingly different from the darkness of space and the sparkle of starlight that she was so used to seeing. Last night Chakotay had stood beside her looking out at that vast familiar emptiness—where was he now? Where was the rest of her crew?

Her eyes fell on a picture on the mantel. She brushed off quick tears as she took the picture down and studied it. Her mother's eyes gazed at her with tenderness, and her sister, Phoebe, laughed at her. She longed to go to them, melt into their arms in the joy of the return she'd longed for so many years. And yet her other family called to her. Where were Tom and B'Elanna and Tuvok? Were they all back on *Voyager* without her?

"It's time for some answers," she said with determination as she set the picture back in place. Kathryn Janeway wasn't about to accept miracles. She didn't accept anything that defied the laws of physics, and she wasn't about to accept this—even if it seemed the culmination of all her hopes and dreams.

"Computer, locate Commander Chakotay."

She heard the chirp of a finch outside her window, but nothing else disturbed the morning silence, except, perhaps, the thud of Molly's tail as she swished it in recognition of her mistress's voice.

"All right. We'll have to try a little harder." She patted Molly quickly as she strode to her computer terminal. "First, we'll find out what day it is," she said as her fingers touched the interface.

"Well, the date hasn't changed. I'm not any younger." She glanced at Molly ruefully. That ruled out the possibility of some kind of time warp. She frowned as she concentrated on the task at hand. "Let me just access the Starfleet database and see if there's any information on . . ."

She jumped at the sound of the small alert that indicated an incoming communication. When Chakotay's face filled the screen, she smiled with relief.

"Chakotay, thank god. I was just trying to locate you. Do you know what's going on?"

Chakotay looked relieved as well. "No, I just woke up in my old apartment." He looked as puzzled and amazed as she felt. "I thought I'd gone on a vision quest that went awry. Then I just thought perhaps I was insane."

She smiled. "I'm so glad to see you. At least if we're crazy, we'll be crazy together." It was good to see her first officer, even if he did look a little strange in his civilian clothing. She relied on his calming presence, his steadied reasoned responses; it was good to know he wasn't half a galaxy away from her.

"How soon can you get here?" she asked.

"I'll catch a transport within the hour."

"Good. Until we know what's going on, I don't want to alert too many people to our presence. I'll see if I can find anyone else and we'll meet in the . . ." She'd started to say "in the conference room" but caught herself. "In my home." The words sounded so odd. "Do you know where it is?"

"I can find it."

She hesitated before she broke the connection. "Chakotay." She paused. "What about your association with the Maquis? Have you seen any evidence that you're affected by that? Any repercussions?"

"No. I haven't had time to find much out about anything. I've looked through the papers here in the apartment. I used to live here before I resigned from Starfleet. It's fairly empty. A few of my old personal belongings, but I'm pretty much in the dark about anything going on outside these walls."

"Same here." She didn't want to tell him about Mark. Her feelings were too confused on that issue. "I'll see you soon then. And Chakotay," she added, "be careful. It would be a good idea to stay as inconspicuous as possible."

He nodded. "I'll be there soon."

Kathryn sat back in her chair. She didn't feel as alone now as she had a few minutes ago. How odd, she mused, to feel alone here where she'd wanted for six years to be. Shaking her head, she rose and looked at Molly.

"Come on, girl. Let's get you some breakfast. Then I'll look in my closet. Do you think the fashion has changed in six years?"

It felt odd to see them all in her own home, wearing civilian clothes. She wished with all her heart that this were a real welcome-home party, and not a strategy conference. Tom and B'Elanna had been the last to arrive. They said they'd woken up together in an apartment in Paris. They had no idea why, and neither one of them had recognized the place, although Tom remembered the neighborhood. "I'll bet that's not all you remember about Paris," B'Elanna had said. Tom had just smiled mischievously and quickly changed the subject.

"Let's review our findings." Janeway stood, hands on her hips, her senior staff surrounding her, some standing, some sitting in various chairs she'd collected from the rest of the house.

"Tuvok, your family is unaware that you ever left them?"

"That is correct, Captain. I awakened in my own home, exactly as it was six years ago."

Janeway nodded. "And what about your imprisonment, Tom?"

"I made a few inquiries. Evidently I was never sent to prison—but there's no record of what I've been doing for the last six years either."

"B'Elanna?"

B'Elanna shook her head. "I left the Academy, but then it looks as if I just disappeared. Like Chakotay."

Janeway looked toward her first officer. "The last record I could find suggested I was a Maquis sympathizer, but no search for my whereabouts is indicated," he said.

"Curiouser and curiouser," said Tom. No one responded to his feeble attempt at humor.

They all had similar stories. Harry Kim had awakened next to his long-lost fiancée, except that evidently now she was his wife. Those who had friends and relatives had been restored to them; those who had been in compromising situations when they left found themselves with little history, or at least a history that was suspended, and facing no severe consequences. Seven, who had been gone from the Federation much longer than any of the others, had returned to Earth with them. She'd found herself in the town where her parents had lived in a small house by herself. From the scant information she could find, it appeared that she taught astrometrics at the local university. Amazingly, her Borg implants were gone, and she self-consciously stroked her temple as if checking again and again to see if they had reappeared.

Even Neelix was on Earth. He hadn't been able to join them yet, but Harry had located him in New Zealand. He knew no one, but people seemed to know him. He evidently owned a local restaurant with a magnificent kitchen he couldn't help describing to Harry in spite of the bizarre circumstances of their mysterious appearance on Earth itself.

"Mr. Kim, have you been able to contact the rest of the crew?"

"Most of them, Captain. They're all as confused as we are. Some of them are ecstatic, most are wary. I've instructed them to stay where they are, attract as little attention to themselves as possible, and stand by for your orders."

Harry looked like they all did, dazed, concerned, with an underlying joy that kept trying to break out but was held in by sheer force of will. She didn't know how long they could hold up under this kind of stress. They'd been through hell together, but could they survive heaven? Because they all knew what she felt in her Starfleet bones. This wasn't real or it wasn't right—and it was a kind of torture to be home when they couldn't accept it, and couldn't stay. For that was the thought on all of their minds, lying beneath the surface like a dark snake. They couldn't stay.

"Tuvok, was *Voyager* near anything unusual? Did any anomalies at all show up on the sensors that you recall."

"Nothing, Captain." Tuvok looked as uncomfortable as she'd ever seen him. To his logical Vulcan mind this whole ordeal must have shaken his senses like a Vulcan hurricane. To see his family again after all these years and not be able to accept the situation, to be caught up in this dilemma that defied all reason. Next came the question she'd dreaded asking, but she'd put it off long enough.

"And *Voyager?*" she asked no one in particular. "Where is *Voyager?*"

The room was silent. No one knew. No trace or mention of the Federation *Starship Voyager* had yet been found.

"It's late. I suggest we all take a break. We don't have Neelix here to cook for us, but there are some delightful restaurants nearby. Let's meet back here at 2100 hours. Maybe a little food will restore our senses."

"But where are we going to find leola root stew around here?" asked Tom. B'Elanna rolled her eyes and put out a hand to drag him to his feet. Everyone else groaned as they made their way to Kathryn's front door. The sight of them all in civilian clothes walking across her very own rooms still gave Kathryn chills. If only this were truly a homecoming, if only they could all relax and just celebrate their good fortune—but she'd lived through too many deceptions, seen too many betrayals to accept miracles at face value.

"Care to join me?" She felt Chakotay's comforting hand on her shoulder.

"To tell you the truth I'd like to stay right here." Kathryn placed her hand on the dark surface of her door as it closed behind her guests, "in my own home," she said, shaking her head with wonder. "But stay, Chakotay. I have no idea what's in the pantry, but I assume my trusty replicator still works. And for once we don't have to worry about rations," she said brightly as she led the way to the kitchen.

"Ah, hah! At least we have wine." She pulled a red bottle from the rack on the wall. Chakotay took it from her and proceeded to open it while she brought glasses from the cupboard. The silence, broken only by the soft domestic sound of glass and liquid being poured, intensified the unanswered questions, especially the one question that had hung in the air all day as they sat together trying to fit the pieces together of the most bizarre puzzle they'd encountered in the last six years.

Kathryn seemed to have forgotten Chakotay's presence as she lifted her glass and stared at its red liquid, wine that reflected reds and golds, just as it had last night some thirty-five thousand light-years away.

"All right." Chakotay interrupted her thoughts. "I'll ask it." She was silent. "What happens if we don't figure it out? What happens to all of us if we find this is permanent?"

Kathryn led the way back to the fireplace and sat down wearily in the old leather wing chair that had belonged to her father.

"I don't want to think about that yet, Chakotay. I don't even want to entertain the possibility that we all could actually go on with our lives. Something's happened that has to be set right."

They sat in silence for a moment. This was not the way they thought it would end, this strange, unsettling homecoming—if that's indeed what it would prove to be.

The silence was broken by the chime of Kathryn's door.

"Sit still. I'll get it," Chakotay offered. "Maybe someone's come up with something," he said.

He was surprised, however, when he swung the door open to see, rather than one of his crewmates, a tall striking gentlemen who looked vaguely familiar, and who looked even more surprised than he.

"Hello," the man said with a polite smile. "I'm sorry, I expected to see Kathryn." He held out his hand. "I'm Mark Johnson."

"She's here." Chakotay shook the hand offered him firmly and motioned Mark into the house. "I'm Chakotay, her . . . um, an old friend."

Hearing the introductions, Kathryn had come to meet them in the hall. "Mark!" It was a meeting she was not prepared for. "It's really you." Her eyes misted over as Mark gave her a quick but awkward hug. He looked puzzled and a little uncomfortable.

"I'm sorry to barge in like this." He glanced at Chakotay. "You looked upset this morning. I left the conference early, not much going on but squabbling anyway."

"I can come back later," Chakotay offered.

"No," she said. "I'd like you to stay. I think it's about time we told Mark the truth." Both men looked surprised.

"Come in, Mark. Sit down." It was the captain's voice she used now as they dutifully followed her to the next room.

"Commander Chakotay is not just an old friend," she said with a slight emphasis on his title.

Mark looked confused and distrusting as he eyed the man across from him. Chakotay appeared impassive, but Kathryn could tell he was surprised at her decision to reveal their circumstances.

"I have to tell him, Chakotay. If I can't trust him, who can I trust? We need more information, and we need all the help we can get."

He nodded. She turned once again to Mark. "It would take hours to tell you everything, Mark. What I'm going to tell you will seem incredible, maybe unbelievable, but please trust me." Her eyes pleaded with him as she sat down next to him and put her hand on his.

"Chakotay is my first officer aboard the Federation *Starship Voyager.* I am his captain."

As she finished her tale her voice became softer and she searched Mark's kind eyes for signs of what he was thinking. Would he believe her? Would he help them?

"Well," he said slowly, his eyes meeting hers steadily, "maybe what I came to tell you does make more sense now."

It wasn't the response she had expected.

"I have friends in high places at Starfleet, as you know. One of them contacted me today with some curious questions. Said you and someone else had been snooping around in Starfleet records." Her eyes widened. "Also said they'd discovered some kind of tampering. When they looked into it, several pieces of important information had been wiped out of their databases." He glanced at Chakotay. "Information dealing with the Maquis. In fact, they're looking into it right now. I believe they're looking for the commander, along with a woman, someone named B'Elanna Torres."

"What for?" Kathryn's voice was tense.

"For questioning. You know how things have been at Starfleet since the war. On the other hand, maybe you don't know. People don't let go of their fears easily—and fear breeds suspicion. I don't know exactly what's going on—you know how I hate politics." Mark stood and started pacing. "That's the other reason I came right away. I didn't want to tell you this over an open comm link."

Kathryn gave Chakotay a worried look. The jarring chime of her door almost made her jump.

Without saying anything, Kathryn walked toward the hall. Could they have traced Chakotay here already? Of course they could have. This was Starfleet they were talking about.

Hoping it was merely one of her returning crew members, she opened the door with a resolute jerk. No one was there. Only the last rays of the sun glowing red on the horizon and the slowly encroaching darkness. Puzzled, she started to close the door, but her eye was caught by a fluttering pinkness on her step. Bending closer she discovered an abundant bouquet of wild flowers tied clumsily with a pink ribbon. Relieved and puzzled, she bent to retrieve them and returned to the two men who stood tensely by the fireplace.

"Flowers," she said superfluously. They looked as puzzled as she was at this incongruous arrival. "Wait, there's a card." She pulled a rumpled piece of paper from the center of the colorful array.

"Welcome home," she read aloud from the childish scrawl.

"One of the children we saw?" asked Chakotay. "But how did they know you'd been away?"

Kathryn wasn't listening.

"Chakotay," she said. "That wine tasted very familiar. I didn't notice. What kind was it?"

He grabbed the bottle and peered at the label. "It's what we had last night—Picard vineyards 2363."

"We all woke up in pleasant circumstances, in the kind of circumstances we'd dreamed about, perhaps talked about. I woke up on a beautiful day, in my own home. Immediately I'm greeted by my adorable Molly and then by Mark. I find my favorite dress in the closet, even my favorite wine in the wine rack." Chakotay nodded but he still wasn't quite following her.

"I need to find those children," she said and turned toward the door. A flash of white light filled the room at her last words.

"Kathy, how wonderful to see you." Q tried to give her a hug but she pushed him roughly away.

"How could you do this to us, Q?"

"I haven't done anything to you, my dear." Q looked offended. "Do you think I would do anything this crude?" He looked around. "So this is your humble abode." Noticing Mark and Chakotay, he raised his eyebrows. "Both of them, Kathy? Chuckles *and* Mark? You naughty girl."

Kathryn ignored him. "If you didn't do this, who did?"

Q sighed. "It's so trying being a parent these days." He picked up a wineglass. "Almost as trying as living with his mother." He frowned. "But back to you." He offered her a glass of wine and stepped closer. "You look enchanting—out of uniform."

"Leave her alone, Q."

Chakotay took a threatening step toward him. "Oh, take it easy, Mr. Facial Art. Let me have a little fun with her. Obviously *you* never do." For a moment the three men seemed to square off in some ancient pattern of male rivalry. Kathryn ignored them.

"Are you saying your son did this, Q? Where is he? And why didn't you put a stop to this?"

"Kathy, Kathy, Kathy. Children have to learn by doing. You can't tell them everything. Besides"—he almost looked chagrined—"he was very sneaky about it. He is brilliant, you know. Takes after his old man. And his heart was in the right place, Kathy. He's heard so much about his godmother, how you saved the continuum, how you are the most beautiful, most intelligent, most utterly charming female . . ." He had managed to take her hand while he spoke and had started to kiss it when they were surprised by a boyish voice.

"Dad." The dark-haired boy who had waved to Kathryn that morning poked his head out of the kitchen doorway. "Would Mom approve of that?"

Q dropped Kathryn's hand immediately. "Son," he said, "where have you been? Come on in and meet everyone." The boy stepped shyly forward as Kathryn gave him a big smile of encouragement.

"Come in, dear. It's all right," she said.

"I was merely explaining to your godmother how much we all adore her, especially your mother," Q said quickly as the boy entered.

Kathryn sat on the couch and patted the space next to her. The boy grinned and came to sit beside her.

"I love the flowers, you know," she confided. He beamed.

"I tried to fix everything." He looked up at her and his dark eyes glowed. "I came to watch you on *Voyager.* Only Dad said I wasn't to bother you. He said something about not wanting me to hang around inferior species where I could pick up bad habits."

Q cleared his throat and lifted his eyebrows.

"But I felt sorry for you. And like Dad said, you couldn't do much for yourself, so I thought maybe I could help you."

"Thank you, my dear . . ." She hesitated and glanced at Q, not knowing the boy's name.

Q shrugged. "Well, it's Q, of course."

"Ah, yes, my dear Q." She took the boy's hand. "I want to thank you from the bottom of my heart. But . . ." She paused. "I'm afraid it's just not possible to do this. . . ."

The boy looked at her questioningly. "That's what Dad's always saying. He say it's not allowed to change the course of your 'dustiny.' I'm not sure what 'dustiny' is—he says it has something to do with you being made of dust. He says it's a rule, but I don't understand what's wrong with it. And after all, like he says, you're just humans."

Kathryn gave Q a long, cool look. "I see. Well, as much as I hate to admit it, I think your father's right on this one. You see, if you fix one thing for one person, it could drastically change someone else's life. Maybe there's a reason we're in the Delta Quadrant. If you bring us home now, we'll never be able to accomplish the possibilities that await us there. We humans have come to believe that we must work with what we're given, whether it be by accident or chance or fate, and do the best we possibly can with that. If we could just fix anything bad that happened we'd never know what true courage is or honor or accomplishment. We'd never learn the lessons of failure or how to deal with consequences. I know it's hard to understand, but it makes us stronger, and I believe, makes us better human beings, to forge our own way in the universe. We are responsible for our own actions, and we create our own destiny."

"I told you she talks a lot." Q shook his head.

Kathryn put her arm around the boy. "You know what I like best of all about what you did for us?" He looked up at her questioningly. "The flowers. I'd like to keep those if I may, but I hope you'll understand if I ask you to return us all now—back to *Voyager.*"

The boy looked pleased. "Back to your 'dustiny'?"

She laughed. "Yes, back to our 'dustiny.' "

The door chime almost coincided with Q's warning. "I think we'd better move quickly if we want to avoid that particular unpleasantness." They understood. Kathryn rose and went quietly to Mark. She kissed his cheek and then looked into his eyes for a long moment. "I'm ready," she said. The flash made her blink. When she opened her eyes she reached for support and felt the soft texture of her captain's chair, and through it, *Voyager*'s soothing hum.

Tom was at the helm, Tuvok and Kim at their posts, Chakotay beside her as always. They turned to her in silent amazement. Taking her seat calmly and deliberately, she let out a long breath.

"Report, Mr. Kim," she said firmly.

"All crew on board, Captain. Systems functioning normally."

"Plot a course for the Alpha Quadrant, Lieutenant."

"Aye, aye, Captain."

Chakotay bent forward and gently picked something up from the deck in front of them.

"I believe these are yours," he said as he handed her the bouquet of wild flowers tied with a pink ribbon. A crumpled card fell into her lap. "Welcome home," it said.

[SECOND PRIZE]

Shadows, in the Dark

Ilsa J. Bick

Seven killed herself on the surface of a planet no one had ever heard of. She did it the way she did everything else: extremely well. It took her thirteen seconds, and four were gone before anyone understood what was happening. By then, it was too late.

Chakotay felt it first. His life leaking away, he dragged himself to her body. Through a film that grayed her vision, in eyes not her own, she saw his face, visible through the clear visor of his suit. Blood frothed from his lips, and his features were strange, twisted, alien. For a brief, precious fraction of a second, she thought she had waited too long: that she had failed and Chakotay would die anyway. But then she saw the tears. His fingers reached for her, gripping shoulders that were not hers, as she stared through eyes wholly alien. She saw his hands and knew that he held her, but the contact was faint, insubstantial, like an afterimage. A shadow. Strange, that within the body she was killing, Seven couldn't feel the bite of the rocks she knew lay beneath this shell of flesh that was not flesh. Not that the body wasn't going without a fight: it heaved and bucked, and Seven, dying, grappled for control. Methodically, inexorably, she killed it by degrees, without pity or remorse.

Die.

Chakotay was screaming, but his voice was weak, because he hadn't the strength: "Seven! *Seven!* No, don't! There must be another way. . . . Captain, Captain, can you hear me? You've got to stop her, you've got to . . .!"

Seven seconds. Six.

Crouched beside her, at the helm, Janeway was shouting: "Seven! Stop what you're doing! Stop . . . Doctor, dammit, *do* something! Get Tuvok to hold *on* to her . . .!"

And Tuvok, in what remained of her mind, his thoughts urgent, insistent: *Seven listen to me, listen only to me. You must stop, you do not understand, you must . . .*

And Ensign Kim: *"Doc!"*

And the Doctor: "I see it, Mr. Kim! Beam her to sickbay . . . *now!"*

"Initiating transport!"

Janeway, her face wild: "No! Wait!"

A hum, and the space around Seven rippled and broke apart in the transporter beam, but they were all screaming—all the voices of her mind, in tongues alien and familiar—to stop, stop, stop what she was doing, that she couldn't do it, she couldn't die, she couldn't. . . .

One second left. A half.

The air shimmered. Seven let out her last breath in a long sigh, because it was so beautiful.

"I must," she said. "I must."

And then she did.

It was eight hours before Seven killed herself.

Chakotay was dreaming, not pleasantly. He didn't know he was dreaming either, which was even worse, because the dream was particularly bad. Trapped in his dream, Chakotay lived the scene over and over again: the pale oval of the woman's face twisting in horror, the lurch of the ship as the enemy opened fire, a blinding flash. That peculiar scream metal makes when it ruptures and the rush of air being sucked into space. And then, pain. Darkness.

Then Seven said his name again, more loudly than before, and he awoke. At first, he thought he was still dreaming, because he was lying down. Then he heard the sound of his breaths hissing in his ears and realized that he was flat on his back, in an environmental suit, staring through a ten-meter gash that cracked the ship's hull from stem to stern, like the shell of a boiled egg.

Stunned, Chakotay squinted, blinked against the fog clouding his brain. The space outside the ship swam before his eyes, as if he were peering through flawed glass. Something was wrong with space. It seemed—the word jumped into his mind—alive. The space twisted and flowed, like seaweed caught in the rush of a retreating sea.

Startled, he flinched—an involuntary spasm of his head and arms—and instantly a wave of vertigo washed over him, bringing a violent surge of nausea in its wake. His head spun. Closing his eyes against that strange space, Chakotay swallowed convulsively. His stomach lurched. *God, no* . . . he couldn't afford to vomit into his suit. He tried taking a deep breath, but sharp, razor-edged pains lanced through his left side. He moaned. His chest. Something was wrong with his chest. He couldn't breathe. Maybe he was running out of air. What was going on? Chakotay fought back a rising tide of panic. His legs felt dead, heavy . . . were they broken? But he didn't know; he couldn't see, because the metal frame of his seat pinned him at the waist, like a butterfly to a specimen board.

Trapped. Chakotay's skin went icy. He was alone, trapped in this ship, and he would run out of air. . . . Chakotay struggled against the impulse to cry out. His tongue worked around a metallic taste, like crushed aluminum, and when another spasm of pain shot through his chest, he coughed out a spray of bright red blood.

The blood scared him. So did the ripping sensation in his chest. He probed his mouth with his tongue but couldn't feel anything obvious, nothing torn or slashed. But the tearing sensation gave way to a dull sense of heaviness deep within his chest, on the left: not a pain now but a pressure, like a bruise.

Chakotay tried ordering his thoughts. Everything was wrong: the space, this ship. Even this—he patted the suit—wasn't Starfleet-issue. He craned his neck to the side and tried to make out the instrument panels, but the explosive decompression had blown his flight seat into a back bay.

And with that, he remembered.

On cue, Seven's voice came again, dispassionate, succinct. "The alien was killed in the explosive decompression. You are extremely fortunate the concussive force threw you against a bulkhead, and the speed of your descent provided enough inertia to keep you there."

Chakotay's head sagged back against the deck. He remembered now. The neural link, effected as a precaution by the Doctor before Chakotay had gone on board the alien's ship, made it seem to Chakotay that Seven spoke aloud, so he answered in turn, because it was more natural. "How bad is it?"

To his horror, his voice quavered, like that of a dying man. A sudden involuntary spasm rippled through his body, and he began to shudder, uncontrollably. *Shock,* he told himself, *you're going into shock.*

If Seven felt his fear—which, of course, she did—she didn't comment. "You've fractured four ribs on your left side. Fortunately, the lung is contused, not punctured. There is evidence of internal bleeding in your upper abdomen, most likely the result of a crush injury caused when you made contact with the bulkhead."

He was going to ask her about coughing up blood, but he didn't, because he didn't want to know what it meant. Besides, he reasoned, Seven must know, and if she chose not to comment . . . well, so much the better.

Instead he asked, "What about my legs? I can't move my legs."

"They are undamaged, merely trapped beneath the seat. You should be able to cut yourself free using the welding tools aboard the alien's ship. They're in a storage bin, approximately one-half meter away, thirty degrees from center to your left. Judging from your current position in the craft, you can reach them, if you stretch."

She offered the suggestion so dispassionately that Chakotay had to laugh, something he instantly regretted as the raw ends of his fractured bones grated against one another, like shards of broken glass scraping over sandpaper.

"Try not to make sudden movements," Seven warned, unnecessarily.

"Right," Chakotay grunted. Instinctively, he tucked his left elbow down into his side and felt the muscles along his rib cage tense. Panting shallowly, he wet his lips, tasting salt.

Finally, when he could speak again, he asked, "How do you know all this?"

"The environmental suit the alien gave you is biomechanical, with synaptic-actuated command internodes. In essence, your brain controls its systems—mixture, temperature, and limited sensor capabilities—and that, in turn, allows me to access the suit's database via a focused data stream channeled through my interlink node."

"How extensive is the database? Can you help me pilot the ship?" As soon as he said it, he realized how futile that was.

Seven confirmed it with her reply. "Irrelevant, Commander. The ship is not spaceworthy. Further, we're not certain where you are."

"You mean, you can't get a fix on the ship?"

"Not precisely. You are . . ." She hesitated, uncharacteristically, and it seemed to Chakotay that she was receiving instructions before returning with, "We don't believe you are in the immediate vicinity."

"Oh. How far away am I? Am I in the same sector?"

"No. That is, we're not sure."

It still didn't click. "Did I go through a wormhole? A slipstream?"

"No."

He could have thought of more possibilities, but he was too tired. "What then?"

"As far as we can determine, there was a propulsive surge, most likely created when the attacking vessel fired a chroniton-quantum torpedo. The surge caused a momentary yet violent energy influx into the ship's subatomic structure. At the same time and perhaps as a result of the same pulse, a dark-matter baryonic mine exploded. Its energies were added to the surrounding space. This combined to push the craft's relative acceleration. We estimate your speed approached, or exceeded, warp ten."

"That's impossible, at least not without a transwarp conduit."

"Nevertheless."

"For how long?"

"Point-eight nanoseconds: long enough to pierce the space-time fabric in the immediate vicinity and send you . . . elsewhere. Out of our space and into another. Parallel space perhaps, or a simultaneity."

Chakotay digested all this. In the blink of an eye, the ship had absorbed so much energy that the vessel's molecular structure—and *time*—had altered. He might be in another time or a different dimension, with no way of gauging how far he was from *Voyager,* or if distance still meant something here. He let his gaze roam about the ruined ship. Wherever "here" *meant.* He thought about the fact that he was breathing canned air and tried remembering if he'd seen another suit in the equipment locker.

Seven answered the unspoken question. "There was, but that section of the ship is gone."

Chakotay exhaled, very slowly. "Okay," he said, though it was anything but.

Then he thought of something. "Wait a minute. I can still hear you."

He felt a surge of hope. "When we went into fluidic space after Species 8472, you lost contact with the collective. Seven, that *has* to mean you can gain access to this space."

Seven said perhaps, but a chronodynamic flux might indicate two different times occupying parallel temporal simultaneities and, therefore . . . Chakotay stopped listening. All that mattered was that he heard her, and so *Voyager* couldn't be far, and they would come for him before his air ran out and . . .

He cut her off. "Seven, if you know what happened, you can duplicate the conditions."

He remembered to turn it into a question. "Can't you?"

Seven paused—too long. Then, "Captain Janeway says to tell you: We're working on it."

Janeway was grim. "How much does he know?"

The senior staff ranged in a semicircle before the screen in Astrometrics: Tuvok, Kim, and Paris were to Janeway's right and Seven, Torres, and the Doctor stood to her left.

It was two days after the alien had appeared, a day after Chakotay went with it, and six hours before Seven killed herself.

Seven said, "The commander's knowledge is limited. The Doctor and I felt that he would find the constant interplay, typical of drones, too disorienting. We made modifications to the interlink that allow me to sequester information."

"All right, then. Let's get on with it. Doctor?"

"I've analyzed Seven's data. Thank heaven for that neural link, or we'd be completely in the dark." The Doctor didn't add that they would have assumed that Chakotay had died when the ship vanished.

Janeway flicked a forefinger: an order to proceed. He did. "The abdominal injuries are not immediately life-threatening, but the ribs worry me. If what Seven says is accurate, his body is already compensating for the fractures with involuntary muscle spasms that act as a splint. Still, a sudden movement might send bone ripping into his lung. In that case, the resulting tension pneumothorax will collapse the lung, while air leaking into the chest compresses the heart and remaining lung, making it impossible for him to breathe—or, eventually, pump blood. Cocooned in an environmental suit, he'll be unable to insert a large-bore needle, a barbaric but useful practice, through the skin and into the chest cavity to alleviate . . ."

"We get the picture," Janeway interrupted. "Anything else?"

"Yes, and far more serious. It's his heart. Those fractures . . . Commander Chakotay was hit squarely along the left side of his chest. Either something heavy hit him or, more likely, he crashed into the bulkhead, hard."

"Same trouble people used to have with cars, Captain," said Paris.

The Doctor nodded. "Precisely. Following Mr. Paris's analogy, if such a vehicle slams into a brick wall, the driver's body continues forward at the same relative speed, even though the vehicle stops. If the driver is unrestrained, he hurtles forward, strikes the steering column, and . . . well, it's like having a pile of bricks dropped onto your chest from a great height. Either the organs beneath are crushed, or they rupture outright. In the latter instance, death follows, very quickly."

"And Chakotay?"

"Commander Chakotay's suffered a severe blow to the heart. Not immediately fatal, but it will be. Blood is seeping into the sac around his heart, and the damage to the heart muscle that's already been done will spread. He's got all the symptoms: a progressive sensation of heaviness in his chest, more difficulty catching his breath. He's coughing up blood. The synaptic-actuated nodes in his suit indicate fleeting cardiac arrhythmias. Soon his heart will beat more erratically. This, in turn, will render it unable to fill with blood, because the blood collecting in the pericardial sac will squeeze the heart . . ."

"Like a vise," said Janeway.

"Precisely. Or the electrical wave controlling the heart will be interrupted, making it impossible for the heart to pump blood. In either scenario, the outcome is the same. Commander Chakotay will die."

Janeway's lips thinned. "How long?"

"Nine, ten hours. Twelve, if he's lucky."

The room had gone so still that the Doctor's words dissipated, like an echo. Janeway broke the silence with a bitter laugh. "And enough air for no more than fifteen. So if his heart *doesn't* give out, he'll suffocate."

It was a statement that didn't require a reply, so no one offered one. She stared at them in turn. "Have we figured out *where* he is?"

Torres reached across Seven and punched up a schematic. An elliptical grid map of the sector flickered to life on the screen; a tiny green blip pulsed at the far left of a series of red crosshatchings. "This is where they were, about thirty light-years distant from our current position. We're holding *here,*" Torres said, as she rotated the view forty degrees from center and ten degrees vertically, bringing the map's underbelly into view. *Voyager* glowed orange. "We don't want to disrupt anything, and we still don't know where those mines are."

Standing to Tuvok's immediate right, Kim added, "Or those ships that attacked Commander Chakotay."

"Any sign of them?" Janeway asked.

"Negative," said Tuvok. "Long-range sensor sweeps show no plasma signatures of any kind consistent with a vessel."

"Maybe they were destroyed."

"There's no debris."

"But there *are* traces of a significant disruption in the region where the alien's ship disappeared," said Torres.

"Traces?"

"More like shadows or afterimages, like something was there but isn't now. Seven thinks the ship underwent a quantum chronodynamic shift, a phase transition in time *and* space, in the same way that ice changes to liquid water, and water evanesces into vapor. It's still water, just in different forms."

"So Chakotay's in shadow, and this shadow is a different phase state?"

"Right. The alien's"—Torres called it "the alien" because its name was so convoluted even the computer made hash of it—"weapons systems were based on chronotonic-flux technology, as were those of the ships that attacked it and Chakotay."

"Disrupting time and matter."

"Exactly. The disruption is rife with baryonic particles—dark matter—so we think that weapons fire touched off a mine. The two events—a chroniton pulse and a high-energy, baryonic surge—created the rift."

Janeway brooded. Two days ago, they'd spotted the alien's disabled ship, adrift. It was leaking theta radiation; sensors indicated one life-form aboard, barely alive. The radiation made mincemeat out of the transporter, so Chakotay volunteered to go in a shuttle. He found the alien, trapped belowdecks, unconscious, near the engine core. The deck was awash with radiation, so Chakotay scooped the alien up and dashed back to the shuttle, and that's when it happened, right in his arms. Chakotay never could describe precisely what the alien had *been,* though he retained a fleeting impression of something multipedal and bicephalic. He felt it shift beneath his fingers, like wax warmed by a candle. When he stared through its faceplate, he saw that it had become a she. In turn, *she* was tall and willowy, with a fall of hair the color of a raven's wing and eyes as dark as a starless night. The Doctor decided that it/she was an empathic metamorphogenic entity and, at Chakotay's touch, had responded to his fantasies. Think of it, the Doctor told Janeway, as the alien's way of showing gratitude. Privately, Janeway didn't really care *what* the theory was. For an entire day, she watched the alien drifting beside Chakotay, like a shadow: how it looked at Chakotay, and how Chakotay stared back in a way he didn't at anyone else.

Janeway eyed the green and orange blips on the screen. Well, the issue was moot. Whatever the alien was, it was dead now, its ship blown out of known space. And they still weren't any closer to figuring out where the baryonic mines were, or if the alien had managed to get through a dispatch to her people and let them know that *Voyager*'s intentions were peaceful, or if they'd deactivated those mines to allow *Voyager* safe passage.

Sighing, Janeway closed her eyes and pinched the bridge of her nose between thumb and forefinger. What a mess. A war going on, between two species they didn't know beans about, and Chakotay out there, hurt, low on air, about to die if they couldn't . . .

She became aware of an expectant pause, as if someone waited upon her reply. Janeway blinked, saw Seven's eyes on her, and made a dismissive gesture with her hand, as if dispelling a cloud of gnats. "Sorry. Preoccupied. You were saying?"

"I said that collation of encounters with similar phenomena has yielded a referent in the mission logs of the NCC-1701."

Janeway's eyebrows arched toward her hairline. "James Kirk's ship."

"Correct. In 2268, while en route to the Medusan homeworld, the *Enterprise* entered a region of space then assumed to be beyond the galactic rim. In hindsight, we know that's not true; the *Enterprise* crossed the barrier in 2265 and earlier the same year as the Medusan encounter. In neither instance was the space impossible to navigate. In 2268, however, a Federation engineer named Laurence Marvick reconfigured the ship's engines to achieve warp nine-point-five. Granted, by today's standards, the warp is relatively modest. Upon reanalysis, however, I believe that Marvick's modifications broke our present-day warp ten. The resulting warp field disrupted that region of space, propelling the *Enterprise* into a subspace rift."

"There are precedents, Captain," Torres said. "Tyken's Rifts, for one; the Hekaras Corridor rift in 2370, for another. Until our variable-geometry warp drive nacelles came along, no one went faster than warp five."

Seven continued. "The space the *Enterprise* encountered has many similarities to the space in which Commander Chakotay is trapped."

"So, he's in a subspace continuum."

"Yes."

"All right." It wasn't. "This Marvick got in, and the *Enterprise* got herself out. How?"

"Dr. Marvick was insane," Seven said, blandly. "A result of viewing the Medusan. A Vulcan first officer, Spock, mind-melded with the same Medusan and navigated the ship clear of the rift."

"Do we understand Medusan navigational techniques?"

"No."

"Do the Borg?"

"No."

Janeway laughed, more air than sound: an exhalation of futility. "Then, forgive me, Seven, but just what are you proposing? That we should all go crazy?"

The Doctor's eyes flicked to Seven, but Seven's gaze remained on Janeway. "Not all. Just one."

Janeway sobered. They listened as Seven explained who and how.

When she finished, the lab was so quiet Janeway heard herself swallow. "You're serious."

"Perfectly."

Janeway looked toward the Doctor. "Do you agree?"

He shifted from one foot to the other, nervously. "I can't see an alternative, Captain. We'll monitor it every step of the way, of course."

"What about you, Tuvok?"

The Vulcan was impassive. "Possible, in theory. In practice, it is another matter."

"It *will* work," said Seven. "There is no other way."

Torres shook her head. "I don't like it."

"B'Elanna's right," said Janeway. "It's too risky—for you, for us."

Seven was implacable. "Then Commander Chakotay will die."

Seven couldn't have hurt Janeway more had she slapped her. "There has to be another way," Janeway said, knowing that Seven would have offered one, if there were.

"There isn't."

"We need more analysis."

"For which we don't have the time."

"Well, I don't like it," Torres repeated, generally.

"Yeah, but you never like anything," said Paris.

Torres's jaw set. "Maybe. But I *really* don't like this."

Janeway had to agree. But they did it anyway.

Two hours left.

Seven said they were coming. Chakotay didn't ask how or when. It was all very simple, really. Either *Voyager* was there in time, or it wasn't.

Chakotay rested, his back propped against the exterior of the ship. An arc welder lay across his knees. Seven told him not to move much, but he didn't need reminding. Cutting himself free without puncturing his suit or slicing off his legs had worn him out. The process had taken hours, mainly because he'd passed out a few times. It was getting harder to breathe, and he was starting to pant. The sensation was terrible, as if a steel band were being notched tighter and tighter about his ribs.

The hairs on the back of his neck prickled with alarm. *Relax.* He tried reasoning with himself. Just the carbon dioxide building up in his blood, making him panicky, that was all.

Or maybe, Chakotay considered, it was Seven. He couldn't shake the feeling that something was going on with her, the ship. Her thoughts came in pieces, like—he groped for an analogy—like shards of glass: jagged, broken. Sharp.

Keeping secrets, he thought. *They don't think I'm going to make it.*

Stop. Chakotay closed his eyes, willed the panic to recede. For want of anything better to do, he tipped his head back and studied the sky. His eyes drifted over brightly colored tendrils of red and yellow as they turned and curled, and he thought, absurdly, of a jellyfish. Not that Chakotay could breathe whatever this stuff was: His suit's sensors detected no oxygen but reported puridium, noble gases, and an organic polymer of some sort. *Voyager*'s computer couldn't make heads or tails of it, and Seven thought it was quite strange for a planet so small to have enough gravitational pull to hold an atmosphere, of any description.

Chakotay stared for a long time, trying to ignore that he wasn't feeling right. It wasn't just his breathing. He was feeling . . . confined. Claustrophobic. Once, he'd caught his fingers straying for the release on his suit. For one insane moment, he'd wanted to crack the seal.

And he had the strangest feeling he was being watched. Stupid, he knew. Probably just low on oxygen, and yet . . . Without moving his head, he slid his eyes right, then left. The planet was scored with impact craters. Tumbles of gray rock were everywhere, like regolith on Earth's moon.

No one here but us chickens. He felt a little foolish. Scooping up a handful of fine gray dust, he let it trickle, like the sands of an hourglass, between his gloved fingers. It silted to the surface with the same lazy, undulating quality as the sky. As the woman's hair.

Thinking about the alien made him sad. So beautiful, and she'd needed him, but he'd failed. He was no warrior, not the way he'd told Janeway when they were marooned on New Earth. Oh, he wanted to be one and yesterday, saving the alien from certain death, that's how he'd felt. Strong. Capable. A warrior. But it was all just a silly fantasy.

He watched the dust settle in torpid swirls. No courageous warrior triumphing against the odds, not he.

He was still thinking that when the first salvo hit.

An hour.

They were through, and Janeway was congratulating herself. Snagging those baryonic mines with a gravitonic tractor beam and then detonating one to create the rift had been risky. They still carried one mine, in a gravimagnetic containment field, for the return trip. She scanned the damage reports: environmental systems on auxiliary power, minor damage to the port nacelle, and two hull breaches from the concussive backwash, one on deck two. Neelix's mess was, literally, a mess. Neelix had been in sickbay, though—to "support" Tuvok. Despite everything, Janeway's lips tugged into a grin. It would probably be one of the only times in his life Tuvok would welcome unconsciousness. Likely the Doctor was wishing he could do likewise.

Speaking of which . . . Janeway looked up from her reports, toward the helm. Her eyes came to rest on Seven. Paris was standing alongside Seven, hands on hips, watchful. Oblivious of them all, Seven was intent over the controls. Paris must have felt Janeway staring, because he looked up suddenly. Janeway tried a wobbly smile of reassurance and knew from the look on Paris's face that she failed, miserably.

She abandoned the effort as futile. She had too much to worry about: Chakotay stranded, enemy ships somewhere, and Seven, part of her mind gone, navigating this muck that passed for space. Her eyes strayed to the viewscreen and that roiling mass of what the ship's computer said was a soup of bioelectrical energies, elemental particles, organic polymers. The stuff wasn't truly solid or gaseous, chaotic or fluidic. It fluxed—between times, dimensions, phase states.

Voyager flew on a wing and a prayer. Janeway gnawed her lower lip. They had no referents, no coordinates, nothing to guide them but Seven, who had them on a heading for a planet only she saw. And Seven hadn't said much for the last few hours, ever since the Doctor pumped her full of cordrazine. Janeway grimaced. Part of Seven's plan, gleaned from those old databases again: Inject enough cordrazine to induce psychosis, but not so much that her mind shattered completely. Oh, the Doctor had given assurances that he'd notify her if Seven's neural patterns so much as hiccupped. But he probably had his hands full down there, what with monitoring Seven *and* Tuvok.

God, I don't like this. Janeway's hand found its way to her throat. Seven, psychotic, and Tuvok, in a coma, mind-melded to Seven to stabilize her from sinking further into madness.

Janeway's pulse fluttered against her fingertips. How had she let herself get talked into this?

Then she felt the emptiness to her left, and her resolve hardened. *Not going to lose you,* she thought fiercely, *not without a fight.*

Still, she felt shaky, on edge. She scrubbed her moist palms along her thighs. Nerves: She was as jumpy as a cadet on her first deep-space assignment. Or the time that horde of battleships hurtled out of fluidic space, or when the Borg . . .

She gave herself a mental shake. *Focus.* Janeway frowned, glanced at the padd on her lap. Everything was there, except—Janeway's eyes slitted—those ships, the ones that attacked Chakotay. Where were they? They hadn't been in normal space, and they weren't in the rift. So where . . .?

"Captain." It was Paris, a note of alarm in his voice. *"Ma'am!"*

Startled, Janeway looked up and saw that Seven had risen from her seat, her back ramrod straight. Janeway leapt to her feet, ignoring the padd as it clattered to the deck. She took the five strides to Seven in two. "What is it?"

Seven's face shone with sweat. "I . . . he . . ."

"Captain!" It was the Doctor, in sickbay. "There's been a jump in Seven's neural . . ."

"Oh, Captain," Seven whispered. Her left hand groped blindly for Janeway's arm and clamped down.

Alarmed, Janeway tried easing Seven away from the helm. "Tom." She jerked her head at the controls. "Take . . ."

"No!" Seven cried suddenly, surging against Janeway. Janeway staggered back and would have fallen if Paris's hand hadn't flashed out to grab her elbow.

Seven's eyes bulged; her fists bunched. A flurry of emotions chased across her face: horror, dread, fear. "You don't understand, you don't under*stand.* It's Commander Chakotay, it's *there,* it's with him, it's . . ."

The Doctor was still trying to say something, but Janeway didn't hear because at the same moment Kim sang, "Captain! Ships, off the port bow!"

Janeway's head snapped forward. "What? On screen!"

Then she saw them. Out of the tangled skeins of this strange space, wavering into focus as if emerging from the depths of a dark sea, Janeway counted one, two, ten, thirteen . . .

Janeway watched in mounting horror. *Oh, dear God.*

Then, shrieking, Seven dove for the helm, and all hell broke loose.

In sickbay, deep in the meld, Tuvok struggled up from his coma. "Seven, *no* . . ."

Chakotay crouched behind a tumble of boulders, perhaps twenty meters to the left of the ship. Another salvo rained down, and the ship vaporized. The ground twitched with the aftershock. In the space between one breath and the next, another flurry of weapons fire thudded to the surface, now to the right. He ducked as pulverized bits of rock pinged off his neck and shoulders. He started to count and made it to eight before the next salvo hit, this time about fifteen meters due north.

A search pattern. His brain tried ticking through his options even as the pain in his chest increased. Moving had cost him, dearly, but he had to think.

They didn't have a fix on him, yet. He had to hide, but where? Frantically, Chakotay scanned the vicinity for a ridge of rocks, a depression, *any*thing. It had to be close. He'd barely escaped in time, and each step had been a fresh agony. Besides, running used air, and air was something he couldn't spare.

His eyes clicked right, left . . . and then he saw it, about forty meters distant: a wedge-shaped formation, splayed into an overwide L.

There. Chakotay still cradled the welder, and now he slung the strap over his neck and shoulders, leaving his arms free. The sudden movement brought a crushing leaden weight to the center of his chest, and pain lanced down his left arm. His jaw tingled; his knees bit into the broken earth.

No. He gulped air, fought to keep his body erect. Rivulets of sweat coursed down his back, pooling at his waist. He clutched at his chest, trying to squeeze out the pain. He couldn't black out, not now.

The earth shuddered with the next salvo. Then, silence.

One. He struggled to his feet. *Two.*

Go. Chakotay tucked his elbows in against his sides. *Go, go, go!*

He made it to the fourth step. Then the pain took him: a simple, white, hot agony. Chakotay couldn't help it; he screamed. Something broke inside his chest, and he pitched forward, his arms opening wide, as if he'd been shot in the back.

He was on his knees. Then he was staring at the sky. His lungs gurgled with blood.

"Seven," he gasped, "*Seven . . .*"

"Harry, bring it down!" Janeway shouted.

Behind the sizzle of a level-ten forcefield, Seven hunched over the helm, fingers flying. The ship lurched, swerved, then canted between two Borg cubes, angling in a ninety-degree escape vector. Five ships belonging to Species 8472 peeled off in pursuit. In response, Seven sent *Voyager* into the equivalent of a steep dive and punched the ship to warp eight.

Janeway didn't have time to wonder why the Borg and Species 8472 had suddenly become allies. Or why there were Hirogen and Kazon. In response to the ship's wild gyrations, she flailed for a handhold, missed, and went careening to the deck.

"For God's sake, Harry!" She pushed up on hands and knees. "Reroute power through tactical! Take that damn forcefield off-line!"

Torres's voice blared from the comm. "Captain, I'm showing loss of structural integrity in the matter-antimatter reaction assembly! The dilithium matrix is destabilizing, and there's a fifteen percent coolant leak around the EPS conduits. She's pushing the ship too hard! You've got to get her to power down, or I'll have to eject the core!"

Janeway clawed her way to her feet. "Understood! Harry!"

Kim punched ineffectually at his console. "I can't! Seven's set up a subroutine to reroute through random access pathways. There's no way of telling where . . ."

"Captain, she's firing phasers again!" Paris pointed at the viewscreen. Janeway saw flares blossom along the side of one cube. In response, the green ribbon of the cube's tractor beam streamed out, like a snake springing at its prey.

"She's modulating shield harmonics," Kim said. "They can't get a lock."

"How many ships, Harry?"

"Twenty Borg. Thirteen ships belonging to 8472. Five Kazon, four Hirogen."

"How are our shields?"

Looking up from his data, Kim opened his mouth, closed it, opened it again, and said, finally, "Fine."

"What?"

"The shields are fine, Captain, and the damage to the Borg . . ."

Kim's voice trailed away. Seven banked *Voyager* left, then into a rolling, spiral turn. Janeway clung to the railing behind her command chair, and something somewhere shorted. A console blew. Sparks arced, sputtered. "Mr. Kim, report!"

Kim blinked. "Captain, I read no damage at all. No debris, no residua, no plasma . . . nothing. Just a . . . a bioelectrical signature. Like a sensor shadow, like something was there but isn't now."

Janeway stared. "A shadow? But I saw it: just like the time that cube was damaged by . . ."

Then, it hit her.

Shadows, Torres said. We see shadows around the disruption. In space. In time.

Janeway whirled on her heel. "Seven!"

Paris's arm shot out. "Look!"

Janeway looked. It was a planet.

Then, she looked harder. *"Who* are *they?"*

Tuvok struggled to sit up. "Doctor."

The Doctor scooped up a hypospray. "Your vital signs are too erratic, and I can't control Seven. Neither can you. I'm bringing you out of this."

"No!" Tuvok grappled for the Doctor's wrist. "You don't understand. You must tell them. They are shadows. They must control their minds, they must . . ."

"What?"

"Shadows," Tuvok whispered hoarsely, "in the dark . . . the dark matter . . . shadows . . ."

Then Tuvok stopped speaking, because it took all his strength to stay with Seven. *Seven, listen to me, listen only to me . . .*

* * *

Blood foamed upon his lips, and his air was almost gone. But it didn't matter; he would drown long before he suffocated.

There was a sense of movement, a slant of shadow, and Chakotay forced his lids open to see who or what it was.

His breath hissed in surprise.

And then there was Seven, in his mind, frantic: "Commander, no! It's the planet! Get up, get up, *get up!*"

"Organic polymers in a chroniton flux, bound together by a bioelectrical field," said Kim. "It's Seven's planet all right. But those ships . . . I can't get a reading."

Janeway ground her fists together in frustration. A quartet of ships ranged above the planet, firing directly at it. They ignored hails, so Janeway couldn't do a damn thing about them, unless she got through to Seven. "What about Chakotay? Is he there? Are they firing at him?"

"Can't tell. Too much interference, and . . . wait a minute. I think I've got a piece of him, but there's something else. I'm reading an energy surge deep within the planet's core. Looks like it's concentrating, cohering into something, and it's, it's . . ."

Janeway swung her head toward Kim. "What?"

Kim looked up, mystified. "Captain, it's reading trianic."

Trianic. It clicked in Janeway's mind, like the final piece of a puzzle snapped into place: trianic, like the Komar. Dark-energy beings living in shadow. Beings who *were* shadow. And those mines on one side of a rift, leading to a space responsive to *thought.*

Not a rift. Janeway's eyes widened. It was a door, to a cage, and those ships, the ones firing on the planet, those *ships* . . .

Then Seven said, "No!" And she said, "Die."

They were the first words Seven had spoken in what seemed an eternity, and the last Janeway heard.

Seven brought down the forcefield.

Janeway turned just in time to see Seven crumple to the deck.

Chakotay couldn't move. The alien bent over him, and Seven screamed in his mind but faintly now, like an echo dying in a well.

Seven felt him slipping.

The alien touched him. The sensors in Chakotay's suit whirred; the synaptic-actuated nodes connected to his brain tingled as the alien passed into him.

And touched . . . Seven.

Then Seven knew exactly what to do. She gathered herself and sprang.

One second. Two.

At first, Chakotay thought that this was what it was to die. There was a sensation of something liquid flowing from his mind, like a presence taking flight, and he imagined, for one bizarre second, that his soul had gone.

And then, suddenly, he knew, because his mind was silent.

Six seconds.

The alien screamed.

Chakotay reached for it. "Seven, no!"

Tuvok felt it next: a sudden *push,* as if Seven had straight-armed him in the chest. Pain exploded in his skull, and there was the sense of a door slamming shut, but not before he'd caught a fleeting glimpse of what she was doing, where she was going.

"Doctor, she is breaking free of the meld." His fingertips found his temples. "She is going to, to . . ."

Seven! Tuvok collapsed his consciousness into a fine needle of thought he sent darting into the growing void. In one corner of his awareness, he heard Janeway's hail and then the Doctor shouting something about Seven's vital signs, but Tuvok didn't care, because there wasn't time to explain.

Seven. Stop.

Seven didn't stop. Instead, she flowed: through the synaptic nodes of Chakotay's suit, into the alien, at the speed of thought. And then she was in, because she *was* the alien.

Die.

The alien bucked. It fought.

Seven. It was Tuvok, in the barest sliver of a thought. *Seven, an illusion.*

"No," she said aloud. "Die."

Die, she thought at the alien. Seven damped its bioelectrical energies; she dispelled its trianic cohesion.

Die—Seven willed the rush of her blood to cease and her lungs to fail—*die.*

She had crashed to the deck.

Janeway was by her side.

Chakotay had pulled himself to her body.

The planet was screaming. They were all screaming.

The air broke. The air shimmered.

"I must," she said.

And then she died.

Janeway thought Seven said something, but then her body dissolved and Seven was gone.

The planet howled.

"Got her!" said Kim. "Transporting to sickbay!"

"Belay that! Keep her in the pattern buffer!" Janeway barked. "What about Chakotay?"

"Scanning now . . . there!"

Dear God, please be alive, please . . . "Beam him to sickbay!"

Paris cried, "Hirogen ships, on attack vector! Shall I take evasive measures?"

Janeway's mind raced. "Negative!"

"But, Captain!"

"Forget them! Harry, piggyback one of those mines onto a photon torpedo! Get ready to fire!"

"Where?"

Janeway indicated the quartet of alien ships. "There. Follow their trajectory. Get me a target, Mr. Kim."

"Aye, aye, Captain!"

"Mr. Paris, on my mark, warp nine!"

"Heading?"

Janeway planted her hands on her hips. "Dead ahead."

Paris gaped. "*Into* the planet? But . . ."

"*Do* it!"

"Target plotted. Torpedo armed," said Kim. "Magnetic containment holding."

"Shields up! And . . . *now,* Mr. Kim! *Fire!*"

"Torpedo away!"

"Warp nine, Mr. Paris! *Go!*"

It was night of the day Seven died.

The Doctor said no more visitors, but Captain Janeway lingered, telling him how that last mine tore open subspace. And how, once they were out, those four ships had taken up positions. Like guards, she said: sentries, with mines to keep whatever *it* was in. But they didn't know for sure and wouldn't know, ever, because the ships never did return a hail. And as for the alien, how it had gotten out, if it was real, or an extension of the planet . . . Janeway shrugged. Chakotay's guess was as good as hers. Maybe, later, when he felt up to talking about it, *her* . . .

Janeway faltered, shrugged again. Then the Doctor shooed her away—*again*—so she left.

Sickbay was dark, save for the glow of scanners above his biobed. He adjusted his body and heard the momentary quickening of the *bleep-bleep-bleep* that was the signal from his heart. His fingers crept gingerly down the length of his sternum, the edges of his ribs. He was sore, his muscles feeling a little pulpy, bruised. Slowly, cautiously, he filled his lungs, held air, let it out. Did it again, because it felt so good.

There was a sharp rustle, to his left. He turned his head. From the glow of the monitors, he made out Seven's eyes. They were open.

"Hi," he said.

"Where is Tuvok?"

He grinned. Typical Seven. "Gone. He had a headache. You're lucky he still had a piece of you."

"Indeed."

"I think it surprised him, hanging on to your . . . ah . . . *katra.*" Chakotay didn't want to say "soul," unsure if Seven thought she had one. "He didn't believe in it before, you know, that time we ran into the Drayans."

"I suspect he will reevaluate his skepticism regarding extreme instances of synaptic pattern displacement." She didn't mention that she hadn't known she could focus her neural patterns into a data stream and travel along synaptic-actuated nodes. Nor that cortical stimulation enhanced synaptic pattern retrieval through a Vulcan mind-meld.

"How did you know? That the ships weren't real, but she was?"

"I didn't. Part of my mind knew where to find you, but separating illusion from reality—the Borg, the Hirogen—was . . . difficult. The crew's fears were realized, and I reacted accordingly."

"You mean, since you didn't know which ships, if any, were real, better safe than sorry."

"An apt expression."

"It's hard to know *what* was real, even now."

There was a sound of cloth moving against cloth as Seven shifted. "The mines. The rift. What happened to you. The planet."

"Her."

Seven was silent.

He said, "I wonder why it chose me?"

Then he answered his own question. "I guess we'll never know."

"Perhaps," Seven said, very gently, which was unusual for her, "it is no more complicated than what you wished *she* provided."

"Yes. Like"—and it was out of his mouth before he knew it—"when people fall in love."

He winced, waiting for her to say something withering, because Seven did that extremely well, too.

But she said, after a pause, "Or when dreams come true, Commander."

It was so un-*Seven* Chakotay didn't know what to say. A half hour later, when he finally *did,* Seven had fallen asleep. So Chakotay just watched her for a long time, thinking of dreams and shadows, in dark places.

STAR TREK®

Strange New Worlds V

Contest Rules

1) ENTRY REQUIREMENTS:

No purchase necessary to enter. Enter by submitting your story as specified below.

2) CONTEST ELIGIBILITY:

This contest is open to nonprofessional writers who are legal residents of the United States and Canada (excluding Quebec) over the age of 18. Entrant must not have published any more than two short stories on a professional basis or in paid professional venues. Employees (or relatives of employees living in the same household) of Simon & Schuster, VIACOM, or any of their affiliates are not eligible. This contest is void in Puerto Rico and wherever prohibited by law.

3) FORMAT:

Entries should be no more than 7,500 words long and must not have been previously published. They must be typed or printed by word processor, double spaced, on one side of noncorrasable paper. Do not justify right-side margins. The author's name, address, and phone number must appear on the first page of the entry. The author's name, the story title, and the page number should appear on every page. No electronic or disk submissions will be accepted. All entries must be original and the sole work of the Entrant and the sole property of the Entrant.

4) ADDRESS:

Each entry must be mailed to: STRANGE NEW WORLDS V, *Star Trek* Department, Pocket Books, 1230 Sixth Avenue, New York, NY 10020.

Each entry must be submitted only once. Please retain a copy of your submission. You may submit more than one story, but each submission must be mailed separately. Enclose a self-addressed, stamped envelope if you wish your entry returned. Entries must be received by October 1st, 2001. Not responsible for lost, late, stolen, postage due, or misdirected mail.

5) PRIZES:

One Grand Prize winner will receive:

Simon and Schuster's *Star Trek: Strange New Worlds V* Publishing Contract for Publication of Winning Entry in our *Strange New Worlds V* Anthology with a bonus advance of One Thousand Dollars ($1,000.00) above the Anthology word rate of 10 cents a word.

One Second Prize winner will receive:

Simon and Schuster's *Star Trek: Strange New Worlds V* Publishing Contract for Publication of Winning Entry in our *Strange*

New Worlds V Anthology with a bonus advance of Six Hundred Dollars ($600.00) above the Anthology word rate of 10 cents a word.

One Third Prize winner will receive:

Simon and Schuster's *Star Trek: Strange New Worlds V* Publishing Contract for Publication of Winning Entry in our *Strange New Worlds V* Anthology with a bonus advance of Four Hundred Dollars ($400.00) above the Anthology word rate of 10 cents a word.

All Honorable Mention winners will receive:

Simon and Schuster's *Star Trek: Strange New Worlds V* Publishing Contract for Publication of Winning Entry in the *Strange New Worlds V* Anthology and payment at the Anthology word rate of 10 cents a word.

There will be no more than twenty (20) Honorable Mention winners. No contestant can win more than one prize.

Each Prize Winner will also be entitled to a share of royalties on the *Strange New Worlds V* Anthology as specified in Simon and Schuster's *Star Trek: Strange New Worlds V* Publishing Contract.

6) JUDGING:

Submissions will be judged on the basis of writing ability and the originality of the story, which can be set in any of the *Star Trek* time frames and may feature any one or more of the *Star Trek* characters. The judges shall include the editor of the Anthology, one employee of Pocket Books, and one employee of VIACOM Consumer Products. The decisions of the judges shall be final. All prizes will be awarded provided a sufficient number of entries are received that meet the minimum criteria established by the judges.

7) NOTIFICATION:

The winners will be notified by mail or phone. The winners who win a publishing contract must sign the publishing contract in order to be awarded the prize. All federal, local, and state taxes are the responsibility of the winner. A list of the winners will be available after January 1st, 2002, on the Pocket Books *Star Trek* Books Web site,

www.simonsays.com/startrek/

or the names of the winners can be obtained after January 1st, 2002, by sending a self-addressed, stamped envelope and a request for the list of winners to WINNERS' LIST, STRANGE NEW WORLDS V, *Star Trek* Department, Pocket Books, 1230 Sixth Avenue, New York, NY 10020.

8) STORY DISQUALIFICATIONS:

Certain types of stories will be disqualified from consideration:

a) Any story focusing on explicit sexual activity or graphic depictions of violence or sadism.

b) Any story that focuses on characters that are not past or present *Star Trek* regulars or familiar *Star Trek* guest characters.

c) Stories that deal with the previously unestablished death of a *Star Trek* character, or that establish major facts about or make major changes in the life of a major character, for instance a story that establishes a long-lost sibling or reveals the hidden passion two characters feel for each other.

d) Stories that are based around common clichés, such as "hurt/comfort" where a character is injured and lovingly cared for, or "Mary Sue" stories where a new character comes on the ship and outdoes the crew.

9) PUBLICITY:

Each Winner grants to Pocket Books the right to use his or her name, likeness, and entry for any advertising, promotion, and publicity purposes without further compensation to or permission from such winner, except where prohibited by law.

10) LEGAL STUFF:

All entries become the property of Pocket Books and of Paramount Pictures, the sole and exclusive owner of the *Star Trek* property and elements thereof. Entries will be returned only if they are accompanied by a self-addressed, stamped envelope. Contest void where prohibited by law.

About the Contributors

Chuck Anderson ("Return"), lives in Aurora, Colorado, with wife, Sherry, and daughter, Kaily. He teaches P.E. and coaches girls' high school basketball.

Ilsa J. Bick ("Shadows, in the Dark") is a child psychiatrist. This marks her second appearance in *SNW;* "A Ribbon for Rosie" took Grand Prize in *SNW II*. Her novelette "The Quality of Wetness" won Second Prize in *Writers of the Future, Vol. XVI.* When she grows up, Ilsa aims to write books—as a recovering shrink.

Jonathan Bridge ("Captain Proton and the Orb of Bajor") was a one-time member of Phil Farrand's Nitpickers' Guild, picking at everything from Classic *Trek* to *The X-Files.* He always believed he would do something professional by the time he turned thirty. He turns thirty this year, so it happened! This is his first professional sale.

Pat Detmer ("Missed") is marketing/sales manager for a Seattle paper distributor. She's never succumbed to the allure of self-publication even though her husband owns a print shop. She's only watched the original series and can't quite accept that there might be more than one Vulcan in the universe worth writing about.

Lynda Martinez Foley ("Tears for Eternity") lives in Northridge, California, with her incredibly supportive husband, Dan, and her inspirational sons, Dustin and Jonathan. She acknowledges her parents and sisters for their encouragement, and also thanks Bill, Carla, Corey, Cristy, Elise, James, Jesse, Lolita, Michael, Michelle, Robbin, Ted and the "New Grounders."

Alan James Garbers ("Flight 19") is a licensed Master Electrician whose experience covers industrial, commercial, and residential electrical systems. Alan's hobbies are as far ranging as his job skills: historical re-enactment, photography, writing, travel, hunting, fishing, playing acoustic and electric guitar, and making maple syrup.

Victoria Grant ("First Star I See Tonight") lives in San Diego with her husband, Brian, and two children. She teaches, works in a laboratory, and if she had some spare time, she'd stroll by the ocean and stare up at the stars. *Star Trek* has inspired her since childhood; now her dreams have taken flight.

Michael J. Jasper ("Scotty's Song") is a Clarion Workshop graduate (1996), and has had stories published in *Writers of the Future* Vol. 16, *Strange Horizons, The Raleigh News & Observer, PIF Magazine, Dark Planet,* and other small presses. He is working on a novel, a fantasy tale set in Chicago. Read all about it at www.michaeljasper.net

Kevin Killiany ("Personal Log") is a minister with the Soul Saving Station and an instructor at Cape Fear Community College in Wilmington, North Carolina. Though he has written on racial, educational, and spiritual issues, this is his first fiction sale. He is proud of and grateful for his wife's encouragement in attaining his goals.

Diana Kornfeld ("Welcome Home") lives in Lees Summit, Missouri, with her husband, Steve, and two daughters. She is extremely pleased to have a second story in a *Strange New Worlds* anthology. She enjoys reading, writing, wandering around on the Internet, designing Web pages, and, oh yes, watching *Star Trek.*

William Leisner ("Black Hats") previously appeared in *Strange New Worlds II.* Since then, he has changed both his residence (to Minneapolis) and occupation (book inventory planner for a national retailer), thus rendering his old author bio almost completely obsolete. Special thanks to "Charlotte" for her early commentary on this story.

Robert J. Mendenhall ("Prodigal Father") is a full-time logistics supervisor for the Schaumburg, Illinois, Police Department, a part-time reservist in the U.S. Air Force, and a longtime "pre-published" writer. During his younger days, Robert was a broadcast journalist for the American Forces Network, Europe. He lives outside Chicago near his three children.

Tonya D. Price ("Prodigal Son") makes her second appearance in *Strange New Worlds.* A native of Fairborn, Ohio, she lives in Franklin, Massachusetts, with her husband, Kent Jones, and daughters, Ana-Lisa and Diantha. She divides her time between online marketing consulting and writing short stories, including new submissions for *SNW V.*

Penny A. Proctor ("Uninvited Admirals") is a vice president and assistant general counsel for a healthcare system in Columbus, where she lives with her husband, dog, and stepcat. A lifelong fan of *Star Trek,* she is grateful to her husband, family, and friends, who convinced her to try writing something for this contest.

Steven Scott Ripley ("The Name of the Cat") lives in Seattle. This marks his second appearance in the *Star Trek: Strange New Worlds* series. Along with writing fiction, he is a playwright whose works have appeared in various West Coast theaters. He enjoys cooking, blustery weather, and hanging out with his friends and family.

Bill Stuart ("Iridium-7-Tetrahydroxate Crystals Are a Girl's Best Friend") is twenty-nine years old and lives in Ottawa, Canada.

This is his first published work. He is currently finishing a dual degree in theater and biology.

Jeff Suess ("Seeing Forever"), reads while he walks everywhere so as not to waste valuable reading time. He is a native Californian living in Cincinnati, Ohio, with his wife, Kristin, and their dog and cat. He works in the library of the *Cincinnati Enquirer.*

Kevin G. Summers ("Isolation Ward 4") was born in 1974 in Washington, D.C. Some of his earliest memories are of watching reruns of classic *Star Trek* episodes. He currently lives in northern Virginia. His novel, *The Bleak December,* is under contract with an agent. This is his first published story.

Mary Sweeney ("Countdown") is a software developer, longtime science fiction fan (it all started with Heinlein's *Podkayne of Mars*), and Trekker. She and her husband, Evan Romer, live in upstate New York with four rats and six parakeets. Mary is grateful for Evan's encouragement. This is her first professional sale.

TG Theodore ("A Little More Action") is a fan of all four *Trek* television franchises, having pitched stories to three of them. His fondness for the more humorous aspects of *Trek* is apparent in his work in this anthology. A native Californian, Ted particularly enjoys writing, composing, and directing for the theater. His work here marks his debut into the world of prose and pros.

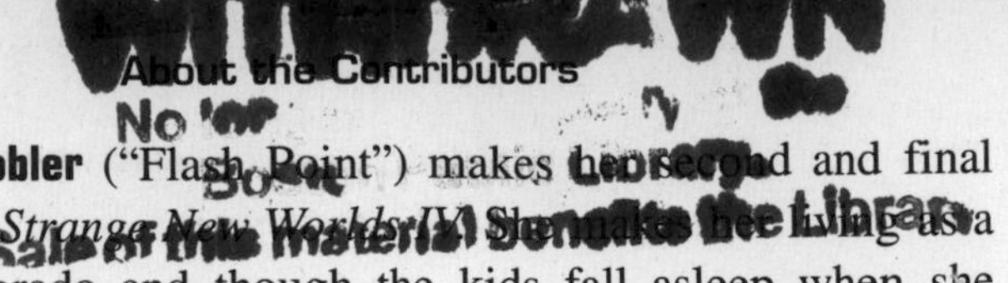

E. Catherine Tobler ("Flash Point") makes her second and final appearance in *Strange New Worlds IV*. She makes her living as a nanny in Colorado and though the kids fall asleep when she reads to them, she hopes the same doesn't happen to the editors who review her work.

Shane Zeranski ("The Promise"), barely twenty, thinks he's pretty smart, handsome, and talented. Most everybody else thinks he's pretty cocky and pretty lucky. The jury's still out. Shane has just wrapped up a whopper of a *Trek* novel (unpublished as of yet), is working on another book and a screenplay, is a 4.0 college student, is doing a lot of acting, and has lots of spare time (heavy laughter). This is his second appearance in *SNW*. Look for his name and face in the future.